Sword of Souls

SWORD OF SOULS

Chronicles of Caledon

Book I

Douglas S. Taylor

iUniverse, Inc.

New York Lincoln Shanghai

Sword of Souls
Chronicles of Caledon

iUniverse books may be ordered through booksellers or by contacting:

iUniverse
2021 Pine Lake Road, Suite 100
Lincoln, NE 68512
www.iuniverse.com
1-800-Authors (1-800-288-4677)

This is a work of fiction. All of the characters, names, incidents, organizations and dialogue in this novel are either the products of the author's imagination or are used fictitiously.

ISBN-13: 978-0-595-40947-1 (pbk)
ISBN-13: 978-0-595-85306-9 (ebk)
ISBN-10: 0-595-40947-4 (pbk)
ISBN-10: 0-595-85306-4 (ebk)

Printed in the United States of America

FOR LAURA AND "*KERWOOD*".

Just a few things on my mind to share with anyone
who would care to bend an ear.

It's been one long ride up to this point and many things I had to traverse before reaching this wonderment. Actually, this is the first novel of mine to make it to completion and finally to print, though I must admit, I would wager that I would have never finished it on my own. It has taken the better part of three years to finish. Sure, there were some pretty darn feverish days and a few weeks of pounding out the story, the story like a movie in my mind across the vast seas of my imagination, but these seas had a lot of shoals and sandbars along the way.

During this time, as a part-time writer and like many of you, a full time 8 to 5'er, there didn't seem a whole lot of time to peer into the abyss of this new found and troubling world, this story, and the characters thereof.

It took determination, time, and energy to go to this dark world from deep within, and after making the voyage, it was all I could do to make it back to this bleak reality of the Midwest. At times, it was all I could do as to keep up with all I was seeing and experiencing in what seemed to be a limited time of looking into Alice's "Looking Glass" before dropping the mirror and striking up another seven years of bad luck.

Yes, that's it—Work in this journey wasn't coming up with this unique world, it was getting to this amazing place, this dimension, and time. Life in reality does its part to pull me quickly out of these sacred scenes within that I sometimes so excitably strive to write as the story begins to unfold.

This journey, this trek of writing down all that I experience as this story, the first of this series literally sprang into life, least for me, offered a safe disconnect from my somewhat uneventful lifestyle here in Pierre, South Dakota.

I mean to say, there is a lot in common with a person being whisked away to a world to write about, and one such as yourself reading about, isn't there?

There were times I thought that this writing or the ability to write was more therapeutic, more relaxing, and more often than not, a drug for me that opened my mind and spirit. Yet again, there is another commonality with the writer, or the storyteller and the reader, ah yes, the relationship between the two, now there's something to be said.

Writing, creative writing that is has always been more or less my escape hatch on reality that over time, I have used throughout my life just as those that love to read, and I too am no exception to this fact.

I will share with you a little secret of mine, a nasty tendency if you will and that is this, I would start in on a project and through life's little fucking twists of ironies something would prevent me from finishing my writing, unfortunately, I would never finish.

Since my life has settled down in the Midwest and has become more secure, it has allowed me time to journey deep into my imagination and write down all the things that come to mind of this world I would occasionally see through the façade of this reality.

Oh, by the time it would seem that my mind's eye would begin to focus and I would become aware that I am catching a magical glimpse, damn it; I would loose sight of it again—Gone, gone, and gone.

Oh not to fret, here is proof of a couple of things straight forth, and the first is, I actually seized enough of this dark world and this enchanted universe or characters, places and things to realize there is so much more to it…and the other? To write it down, bind it long enough to get it published before the demonic forces of reality would scatter the evidence if you would, to the four corners of the world!

I would like to interject something right here for you to merely dine upon, and that is, I have had help in getting this first book and consequently the series out into the light of day, aka, reality. Sure, there were many a night wrestling with my own demons, wrestling other demonic forces beyond my own, but I was certainly never alone, and in this life, it is never good to be alone!

My love for science fiction, fantasy, and horror wasn't enough to keep my spirits and wits about me, no there were others. Again, I would be literally a fool if I thought it was just me all along. You as a reader and I am certain this is not your first science fiction (slash) fantasy, (slash) horror novel, if it is, oh my god, run!

I would like be as transparent as I possibly can here with you and that is this, over the centuries (though it seems on some days) my meager existence there has been so many writers and storytellers has in so many ways, enriched, engulfed to a noticeable measure, impacted my world, the world and series of the Chronicles of Caledon.

What in the world, am I talking about? Yes, this is a fair question, and here's my point to my rambling, as you read the first book of the series, you'll see shadowy reminders of things you, the seasoned sci-fi reader will no doubt, pick up on, and that is some similarities of all those fantastic storytellers who have touched my spirit, my soul.

Yes, the altered universe of science fiction and fantasy that was introduced to me as a youth with master craftsman like Robert E. Howard's "People of the Black Circle", JRR Tolkien, "Lord of the Rings", Robert Heinlein's "Stormtrooper", and so many others. From Conan the Cimmerian to the Dragons of Perth, oh these mystic lands and tales I traveled mostly in my youth while listening to Led Zeppelin, Areosmith, and….

As you can see, yet another monumental and all consuming influence of mine is my love for music, and trust me in saying, this world, this series would not be a "reality" if it were not for these major forces in my life.

Oh, there was many a night I traveled and would visit the Shire in relaxation in the summer twilight on the grassy knoll and reflect upon the true talent I have read from these fantastic storytellers that graciously shared amongst the world. It is these very things I mention and convey that have "seasoned" my creativity and wonder that you will no doubt notice.

Okay, so how did this all begin for a poor south-side boy from the "Windy City?"

Another fine question, even if you hadn't asked. You know the saying, "It all started many years ago…?"

Allow me one simple indulgence of sharing with you of something that began to burn deep within me at an early age, the gift of storytelling, and the desire to write about it all. Yes, that is when the trouble of it all began…

It was when I was a young boy, with my last four dollars I had in my pocket as a child from my weekly wage of allowances combined with mowing yards, I bought a small dictionary, spiral notebook and a pen and I began to write my first lengthy account of a place that my imagination had been taking me. Aye, this was the summer of 1976 and it was sometime after a death of my young friend. In fact, I was planning to write about this kid, a friend like so many of us that was raised by just a single parent. His name was Jonathan (last name withholding) who spent much of his time daydreaming about his father. Jonathan unfortunately like so many of us never met or came to know who his father was, what he was like, or for that matter, even his name.

For Jonathan as it turns out, he never did find out anything about his natural father. As a child, Jonathan spent a great many hours fantasizing about his dad and spending too much time being ridiculed by the cruel realities of this very situation by others made aware of this fact who did not have the betterment of keeping their mindless comments to themselves—Life can be most cruel and intolerable to say the least.

As I can remember, it was on a cold April morning, you see, the phone rang and at my father's house, if it were too early or too late in the day, my dad would answers all calls. I remembered peering around the corner of the doorway of my bedroom, it was still rather dark out and couldn't have been 7:00 a.m. My father, in his soft sober voice, said, "I am so very sorry to hear that…So very sorry" I remember walking down the hallway to meet with my dad who stood there in the shadows and as I could see, he was struggling on how to break the news to me while he was still on the phone. I drew nearer to the giant of a man, a man who easily cleared 6'8" and blocked out the sun towering over you, signaling without a doubt, you've had it.

I knew what the news was, who it was about, and knew without a doubt who called him, but still I was hoping against all hope, I remember cursing within that, "No it can't fucking happen, tell me its not so!"

My father received news that Jonathan had succumbed to a vile and wretched disease that literally robbed him of his life, but not only that fact alone, it had caused him to suffer for too long a measure in pain and agony that fetches the soul of a child and without mercy, drags it into the depths of desperation. What fucking enemy of life would or could ever do such a horrid thing to an innocent soul? Mind you, I am talking about a human soul of a child who never asked for such a painful and horrifying death in a long drawn-out painful battle that he was forced to fight alone with the exception of his mother and those closest around him. Just looking back on this tragic event causes my eyes to water and the bitter taste to well up to the surface. I had come to understand something at that moment while my father was still on the phone; you cannot suffer this life without wounds, bumps or at the very least, bruises.

I remember how depressing that moment was for me and later to my friends as the news spread. My father attempted to comfort me by saying things like, "He's better off Son, he's better off..." Perhaps he was, and no matter who you are, unless you are the coldest and hardest bastard I can imagine, you would want to think these thoughts, no matter how distraught I may have felt, there was this one comfort.

In the coming days to follow, it was another rainy drizzling and damp moment, it was now Jonathan's funeral. His mother, his brother and young sister, spared only by the innocence of their age, they were so very young as I remembered looking at them next to the gravesite and memorial service. I wondered even in that moment so long ago, if his remaining brothers and sisters could understand the finality of that day. Would they, or could they understand that their big brother would never return home and for that matter, do any of us really understand?

Coincidently, I never saw his mother, or any one from Jonathan's family again after that wretched drizzling day. It was as if some mythical force came down and separated Jonathan's remaining family members away—Odd?

On the way home in my dad's sedan the ride was quiet in reflection. I know, I mean, I could sense my father struggling with something to say, something that would bring some sort of healing process, some comfort. He couldn't find the words, and even if he could, it would only have been like a band-aid over a bullet-hole. Besides, the only sound was the rain hitting the windshield and the old windshield wipers and motor frantically attempting to keep the windshield clear enough to safely view the surrounding.

We were nearly home when I turned to look to my father and said at the point of loosing what little composure I was struggling to keep as I blurted out, "The only thing he ever wanted was to know his dad, to know his own father, who and what his father might have been?" I remembered feeling my heart crack right in two at that moment; this would be the first of many times since I would experience this sort of pain.

I remembered my fist of my left hand smashing down on the seat, as I couldn't hold back the tears any longer; I was never so angry, so bitter, and so very grieved stricken…

Now moving fast-forward to the summer of 1976 armed with pen in hand, I wrote a story about a youth in a fantasy world who was in search of his father.

Jonathan was in life, very poor, his mother obviously on welfare now called public assistance. Nevertheless, I was the architect of this new world and in control of this newfound situation I was about to bring forth in writing. I was realizing in this pristine revelation that I had the power, the thought to set things right and in this vigor I would not stop until the beginning of the school year.

It was now October 1976 and I submitted my work to my creative writing teacher. In a week after my submission, I received grades upon my work from a tough old German woman called, and I shit you not, Mrs. Slaughter. She was perhaps the coldest and hardest physically looking woman I have ever seen and with barely any sign of femininity that I could sense at the time.

Mrs. Slaughter stood nearly six-five, and even today's standards, she is considered right up there with the California Redwoods for a woman, and as a child, I figured as old as one of those trees too.

I could only imagine she has passed on after all these years in my reflection. Hey, if you were a kid, no matter if you were up to no good, or one of those goddamned "good kids," everyone felt as guilty as discovered thief caught in her steel-blue glare, shit you not. Whatever you thought, or plan to do, in that instant, it was over and done with and you felt exposed as you can feel her gaze burning into your very soul!

Nevertheless, again, it was some time before she finished grading the story that completely filled two spiral books.

She successfully navigated through the bad grammar, the misspellings, and plenty of blotted ink filled pages to choke a horse. I remembered when I turned the work in, the work was on a creative story, whatever you wanted to write about to the best of my recollection and a minimum length, 500 words. "Cripes!" I thought, "I could do that before breaking into a finger cramp, please!"

Aye yes, it was one of the very few times I needn't do any homework; this stuff was already done, completed, and finished and all I had to do was to turn it in!

This was so very important to me; my whole world came down to this single moment and with the mental clarity as if it all occurred just yesterday as I recollect.

Mrs. Slaughter was comfortably sitting at her desk, one of the very few times without any sign of pain or discomfort. I remember she suffered from back problems and I always thought it was from her wounds that she might have sustained from her many ancient battles with the Franks or the Gauls "back in the day!"

I remembered her eyes beaming through her cat eye horned-rimmed glasses; if you grew up in the 1960's and 70's you know the kind with the "chains" on each side of the glasses that goes around the neck so they wouldn't fall off to the floor. You see, she had a porcelain slender and elongated nose. These chains in any event kept her glasses from falling off in the "heat of battle" and the prevention of shattering on the floor as her intensive focus would be in feeding the end of her swatting paddle on some youthful flesh.

Yeah, she sat there looking at me while attempting to conceal some measure of restraint as to the surprise of me lobbing down upon her very organized desk my work in its entirety.

Her desk was without no doubt, the diligent display of the very same organization skills she acquired while beating back the Roman Invasion.

Yes, yes, the Germans lost that one, and if you ask, she probably never got over that particular loss and eventually took the experience I speak of to her grave.

In reality, she was probably a sweet woman, kind in nature, and after all, I did catch a glimpse of that now and again.

Eventually Mrs. Slaughter found time to read my work. She navigated through all of that to see the talent, or the possible lack of talent I had. I can also remember her smiling in the end when some time had passed. I remember that this very process was so very nerve-wracking for me. I remembered fretting, not so much about a grade, but rather something closer to my heart and that was simply, would it do Jonathan some justice, would he be smiling down from heaven and give me the nod of some sign of approval?

I don't recall the skies parting and a glowing golden ray of heaven's sunshine cutting through the dismal and dingy glass window up high above Mrs. Slaughter shining down upon me in that instant.

So what did happen, what did come about from all of this?

Well, let's see, Mrs. Slaughter finished the evaluation process and I survived!

Mrs. Slaughter was mysteriously warm and sensitive as she instructed me to be seated; both of the things I noticed were very rare indeed, the warm, and the sensitive.

Mrs. Slaughter began by discussing the grades. She separated them into categories and because of the length and nature of my work. She wanted to afford me the time to respond. I must have sat there forever in that little wooden chair next to the dark but highly polished table. I sat there on her left side facing the highly organized desktop and nearly paralyzed with anxiety.

She said so much, but there was something more, there was something deeper she wanted to tell me. I could feel it, nor did I have the skill or the courage to bring forth whatever that was, besides this was long before Star Wars showed me "the ways of the force" and the "Jedi" power of mind control—Curses, if only I know now what I could of known then!

She never told me what it was. It wasn't until later on that year during a parent-teacher conference that my father went and met with my teachers. He also, met Mrs. Slaughter on which she shared with him those things she had kept from me.

She knew Jonathan too, who didn't? She knew of the tragedy. She knew the story that I worked all summer and through the autumn was all about him, and dedicated to him. Anyone who knew Jonathan obviously knew the fact that is if others had a chance to read the work. It touched her emotionally and she refrained from telling me this. After all, I was a child and might misinterpret it the wrong way or something.

She confided in my father, even in spite of my dyslexia I was and for the matter is battling to this very day against armed in axe and shield. At the time, back in 1976, the school system or the medical profession knew little about. Anyway, Mrs. Slaughter confided in my father that there was this genuine gift, this gift of imagination of mine and how important, wait, nixed that, but how sacred that this gift is.

My father knew I was working feverishly on something during those months but would not disturb me on the work of mine, this seemingly paramount project—And it was!

After the conference with Mrs. Slaughter, My father then asked for the writing that I gave him to read, and I remembered feeling reluctant in doing so.

My father opened the first of two spiral notebooks and there was a piece of paper separate from my work that was Mrs. Slaughter's evaluation notes drawn out in the traditional red ink. My father began looking at her evaluation and smiled, looked at me once more, as he shooed her notes away behind my writing within the book, closed the spiral notebook, and walked away.

Again, as with Mrs. Slaughter, my father found just enough time to read both spiral notebooks and over a cup of coffee early one morning informed me as I was cooking us something to eat for breakfast, that he just finished reading the story.

"Oh God!" I exasperated so very loudly within me as my heart shot up to my throat, "Now what, what does he think, what will he say, *what will he say...*"

Yes, I probably could have been slapped to help me with my nerves, but he didn't notice, or closer to the truth, he may have chosen not to see the worried look of insurmountable dread encroach my very existence.

My father was always short on words, he got up, and he hugged me. I guess as to catch me and in doing so, he smiled as the tears welled up in his eyes.

My father said it was a magnificent story that young Jonathan would really love and would have really enjoyed it. He encouraged me, rewarding me in something that he said he could never do, and that was to sit down and create something like this up. For me it was an attempt to put things right between Jonathan, life as in reality, and his father in a proper perspective as a child with my skill and talent could possibly do. You don't need a "barnyard degree" in psychology to figure that one out!

I eventually put the work up and no one ever read it again. It was also the beginning of that nasty trait of mine; writing and putting the work up so nobody would or could ever read it. This was also the beginning of building an imaginary world and altered states of the shadowy reflections of the sometimes-harsh realities surrounding my youth.

Fast-Forward: Present Day; So you know how or what cataclysmic forces ignited me to write such an undertaking and mind you, I have began creative writing before 1976, but those, the works and tales were short stories, nothing like the magnitude of "Lord Jonathan…" My first "real" novel that I have ever written and I can sense that there still may be a question or two from whomever is reading this, what grade did I receive from Mrs. Slaughter, what did she say in her evaluation?

I will share this with you this tidbit fact; it was all positive, and the first seed of true encouragement to continue writing and something I will take with me when I meet up with Jonathan and his father.

"Yeah, boy that was a round-about way of telling everyone what forces caused you to inspire to write long stories…"

Maybe so indeed, well as for the Chronicles of Caledon and my nasty little habit, you know putting or hiding my work away. Yeah that can't happen any longer. You see, I am married to a woman who loves to read novels and stories will not allow me to write only to archive away and eventually loose. This book is dedicated to her as well as to a dear friend of mine that has in his own way, pushed me to complete it in a supportive way that I cannot adequately express into words.

I thank them both deeply for their support in this endeavor that has brought out both the creativeness and the ability now to share this with the world. Without either of these two people, the world of Caledon and all that's within would have been locked away from the world and this would be nearly as tragic to some as it would have been to my dear childhood friend that I would like to believe is now with his father.

Besides, I know there were times in the creative writing, the troublesome portions, and in the wee hours of the morning while crafting this work that Jonathan would come visit and look over the shoulder of his childhood friend and take notice and in some mysterious way, encourage me to forge on ahead and taking no prisoners in my wake!

Thanks Jonathan, and God Rest…

Introduction

Historical Linage of the Draccus Kingdom:
Accounts taken from the Sacred Scrolls of Adajahara

In the end of the First Age, the First Age, a time on where all Caledons looked to the heavens and wondered, "What powerful gods have made such wonders to include the two moons that watch over us, and to what knowledge, what life is lurking out there among the lights in the night sky?"

The innocent Caledons, though it seems by the historical account of the Ancient Sages would have come to know there was indeed life beyond the stars, and for the matter, the children of Caledon would have been far the better if this question was never resolved and left in their ignorance.

The end of the First Age came to a violent and bloody end as the invaders, the Taltakkurdg-Kevnaps, a distant humanoid race of savage cruelty brought with them the heavy shackled yokes of bondage and the terror to the likes that the Caledons had never experienced.

The first of the great Taltakkurdg-Kevnaps, the head admiral of the massive fleet have decided through self-proclamation as king, or in the Taltakkurdg-Kevnaps forked tongue, Pitah of all Caledon, the entire planet. The Pitah diverted his military forces into smashing any resistance that stood in his bloody way. Pitah Alohaim Rystak, with his dark emerald eyes gazed upon peaceful isle of Draccus, formerly called the Isle of the Dragons, home to the sacred winged beasts thought to be believed creatures sent by the gods of the netherworld to protect the faithful and innocent of the land in the traditional Caledon ancient religion.

With the aid of the Pitah's crafts and his armies invaded, the serene island landscape covered in dark oak and mist, he spared no one and brought those that surrendered to slaughter to set an example of his utmost mercilessness that he wore as a crone upon his raven scalped head to all the inhabitants of the planet.

Pitah Alohaim Rystak, in his ascension to the bloody throne of Caledon and the isle of Draccus, so renamed by the Pitah himself became his chosen center of his empire. The battle that indeed took less than a day, Pitah Alohaim Rystak secured his ambition for many generations to come.

In just a few short years, the first linage of successful and equally cruel Pitahs to reign from the great city Pitah Alohaim Rystak would later build offing a port to the Taltakkurdg-Kevnaps forces that traveled far from across the galaxy. For the Taltakkurdg-Kevnaps, this spaceport was a valuable staging point to expand their empire across the galaxy. This great city upon the Isle of Draccus was the first of the major cities ever constructed by the Taltakkurdg-Kevnaps and necessary for the Taltakkurdg-Kevnaps ambitions in dominating the galaxy, this city is called Draccarium, the greatest of the Taltakkurdg-Kevnaps cities and home of the first Pitah, served as a major military and fleet depot for the humanoid race.

Nearly two centuries continued with hard bondage as the children of Caledon prayed for the deliverance from the pale green-skinned giants with a hope and faith that someday indeed a deliverer would come. In a series of events, their deliver, the mighty foes of the Taltakkurdg-Kevnaps, the people from the "Blue Planet" as the Caledons answered the Caledon call. These people, these humans traveled across space and time from an equally distant planet like that of the Taltakkurdg-Kevnaps had arrived in the great northern expanse of the continent north of the isle and the sea of Caledon.

With this invasion of the people of the "Blue Planet" that were challenging the tyrannical grip of the Taltakkurdg-Kevnaps on the surface of the planet had already defeated the ambitions of the green-skinned demons from advancing to other systems in the galaxy, this was to be known as the beginning of the Third Age.

The "Blue Planet" peoples began liberating the northern tribes from the Taltakkurdg-Kevnaps occupation with the exception of the great Pitah of the north, a Taltakkurdg-Kevnaps descendant named Pitah Valgas, cousin of Pitah Alohaim Rystak. Pitah Valgas built a massive stronghold in Adajahara high along the mesa of the land to withstand the relentless attacks from the people of the "Blue Planet" and the children of Caledon. Pitah Valgas, a highly spiritual and mythical king of Adajahara eventually lost his grip and the conquerors; the people of the "Blue Planet" quickly freed the inhabitants and built a great city named after the land they liberated from the Taltakkurdg-Kevnaps.

The people of the "Blue Planet" build a huge spaceport allowing many from their world enter and flourish among the indigenous people of the region further driving away the influences and control of the Taltakkurdg-Kevnaps.

However, the great sons of Pitah Valgas that mostly consisted of shamans and priests of the Taltakkurdg-Kevnaps faith arose with the aid of their great uncle, Pitah Alohaim Rystak to reclaim the land of Adajahara. The holy war, through the newborn kingdom of Kahlarium, it was there, the bloodiest land feud fueled by religious and spiritual differences finally sacked Adajahara.

Once again, Adajahara was under the rule of the Pitahs only for a season as the children of the "Blue Planet" and Kahlarium arose through a siege starving out the ruminants in return. Pitah Alohaim Rystak fled for his ancient and unnaturally long life in a hasty retreat back to Draccus when the siege broke and the Taltakkurdg-Kevnaps and those armies under the Pitah were devastated.

Kahlarium, now strong enough assumed the region of Adajahara for herself, but for Adajahara, the priests of the land guarded her secrets and persuaded the kingdom of Kahlarium in an uneasy truce to serve as a spiritual place shrouded by mystery and secrets preventing, at the time, further bloodshed.

In the twentieth year of the Third Age, the black sails of Draccus reached Kahlarium and through the driven military force, Pitah Alohaim Rystak lead a force against the greatest of all the kings of Kahlarium, King Atridius. The son of Pitah Alohaim Rystak, the planned successor of Draccus, Pitah Alohaim II, eventually defeated King Atridius.

Kahlarium fell to Pitah Alohaim II as the Ramadans raised spear and axe under the leadership of Kronos, Pitah Alohaim II beheaded the rightful heir of Kahlarium, for the great king.

Only in three meager years, Pitah Alohaim II ruled Kahlarium and its province in the north, Adajahara. Adajahara again fell under an uneasy truce with the immediate withdraw of all Draccus military while maintaining their priests and the religious or spiritual temples in the region. Pitah Alohaim Rystak angered by his son's unsuccessful attempts in expanding the kingdom of Draccus, removed Alohaim II from power as the Pitah of the Draccus Northern Lands, and imprisoned him within the heart of Thuma-Attarrach. Consequently, Alohaim II was never seen again.

Legend of the early sages believed that the spirits of the Taltakkurdg-Kevnaps faith visited Pitah Alohaim Rystak from Adajahara, in this visitation; he was commanded to go to the Catanbar Mountains far to the east of Adajahara and bring all those under the faith and rule of his hand. In the sixth year of the fall of King Atridius, Pitah Alohaim Rystak did as instructed, doubling the landmass of Draccus.

Like a great wind, Pitah Alohaim Rystak rolled his forces down from the silver peaks with his newfound armies of the red bearded Tarvas; he burned his way from the east into the lands of Kranos, the homeland of Kronos. From here, the great bowman of Kranos and their light nimble forces pinned down the ancient Pitah Alohaim Rystak and severing the Pitah's reinforcements and consequently, Pitah Alohaim Rystak was captured and returning the favor, the Pitah's head was found severed from his ancient body and his unnatural long life came to an abrupt and overdue end.

Pitah Alohaim Rystak's remaining forces, those that managed to escape with their lives headed across the burning steppes of the region to the Catanbar Mountains. The armies of Kranos liberated the landscape of the black sails and banners of Pitah Alohaim Rystak and the rising Gwarvarik, the great nation of kings were born.

Draccus entered into a bloody civil war over the next ruling Pitah ensued and with the outcome, the cousin of Pitah Alohaim Rystak, Vandormirk ascended to the throne. Pitah Vandormirk, a cunning Pitah with interests of rebuilding a strong relationship with the barbaric tribes of the Tarvas to guard the dark isle from any northern reprise. Pitah Vandormirk had successfully won the hearts of his fellow countrymen and ending the civil war. The Pitah had begun rebuilding Draccus militarily as well as culturally. Pitah Vandormirk eventually died of extreme old age, his successor, his grandson Pitah Vandormirk II arose, and the first order of business was the re-introduction of the Drakkars, the ancient dragons captured in the Tarvas lands into Draccus and fulfilling his Grandfather's ambitions. Draccus during these times under the rule of Pitah Vandormirk II prospered in trade with Faedaria to the south as well as with Gwarvarik in the north.

Late in Pitah Vandormirk II's life, a dark heavy-handed movement was stirring unrest as a portion of the purest of the Taltakkurdg-Kevnaps fueled by the hateful tongues of the Taltakkurdg-Kevnaps priest conjured his assassination. Pitah Vandormirk II was forced politically to establish the Taltakkurdg-Draccus Senate that eventually closed its borders to the world of Caledon, the Fourth Age was born with the Draccus Republic and the ultimately the death of Vandormirk II.

The Taltakkurdg-Draccus Senate ruled all the districts in Draccus including any Draccian occupied lands, interests, and eventually broke treaty with the Tarvas.

With greed and the bloodlust for war, Draccus sacked the northern regions of Caledon, Gaelund, and Faedaria. The Taltakkurdg-Draccus Senate ruled these regions for nearly twelve decades before another civil war drove the Taltakkurdg-Draccus Senate into relinquishing its power to the new Pitah, Pitah

Karvadir who through a new form of government allowed the Taltakkurdg-Draccus Senate to co-exist with limited and controlling power of the Senate.

Pitah Karvadir, during his rule saw the second major invasion from the stars, the return of the Taltakkurdg-Kevnaps, though brief, Draccus remained sovereign and at an exhaustive cost. The great ancestral invasion of the Taltakkurdg-Kevnaps failed miserably. The children of the "Blue Planet" who for many centuries remained off the Caledon surface regain it's footing on the stellar region driving back the Taltakkurdg-Kevnaps once and for all as the Taltakkurdg-Kevnaps home world across the great expanse of space was utterly destroyed. The legacy of the Taltakkurdg-Kevnaps was scattered throughout the distant planets and eventually the children of the "Blue Planet" also withdrawn their interests of Caledon.

Pitah Karvadir eventually lost all of the Draccus lands south of the isle due to the struggling battles with the Taltakkurdg-Kevnaps and eventually, Pitah Karvadir died giving the throne to the first female Pitah, his only daughter, Vangosa.

Pitah Vangosa first order as she assumed the throne was the rebuilding of the Draccus culture to the restoration of the golden age of Pitah Vandormirk II. In doing so, she opened up her borders for trade and peaceful settlements of the Gundish, Pictish tribes, and Caledon kingdoms abroad.

The Draccus land and kingdom prospered and other great cities were built along with these great works, also the ancient Taltakkurdg-Kevnaps faiths were abolished, and with them new faiths, though short lived and popular arose.

Pitah Vangosa eventually married a suitor, one from a long ancient linage of Taltakkurdg-Kevnaps bloodline. Succession of Pitahs from this union arose to this day, though nothing as noble as one of the greatest Pitah diplomats that ever arose, Pitah Vangosa was deemed as the greatest of all the Pitahs in both popularity and surpassing her predecessors in peace.

Pitah Vangosa outlived most of her children, and three husbands before she passed. Her attributes in the history of Draccus were nothing short of miraculous, and for many years, Draccus found a simple peace. Her grandson, Pitah Dariuabk whose interests were much darker reinstated the ancient religion and a heart bitterly filled full of hatred once again proven to the rest of the kingdoms of Caledon, that the kingdom of Draccus was the center of military strength and vengeance.

Pitah Dariuabk's first order was the abolishment and execution of the senate and then the totalitarian reign upon all of Draccus. All non-Draccus born were exiled from its lands as he concentrated on his military forces. Before Pitah Dariuabk could unleash perhaps the greatest military fleet into the open seas, he died, some believed assassinated through poison by Vangosa or Senate sympathizers. Dariuabk son, Pitah Ikar assumed the throne and following his father's footsteps, pursued ambitions on Gaelund than eventually secured firm occupation in Northern Gaelund.

Pitah Dariuabk continued raising his army and securing the southern regions of Gwarvarik. Pitah Dariuabk died after ruling for nearly seven decades and seeing the expanse of his kingdom doubled.

His eldest son, Pitah Hamada ruled for nearly two decades maintaining the regions his father conquered without little resistance or the ambition of scorching his mark on the Caledon landscape.

Pitah Hamada great nephew, Pitah Amadrok ascended the throne only for just a few years before he died of natural causes leaving also Draccus and for that matter, Caledon in the same state.

Amadrok III, then assumed the throne, a grandson of Pitah Hamada fought against the liberation of Southern Gwarvarik. However, not a successful warrior, Pitah Amadrok III maintained the unruly occupied northern lands of Faedaria, Gaelund, and Caledon up to his death.

Accounts Taken from the Sacred Historical Scrolls of Caledon and Gwarvarik:

By the time his great grandson, Morderra-Atrauis arrived as Pitah, all lands outside the Isle were lost to Draccus. The treaties with Tarvas that were again bonded before the reign of Morderra-Atrauis was straining, fueled by the Tarvas conquest of the Ramadan tribal kingdom and the increasing threat of the Gwarvarik kingdom. The Tarvas, pressuring Morderra-Atrauis to aid in overcoming Gwarvarik was preoccupied with his dark intentions into regaining the northern region of Gaelund offered minimal forces under the guise of peace with Gwarvarik. Morderra-Atrauis' dark plan was to send a façade of peace and negotiations with the King of Gwarvarik in trade and diplomatic offerings. Morderra-Atrauis began trading the Black Lotus, a highly addictive and mind altering herb that grew in abundance in Draccus to weaken the Gwarvarik kingdom enough to give the Tarvas barbarian armies the winning edge and to alleviate the pressures of a reprise from the Tarvas tribes upon Draccus and maintaining his press on Gaelund.

As the deceitful trade between Gwarvarik and Draccus continued, Gaelund eventually won the war in its northern forests and repelling any further attempts by Morderra-Atrauis. Draccus, heavily drained from years of war and a dwindling population enraged by the Pitah's Black Corsairs, his most elite of his personal army froth with corruption raping the landscape of Draccus from its limited wealth began rising up against the Pitah. Dearth, a small village was the first to strike out against the cruel intolerable Black Corsairs. The battle though small, costing nearly all the inhabitants of Dearth through the aid of a rumored mythical leader defeated the small army and sparking a new civil war in the land.

With the return of the remaining military forces, returning home joined in the rebellion against the Pitah. However, Morderra-Atrauis was never found and shrouded in mystery and the uncovering of his evil acolyte leaders, Draccus quickly dispatched the remaining Pitah government.

Upon the sacking of the most sacred temples and holy places in Draccus by the rebellion, Thuma-Attarrach, the throne of Draccus fell to a new Pitah, a non-Draccus born outsider, a former admiral that was hand chosen by Morderra-Atrauis himself, a man named Tiberius, a Gundish native.

To this day, Pitah Tiberius governs his land, and through his leadership rests peace and prosperity with the land and his new people. However, Morderra-Atrauis was never found along with two of his highest-ranking acolytes, the ancient and oldest living Draccian former leader is presumed dead. There is, of course, speculation and to his whereabouts and or his demise.

Historical accounts through the fall of Draccus by this civil war and the ascension of Tiberius to the thrown are at best, hidden by secrecy and legend, but the sages did recover some hidden scrolls on this mystifying subject, known as the Thuma-Attarrach Scrolls.

The Thuma-Attarrach scrolls and those written accounts of what had taken place upon the arrival and the discoveries of Tiberius and his army are adamantly denied by Pitah Tiberius himself, and he denies its accurate and historical account of events. The Thuma-Attarrach scrolls are considered contraband and illegal under the possession of any Draccian.

Excerpts taken directly from the Sacred Historical Scrolls of Caledon and Gwarvarik Thuma-Attarrach Scrolls:

Upon the immediate execution of the orders of Tiberius, all Lycoi, deemed to by the mystical beast of the evil Morderra-Atrauis, order was given and dispatched that the Lycoi would be gathered and executed sparing no beast to surfer with its life, regardless of gender or age. The Lycoi tribes in the ancient woods and hills were gathered and executed along with any whom found aiding these beasts. Great in numbers, the Lycoi are undergoing extermination and Tiberius has offered a bounty to any hide, mane, or head of these horrid beasts...

...The fall of Thuma-Attarrach finally came in the Month of the Lion and Tiberius with his leading generals lead a brilliant campaign against the last of the mighty Lycoi and eventually the surrender of the former Pitah soldiers, the wretched Black Corsairs. Those that resisted were put to death in the end along with any Tarvas born found among them...

...As reinforcements arrived at the siege of the former castle, the Illua Falls ran down in blood as Tiberius carved his way into the inner sanctum of the throne of the Pitahs. It was in the inner most part of the former throne, the Castle when order was given that none shall enter except of those of the most brilliant of minds and those with the strongest of stomachs...

...Many evil wonders were uncovered and studied on behalf of the new Pitah of Draccus, in the bowels of the black mountain was discovered a den of blood feeding creatures who waged a high cost upon the most trusted of the Tiberius' men. The blood feeding creatures, though Draccian originating was somehow changed by the curse to feed upon the blood of men. As these men were attacked by these creatures whom is forbidden to speak of, and those that did not die by the attack, would in the course of several days, no more than three or four, would become these beasts...

...Two of Tiberius's closest fell victim to this curse and were put down in such a way that they would not arise again...

...Fire and beheading were the final resolve for many of the blood-feasting creatures who withstood against Tiberius and his soldiers...

...For those blood feeding fanged abominations, some were taken in captivity alive, though impossibly strong and swift were subdued and taken from the heart of the mountain. However, upon the light of day, these captives burst into flames and ashes and were of no more...

...Becoming too costly, the remaining creatures were buried within the mountain and the passage sealed for all time...

...There was a great hall that contained columns of thick glass, and behind this glass were strange creatures, some almost human, and some not. Though dead and many encased in these glass tombs for many untold years seemed to be rather a horrid collection of both Morderra-Atrauis and his fathers. For no living person has ever seen such a collection of strange creatures than this mountain contains...

...There were signs of a great battle waged within the mountain that was also uncovered. This battle was fought showing large numbers of Lycoi and these blood-feeding acolyte creatures, the remnants of the Black Corsairs and the other evil minions of

Morderra-Atrauis. Nowhere are there signs of those fallen in battle of their attackers...

...A great dungeon was also recovered and many doorways sealed and remained sealed, there were no survivors found...

...Great works, those deemed by the most ancient of the Pitah and Draccus bloodline were found and are studied by the most brilliant scribes appointed by Tiberius as to their nature and purpose...

...It was in these works an ancient man, a man of extreme old age, a priest of a forgotten order was found still barely alive and eating on rats and other creatures. His name was Kronus, though mad and old, he was treated for his wounds and though many ailments beyond treating, he succumbed to the horrendous years in the dungeon as prisoner of Morderra-Atrauis...

...Before he died, though blind by his disease and harsh lifestyle, he told Tiberius of a young man, a Ramadan that is the keeper of some mystical weapon, a sword, a sword of greatness and mystery. Kronus spoke of his encounter of this Ramadan boy in Adajahara many years ago and that this boy traveled through the northlands and eventually taken to Draccus by ship disguised as a Draccian. The boy then grew to become a man who, according to Kronus, had become a powerful sorcerer through the sword and fought against Morderra-Atrauis and this man, responsible for the death of many that Tiberius had uncovered...

...When asked by the Pitah who this man's name was, Kronus expired before saying the identity of this person...

...As time progressed the mysteries surrounding Thuma-Attarrach have been sealed this day, all accounts of the ancient castle have been put away save for this, the last remaining scroll.

Many began speaking of the horror and those things recovered and destroyed. The castle was finally destroyed and her secrets with it by the order of Pitah Tiberius and all banished from the top of the mountain where once again the Drakkars find safe haven...

CHAPTER 1

━━━━━━━━━━━━━ ▼ ━━━━━━━━━━━━━

"Oh, from afar shall come the Deliverer that will smite the terrible army of the Wicked and bind the hearts of men into one against the Iniquity..."

—From an ancient Rune Kobarian prophecy.

Long before the fall of the central kingdoms and the dark sails of Draccus pierced the hearts of both men and beasts into a great war, a tribal battle in the frozen north is drawing to a final close. The battle, these barbaric skirmishes have lasted nearly four generations before the silence of near genocide befell the weaker, the quieter and peaceful, as it does so many times before. Now, beneath the audience of the dark granite peaks and across the bloodstained snowfields the spoils of war belongs to the victor. For the victor, the fierce Tarvas who dwelt over timeless seas of generations high in the Catanbar Mountains region had finally come to them. The lands below the snowfields beyond the Iratirus River, the lands of their foes, lay the Ramadan lands. The great Chieftain, Y'llian-Talbok lay dead in the snow, his strong powerful body separated from his head in a pool of freezing blood, along with countless of other bodies that dotted the pristine landscape. The Tarvas warriors raced through the winding pass wreaking havoc upon the villages below like a great pestilence of locusts, and the fall of the Ramadans has now begun.

Soon, pillars of smoke rose from the landscape of the forest canopy below the mountains, and the air filled with screams that were suddenly silenced. With the fall of the Ramadans, the Tarvas grew stronger in numbers, enslaving the women and children and putting to the blade, every old and sick Ramadan man over the age of twelve. In chains, those few Ramadans were forced to march under the Tarvas whip. To the north, through the high passes of the Catanbar Mountains on which many imprisoned succumbed to the elements, the death marched continued. A Ramadan boy stood there shackled to his mother who lay in the snow, her body broken and cold, laid still, the boy too exhausted to cry he fell along the side of her, his body barely covered shivered. He looked up into his mother's face; her steel blue eyes had faded as the life left her a few moments before. He knew she was dead, and he realized that he too would be with her, and as he thought, he too would be joined with his father who died months before against the relentless Tarvas masters.

The young child had stopped shivering so uncontrollably now as he could almost hear his mother's voice calling him from afar in a direction he could not quite discern. The taste of blood from his bleeding gums, wounds sustained in beatings from his Tarvas masters. His legs bruised and nearly broken and his skin on his back shown signs of old and fresh marks with the Tarvas whip were now completely exposed to the elements of the bitter cold. A sound much closer in the snowfield came forth from behind him, for he knew this familiar sound; it was the sound of feet in the snow, feet belonging to the Tarvas demons.

The laid still and held his breath, thinking it was his last, "Look here is too more!" growled the menace that loomed just above the boy that concentrated a stare into his dead mother's eyes. "A boy I think and that of a woman, dead!" The voice said. The boy knew the man above him had his head turned to another farther down the pass at a slight distance from all the others who were chained and marching further up the mountains. "Shit, these Ramadans are weak, if this keeps up, we will have none to tend to our goats!" The Tarvas warrior began to laugh as he bent down and unshackled the small boy and woman. "No sense of leaving good steel on this Ramadan trash." The boy could feel only the numbing bitter cold go deep into his body while concentrating as hard as he could in staring into his mother's eyes. He then could hear the footsteps of the Tarvas warrior leave, as he lay there motionless in the snow as the frost began to form on his brow and eyelashes.

Just then, the sun began to shine through the thick brooding clouds, so bright that it nearly blinded him causing him to squint with the reflection off the snow. It has been the first time he has seen the sun in three or four days traveling through the rugged and remote passes of these mountains. He could not move it was now only a matter of time before he too would follow his mother and he accepted it. The young boy thinking that on the other side, somewhere he knew nothing about, only that it had to be a better place, a place that he would find both his mother and his father waiting for him. Tears began to well up in his eyes as he could feel the sun upon his frozen flesh warming his body slowly at first. After a few minutes, the stinging in his legs, feet, and toes were almost too unbearable, but he was still alive. With each passing minute, he grew warmer under the intensive sun. Eventually for whatever reason, he knew that it would be some other day before he would meet his mother and father on the other side of this life, this harsh life he must continue to endure.

"You will do my bidding" The voice sounded sinisterly and far off that was in the young boy's native tongue.

The boy remained motionless, and thought about the direction where the old and sinister voice was coming from, he waited nearly holding his own breath, "I have spared you life so that I may do my work in you." The voice faded off again, and for the boy, this troubled him because he knew that someone out there knew he was yet alive.

"Arise, my child." The voice sounded closer, sounded it was just behind him, but above him. The boy heard no other noise, no footsteps, no breathing, and no sound of armor and steel mail.

"Adajahara, you will go, there you will learn what is already inside you, and there you will also learn much" The voice faded off into the slight breeze and then came back to the boy lying in the frozen snow.

"Arise and head down on where you have came, I will guide you to where you need to be, and be not afraid." The sinister voice seemed colder than that of the boy's surroundings, but he had nothing else to trust, nothing else to go by and he was certainly smart enough to realize if he stayed there in the pass, he would die.

Shortly after all the noise from behind him had passed and he knew he was alone, he arose and looked around and could see no one, except for his mother's frozen body. He then took her outer garments as his own and arose and turned and walked down the pass, in doing so, he turned on final time to his mother's body as his tears flowed from his reddening frost bitten face and said goodbye in his native tongue.

He traveled down the pass as carefully as he could in the blinding sun, he was warmer now, his body was trembling, but not from the cold, but from fear, fears of being caught, but fear knowing he was truly alone.

Soon minutes passed into hours, and hours into a few days. He had now managed to escape the Tarvas's whip and headed south along the foothills of the mountain range behind him. The young orphan ate wild berries to the point it was making him sick, but he was free. The boy did manage to find a small sword, a Ramadan dagger in fact, but in his tiny hands, it was like a sword, and something that would give him an illusion of protection.

The small boy, thoughts filled on where to go, in what direction, and for how long, preoccupied his mind. He had no real sense of direction, and he found it hard to focus, so he decided to follow the direction of the sun as it rose, and as soon it was over him, he would follow his shadow until night, this he knew would keep him heading in on direction. He had done this for several more days.

By his second week of walking through the foothills that opened to the plains of his people, he came across several villages, mostly leveled to the ground; there he found enough bread and clothing to get dressed. He made a pack, crude in nature so that he could haul some meager supplies and an old flask for his drinking water.

The bruising suffered from his beatings was healing in his legs as he grew stronger, and the wounds on his back and arms began to heal as well. The land he was traveling through was unfamiliar to him and at times he thought briefly about turning back, but he did not, he figured to stay with his original plan as best as he could. His fears of being alone gave way to excitement of the adventure that was beginning to unfold before his eyes.

In another week, the mountains were just a purple distant line barely noticeable over his left shoulder. The young boy continued now accompanied by a heavy wooden staff he held firmly in his right hand as he walked. He also had a leather belt tired around his waist held his dagger and kept his dark-blue wool tunic from blowing up over his head in the wind. He managed to find a pair of leather sandals, slightly too big for his small feet, but they were much better than the animal skin rags he was wearing before.

Eventually he left behind him the ruins of his people and crossed over several small streams before he was at the edge of a huge river, too wide, and too swift to cross, and on the other side, as far as he could see in either direction was a huge green forest. As he looked through his green eyes, he could see hills rising from the forest, covered in strange trees like that of the forest, trees he has never seen before, they were not of the pine. As he stood there in the midday sun, his face covered in dirt and sweat he looked down at the small pool of still water from the raging river and could see his dirty reflection. He smiled at the reflection, bent down, washed his face in the cool water, and then filled his flask that was nearly emptied.

"Boy, you must find a way across the river." He arose and turned half-startled and half-expecting to find someone standing behind him, and he recognized the voice to be that of his father.

"What?" He replied clutching his staff with his right-hand looking bewildered. He clearly heard the warning as his heart began to race. "What direction shall I go, I am too small to cross this river, and I would die?" He yelled aloud to the surroundings, and of course, there was no answer as he waited.

He then turned west following the bank of the river half trotting along. He did this until sunset that day and slept during the night. Sometime in the morning, the voice returned to him in the same fashion, "Boy, you must find a way across the river" and there was nothing more. Lithius continued at a fast pace until his sides hurt, it was now midday and still no sign of the river getting any more likely to cross, or any sign of a bridge to aid him.

The boy did not waste time throughout the day, only taking a break long enough to muster enough strength to go again. Eventually he ran up to a large path, a dirt trail that ran up along the upper bank. He decided to go along the path; he would cover even more distance easier than taking his chances along the lower bank next to the water. The day eventually turned toward night, and before it got completely dark on the small boy, he found the safety of a small tree, a tree that looked odd to him, like those in the forest across the water. That night, he ate the rest of what little of the bread he had left, he was now out of food, and this worried him. Throughout the last couple of days, he has seen no sign of wildlife with the exception of an eagle that flew high overhead. The young boy in his tenth season figured the eagle was also searching in hopes to uncover an unsuspecting hare, but eventually the eagle had moved on, perhaps crossing the river to the forest, so the young boy thought.

The boys slept soundly throughout the night, and in the early dawn, he awoke just as the stars were fading from the brightening sky. It was early as he wiped the sleep away, he was cold and slightly stiff, he knew how to build a fire, but since his escape, he decided against it, too easy for someone to spot him, or the Tarvas to find him. As he arose, he could see a twinkling of a different light from the woods across the river. As he looked, he could see they were scattered campfires, he could smell any smoke, or hear anything beyond the sounds of the river, but he could definitely see the light. He stood there for a few moments looking and the voice came again, "Boy, you must find a way across the river." The voice faded quickly, quicker than before and it sounded somewhat different, a voice familiar like his father's, but somehow different, never the less he then grabbed his staff and trotted along the trail that followed along the river that shortly turned with the waters south.

By midmorning the young boy ran across large number of tracks, mostly sandaled footprints of what looked like young children, women, and others he would assume would be of men. Oddly, there were no tracks of livestock, no other creatures, and one other thing that he seemed thankful for, no signs of the Tarvas. The tracks, weeks old all was heading to the same direction that the child was heading. He continued as best as he could that eventually led to a small cluster of trees, trees like that from across the river.

Once inside the shade of these trees, the dirt path widened into a stony path that was three times as wide as the boy was tall. He found this path odd and he has never seen such a path made of such a stone. The boy then looked directly across this path and could see another dirt path, like the very same he was on. He crossed the stony pathway to the dirt, there he could see the footprints, and they were different from the ones he was following, other people traveling toward the stony pathway. He looked north along the stony path and could see no sign of tracks, he turned south and could not find any available due to the stones. He wiped the sweat from his brow that was stinging his eyes, as it was silent in the small patch of trees and with the exception of crickets and a few grasshoppers singing.

He realized that the people, those that left the tracks from both trails were in a hurry. There was no sign of livestock headed to this point from both directions, and as the boy concluded, perhaps they were chased, but there was no sign of the Tarvas. He looked south as the path lead slightly west down from the small hill along to a thicker cluster of trees. He figured this was his best bet, which is if he wanted to see his eleventh season.

The boy followed the stony path through the ever-thickening woods, the shade offered coolness as his lungs were on fire and his sides aching from the fast pace. He could not see the mountains any longer, or the plains behind him. He spent a few minutes catching his breath and taking in some water. "Almost there. You must keep going, you are in danger here" It was the voice, not as faint as before, the voice still sounded near the boy, but the boy realized that the voice was more like coming from within him.

"Who are you?" The boy insisted, but there was no answer. "What danger?" the boy asked, and like before no reply.

The boy forced himself to go on as best as he could through the thickening woods on where it was becoming quite dark. At least, he could hear small birds and the sound of small game scurrying through the brush. By late afternoon, the boy could not continue to run any longer and found a dark cool shaded spot that concealed him from view as he fought hard to regain his breath and collapsed.

It was late in the day when he came around out of his slumber, he felt rested but hungry, and he drank from his flask, his lips parched, and his limbs trembling from the lack of food and strength. As he arose, he looked across the stony path, found a small shrub of berries, and crossed the path and picked them; he recognized them as a safe berry that tasted especially sweet, not as bitter as the ones before. After he carefully picked them, he put what he could not eat into his small pack and headed once again down the stone path.

By sunset, it was entirely too dark within the woods for him to see clearly, he found shelter like before and rested there until morning. When he arose again, it was due to the sound of thundering hooves quickly approaching. The sound filled the forest and he could sense the sounds of many riders were coming from the north. As the riders came into view, he could see they were Tarvas Warriors on Larnges, huge and fast six legged wholly beasts, larger than the horses sent from the gods of the time of old. The boy only saw these horses, the creatures that by the stories of the great elders of his camp said that come from another world far away. As far as the Larnges, these creatures were of this world, but for the boy, he had only seen a couple few in the wild as he was growing up. He knew of no one from his tribe that rode such creatures. His father told him that there was other Ramadans farther east and to the south that did, and of course only a few Tarvas.

As the Warriors' foes rode in a hurry passed the view of the small boy, he could see that these warriors were not the same as those that captured him and his mother. They were slightly different, the color and markings upon their faces in paint were of something the boy has never seen before. There must have been fifty or so riders kicking up the dust and heading in a great hurry with weapons drawn, mostly spears, and swords.

The Warriors, as soon as they had appeared, they were gone as the thunderous sound faded off into the south and out of the eyesight of the small boy. At first he thought, perhaps they were after him, but quickly dismissed it, if he could not find tracks along the stony path, how could they? Besides, they were traveling toward some sort of a blistering attack.

The boy then gathered his belongings and began walking toward the stony path, "If they would have found you, they would have killed you." It was the voice again, sounding even stronger, and more unlike the boy's voice of his father.

"Who are you?" The boys said.

"Someone who has been watching you from afar" The voice replied somewhat reassuring as it could not to alarm the boy who was looking in all directions for the source of the boy.

"Were you the eagle?" The boys asked bewildered and scared.

"No, though I did see him aloft wondering about the same thing as I was"

"What is it that you are wondering?" The boy asked still trying to uncover the source of the voice.

"Why a small boy alone travels great distance alone?" The voice asked as it transformed fully from the voice of the boy's father to an older voice, a voice belonging to an older man, a foreigner that knew the tongue of the Ramadan.

"Not to worry, I mean you no harm man-cub…"

The boy quipped.

"A young Ramadan, and by the looks of it, a young lad who's been through a lot in recent days" The boy remained silent as the voice, a dialect in it that the young Ramadan has never heard before.

"If I spoke to you in such a fashion a couple of days ago without any familiarity you would bolt away and I could not guide you."

"Guide me where?" The boy insisted as he drew his free hand to the hilt of his dagger.

"No need for that, I will not harm you." The voice said. The boy could feel eyes, unseen eyes upon him.

"How did you know the voice of my father?" The boy asked as his heart raced.

"I read it in your mind; I thought at first you knew I was running around in your thoughts. I also know that you are alone." The boy remained now motionless except for his probing green eyes looking around the forest for the sign of this trick.

"…I am sorry about your mother as well The Tarvas are ruthless people who do not appreciate the value of their won life let alone a life of one of their slaves I'm afraid. But yet a child was able to fool them and escape" Then the boy felt something, like a hand inside of his thoughts unrolling the scrolls of his thoughts.

"I feel you now, demon!" The boy drew out the dagger.

"Demon?" The voice quizzed, "No, not a demon, I am afraid you are a little wrong on that one." The feeling of someone inside of his head grew probing his every thought and the young boy did not like it and closed his eyes and strained to find the culprit in his head and once doing so, he has seized the silhouette of a dark figure like a twisted man without features, a face he could not see.

The boy could see the phantom in his head clearly enough to see it seemed surprised that the boy's thoughts were looking back at the figure. "Release me?" the figure warned inside the boy's head.

"No, I will not!" The child warned as beads of sweat began dripping down from his forehead. The figure then broke free, knocking the boy down physically and removed itself from the boy's mind.

"Amazing, a man-cub, who caught me?" The boy could hear the amazement in the wolf's words. The young boy continued to guard his thoughts. In a way, he was both astonished and could not readily explain this gift.

"I am Naverron, great druidic wolf of the Najar." The boy never heard of such a thing and still on his guard became somewhat curious.

"A wolf?" the boy asked.

"Yes, a wolf" The voice was clearer now than ever before as it began to continue to speak.

"I saw you several days ago when I first came to you. However, I spotted you from the other side of the river. First, I noticed the sent, I knew you were Ramadan, and everyone knows what has been happening to the Ramadans with the Tarvas. So I went to seek you out, found out more about you, and well, I guided you here and thus far, you aren't dead." The voice paused for only a moment, "I took pity on your loss"

"I do not need your pity!" The boy raised his dagger in plain sight.

"That is pride talking their man-cub, and for the dagger would not be much use in your hands against me if I chose to harm you, on which, as I said before, I do not."

"Show yourself, wolf!" The boy firmly demanded the actions of his words.

"Certainly." The voice grew quiet and the boy could see from the settling dust from across the stony pathway arose two intensive red eyes, the color of rubies catching what little light there was being offered by the dense foliage. As the wolf entered the stony pathway, the light caught the shining pitch-black fur of the huge beast, its glaring red eyes focused on the boy with the dagger in his hand, not to mention, and the staff in the other. The huge wolf, an animal that outsized the boy in weight and height, then stopped and rested its backside firmly on the stony path never looking away from the boy in the foliage beyond.

The boy could sense the glaring red eyes upon him, and he knew if the wolf wanted to, the wolf could easily take the small boy. "What kind of wolf can speak to a, a, a"

"Man-cub?" the wolf responded.

"Yes." The boy answered back.

"As I said, I am a Najar."

"I do not know what a Najar is, is it a type of wolf?" The boy was having some difficulty speaking because of the surmounting fear from the sight of such a powerful wolf, a wolf that was at least twice the size of any wolf that the boy seen growing up.

"Najar, no, not a wolf but of the people far away from here, though you see a wolf before you, I was indeed a man before." The wolf spoke through its telepathic powers to the child standing on the other side.

"What trick is this?" The boy was becoming even more bewildered by all of this as the wolf could clearly see.

"I was once a man, a powerful man, a druid of my people the Najar"

"A druid, what is a druid?" The boy asked.

"A shaman to your people, you do know what a shaman is, right?" The wolf asked with an element of understanding.

"Yes, yes, my father was a shaman before he died." The boy insisted.

"Pretty much the same in so many ways I suppose. So I chose long ago of being a wolf instead of being a human. A wolf is a sacred animal, but I am still very much a man as I was inside, this is how I can clearly talk with you through the powers of telepathy." Naverron added.

Naverron's voice did not sound cold, or sinister like the voice in the mountains. Therefore, the young boy decided he would keep that part, the part of the sinister voice to himself.

"So you are a man in a wolf's body?" The boy asked looking as bewildered as before.

"No, I am a wolf, just with a spirit of a man. Before I was a man with a spirit of a wolf in him, do you understand?"

"Not really, but I hear your words though you do not open your mouth only to pant or yawn. Why should I trust you?" The boy asked, looking curious at the huge wolf.

"That is a good question, why would you trust me?" Naverron concluded looking down at his two front paws and then back up at the boy who was still concealed in the brush across the path.

"Who taught you the tongue of the Ramadan?" The boy quipped as he held the dagger firmly in his left hand.

"I learned some of it, well, long ago when I first traveled into the Great Plains, long before the Tarvas, and some of it from you since the other day." The wolf answered.

"If you do not make it to the other side of this river, you will most certainly be caught, more likely than not, killed. If you follow me, I will guide you safely to the other side to the land of the Gwarvarik people. The forestland you have been seeing since you arrived at the great river. There you will travel to the temple ruins of Adajahara. It will be at Adajahara that you will take your leave from me, and we will go our separate ways." The wolf then grew silent.

"Why have you really chosen to help me?" The boy insisted.

"It's a long, long story, and if you do not mind, we must go. Adajahara is at the least three days travel from here." The wolf then arose to all fours and then trotted off only looking once more at the direction of the small boy.

"You can choose life, or you can take your chances with death there in the fallen lands of the Ramadan boy."

The boy stood there thinking on the words of the Najar wolf and decided to take his chances with the black creature. In doing so, the boy followed behind him to a great bridge that crossed only halfway across the river to a huge island in the middle. The direct sunlight nearly blinded the boy as he stood there watching the wolf continuing to cross the cobblestone bridge.

The boy had put his dagger away and trotted off after the large wolf as he led the way to the tall trees on the other side of the bridge.

Naverron was the first to cross over into the island, "Come man-cub, we are halfway there to the land of the Gwarvarik." Naverron said without turning around. The boy focused his thoughts toward the wolf far above in front of him, "Can you hear me?" the boy thought without saying a word physically.

"What?" Naverron said suddenly as if he half heard the boy.

"Can you hear me?" The young boy focused with all of his strength.

"Yes, I can, how far back are you?" The wolf turned and trotted back and could see the astonished boy's face halfway to the island, "Come, quit dragging your feet." The wolf said as urgently as he could.

"Okay, I am coming." The boy could see that the wolf realized what he was doing, he was talking to the wolf in a like manner, this of course, and the boy could sense that the wolf was a bit nerved by this.

The wolf turned and trotted back toward the island, "I know you can hear me Naverron" The boy concentrated as he ran headlong toward Naverron. "Yes, yes." The wolf replied as he continued along the path that ran up higher along the island.

Eventually, the cobblestone trail headed to the steep hill of the island, and from there, the boy and the wolf could see in either direction for a great distance. The two could see another bridge on the other side of the island toward the Gwarvarik forestland made of the same stone as the other bridge in like fashion. More importantly, the boy could see that the Tarvas riders were nowhere to be seen.

"So what happened to the riders?" the boy asked Naverron using the new found gift, and with it, the boy could see enough into Naverron's thoughts that he truly was not there to hurt the boy. The wolf was there to help him, and the boy could sense that Naverron was actually sent, "…sent by whom?" the boy thought. Nevertheless, he was trying to be as careful as he could not to raise the suspicion in Naverron. He knew for whatever reason unknown to the boy that the gift had come natural and easy enough, but did not understand how.

"Whom did I come across this gift Naverron?" the boy asked while he was attempting to catch his breath.

Naverron was preoccupied by something; something far more important than the boy stumbling upon the gift of telepathy and the boy was sensing this as he noticed the large wolf looking on behind them to the huge plains. The boy turned to face the same direction, and with his left hand, he put on the top of the front shoulders of Naverron. "What do you see?" the boy asked.

"The bloodshed will continue until your people are destroyed and have become the ashes and dust of the land. I am also afraid that the Gwarvarik is next, we must go, climb upon me, I can support you and grab hold of my mane." Naverron warned.

The boy did so, Naverron trotted down the hill along the winding path into the forest below, and within a few minutes, they crossed to the other side into Gwarvarik. Upon there, Naverron found yet another path leading south and the boy suspected that this path also made of stone would lead to Adajahara.

"What is Adajahara?" The boy asked as he realized that this could be a name of a place.

"A sacred ancient places of people long ago, a place that I must take you." Naverron said as he panted along the winding trail at a great speed.

"Are these the Gwarvarik people you talk about?"

"No, an ancient race of people long forgotten that very little of the Gwarvarik know about and more importantly, the Tarvas knows nothing about. Be still so that I may concentrate on the way." He warned, as the boy grew silent.

The wolf raced through the winding woods with great speed and with the boy on his back. This was the case for the remainder of that day. By night, the two rested by a small stream of fresh cold water.

"What of the Tarvas Warriors that we saw earlier?" the boy asked.

"They remained on the first path. The first path will lead eventually to a city of the Gwarvarik, their will they meet with the others already outside the walls of the city, and it will be there that they will find their deaths. The city will eventually fall to the Tarvas, but not for a while yet to come. Already there are soldiers from other villages along the river's edge that has joined to do battle against the savages from the mountains, and the Gwarvarik is not as simple as your people

man-cub." The wolf then grew quiet as it took a cool drink from the small bubbling stream of moss-covered rocks.

The boy thought about the campfires he caught a glimpse from earlier, "So
that was them?" He thought to himself.

"That was who?" The wolf said.

"Oh the soldiers from the campfires I saw from when I was on the other side
of the river a couple of days ago." The boy whispered.

"Build us a fire if you know how, and I will fetch us supper." Naverron said
looking back at the boy standing there looking somewhat amazed.

"Is it safe?"

"Safe enough" The boy then turned back to the wolf, but the wolf was gone
without a sound. A few minutes later, the boy had started a small fire and went to
go fetch larger sticks close by and on his return; he saw the large wolf that just
dropped a huge hare before the flames.

"It has been a very long time since I have had a cooked rabbit." The wolf
added looking up over at the small boy who was pleasantly surprised.

After supper, the boy filled with meat inside of him grew tired and slept
throughout the night. The wolf, Naverron spent most of the evening looking and
sniffing about in the night air, looking for something or someone in the distance,
someone who hadn't come.

By morning, Naverron woke up the small boy. Like the manner before, the
boy saddled the wolf. The two headed deeper into the forest along the path that
out skirted a small village and traveling along the steep hillside of the mountains
along the dirt path that faded to nothing. By the evening of the second night in
the land of Gwarvarik, up high in the mountains on where the thick forest below
tapers considerably, the two had covered great distances. Again, Naverron was
treated to cooked meat, and the boy to fresh rabbit. By the third day with little
said from Naverron, the two headed up along the crest of the jaded mountains,
and to a forest of pines and heavy mountain forest timber. "These trees I know
of," the boy said.

"What of the heavy oaks below?" Naverron asked.

"No, they are strange to me?" The boy admitted.

"I see" Naverron said as his attention turned toward Adajahara.

"Up ahead are the ancient ruins, the temples of Adajahara, and it will be here
that I will leave you. This is where we will our separate paths." The wolf said
soberly.

"Why, why must we separate?" The young boy, who over the last three days grew closer to Naverron as a friend gaining trust as they went on in this adventure.

"It is the way it is supposed to be, this is they way it is intended, do you feel that?" Naverron said.

"Yes, but I do not know why, can I go with you?" the boy asked desperately.

"No, I go to Najar now; it is a very long way from here, very long across the sea and leagues, and passed the shores on the other side."

The boy who had grown close to the wolf, his heart was becoming heavy, "Will I ever see you again?" This caused the wolf to stop in his tracks.

"The next time you will see me, things will be different I'm afraid, and you will be a man, but you will see me again." Then Naverron grew quiet as the boy held back the welling tears as best he could in his green eyes.

"Many things are not without some sacrifice in this world my young friend, just as you and too many others. I'm afraid has paid too dear of a price, but do not become bitter, do not allow your heart to grow cold whatever you do. I sense that you will become a very powerful man, a man, that will surpass the powers of your father and will lead men, but that is all I can see, other than a dark future of a storm on where I will see you once more, but as a man." Naverron grew silent and without another word delivered the young boy to the high table rock, a mesa that had a few ancient building covered in moss and vines. From the distance, the boy could see the buildings were made of white stone under the green growth.

"Adajahara" Naverron stopped, "I am afraid my back is rather tired man-cub, could you please get down." Naverron asked politely.

The boy slipped off and looked at the ancient site. "As you can see, the path down there, follow that up to the temples, there you shall see the main temple, look, it's the one with a huge dome, and do you see?" The wolf asked.

The boy could see a huge building with a white dome. Upon this white dome, a huge groove or gap that started at the top of the structure's roof that ran straight down to the base of the dome. "Yes, I see it?"

"Good, and do you see those animals in the field nest to the great temple through the mist?"

"Sheep?" the boy half asked.

"Yes, they are sheep, they are Adajahara temple sheep, they are your sheep, take care of them, and they will take care of you." Naverron said softly.

"Why are you brining me here?" The boy turned to face Naverron.

"To keep you safe, safe from the war below that will soon sweep this land, and like I said there are only a handful of people that know of this place. There is no one down there in Adajahara, just the sheep and you." There was something that Naverron wasn't saying, and the boy could sense it. The boy could sense that the wolf knew that the boy was attempting to peer into his mind in like fashion as the wolf did earlier.

"Now mind what I say, you will be safe young Ramadan, grow wise in the wisdom of the temples below and take care of yourself, already I am late." The wolf warned.

"You have not answered my question Naverron, why are we really here?" the boy insisted.

"In time there will be another who will come and answer that, and of course, other questions. Now listen, there is a great cistern below the temples, there is fresh water, a lake really, but be careful when going down there, draw from the rain water for the livestock as best as you can, the rain season will be in the fall, and in the winter, the snow, but not a lot, least so I am told. Look at the orchard south passed the pasture; they are of trees not of this world that bare fruit in the late spring and summer, they are ripening even now, as we speak. Store this fruit well; you will draw from them time to time"

The boy turned once more, looking at the three tightly organized rows of trees toward Naverron, but the wolf was gone. "You never did get my name" The boy said through his telepathic power, but no response from Naverron as tears welled up in his eyes as he realized that he was once again very alone, and his future, uncertain.

CHAPTER 2

▼

The remainders of the summer, the boy tended to the sheep and orchard of Adajahara, the nights were mild, and the days warm, but he spent them alone. As time passed into the early fall, the young boy learned to catch wild game, mostly small hares. He would go on adventures, mostly exploring the ancient ruins of Adajahara. There in the various temples he found scrolls of pictures and strange writings that he could not read and decipher. There were things amongst him that he has never seen before, large glass and translucent objects, some of these things were obviously broke, decayed or in disarray. He decided to clean and get things in the best order before winter would finally arrive. With winter would be hardships as the nights were now growing colder and the leaves turning gold, red, and yellow falling from the trees in the orchard, and already, he had gathered the fruit from the trees on which he found both sweet and fulfilling.

In his adventures in Adajahara, he had found the great cistern by a cave entrance in one of the temples. Made of the solid white stone, the entrance stood, and the steps that went down into the cool earth into utter darkness. Save for the torch he would make from the wool and a liquid substance, a strange oil he found in large metal barrels. These too had strange writings on them he could not discern, but there were these red and yellow faded symbols that shown something like a flame on them. From these symbols, he suspected that these could be used to start some sort of fire. Earlier that fall, he took some of this oil and in a cup, he poured it on wood and lit the wood with "fire sticks," small sticks with a smaller red top, when rubbed against a rough surface would ignite on their own, and from these "fire sticks", he could start a fire within a few seconds. With the oil, a large fire in a matter of moments as he continued to study these magical devices that he thought were without a doubt from the gods they left to the shamans of these temples.

He would occasionally thumb through large texts, scrolls, and devices that held the ancient papers, still he could not read, but he saw pictures from the heavens, and these too were maps of the gods as he thought.

In the biggest of the temples, the one with the dome, there he found a great tubular device that looked up toward the heavens. There were throughout the building, scrolls, and scrolls everywhere. The boy found one on the subject, the long tubular device. However, it was all beyond him, for now. He figured that perhaps with time, and after all, that's seemed like he had a serious abundance of in the first place. The boy would also continue exploring that lead up to the cistern.

The dark entrance leads down further. With one hand on a still rail, the other hand holding the torch that would stay lit for quite some time. He manages to enter the second level of the long dark stairwell, from there the air filled with moister, and the sound of dripping water was heard. As he continued down further along the way, the light from above faded. He was now at the bottom as he could just barely see enough to tell that the hall opened into a great cathedral ceiling. Next to him, he could see the reflection of the water, and from the bottom, he could see lines, strange markings running parallel from one another going off into the darkness. He could see nothing else except for some sort of plant life below and some sort of small fish. He then continued passed the cistern that Naverron had spoken. He moved to yet another entrance that he gained passage to yet another room, a room filled with many metal, mostly rusted small doors, some were open that when he looked in these small cubicles, he saw rotting fabric; some looked like clothing of a strange fabric. He continued to another entrance, one that took him further along a dark hallway on where the faded white stone turned to earth and rock. There, a huge door of sorts faced him; the door was open only about two to three feet. The door itself was perhaps ten feet high, and eight or so feet wide and over two feet thick held by huge hinges. The boy would grow to suspect that the door weights a staggering amount and would come to know this doorway as the door of the gods. As soon as he would go to the top from where he came, he would mark this in his map. He was at the farthest point underground, but for now, this would have to be the farthest he would venture, he felt a sense of urgency to prepare the best he knew how for winter.

The winter came, and with it, the first of the snows, mild in the comparison to the winters of his homeland. The sheep were fine, plenty of winter grass and little worry of wolves or other predators, Adajahara, though very mysterious in its own right, offered sanctuary for the young boy. At times though, usually toward dusk, the boy would hear conversations, voices in the distances, echoing through rooms within the temple buildings. The languages, though faint and fleeting as if "they" knew someone was listening were indeed foreign to the boy. When the boy was much younger, in his village, there was talk of the spirit world. Sometimes these spirits would visit upon the living, and to him, on these occasions; he assumed that it was indeed the spirit world coming to pay him a visit. He didn't worry about it, or dwelled on the subject when the experience happens, he just went along his business of tending to the flock and continuing his adventures and studies.

On the shortest day in winter, the boy growing restless prepared to see what was behind the great door that he referred to as the "Door of the Gods." This he marked on his map, he packed it away in a pack he found in the summer before, and with several torches, water, the fruit from the orchard and cooked meat from game he had captured. Within a few minutes, he was down past the cistern from where he would occasionally draw drinking water and continued through the room of the "many small doors" that lead to the huge door on the white stone pad. From there, he carefully removed his pack and slid that through the opening and once that was accomplished, he would then slide himself passed the doorway and to the other side.

Once he was safely on the other side of the huge door, he put his pack, a dark red, and yellow pack and headed carefully down the stone and earth path. The area around him, a tunnel was made of chiseled rock and earth, the air was growing even more musty and drier. He continued until he reached a stairway made of an iron grate, rusty and old. He knew he would have to be careful going down, for as far as he could see, the stairway looked sturdy enough, but he realized how very old it was, and his light from the torch was limited, he knew he was in a larger chamber, but he couldn't see, the slightest sound he made echoed throughout this large place. He then decided to continue down the iron grate stairs with considerable caution.

As he continued down, the air grew even mustier and his eyes could catch the reflection from his torch from unseen things below. He knew that the reflection might be from glass or translucent objects, they were not certainly living animals, and not down this, far he thought to himself as he swallowed hard. His torch was now beginning to burn out; after all, it was the torch he used several times in the past. He then grabbed a fresh torch he made from the pack, lit it, and continued until he reached the bottom of the iron stairs. From there he realized the room was indeed much bigger than before, the floor was of earth after the stone pad that the bottom of the stairs rested on. He then could see large objects, some made of steel, and others made of glass; the objects looked like some ancient fire damaged them long ago. The boy then noticed several skeletons, human skeletons covered in cobwebs and dust. The sight frightened him but he realized that these skeletons could do no harm; they were already dead and dead by the looks for hundreds of years at least. The boy then continued through the skeletons, ten in all that must have died by the fire the boy thought; in the hands of some of these skeletons were some sort of metallic black "L" shaped devices, all the same, except for one skeleton who had a longer black device, a device with some sort of a steel tube. The boy picked it up from the clutches of the skeleton's right hand and then sticking his torch's handle securely in the rib cage of the skeleton, he concentrated on the device.

The device had some sort of contraption on the top, also made of some sort of metallic substance. The boy could see that this might be of some sort of a weapon but wasn't sure. He then put it securely in the pack along with one of those smaller "L" shaped devises and continued toward the other side of the room on where he found several other skeletons.

Some of them, the skeletons had arrows in them, the arrows were very old, and these arrows were similar to those used by his people, the tips were small stone arrowheads. He then looked back at the equipment and the direction of the other skeletons. "Must of been some sort of a battle, a fire started, and…" he wasn't sure about the rest and continued on until he found another door, a smaller door than before and it was nearly off the last hinge, and as he opened it, the door fell and the sound filled the room. The boy remained motionless until he could not hear another sound except for his own breathing. Feeling somewhat safe, he went into the chamber passed the fallen door. Continuing, he nearly walked on the bones of other skeletons, some he realized by the looks of them were fighting some sort of a battle, and he could see small crude hatchets, bows, swords and knives. He examined some of the weapons and concluded the ancient battle fought were not of his people, and the other skeletons bearing the "L" shaped weapons and longer devises like he had been the Adajahara, and perhaps as he realized, the voices he has been hearing from time to time have belonged to the dead here.

He quickly dismissed the thought, concentrated on the journey, and walked as carefully as he could around the dead. Eventually this led directly to another room, a room filled full of broken equipment and strange objects. He continued and eventually found another chamber that directly led to a stairway, unlike the others, this stairway was carved right out of the earth and rock and looked far older. As he continued down the spiral staircase encased in the great walls of the mesa, he continued until eventually deep within the mesa he realized he was hundreds of feet below ground. There at the end of the stairway was honed from rock a bridge, on each side of the beginning of the bridge on his side was two great torches. He lit them with his torch and now with the added light he awaited for his eyes to adjust could see that the bridge was far longer spanning the great darkness. On either side of the stone bridge, he could not see the bottom of the chasm. He then turned and found a small stone and tossed it off the bridge. He listened and could only hear the flickering of the torches. He looked up and could not see the top or the ceiling of this great place. He carefully decided to cross the stone bride to the other side on where he lit the torches there and could see only little more.

Eventually he found a two or three more skeletons. One had a small hatchet embedded in the skull as the skeleton rested up against the wall. The other skeleton next to it, the one that look like killed the other lies died next to it with its face looking burnt with a whole in the forehead. The one with the hatchet in the skull had an "L" shape device in its right hand. The boy turned his attention toward the third; it was one of the ancient warriors with a sword in his hand. The sword broke from over time, and its skull had a hole in it and the same-burned marks like the other.

There was a solid rusty steel door and was nearly coming off the hinges, and like the other door, it fell when the boy struggled to open it, and from there he encountered some sort of ruin, perhaps it was some sort of door made of stone that it looks like was half destroyed somehow. He quickly climbed up across the rubble to the entrance of a doorway that was at least ten feet high. At the op, he peered in and at first could see nothing but ancient dust in the air that he had disturbed.

He crossed over to the other side and down into the floor of this chamber, on the wall on his right-hand side he noticed strange writings, pictures chiseled into rock. He looked up at all of this in great amazement, the pictures as he could see were telling a story. In the upper portion on the left, he could see a picture, a drawing that looked like the shining sun, the next a vessel of some sort coming from the sky from the sun. The third, a picture of the vessel on top of a flat surface, and around it, sticks figures of what looked like hunters or villages. A primitive lot perhaps, under each of these pictures where symbols and words that he could not read. He continued, and there from the strange vessel were tall warrior looking creatures, he thought, perhaps gods, some had different shaped heads that the heads of humans, but he could not tell what, there was nothing as far as the animals that he ever saw that reminded a resemblance of these people etched and carved into this stone.

As he continued to view the drawings, the next showed these gods began killing the villagers around them and these gods enslaved burning villages and those that did not die, and as he looked up, he saw the similarity with his people and that of the Tarvas and this angered him. He then looked upon the next and could see one of the creatures, the biggest and most powerful sitting upon the huge chair. Next to him, many smaller ones like him on his right side, ten in all, they looked like the bigger one, a chieftain of great power the boy thought. As he continued, he then saw another vessel coming from the "stars" and the sun. This vessel was different, and this vessel had different gods in the windows of this great ship. The great ship landed, there were other ships or vessels that came from the sky just like it and from these, the gods came out and those gods from the previous vessels fought a great war against the gods of the new vessels. As the boy looked on, he could see that great armies were destroyed on both sides, but the gods from the second vessel eventually won, and with it, all the gods from the first ship that didn't leave, were chained up and cast into a great fire. There were others, even stranger and more problematic, the offspring of the first to arrive. There, the young boy could see these creatures raged by some great evil attacking all those around them, biting and dismembering those, they captured, but then a great fire engulfed them. The slaves from the first gods were set free and lived in harmony with the second gods. That was the last of the drawings. As the boy looking from beginning to end at least three or four more times, as the images were etched into his brain, the second set of gods looked more like the people of his world than the former. The boy also understood that this was some sort of story being told in these drawings. Just like the great elders of his people telling of things that happened long before his father and his father's father life. He also could see that the weapons that were used from the second gods were like the ones he found on the skeletons.

He then turned his attention toward the center of the room and the torch caught a reflection of something metallic and gold in color just off at the distance. The boy walked up to a great dais of stone, and ancient green polished stone under the dust, as he looked up, he could see two very large skeletal feet. He arose up to the second level of the dais, and like that in the drawings, he could see the huge skeleton sitting in a stone chair before him. It was one of the great chieftains, the first gods sitting in the chair upon his death. The gold and silver armor caught the light, and above high on the brow of the skull rested a huge golden crown covered in dust and cobwebs. The skull was not human, though it was similar like the ones he had seen before; he realized that this was truly a skeleton of a god. He looked on at the remains that must have stood nearly ten feet tall in life.

Both skeletal hands rested on each side of the huge stone chair carved from the wall behind him. The skeleton looked at the boy and though void of eyes, the boy could sense that the skeleton was peering deep within him and this was quite daunting.

The boy also noticed several things next to the chair; one was some sort of sword, least a handle, a black handle, or hilt of the sword. The boy noticed, unlike the others, this one was not rusty, and a closer examination showed it was some sort of translucent material. He then carefully picked up the sword and scabbard, the scabbard was of a darker color that felt more like stone than metal, but he wasn't sure of what it was made from. The sword and scabbard looked like nearly five feet long and extremely lighter than the boy had expected, but not as light as he hoped for; it would be heavy but manageable to take out with him. He was careful not to disrupt the other items, items made of both gold and silver covered in dust.

The sword was something the boy wanted to take back within, something he "needed" somehow. He looked back up at the great chieftain, "You have been dead a very long time, and this sword belonged to you in life, this I know. Your people had left it for you. I will take good care of this for you as long as I shall live, that is if it is all right with you a great chieftain of the first gods?" The boy was now looking directly into the eye sockets of the skeleton, but naturally nothing was said from the dead but only silence filled the room with the exception of the torch.

The boy turned and stored the sword carefully to its scabbard as he could strap it to the pack with twine and rope above. He then put on his pack and headed the rubble to the top, as he climbed, he heard a noise from behind him, and as he turned, he could see in the terror of the torchlight the skeleton arose from the chair and lunged forward to the small boy that screamed.

The skeleton fell flat on the dusty floor sending up a plume of dust as the bones broke up in pieces. The boy did not waste another second, he quickly left the chamber and headed directly back form where he came. He made it to the bridge when a tremor was being felt growing stronger. The boy ran across the bridge and made it to the other side when the ceiling was beginning to give way from above sending huge boulders hurling down crushing the bridge as it collapsed. The boy knew somehow that this was meant for him. He ran up the stairs as fast as he could and did not stop, he couldn't, the whole place was giving way. He finally made it to the large room on where the tremors had certainly faded away and began climbing the iron steps to the top as his lungs and legs burnt from the pace. Just then, toward the top, the lower staircase collapsed as it sounded like the entire mesa was falling in on itself. He quickly made it to the top when the entire iron stairwell fell, hurling down to the ground.

The boy yelled, "No, not the door!" His thoughts were on the huge door, the door of the gods, with the earthquake and tremors, it could in fact cause the door to shift, and perhaps close sealing him in forever.

As the boy raced toward the huge door, he could see that the door was swaying shut as the sound of the heavy hinges buckled. The boy ran headlong to the door as he removed his pack as the air filled with a sinister laughter from below and the boy did not turn around, there was no time.

He raced up to the door and slid through the shrinking gap just barely. On the other side, he dropped the torch in doing so, and struggled to get his pack through, but the gap was closing and the pack was now stuck. He then quickly grabbed the sword, and its scabbard was of course fastened to the pack, is pulled on the sword, and the sword came free sending the boy flat on his back as the door began to shake under the stress. In the failing light of the dropped torch, he could see that the door was coming off its hinges as it failed to keep him on the other side. The boy understood somehow that the forces below did not want to part with the sword and it was using the door to crush him. Without a moment to spare, the boy got up with the sword and raced away as the huge door nearly came down upon him. The crash of the door sent out a thunderous rumble and with it, a cloud of dust and debris sending the small boy into the wall, knocking him senseless. The boy was unconscious laid there in the settling dust with his right hand gripping the long double-bladed translucent sword. As he lay there, the sword illuminated a dull amber and green color. From behind the boy and the fallen tonnage of debris, the sounds of man unseen beings whispered and spoke amongst themselves. In the doorway leading to the room with many small doors, the very same the boy practically made it too stood a dark figure in a crimson red robe that vanished into the darkness looking on at the boy.

The blade stopped its glowing and the voices from below faded away as the boy came around. The boy's ears rang, and there were spots of color in his eyes as he arose slowly realizing that he had struck his head against the wall. It took a few moments for him to realize that he was almost to the cistern. He also realized that he had the sword and he decided to go to retrieve his pack if he could, there, he would find the torches and finish his journey. He somehow sensed that he was all right now and the forces that were trying to kill him were gone least he hoped so. It took him a few minutes but he found the pack after reaching around in the dark, he put the sword back in the scabbard. The boy found a torch, and lit it with one of the smaller fire sticks that gave off a smell that was rather pungent. Once the torch was lit, he arose and walked out of the area and found his way back up to the top of the stairs, and from there he was in one of the temple buildings. By now, the sun was setting; he had been down there for quite some time. Judging by the knot on his head, he didn't make it unscathed, but he had the sword and the other artifacts to examine.

He walked out of the building covered in dust outside in the cool dry air and with his vision now clearing up walked toward the small heard of sheep. The sheep that were peaceful looking back at him that managed to escape their pen that he used to store them away from the night. He gathered the sheep together and put them safely back into the pen. It was now nightfall, and he washed away the dust and grime from his latest adventure and slept in the dome temple building for the remained of the night, his dreams were filled from the adventure and hideous creatures that plagued him and things of little or no understanding that were being revealed to him. When he awoke, he heard the voices again, but this time, he understood them at first. He lay motionless as if he was still deep asleep.

"The boy has the sword," the voice sounded very spiteful and angry.

"Meddling youth, we should kill him once and for all and then take the sword." The voice was that of a bitter woman.

"Enough, he has the sword, the sword is his, Pitah Valgas tried to kill him nearly sending the mountain down on him, and he failed, what little so you think you two can do?" The man's voice was stern.

"He cannot leave here with it, which are just the rules. Do you think just asking for it back, he would comply and just give it back and say, sorry, take the sword?" The scornful woman said.

"Shut up, just shut up, I can barely think." The man's voice seemed a bit nerved, the dialects were very unfamiliar to the boy, and as time progressed, it was becoming hard causing him to grip the sword's hilt firmly.

"Okay, we kill him like we did the others; make it look like an accident and we will let Pitah Valgas deal with the sword, okay, will that do you two fucking bitches just good enough or what?" The man's voice was becoming angry.

"Listen here Roy, I didn't ask to die on this god forsaken planet, now did I?" The voice of the bitter woman said.

"No of us did, you pigheaded sow." The other voice, sounding more of that of an older woman spoke up.

"I like the boy, are you sure we have to kill him Roy, let's rethink this a second." It was a new voice, a voice of a younger, softer woman.

"Shit, I don't fucking know!" It was Roy's voice contemplating.

"He's asleep over their Susan, scare the hell out of him, and he might just run away leaving the sword there" The older woman was cut off by Roy's voice.

"Sure and then what, he saw a ghost, he would just come back, he doesn't seem to scare easily, and what of the sword, none of us can touch it, and unlike other things we try to touch in the physical world, this one has a nice little surprise, remember?" The voices grew quiet for a moment.

The young boy gripping the handle of the sword firmly gave him strength to understand the foreign language giving him the ability to understand.

"Listen he is gifted, he has special power or why else would that druid bring him here?" It was the voice of Susan.

"You mean the wolf?" The older bitter woman suggested curling her top lip.

"Right, the wolf, the fucking druid, and this whole fucking planet just fucking stinks." It was the voice of the other woman.

"A shit hole of the universe, yeah and where stuck here, looks like its forever." The voice of Susan continued.

"But the boy is certainly special; who would think that he would have been brave enough to face Pitah Valgas in his very own crept and literally walks right out of there. You know I never liked that son of a bitch anyway."

"Please, I hate it when people mention his name, I just hate it!" The older woman voice peppered in dismay as her face covered in a blanket of scorn spoke.

"Would it be that he had us killed, do you think that might have had something to do with it?" Roy mocked sarcastically.

"Besides Susan, I wonder if the boy saw your remains with an ax stuck in your in your fucking head?" Roy chuckled.

"That's not a bit funny, asshole!" Susan replied as the boy realized that the skeleton resting up against the wall belonged to her.

"Well we got to do something, something fast because if he realizes the power of the sword, he will never release it and we are all fucking in for it. Just think the kid could be playing with it, one of us comes in, and bam, we're fucked but good." The older woman said as the others agreed.

"Okay Susan, beings you like the kid so much. Get the fuck out of here and the rest of us will just have to kill him ourselves." Roy warned.

"Fuck him!" Susan unleashed.

"The boy?" Roy asked.

"No, Pitah Valgas, that's who, let him deal with the boy and the sword; whys do we have to do his shit for!" Susan was growing upset.

"You know the rules!" Hissed one of the other women standing there talking.

"If we do not do his bidding, then he torments us, the prick bastard enjoys nothing more than doing just that." The old woman then spat.

"Curses his unholy name" She then grew silent.

"We have no choice regardless, if we do not do Pitah Valgas's bidding and kill the boy, the boy will uncover the power of the sword and finish one or all of us in. Besides, Susan, we'll make it as peaceful as we can for your sake as well as the kid's, and you're right, he's a good kid." Roy concluded.

"Fucking well then, that's it. Okay I tell you what you assholes, after he is dead, then you can explain why he had to die then, 'cause I'm tired of being the one that has to tell the bad news all the time." Susan warned.

"I never did catch his name?" The bitter woman wondered.

"Ask him after you have killed him" The boy could sense that the one who is called Susan had left the room.

The boy drew out the weapon from the scabbard as the three others went into detail on what to do in killing the boy that they did not pay attention as he lifted the point toward them. The boy was far from being a swordsman, and with the sword gave him the advantage of having some sort of a weapon that he realized that would or could protect him from the spirits, and as he was just coming to realize the sword gave him the power to see the spirits standing there as he quietly arose.

Roy, was a tall middle-aged balding black man, and the two women standing before him, both lighter in comparison and dressed in the same unfamiliar fashion as the black man. The older woman had long white and silver hair tied back in a tight bun, and the other a blue-eyed redheaded woman younger than the other two.

"You two, hold him down, and I will suffocate him, and I'll explain to him why he had to be let go, deal?" Roy said.

"It's just bad business, this whole fucking thing stinks, and how many more do we gotta kill before Pitah Valgas let's us go, shit…" The redhead said.

The blade of the translucent black sword began to glow an amber color with pulses of green illuminated catching the eyes of the spirits.

"Shit!" the older woman pointed up at the boy upon the pile of rubble.

"We're fucking done for!" The old woman concluded.

"Shut the fuck up, he doesn't know what we're saying, doesn't understand a damned word we're talking about. Bonnie" He pointed to the redhead, "…Go around over there and let's circle him, Anita, you go over and around there, now we have no choice but to kill him." Roy said to direct the other two women.

Flashes blinded the mind of the boy as he saw things, things in his mind that he did not understand, and felt the wisdom of the sword growing in him. He then motioned the blade toward Roy's spirit.

"You sure, he doesn't know how to use a sword?" Bonnie asked sarcastically.

"He certainly sees us!" Anita warned.

"Shut up and move in," warned Roy.

Just then, the boy's mind grew clear and lunged for Roy, and this surprised Roy as he fell back as the point of the sword penetrated his chest, and in amazement, to all, and especially to Roy, the sword absorbed his spirit. With blinding speed, the sword removed Bonnie's head from her shoulders as her eyes rolled ghastly back into her head as the boy turned his cunning new skill toward the breast of Anita. Like that of Roy, she was dispatched into the blade as it glowed even brighter into an orange yellow color. In blinding furry, especially that for a boy who has never held a sword before, disemboweled Bonnie's body still standing that fell to its knees spilling out her intestines onto the floor before her body being absorbed by the blade.

Her head looking up at him in a pool of blood, though not actual blood, her eyes came down looking up at the boy who wore a grimace, "So this is how it ends?" she said as her head was absorbed into the blade, the blade which stopped glowing. He then put the sword back into the scabbard and with it, he felt some of the power and knowledge drain from him, but there was still so much to learn.

By early spring, the young boy learned the secrets of Adajahara, which it in fact was some sort of a settlement for the first gods. Which he later discovered as the Taltakkurdg-Kevnaps originated from a distant planet in the galaxy. These beings came in moderate numbers and enslaved all those around them for at least ten generations by the looks of things. From this point, the invasion of the second god, those from a distant blue planet that killed the Taltakkurdg-Kevnaps eventually develop a virus that would attack specifically the foe, but somehow the virus mutates. Upon the defeat, the remaining bodies destroyed by the virus were then consumed by fire. The virus then mutated and killed many from the blue planet and eventually those tribes surrounding the mesa to be later called Adajahara from the distant descendants from both the blue planet and the ancient tribes of this land. The mutated virus affected the host bodies, causing madness and evil that spread like a wildfire throughout the land.

However, there was one survivor from the great Taltakkurdg-Kevnaps chieftains, the called Pitah Valgas. Pitah Valgas, a powerful ruler who dwelt in the lands far off from the virus's reach initially; there he developed strong magic and incantations raising an army. The army, mostly those that consisted from those that survived the virus attack and the mutant strain. The ones that freed the ancient tribes were few in numbers chose to protect Adajahara, fought to their deaths against the sorcerers' chieftain Pitah Valgas. However, not before sealing him into a crypt that would have permanently held him, they literally walled him in. Years later, Pitah Valgas body's expired in the crypt that they used to deceive him. They filled the room with the original virus to insure his death. All writings of this were sketchy and parts missing.

A few years later, the children of Pitah Valgas rose in numbers and manage to overtake Adajahara and free what was believed by them to rescue Pitah Valgas, these children slain the remnants of the blue planet and attempted to free Pitah Valgas only to find him indeed dead. They performed a great ceremony, resealing the room with his most valued possessions.

As the young Ramadan read from the scrolls that were written by the ancient sages of old spoke of events of long ago. The scrolls spoke of the temples of Adajahara and the history passed the deaths of Pitah Valgas the sorcerer and those from the blue planet that he found oddly fascinating.

"…*Pitah Alohaim Rystak, vile pestilence of the dark isle of the dragons, the beasts of the netherworld spilling the hatred and the blood of the children of the blue planet and that of the tribes of Kahlarium. From these nations, the priests and shamans perceived that the great sons of the sorcerer Pitah Valgas now only a legend. Indeed, the Pitah commands those closest to his bloodline to avenge his death and resurrect his bones from the forbidden tomb of Adajahara. Great warrior priests from the children of the blue planet and the kingdoms sent forth to find Adajahara, and safeguarded from the scourge from the south, to keep within its dark and powerful secrets.*"

"*In the second year of the Second Age, the black sails of the dragons reached Kahlarium. The great warrior king Atridius ascended in battle against Pitah Alohaim Rystak. Like that of Kahlarium, Atridius fell into the ashes of time; next Kranos was in the view of the dark chancellor of doom, Pitah Alohaim Rystak, and his brooding forces. From across the Great Plains, the Ramadans raised spear, shield and ax against the black wave that kept the torches of Kronos alive sending her light to the darkest of heart of the vile that occupied the fallen Kahlarium.*"

"*The ghosts of the great chieftains visited Pitah Alohaim Rystak and told the Pitah of a great northern passage across the silver capped Catanbar Mountains and imbued his soul with strong magic and from this magic great horrors were released and the*" *nameless kingdoms in the Catanbar Mountains fell to the rule of Pitah Alohaim Rystak in the sixth year.*"

"*Pitah Alohaim Rystak, in the seventh year of the Second Age, led his armies along with that sword to bear his seed for generations to come. The Pitah, drawn upon the Great Plains, and like a world wind of black locusts and all those that dwelt there suffered unspeakable horrors… The dark chancellor of the isle of the Dragons came forth cutting a violent path of pillars of flame and smoke to the steppes and across the Thunder River to Kranos and the jaded hills of Adajahara. The greatest of all the warriors of the kingdoms waged a holy war against the darkest of foes, and with the Ramadans behind the black wave. To the west, the Kranos bowmen, Pitah Alohaim Rystak fell, his severed head removed from his body by a great ax and put away and separated from his rotting corpse, his armies dispersed fleeing from the spear, ax, and bow headed to the Catanbar Mountains, Kranos liberated the sons and daughters of Kahlarium and Gwarvarik was born.*" The young boy continued reading from the ancient text, scrolls put away in ceramic vases, preserved by dried herbs and incantations.

"*…In the two-hundredth year of the Second Age, the children of the Dragon Lords, those led by dark chancellor, known as the Tarvas once again befriended their dark fathers now led by non other than Pitah Nabnugen. In a sacred treaty against the people of the Great Plains, it was his dark hope of seizing the Holy Land of Adajahara. Pitah Nabnugen visited neighboring kingdoms of the great north and many tribes to gain favor and alliances but his witchcraft was thwarted and he too was destroyed, and so with it, the Tarvas alliance was resolved. Peace ruled the kingdoms as the dark isle of the Dragons gleamed to kingdoms south.*"

In the passing weeks, the young boy continued his studies from the ancient scrolls until he found a particular scroll on which perked his fascination somewhat more than the others did. "*In the two-hundredth and seventy-second year of the Second Age, the great priests of Adajahara fell into utter madness. These priests in murderous rage speaking in a forgotten language proclaiming that a great and terrible sorcerer would rise from the holy mountain, killing all in their wake, who withstood them. Others said that they have seen the spirits of the dead afoot, others heard voices, strange voices chanting evil and vile spells feeding on the blood of the righteous and innocent. By order of King Melendor, guardian of Gwarvarik summonses the closure of Adajahara and the destruction of the road to the holy land. The priests, those that survived from the madness, only a handful indeed, they were sent to the four corners of the kingdom to live out their natural lives in service to the gods. As for those stricken with the madness, they were put to the blade for corruption of the soul and mind, but they would not die, die like that of the man but had to be destroyed by fire. King*

Melendor forbade anyone to enter Adajahara, anyone would be put to the blade and fire, and this law were sent forth through his sons and his son's sons."

CHAPTER 3

▼

The boy then resealed the vases and put them away, he had come to know more with each passing day as the snow melted to greener days of spring. By the time of the rains, the boy grew tired of this place. Though it was safe, he was realizing the world was pressing on without him. He wanted to be a part of it and on the day of his sword practicing that his sheep, growing in numbers as the heard grew larger. His audience watched. A figure of a red robed man, his face concealed by a black grill under the crimson red cape concealed his eyes carrying a large oak staff caught the attention of the boy as well as the sheep.

The boy quickly realized that the figure he was seeing didn't appear to be of the spirit world, but of one of this world. There was also something else, something that caught his attention as the figure walked up to the boy, and uneasy feeling.

"Are you the one that Naverron had told me about?" The boys said this through his telepathic power that stopped the figure in his tracks shortly.

"Yes, I am Kronus, high priest of the Temple of Jah-Hadeim, the temple of" His older friendly voice that had a flare of authority was cut off by the boy's thoughts.

"God's Hand, yes, that is the name of the temple, yes?" the boy said telepathically.

"Why yes that is right, Naverron did say you have been especially gifted, my young friend."

"Yes that was it!" that was something the boy was feeling, that this is the one that Naverron was hiding from him, but he also realized that Kronus was beginning to pry into his own thoughts.

"A friend doesn't pry into the thoughts of another, I don't consider an unwelcome visit, and shall I say, friendly?" the boy challenged sending a powerful wave of strength back to the crimson robed figure.

"No, I guess not, I was seeing if Naverron was indeed right about the gift." In that instant, the young boy knew that Kronus was a terrible liar. The boy realized there was something, something that Kronus was hiding and indeed was approaching him under false pretenses.

This voice was not of the sinister voice that came to the boy after his mother had expired, there was something though, something about the old man that the boy did not like just the same.

"That is not true, you wanted to know what or who I really am, and I would tell you that I am Ramadan, all you have to do is ask." The boys warned, and again, made the one in the crimson robe stop and ponder a bit struggling for the next line of words.

"Though you hide your face from me, I can still see your face clearly enough old man from the desert places." Just then, Kronus could sense that the boy was already inside of his, the priest's own head; his thoughts open to the boy.

"You have underestimated me; perhaps it was because of my youthful appearance, true, that I am just a boy." The young boy projected these thoughts through his telepathy gift.

"Know your place boy!" Kronus returned a strong wave of strength in his telepathic warning, but he also knew the boy could see through the black grill and was still in his thoughts and mind, and the boy did not show any fear.

The boy could feel the anger welling up in the old man, so he withdrew knowing that his own mind had become stronger. The boy thought it wise that the old man should not know the extent of his powers, after all Naverron liked this man quite a lot.

"I am sorry to anger you" The boy spoke aloud.

"Accept my apologies." The boys bowed down a little and then back into the black grill of Kronus's mask.

"You have been here for a year, and already you wish to leave?" Kronus asked.

"Yes, tending sheep, well, I believe they tended to me more often than I them." The boy returned a smile. He could clearly see the man's face hiding behind the mask glimmer a ghost of a smile.

"You have been educated beyond your years, by whom?" the boy noticed that Kronus didn't try to probe into his own mind and instead waited for an answer.

"I have taught myself to read and to write on my own, there is no one else here." The boy added.

"I see," the boy could tell without powers needed that Kronus was having a hard time believing that and was wondering about the boy considerably.

"Nevertheless, you have something, something that is very powerful and dangerous, and something that you have little understanding about that I have come for." Kronus were not being deceitful or willing to continue any such façade any longer.

"You mean the sword?" the boy quipped.

"Yes, the sword, the very sword I have seen a moment or two ago." Kronus insisted as he continued.

"The sword you have strapped to your back, the hilt in plane view, it doesn't belong to you." Kronus warned.

"It doesn't belong to you, does it?" the boy added catching Kronus off guard as the boy could see it in Kronus's own mind.

"What do you mean; surly you do not understand what you possess?"

"Pitah Valgas's very own sword, the translucent sword of souls!" this caused Kronus to back up slightly as the boy could see his grey eyes gleam at the hilt, and in doing so, the boy could feel the greed and jealousy well in the priest.

The boy drew out the sword and his mind began filling with pictures, pictures of the sun in the mountains. The very same on the very same day he gained his freedom, and from behind the coincidence of the warming sun. The boy could sense that Kronus was behind it. The boy sensed that the priest was inside of his thoughts and struggling through these images to give a false image, or scheme to show it was the priest behind these events. The boy also saw the huge wolf Naverron waiting by the river for days for the boy to show up, track him down, and befriend him so that he could take the boy to Adajahara. The boy saw the vale of chance and deception fall before him. Kronus were trying to take advantage of the one who really did save the young boy in the mountains.

"So you have arranged me to be here, you were the one that brought the warmth to me as I was dying in the mountains under the whip of the Tarvas. And it was you that sent forth Naverron to take me to this place." The boy paused as he could sense that Kronus was not onto what the boy had just discovered in his thoughts. The boy, rather playing along in the rouse that Kronus was webbing in the boy's mind.

The boy saw more in the mind of the priest standing before him, "You cannot take this sword away from me, and you will never have it!" The boy looked at the reddening face of Kronus.

The boy could see in Kronus's mind that for years, many years, that the priest from the high desert has formulated many attempts to get the sword. After he, the priest had discovered its true powers from ancient scrolls, scrolls much older than anything that the boy had uncovered or knowledge about.

The boy obviously knew Kronus's plan of sending the boy down through the cave, retrieves the sword through a series of subtle suggestions playing into the boy's curiosity. This angered the boy as he realized that Kronus was as crafty as he is deceitful, but more so in the fact that he was very unaware that Kronus was controlling these events from afar.

"You, from afar waited for my death, but more importantly the ownership and possession of this very sword." The boy retorted, as he could see in Kronus's mind the door falling upon the boy. In that instance, the boy realized that the priest was attempting to kill him then, it was the only way that he, the priest could get the sword.

The priest stood there in silence as the boy pierced his brain uncovering the dark and evil thoughts of betrayal. The mind of the priest was filled with lust for the sword, and the power of such a weapon. The power of this sword that the boy could not uncover in Kronus's thoughts through his young gift was safe from him.

"I know it's true so do not deny it, I was a simple pawn in your plan to catch Pitah Valgas off guard, he would not suspect an orphan Ramadan to stumble upon the sword, and oh yes, he tried to get the sword back as you know, but he, like you, has failed, you a murderous priest!" The boy accused flashing the blade quickly.

"Boy gives me the sword, and I promise you will live out the rest of your life naturally in peace." Kronus extended his hand out toward the boy.

"Really, and I can see that my life would only be a few moments long, for I can read your mind as well, viper!" Without warning and blinding speed of the sword, the young boy removed the stretched out arm of Kronus as blood spurted out from the wound.

"You fool, boy!" Kronus reared back in surprise and pain with his other hand; he used his staff against the Ramadan boy.

"Good kill him, he's an old fool that turned away from his divine faith of, what is it they call it, oh yeah, righteousness I think is the word." The sinister voice came back to the boy. The very same that lead him down the mountains that were nearly catching the boy off guard as he cut through the oak staff into, and this act alone terrorized the crimson robed priest.

"Look, see that the sword not only cuts through sinew and bone easy enough, but through so called bullshit religious items like that oak staff from a sacred tree, the very same that these idiots have killed." The mocking voice came back like before.

"End his life, already his blood flows on the ground, it's either you or he, let's make it him, shall we?" It said to encourage the youth to end the priest's life.

"Pitah Valgas wants you dead Kronus, can you hear him?" the boy asked as he stood there poised for his final strike upon the old man whose robe was now cut up and his staff in pieces on the ground before him. The boy knew it was not the voice of Pitah Valgas himself, but of the one that truly saved him.

"Kill the two-bit has-been, and I will increase your knowledge of the black arts, and you will become my son." The sinister voice sounded somewhat frantic and troubled.

"Kill the priest, I command you, boy!" the sinister voice commanded.

"Do it yourself" he turned and snarled as he walked away as his heart hardened by the uncovering of the priest's deceptions.

Then in that instance, the boy realized the hidden power, and the name of the sword he wielded above Kronus who was kept at bay by the deadly point. It was in the priest's own mind that became weaken enough from the physical wound of his missing forearm that lay before him.

The boy could see that the sword contained and gathered souls it has collected over time, and within it, it contained an army of the undead, the sword of souls.

The boy decided for himself to allow Kronus, who fell back on the ground holding his bloody stubble on where his forearm used to be. "I will let you live, I know it wasn't you that saved me high in the mountains, and this plan, like the others I have seen in your mind has failed. You will never have the sword and do not make me regret sparing your life old man."

The boy walked away after sheathing his sword and picked up his pack, looked once more at the wounded priest, "The next time we meet, I will kill you, and hear me, priest, and to that fucking mutt with you!" the boy then turned away as Kronus passed out from the blood loss and pain.

As the boy slipped off into the darkening skies and in doing so, his face darkened and then turned as pale as silver under the full moon, his eyes darkened to two black orbs as his hair, changed to coal black as he walked away from the priest. The boy's anger intensified passed his own comprehension, as he was very unaware of his physical change.

"Already the sword is transcending its dark powers in you, boy, and you shall be condemned to eternal damnation." Kronus yelled aloud as his body began losing blood, too much blood from a wound that the priest was struggling to contain.

The boy, as he gave without another thought of the priest, continued to slip off into the thick woods. The boy was long gone by the time Kronus regained consciousness saved only by conjuring up an old spell to stop the bleeding before he passed out, a spell that no doubt saved his ancient life. Kronus could sense that Pitah Valgas was indeed gone; Kronus wanted the sword even more that the great and powerful spirit of Pitah Valgas was removed somehow.

With this renewed desire of obtaining the sword, Kronus managed to arise to his feet. Kronus realizing that the sword somehow had begun transforming such an innocent boy into something that he had yet to understand other than the fact slipping into a darker power. This power that Kronus was too weak himself to contend with, and at his age of men, had little knowledge about. The boy would have to find Naverron, the black wolf and conjure other things, other plans into his own malevolent course of action.

The boy walked east from Adajahara through the winding mountains down into the emerald woods of Gwarvarik. The boy showed no sign of fear as he deliberately headed further east until he came across an old stone road, a path like that he followed a couple of seasons ago when he met Naverron. The path headed south deeper into the woods, trees that he realized were called oaks from the tablets and scrolls from the temples of Adajahara. These very same trees were once seeds that came from the "Blue Planet" so many centuries ago and grew well in this region; many generations of these trees have grown since then. The boy decided to follow the path until it led to a small abandoned village, a village that showed signs of a battle fought a battle with the Tarvas. It must have been the battle that he heard of some time ago, there were human remains, arrows piercing, but now lying in the skeletal remains where the dead had fallen. He continued following the path that leads behind the huge timber walls into the village. There he could see the skeletons of the Larnges, horses, and more humans that fell by bow and sword. It was obvious to the boy that the Gwarvarik village eventually fell to the Tarvas raiders, but it obviously took a heavy toll on the Tarvas.

The boy found supplies, a good pack, and a warm dark cloak to rap him in and to keep him dry of the impending storm coming from the Steppes in the north. He then thought he heard something from behind him, out from the doorway of the small stone-dilapidated structure that was once a villa. He drew out the sword slowly and cautiously turned to face the source of the noise, the wrestling sound off in the distance. As he turned around, he couldn't see anything just outside the doorway, his hearing focused to detect the slightest of sounds, but he heard nothing more. He then drew closer to the door, and then removed the hood of his newfound cloak and peered ever so carefully from the darkened doorway. Still he could not see anything, but he knew he knew somehow that not only was there something out there, but that something was watching him.

The forest mist and low-lying fog were now beginning to roll into the village. Across the villa and beyond the foundations of destroyed structures, beyond the skeletons of the dead, it was in the dark oak trees he could sense that something was just out of eyesight watching him. The boy withdrew slowly from the shadows of the doorway and slipped back into the darkness. As the fog rolled in on where the boy could barely see the dead, knowing that this something, this presence was beginning to take further advantage of the fog and move closer to him. The boy realized that there was no other way out of this old villa; there was any other window or a hole he could climb.

"I know you are watching me!" The boy shouted in telepathy, but there was no response, nothing, he repeated as before, and like before, still nothing, as the fog grew thicker.

The boy then slipped out of the villa with his sword in hand, his pack over his left shoulder and with stealth-like precision he manages to leave the area of the villa. Through the skeletons and down along the cobblestone path that headed through the village south. The boy thought it might have been Kronus, or perhaps Naverron coming for him, but he didn't since the familiarity of either one. The creature, it was some sort of a creature the boy was sensing, it wasn't human but had a remarkable intelligence the young boy was realizing. The boy was also realizing that the creature knew that the boy slipped off in the fog. The boy wasn't frightened, but he knew if he would give into fear, that fear it would consume him and therefore would be but already dead. He had the sword now and he has now become good enough to defend himself from others as he reassured himself.

He continued down the path, but he was realizing that the creature was now already onto him and following close behind in the blanket of fog. The boy then heard the sounds of hooves from the south, many of them coming to the path, and he could feel the presence behind him closing in. The boy ran headlong toward the sound of the approaching hooves as the creature was giving the chase. The boy then reeled off east of the path and turned to see what it was stalking him and in the vale of the silver mist, a shadow arose from the fog, its blood red eyes gazed upon the boy. The boy could see the shape taking form and could see it certainly was a beast that stood nearly five feet high. On two bowed legs, black fir and an oddly shaped head, its massive arm reached down well passed the creature's knees. In one arm, its rights arm it had a heavy bone, a lower leg bone of a

Larnges. Along the end was a rock tided by what looked like leather straps an axe head fasted to the bone on which the beast raised up into his other hand.

The boy knew this hideous creature meant to kill him, but the boy could clearly see the creature was flesh and blood, and therefore susceptible to his sword's razor sharp edge. The boy made it known to the creature that he was also armed, and not in fear.

"Boy" The creature uttered, and his eyes intensified its hatred and drool ran down its dog-like chin from the large canine teeth.

"I will split you in-two!" The voice was dark and sinister and was more like a growl than words.

"So be it, I am not afraid," The boy uttered in defiance.

The creature then turned slightly toward the thundering hooves, and then back to the boy, its red glowing eyes filled with hatred squinted as the creature realized that there was a bigger danger coming upon him. He then turned around fully and headed off into the fog leaving the boy there poised for battle. The boy could feel the presence leave completely, sheathed his weapon, and picked up his pack as the sound of many hooves thundered by him just outside the blanket of fog concealing the boy. Within moments, there were sounds of screams, all human. Then there were some blood curling screams and sounds from something else. The boy froze and then turned around to hear the clash of steel and men fighting whatever the creature was, and the boy realized the creature was not alone, but there were many like him that fell upon the riders, the boy suspected that the armed riders were some Tarvas raiding party that was in the area. As he stood there for a moment, he could hear the Tarvas cursing their strange foes and battling them. The boy could hear the heavy crude weapons smashing human bone and sinew as well followed by blood curling screams echoing through the forest and stilled eventually by the rain.

"Better them than I" the boy flashed a dreaded cold smile and headed off down the path into the every thickening fog.

By night the rains came and the boy found shelter under an old oak, there he built a small fire to warm him and take away some of the dampness. He wasn't worried about the creatures any longer and witnessed two heavily armed Gwarvarik patrols heading along the path in what the boy thought was, no doubt they had come across the Tarvas raiders. The boy was anything but Tarvas.

The next day, the boy found another path that headed directly east, he followed this throughout the remaining of the day. His direction was leading through the thickest of the forest and through a series of small bridges. He followed it down into the thick moss-covered rocks and brush to where the rail met with the faint path that led south along the ravine of black rock. He followed up the scant path that was cumbersome and dangerous toward the top. Once there, he witnessed large game, birds, and other signs of life. He continued heading along the path headlong into the emerald embrace of the forest. He stayed there until daybreak the following morning and found a large valley. The valley was cleared mostly from the trees that surrounded this large valley; there he could see a spiraling hilltop and a city on the crest of the hill of stone. The city was the biggest that he had ever seen the entire city was enclosed in this thick wall of stone. There were towers that jetted up high above nearly into the clouds. The boys stood there with his mouth agape by the view. Behind the towers, the uppermost building was some sort of architecture made of solid stone and a golden dome that caught the light of day and shined brightly in what little sun bled through the high overcast day.

The boy was tired, and in the safety of the trees, he would rest and wait until darkness before crossing the valley to the city that nearly went into the heavens. The boy eventually fell to sleep after eating some bread that he found from the village in the woods. His sleep was troubled by the dark creature in the foggy mist, its eyes, blood red and filled full of hatred burned even in his dreams. When he awoke, the sun was just setting off in the distance behind him. He then began feeling the presence like before, the same presence from the village. He knew it wasn't the nightmare; he was fully awake and understood once again through his uncanny ability that he was the attention of unseen eyes.

He drew out his sword; the translucent black blade gave off a unique ring from its sheath. He gripped the hilt with both hands firmly and closed his eyes to the world. This as he found out shortly after receiving the blade that he could see silhouettes of living things, he noticed this with his sheep, he could see all of them with his eyes shut. He then turned slowly around with the blade aiming straight up into the sky firmly against his forehead; he could feel the increased strength flow from the dark sword into his bloodstream, burning up into his arms from his hands and into his swelling chest. With his eyes closed, he could see these silhouettes, but they were not yellowish white smoky images against the dark canvas of inside of his eyelids, but a dark burning orange, and there were many of them, five, then six, and finally, eight just in the distance.

"You cannot take me." He said through telepathy at first. He could sense that these creatures did not have the capability or able to successfully block his thought from them. He could see one, a large image that stood a half a head higher than the rest of the eight.

"Come and know your own death!" The boy fumed showing no fear, and his words seeming not his own but of another, a strange voice that sounded much older than he who stood there poised on the edge of the forest.

"Boy, I will gut you while your heart still beats!" growled the tallest now running forward raising clearly an axe of stone, bone and leather. The boy opened his dark orbs of his eyes; the whites of his eyes were now consumed in a sea of darkness giving way to a bottomless pit.

The Beast came down crushingly extending his axe that came down upon the hard earth below sending sparks up into the air just missing the intended target. The boy then swung his sword in blinding speed slashing the exposed rib cage of the beast that then sent up a violent howl into the twilight sky.

"Boy, you will surely die as I raise Bone Crusher, I will split you into!" the beat shrieked. He was seriously wounded and countered with another slash from his crude but deadly axe, and like before, failed to hit the young boy by some small miracle.

The boy much faster again cut deep into the beast. This time opening up his stomach and spilling out his intestines that sent out a vile stench. A blood curling howl as he stumbled and realizing it was he who was dying by his own proclamation he had made just a few moments earlier. The boy raised the sword a third time, severing the head of the Lycoi from his disemboweled body sending blood ejecting from the exposed arteries of the pumping heart as the body fell down.

By now, three other beasts advanced on the young boy, and one by one in blinding fury, he killed each of them separating limbs from their powerful bodies, they were no-match for his cunning skill that certainly surpassed his age.

"Kill that boy and bring me the sword, he must die!" The boy recognized the voice filled full of frenzied bitterness, "Do it now, or I will torment your souls in hell forever!" It was none other than Kronus himself just off in the distance, now there was other Lycoi returning and in the background of the thick forest, sounds of distant howling filled the woods.

The boy then turned and ran headlong toward the open valley. As he turned, he could three or four more of these creatures giving the chase to him, and from behind them, he could see the tall crimson figure of Kronus emerging from the forest. The boy realized his drastic mistake of not finishing the old treacherous priest off earlier and in that instant, he would never make that mistake again as long as he would ever live as it seared into his memory. Now he had found a new enemy, an enemy he was beginning to hate as much as the Tarvas.

"You'll never make it to the city boy!" Kronus said through his telepathy power.

The boy then realizing that he could not out run the beasts turned and killed the first two just behind him. Before the others could approach him, he stood over the two dead beasts where they have just fallen. He then ran the sword over their corpse. A gruesome green plasma as faint as whispering smoke went into the blade, causing a unique high pitch sound that drowned out the sounds of the advancing beasts. These beasts, growling and cursing at him that was quickly approaching with their crude axes through the field of wheat and tares.

"I command the Sword of Souls to release thee into my bidding" the voice from deep within his very own bosom flowed forthwith sending the souls of the two beasts to attack the living creatures. The spirits of the beasts, though translucent, were as horrifying to the living that was now upon the boy. The spirits of the two fallen bodies, picked up their weapons next to their physical bodies and began hacking and killing their living kind before the boy and the sword. The boy then could see the souls of the beast were then going for the remaining that turned and ran headlong in the horrid fear that was unfolding that were moments ago advancing on the field.

"Bring Kronus to me!" The boy commanded.

Before the souls of the two beasts could grab hold of the priest, the old man conjured up a spell that caused the old man to vanish only to reappear a few yards where he was just standing. The spirits of the Lycoi were shortly thrown off only for a moment to reacquire their bearings on the target, the old man in the crimson cloak.

Yet again, the priest managed to escape by a series of vanishing and appearing elsewhere and the boy could see that the priest's powers of distance were limited to twenty or thirty yards at the most. Nevertheless, the boy knew the old man could not keep it up; eventually the Lycoi souls would have him. This gave the boy enough time to collect the other souls just as he did earlier. However, instead of unleashing the souls under his command, he kept them in the power of the sword, a power he was yet to realize fully.

As the boy watched, he could see the old man was tiring as other Lycoi entered the edge of the forest and began to engage the two Lycoi souls only to find their weapons. Those very crude axes made of bone and stone render uselessly as the blades just simply cut through thin air, but for the souls, they violently tore through flesh and bone, invincible against the living.

Finally, the remaining handful of Lycoi ran bewildered into the forest as the two souls turned their attention back to the old man who had vanished in the distraction. The boy seeing this drew his sword back to its scabbard and in doing so released the two souls from afar, as they returned to nothing more than whispering green smoke that evaporated into the twilight sky. The boy knew in that moment that by sheathing his sword had released the souls from his bidding and the control of the sword. As long as the sword was unsheathed, the souls would continue, perhaps indefinitely.

"So old man, you managed to survive me again!" The boy was angered, but he realized now he had in his possession a small but a formidable army that no sword, arrow, nor the axe could silence, and with this, a sinister smile broke across his face as he turned his attention back toward the huge city upon the hill.

CHAPTER 4

—————————— ▼ ——————————

It was now well past sunset by the time, the boy walked up to the massive city gate. From there, he could see two guard towers up high, one on each side of the huge gate, from the towers, one could see well passed the small valley and far along the canopy of the forest. The boy thought for a moment of why those in the towers did not see him fighting, "…if so, why did they not attempt to rescue him from the creatures?" he thought to himself.

"If I saw a young boy fighting for his life against such odds, would you go and help?" This puzzled him as he began to rationalize that perhaps either the priest conjured up some sort of a spell that blinded those up high from seeing, or the cold fact that those in the tower did not care. Would it be that they were afraid of the creatures and that is the reason for the massive walls around the huge city?

The boy then could see has he been walking up next to the torch light that there were others at the gate. Heavily armed guards, men in brass colored armor, helmets that favored the dome he saw earlier with some sort of fur that ran completely around the helmet just above the brows of the men. On the top of the helmet was a spire-like point, the two guard bear pikes in each of their right hands. These guards had a completely different shaped heavy sword that reminded the boy of the second moon, Zantar, the crescent blood red moon. The boy could also see that the guards could see him walking slowly up to the light of the two torches one on each side of the road. One of the guards spoke up; it was the one to the boy's right.

The guard did speak, but the boy did not understand the guard's language. The boy knew the sword could somehow interpret for him. However, the sword was sheathed across his back under his cloak, and using it would look like a sign of aggression. It would look like the boy was going for a weapon and put him once again in a perilous situation that he didn't want. Besides the Gwarvarik people were enemies of the Tarvas, and in the boy's young mind, he figured an enemy of the Tarvas, was an alley of the boy. Besides, he had more than enough enemies, and he could certainly afford some friends.

"I am sorry, but I do not understand what you are asking of me." The boy responded in his natural tongue.

The guard looked at the boy somewhat surprised and flashed a smile to his comrade before turning his attention back to the boy.

"Ramadan?" The guard said in return to the boy's language that suffered from the lack of experience of the language.

"Yes, I am Ramadan, mortal enemy of the Tarvas." The boy insisted that immediately caused the guard to laugh as he turned and translated what the child had said, and this caused the other to laugh and say yet something to the other who was translating.

"He said, 'what you know of the Tarvas, and what is a small child to do against those dogs?'" the guard was half-amused with himself chastising the boy.

The boy's eyes narrowed as his anger began to rise a bit by the questioning. "I know too much about them. They killed my family and left me for dead." The boy returned his answer sharply causing the grins to evaporate quickly from the faces of the two guards.

"Instead I see the work of these strange beasts that is not of man attack the Tarvas raising fear in the hearts of those that invade you lands. Maybe, I talk to them, instead of you." The boy's words were as sharp as his sword.

"What do you know of the Lycoi, boy?" The guard demanded as he drew closer to the boy, and the boy could sense anger in the man.

"I know they attacked Tarvas marauders earlier this day by the ruins of a village that I passed through."

"Oh, and you saw them with your own eyes?" The guard insisted as he brought his left hand up grooming his long black goatee.

"Yes, I saw these creatures with their stone axes attack the Tarvas." The boy grew silent.

"So what business does a young Ramadan have here in Gwarvarik in the city of Gwardara?"

"I am passing through to go to the sea." The boy had no idea on where he was going. He had to tell them something, besides, he knew he was just passing through, and he knew left out of the city, he might not make it alive until morning.

"Passing through to the sea, and once at the sea, where too then, boy?" The guard peered into the Ramadan's eyes.

The Ramadan did not turn his attention away, "There I will cross the sea and go to a distant land, a land far away from the Tarvas until I grow older and stronger so that I will come back and kill every living Tarvas and those that entertains them to their deaths." This caused the guard to bellow out in laughter nearly uncontrollably. The other guard pressed fro a translation of what the boy had just said. In doing so, the other laughed not nearly as loud and then spoke to the translating guard. The two grew silent for a moment and then turned their attention back to the boy.

"All right my young warrior, you may enter the city, but at first light you make straight for the eastern gate, there it will be open and walk straight down the road. It will take you to the farthest edge of the valley. Once there across the farmlands is the forest., Turn right heading south on the fork of the road, follow for three to four days, on this road you will find a village on the sea. The village is called Trestdan; in Trestdan you may find passage across the sea." The guard then put his left hand on the left shoulder of the boy, "When you lead your armies back this way, remember Ivan and my friend Satarus and we will help you, okay?" He nearly laughed aloud again.

"When I have come back through here with my armies, in Gwarvarik in the city of Gwardara will already be of ashes and under the rule of the Tarvas. As for you and Satarus, you will both be resting with your fathers." The boy said without emotion, as if it were a force from deep within him speaking.

"Go on, boys; enter the city before I change my mind!" The guard said as the other was again pressing for a translation, a translation that was not given but dismissed by the guard. There was a small doorway on where yet another guard stood. The signal came from the one who questioned the boy, a simple nod and the heavy small door opened and the boy was allowed to walk through the three-foot thick outer door through this small tunnel-like entrance. Once on the other side, the boy could see the lights of torches, candles, and lamps with the stench of open sewers and rotting debris. He put on his hood tighter over his nostrils and headed the main cobblestone path into the heart of the city.

Once up high along the towering heights, the air was much cleaner, he found a small wooded area toward the center of the magnificent city by the towering golden dome that he recognized as possibly a temple. The small wooded area he was standing in also was well kept, and the grass was cool and green. It was here under a tree he prepared for his sleep. Within minutes fighting the initial excitement of being in the biggest and only cities he has ever been in, sleep had finally overtaken him as his eyes closed from the view of the heavens above him.

By morning, the young Ramadan manages to find a small marketplace where he traded some trinkets and those ancient weapons that he later found out through the manuals found in the scrolls from Adajahara were useless for practical purposes. Two of his weapons sold fetch a surprising price, junk to him, but valuable to those buying the devices at such a cheap price. With his newfound wealth, he quickly purchased a better pack, clothing, food and a good canteen to hold water along with the practical pair of good boots. His small dagger, the very one he found on the way through the Steppes seasons past, was the only weapon that was in plain sight. He had rapped his sword up on his cloak and fastened it to the inner side of his pack to conceal as much of it as he could.

He understood very little about the sword, and littler still, the powers that it possessed. These powers, to those that the sword gifted to its possessor, and surely, he did not want people to see such a weapon especially in the possession of a small boy. He then continued after talking to a couple of traders that looked innocent enough. They spoke Ramadan, and confirmed that the guard Ivan had did not misled him in his directions to the sea, to the Village of Trestdan. He also found out a thing or two about this city. For Gwardara, it was the capital city of the kingdom, and the armed forces from the nearby villages, and garrisons including the huge garrisons surrounding the capital would advance toward the Steppes to drive out the Tarvas. Something deep inside the young boy told him that the next time, though it would be much later in the future perhaps, things would not favor Gwarvarik. The premonition was stronger than before when he uttered the dark warning to Ivan earlier causing a slight dizziness. He then found a shaded quiet corner and began to eat on some fresh fruit, fruit that he had not had in a very long time. The sweetness from these berries where not bitter like the ones he was eating along the way. The apples as he later found out in the orchard of the temples of Adajahara, which he found out being crab apples that sustained him where much more to his liking. He spent no further time dwelling about his past. It was over and his family destroyed would only bring him to pain and anger. The anger that at times would consume him so much he would vomit from the hatred he felt for the Tarvas who mercilessly killed the old, and the sick, and would not ever spare the whip.

"But one day I will return and free my people and the Tarvas will burn like the tares of autumn" he whispered as his dark eyes reflected the inner fire he was feeling. As he sat there in the cool of midmorning, there was some commotion over at the small marketplace. As he looked up, he could see several guards dressed just like Ivan that he met from the night before, four of them talking to the very same merchant he sold the useless weapons found in Adajahara. He couldn't hear what was being said over the noise of the others trading, but he realized that the four guards wanted to know who and where this person was that sold these weapons.

As he could see that the four guards were asking questions, it would be a matter of time before they would find him. They knew the town, he didn't, and if he would bolt for a dead run down along the path to the eastern gates, no matter how fast he would run, there would be guards waiting for him already there.

Just then, as he thought about his escape, in the distance, stood Kronus in the midst, one of the guards turned to Kronus to show him the weapons that were sold. Kronus drew near the weapons and once he saw them, he knew exactly who it was that sold them these two ancient devices.

"Kronus!" The boy hissed, "You're behind it all." The boy then scurried off into the dark streets away from the marketplace heading south feeling betrayed and realizing his mistake of allowing Kronus to live in the first place, something he felt would never happen again, ever.

Once heading down the path, for an instant he felt Kronus's mental presence. Kronus were attempting to sense where the boy was exactly where in the capital city.

"Boy, I know you are near" It was Kronus, and by no means was the boy going to answer back through telepathic powers. "The sword is mine and I mean to have it!" Kronus warned, however the boy knew that Kronus was attempting to seek him out, and if the boy answered likewise, Kronus would have known his exact location. The boy wasn't scared of the old priest, but he did not want to bring forth the entire attention of the Garrison within the capital, he just needed to escape.

Within a few more moments, a great sound was heard filling up the air above his head. The sound was from trumpets throughout the town, though it was the first time that the boy ever heard of such a thing. A steady blast, he knew it was some sort of warning, that it was nothing good for him.

People he could see began running frantically through the streets running toward homes and businesses and boarding up, closing the windows and doors to the outside. Now he knew he was right as a pit filled in his stomach, they were on to them because of his mistake of suffering Kronus with his life.

Soon the streets were empty and the boy scaled the side of a small building and climbed to the rooftop. There he removed his pack and found shade as he drew out his sword. He did not want to use it on the Gwarvarik people; he also knew that if he released the souls within the sword for his bidding that many would die. Besides, he only wanted one to die, a lying but cunning old man. The sound of the trumpets that rang out through the air had finally stopped with the sound echoing off into the distance, and the sound of soldiers marching and the sounds of hooves began filling the streets below.

"I mean to have what is mine!" It was Kronus's voice threatening the boy.

"Let us end this, give me the sword, and I will have them spare your life," His voice sounded urgent but sincere.

"You see, boys, they know you are from Adajahara, and Adajahara is a sacred and holy place of these people, and a place that is forbidden. Those that are found out to have been from Adajahara are put to death. I have told them that you are from Adajahara that you have stolen what was mine and have hidden there, and with you selling the relics of Adajahara, only proves my story, but" Kronus grew silent for a moment before continuing.

"Give me the sword. I shall talk to the king for me to take mercy on a young Ramadan orphan. The king, he just might put you in the salt mines for the rest of your natural life, what does you say to this most merciful offer?" Kronus were probing but the boy remained quiet as he reached over with his good hand to rub the dark clothing covering the bandage from the limb severed by the boy. Instead, he drew the sword up next to his own face before his nose and closed his eyes. He could see where Kronus was standing, he was now before the huge temple of the golden dome, the very same whose reflection bathed the building around this city in the sunlight.

"Now boys, don't be foolish!" Kronus were realizing the boy wasn't falling to his ploy. The boy drew his sword down and sheathed it. The boy realized that if he unleashed his small army of Lycoi souls that many innocent people would get in the way of his ambition of destroying the old man. This was just something the boy was not prepared to do, something that was holding him back, besides he understood little about the magical properties of the sword, nor understood how much the sword has begun to affect him.

The boy scurried off into the city below and his plan was to wait until darkness falls, he might just have a better chance of escaping the soldiers who would be on every gate waiting for him.

By evening, he was at the southern gate and he could see the heavily armed guards. The guards were safely off at the distance, but he could hear them talk, there were two directly before him amongst the people, mostly villages coming forth before the hour the gates would close. From afar on the top of the wall stood archers, many of them under the light of the torches and he knew even if he manages to escape the guards on the ground, the archers would easily find their mark.

The boy gripped the hilt of his sword, and in doing so, he could understand the language of the two soldiers talking.

"Ivan remembers seeing the boy who stole the sacred relicts, dressed in a black cloak, a Ramadan that had the strange eyes and pale skin like the moonlight looked like he was perhaps his eleventh or twelfth season." One of the guards said.

"Ivan?" The other asked as he continued.

"Why did Ivan allow him in?"

"He didn't know, besides a small boy, a Ramadan to boot, what's the odd?"

"Yeah I thought the Tarvas bastards had rounded them all up, and what they didn't kill, chained them and sent them off back to the frozen tundra." The two laughed a bit.

The two guards laughed and the first spoke, "Yeah I never did care for the Ramadan scum, but they kept to their own and for that, I respect them. Ivan got two weeks worth of additional duties for his oversight." This caused the two laughs aloud again briefly as the first guard continued.

"The boy is still in the city and Kronus, the old friend of the king wants the boy and the relic of Adajahara in tact. So keep your eye out." The guard walked off as additional guards approached readily to close and secure the huge gate.

The boy turned his attention to a large wagon being pulled by a team of horses. The wagon was filled full of wheat and the boy didn't waste any time leaping on the back of the wagon and hiding himself deep within the wheat from eyesight. He clutched the hilt of his sword as he heard the two wagon masters speak.

"Well they all seem to be looking for someone in particular tonight," the older voice said.

"What else is new, every night it is someone in particular?" the younger one laughed a bit.

"Halt!" The boy heard the other guard before.

The wagon suddenly stopped.

"Yes?" The older voice said.

The boy could hear the feet of other guards circling the wagon, and light from their torches reflecting over the grain of wheat, as they were looking for signs of the boy.

"Get those damned torches away from the king's grain you fools!" scowled the older voice.

"Where are you heading, especially at night, have you not heard of the Lycoi?" The guard warned.

"Lycoi?" the older voice raised with keen interest as the other wagon master could be heard bending over giving his ear to the guard. The others then removed their torches and search from the grain shortly as the guard speaking to the wagon masters continued.

"Yes, the Lycoi, many of them were spotted along the edge of the oak wilderness, looked like some sort of skirmish." He was shortly cut off from the older voice from the wagon.

"How many men did we lose in the process?"

"None, it wasn't with us." The guard added.

"Shit, every since the Tarvas crossed the river, it's been nothing but trouble, the whole damned forest is in an uproar, and what of the treaty with the Lycoi?" The older voice added.

"As far as I know, it is still intact; patrols have picked up the tracks of a small Tarvas group marauding northeast of here in the village of Poi attacked by what looked like the Lycoi."

"Any survivors?" the older voice asked the guard.

"No, nothing much left, looks like they rode right into a small pack of them at Poi."

"I hate the Tarvas as much as the Lycoi wished they just kill each other and do the rest of us a big fat favor." The guard laughed with the others listening to the older voice.

"Yes, yes, but the road as far as Trestdan is clear?" The younger wagon master weighed in his concern.

"Yes no sigh of Lycoi, but whatever stirred them up in the first place in the skirmish to the north might be out there still." The guard warned.

"Tarvas raiders?" The older voice quipped.

"No, no sign of Tarvas, some say may be some sort of Lycoi tribal conflict, a rivalry perhaps." The guard retorted.

"Tribes?" The old man recounted.

"Lycoi has no tribes, what makes you say this?" the old voice asked the guard sharply.

"Those that killed the Lycoi with the exception of a few bodies severed by a weapon served under skill exceeding the Lycoi, seemed to attack their own in general."

"Strange, and a damnedest thing I heard of yet." It grew silent for a moment.

"Anyway what of this?" The guard asked as the older voice's body wrestled a bit and the boy could hear him handing the guard some parchment. "As you can see, it is the king's order for us to deliver the wheat at once to Trestdan to board shipment to Draccus to be used as seed."

"Draccus you say?" The guard asked somewhat puzzled.

"The king of Draccus, well they call him" The old man paused for a moment.

"What do they call the king over there?" his voice was directed to the younger wagon master, "Pitah 'er something like that" the younger responded.

"Yeah that's it, Pitah. Some name, right?" the old wagon master said.

In that instant, the boy's mind recollected the ancient scrolls of Adajahara that told of the name called "Pitah." He whispered under his breath as his dark eyes went ablaze with the reeling whirlwind in his mind, "...*Pitah Alohaim Rystak, vile pestilence of the dark isle of the dragons*" he remembered from the sacred scrolls. Then like a bolt out of the darkness, "Draccus could be the isle of the dragons, and if so, then the inhabitants could very well be the descendants of the Taltakkurdg-Kevnaps chieftains told from the scrolls." Then indeed the young boy realized at that moment that the sacred scrolls of Adajahara were indeed based on events. True events that certainly happened and the skeleton of the sorcerer that he himself had obtain by the happenstance somewhat orchestrated by Kronus and Naverron. All of this, was indeed as true and then perhaps the very sword he had in his possession that had the supernatural powers could in fact have belonged to the Taltakkurdg-Kevnaps themselves, or may have come directly from the Taltakkurdg-Kevnaps' distant world. The boy wondered of the possibilities that his young mind was unfolding.

"No shit, Draccus? I would not set a foot on that dark isle of the demon possessed and accursed land of bastard children ill-will inbred witches!"

"Diplomatic channels have opened between the king and this Pitah of Draccus who is sending us Black Lotus by the tons."

"Black Lotus you say old man?" one of the other guards asked.

"Yes so I am told?" The old man said as he continued.

"This wagon must make Trestdan by the evening of morrow to make the ship bound to those people." The old man's voice was filled with a bitter prejudice.

"What of the wheat?" the other guard asked the old wagon master.

"The emissaries of Draccus have requested this, they plan on using it. The seed to mix with their grain they grow for a reason that we are not privilege to" The old wagon master answered and then reminded the guards that he had orders to Trestdan.

"Be on your way." The guard handed back the paperwork to the wagon master and the cart pulled forward with a crack from the whip. The cart then passed through the huge southern gate and the noise from the city fell into a distant silence. The huge oak and iron gates closed behind the cart as it traveled down the winding cobblestone road to the floor of the valley.

Only the two torches lighted the wagon, one on each side of the wagon masters as the darkness consumed them. The boy realized that he was safe and remained hidden listening as the two speak with the aid of the sword.

"I tell you that guard back there didn't tell us everything about the Lycoi," the older wagon master suggested.

"Oh, what else is there?" The younger one asked.

"There were several found in the wheat fields not more than a league away from the main road leading to the city."

"Really and how do you know of this?" the younger of the two asked as if he was challenging.

"I know the city and if you want the truth about things. You just need to know the right people, simple really, never trusts a guard to tell you anything, and mostly they don't know the whole affair, only told what they needed to be told."

"I see," said the younger, "What of the Lycoi in the field, they never have come that close to the city, and they would be seen?"

"I have heard that some believe they were chasing someone through the fields, track of a boy and it was the boy that did the killing with the blade, a sword perhaps. But I also heard that it looked like that they were one of the Lycoi than turned on the others, the others that the boy didn't kill, no sign of a sword at least." The older man grew silent as the younger took this all in.

"A boy?"

"Perhaps" the older man answered.

"What boy would you know that would have that sort of skill or the strength to swing such a weapon?" Without an answer the younger one concluded, "None I say."

"Well goddamn it, let's just get through to Trestdan in one piece shall we?" The older man's voice was filled with a rising fear and concern.

"Something brought the Lycoi very close to the city though," The older man concluded.

The boy found himself drifting off to sleep in the quickened pace of the wagon as it was heading from the cobblestone road to one made of a softer surface of dirt.

The sudden stop of the wagon woke up the boy. His eyes began to focus, he realized that it was daylight and he could hear the sounds of birds, and the faint sent of water in the air, salt water, a scent his nostrils did not know. He carefully arose from his hiding from within the wheat and could catch a glimpse of both the wagon master getting off the wagon and addressing someone on the ground.

The boy wasted no time of leaping down quietly and removing the wheat and dust from his clothing and walking away from the cart. He could see he was at a village, there were people walking about, shopkeepers sweeping off the dirt from the wooden planks that made up a walk way that others walked up and down on both sides of the road. He walked up to the walkway and turned to see a large bay, a body of water that stood directly before him. The largest body of water he has ever seen filled only the horizon on where the clear blue sky met the sea.

"Trestdan." The boy muttered. Along the side of the shore he saw large docks and two ships, both dark with dark maroon and black square-like sails rolled up on a wood cross beam two-thirds up the huge wooden mass. There on either of the ships made of black timbers and he could see huge shields lining the top of the sides what also appeared to be a few of the men loading and unloading the large creates and boxes. The air was generally still like the water before the boy at a distance, and he could see two smaller ships, dark like the other two, but smaller and more slender approaching the village. He could barely make out the maroon symbols on the square sails, but it looks like fire-breathing Drakkars that he has read about in the ancient scrolls of Adajahara.

Something deep within him stirred, he realized above all else that he would go to Draccus, and for the first time in his life he had never felt more certain about something so strong.

CHAPTER 5

▼

"Hey boy, first time in Trestdan?" it was an older man, dressed in garb the boy has never seen before, the same garb as those that was working on the decks of those dark ships, the older man smiled.

The boy realizing that he did not have his hand on the hilt of his sword that wad strapped to his back under his cloak hidden out of eyesight. The dialect and language of the man were like his own.

"Yes" the boy answered sheepishly, he wasn't afraid at the older man in the gray stubble weathered beaten face as his steel blue eyes met the dark orbs of the boy.

"How do you know Ramadan?" The boy looked at the old man. In the light denim shirt and short pants wearing canvas shoes, the old man stood there before him carrying his belongings in an old dingy tan leather bag slung over his left shoulder held by his left hand.

"'Cause I am Ramadan myself, I can spot a fellow Ramadan a mile away!" boasted the tall slender sailor looking down at the young boy waiting for a reply with a smile on his nearly toothless face.

"What tribe are you from?" The Sailor asked.

"The tribes are all gone, there is none living in the Steppes!" The boy words were as sharp as his swords catching the sailor off guard.

"Say again?"

"Did you not know that the Tarvas had killed all of our people except for the women and children, and many of those have died along the way?" The boy was stunned that the sailor did not know as he could see the shock still painted on the old man's face.

"I have been at sea for a good many years, I have not known, news from the northern countries travels a wee slow across the sea." The old sailor looked down at his feet. The sailor was silent only for a moment in reflection of the shocking news that he was receiving.

The Sailor looked back up at the boy, "What of Revendrake boy?"

"Burnt to the ground, nothing left except for this dagger I have found in the ashes when I was passing through." The boy opened up his cloak and handed the old sailor the dagger he had found in which the sailor took carefully from the boy for a closer examination.

"Yes, from the house of Two Lions, the guardians of Revendrake." The Sailor added in a whisper as he spoke.

"I have heard of the battles with the Tarvas, and since the birth of my father's fathers, it has always been so, and there will never be peace." The sailor grew quiet.

"I am afraid there is now." The boy added, "Y'llian-Talbok is dead and all those that followed him against the Tarvas."

The sailor handed back the dagger, "No you keep it, that is all that is left of Revendrake I'm afraid." The boy concluded and began to walk away.

"Wait, and did others like you escaped?" The sailor looked back at the boy as he was holding the dagger in the palm of his hand.

"I do not know of any, you are the first Ramadan I have seen since I have escaped from the slave-masters." The boy said solemnly.

The sailor was still surprised then turns around toward the boy, "Where shall you go, boy, what shall you do?" he said looking at the young boy.

"I shall go where those ships go." He pointed onto the two Draccus ships that were docked. The boy turned back to the old sailor who was now looking onto the two ships.

"Draccus. Lad, those ships are to return to the dark isle, no place for a young Ramadan boy such as you and take my heed. Be content right here, or choose yet another ship bound for another country such as Gaelund, Caledon or some place like that!" The sailor warned.

"Why is that?" the boy insisted turning his full attention back on the sailor, "You are from one of them boats, are you not?

"Yes, I have served enough for Pitah Morderra-Atrauis, no more, no more."

The boy could see the disparagement in the sailor's eyes as he spoke looking on at the ships before a quick glance was given to the boy.

"You go as a new hand on the ship, they will work you to death, goes as a passenger, and they will slice your throat and turn you over the side and feed you to the sea before night fall. Why do you want to go to Draccus, you have never been there?" The sailor walked slowly back to the boy keeping his distance.

"No, but I must go, I have family there?" The boy was lying and hoping the Sailor did not realize the sudden fabrication causing the sailor to look at him once more quickly.

"Really, an uncle or something, perhaps your parents?" the sailor asked handing him back the dagger.

"My mother's brother life's in Draccus and I must tell him the news that she is now dead." The boy was quick with his growing yarn.

"Take back the dagger boy, you'll find a greater need for it than I." The sailor looked sternly at him through his steel blue eyes that were almost silver in color. "I would suspect that is the reason for your dark colored eyes and the color of your skin." The sailor smiled.

"Why is that?" The boy said confused somewhat.

"I can see the Draccus in you, from your mother, but yet you were your hair in the Fashion of a young Ramadan, truth is, and I thought you might be Ramadan, but after all, I was not sure." He said with a smile as the boy took back the dagger as the sailor continued to speak.

The boy was stunned by his words by how much he resembled a person from Draccus; it has been nearly a year since he saw a reflection of himself. He only saw himself in the mental image of his own from a time before the Tarvas razed his village, but he had to attempt to keep his composure so the lie would be convincing.

"If you must go to Draccus, you see the ships still out in the harbor making way inland?" The sailor pointed to the two ships that were now growing much closer than before.

"Yes, yes I do." The boy answered as he felt some relief that perhaps the sailor's mind would be drawn off from his lie.

"Those are the Draccus warships under the flag of a truce with Gwarvarik; they are the ships that carry the Pitah's diplomatic emissary returning for them tonight along with the emissary's soldiers. On the second of the ships you may find boarding. Tell the captain of the ship what you told me, if it is whom I think it is, he will know your tongue, and he will spot out a lie in your words. Do not cross him least you will be spending the night alone at the bottom of the sea. They're on that ship you will be treated well and will survive the travel to Draccus." The sailor then offered a quick hint of a smile.

"Those ships have the Pitah's best soldiers on board, though they are Draccus, but they can be trusted." The sailor added as he looked back to the warships.

The boy was a little nerved by the old sailor's words, "Does he know the truth?" the boy thought to himself looking for a sign, but the old sailor had a weathered face of stone.

"How long shall it take to get to Draccus?" The boy asked.

"Three maybe four days in a ship as cunning as that one, but with the captain I am thinking of, perhaps two full days. Well, the emissaries may be taking guests, I have no idea on how many, but those other boats are off loading Black Lotus, you know of that?" The sailor asked as he bent down closer to the boy.

"Black Lotus, no?" The boy asked.

"Good and keep it that way, it is nothing more than a mind numbing poison that aids in the dark bidding of evil, stay clear of it and never take it to your lips, no not ever." The sailor said most sternly as he put his right hand firmly on the boy's shoulder.

"What is your name son?" The sailor asked with a warmer smile.

"My name?" The boy realized that no one since his capture or escape has asked that question and after a year to him, it took a few moments to answer.

"Lithius, my name is Lithius." The boy replied with a returning smile as the sailor took his right hand off the boy's shoulder and extended his hand in a handshake. Lithius stretched out his hand and shook it firmly.

"My name is Salvan and I wish I could talk you out of going to Draccus, but your uncle must know, and you should be with your family young Lithius." Salvan arose up and then asked one more of the boy before departing, "You have silver for the trip, it will no doubt be about five silver pieces and not one piece less."

"Yes, I have enough." Lithius returned, he had just enough.

"Good my young friend, I shall go and settle down after looking into the interests of my people, perhaps I will find me a young Gwarvarik woman if I cannot find me a Ramadan woman for a wife." Salvan began to laugh, as he turned not giving another look to the boy.

"Good bye my young Ramadan friend, good bye!" Salvan walked up the wooden walkway and beyond the hill out of eyesight as Lithius watched him go until he could not see him any longer.

Lithius could see the two wagon masters yammering to the two sailors now overlooking the load of the wagon as other sailors from one of the ships came down to aid in loading up all the grain and wheat.

Lithius then found a comfortable place and sat down looking on at the two warships coming into the nearby vacant dock that was filling with the Trestdan hands lashing the ships to the dock. By now, Lithius could clearly see the Draccus maroon Drakkars that looked so formidable to those caught in the ship's grips.

Lithius also say a long large horn that followed the curvature of the ships bow from within the long sleek ships that was filled by shields along each sides of the ship. Just then those very same horns blew in a steady blast simultaneously together giving off a very frightful sound that filled the air. The sound was scattering the white and gray sea birds and startling all those that was not from Draccus including Lithius who rose suddenly to his feet looking wide-eyed to the two warships. Then without further notice, the blasts stopped and the valley was filled with the echo from the mighty horns. The sound was so defining that Lithius and many others, especially those villagers closer to the ships had trouble regaining their hearing back right away.

As young Lithius looked on, he could see, unlike the two other ships docked to his left that were still off loading large crates and boxes. These cargo ships had sailors like Salvan dressed in the same fashion, but on the warships, those that he could see were far different. There were tall and powerful men who wore black armor headgear, black armor chest plates with the same maroon Drakkar symbol boldly placed and leather, black colored tunics with long black leather boots and a wide leather belt each armed with a sword and dagger and other smaller weapons that a soldier may need. Some of these soldiers have long lances and spears, other bows and quivers. Those that had the bows, their armor was lighter in both color and in nature than the rest. As Lithius looked on, he could then see a single man come forth to several of the men in the ship. He stood there standing very still by the plank that ran from the ship to the dock as the sails were being lifted and drawn in the same fashion as the two cargo ships. The man was dressed in nothing but crimson and gold. Lithius assumed that this was the leader of all the men on the ship because he could clearly see the respect and admiration that the others had for him.

As the leader approached the three men waiting for him by the plank, the leader then put on his golden color helmet adorn with ruby red jewels and a long crimson single mane that ran from just above the brow of the helmet to its back and below. Lithius were quite taken by the colorful dress. Suddenly a high-pitched whistle from something like a flute that Lithius could only hear was given. Those that were not directly stowing away lines and the sails were drawn to the same single statue position like the other three men all facing their leader. The three brought up their right hands above their brow as the leader did sharply the same and then brought down his arm with the other three men standing before him. The leader then turned and walked down the plank to the dock on where there was another dressed exactly in the same fashion from the other ship that stood a half of a head taller.

Lithius watched on as the two leaders from the ships stood there on the dock for a few moments exchanging words and laughter. The young boy strained but could not hear and he would not risk exposing his sword to the weary eyes of the villagers, the last thing he wanted to do was draw unneeded attention to him.

As he looked on, the two walked down to the dirt rode and behind them the soldiers were forming as they unloaded from the boats, Lithius could see there were fifty or so, five bowmen from each ship that were toward the front of the ship and behind the two soldiers with the banners of Draccus. The rest formed neatly in two columns further behind. The order was given and the army marched down to the dock and as every eye of the village was trained on the soldiers as, they marched. Some broke off and stood guard before the two warships. As for the rest, they were behind the leaders and followed them up to the top of the hill on where many broke ranks on each side of the road. The army evenly distributed guarding the roadway as the sound of horses from afar beyond the hill came, and Lithius could see the swirls of dust clouds rise into the blue clear sky. Within moments, Lithius could see the black and maroon banners of Draccus high the air caught in the breeze of the group that obviously had the Draccus emissary with the soldiers on horseback. As Lithius strained to get a better view of the entourage of the emissary, He could see twelve unarmed men. The older dressed in silk black tunics under black robed cloaks and all twelve wearing golden chains with an emblem made of silver and crimson that looked like they might be symbols of the Drakkars on these pieces. Among the Draccus soldiers that accompanied the Gwarvarik soldiers on the gray and white horses also heavily armed, and behind them, several canopied wagons.

The procession stopped nearly before the leaders of the warships as the two officers saluted in the same fashion as before. Lithius could clearly figure that the emissary was obviously great leaders and admired by those from the ship. Most of the villagers just looked on in silence as those on horses began dismounting the horses as the Gwarvarik gathered the animals that became clear to Lithius that the Draccus came afoot to this land. The wagons then were ordered down toward the docks. From there, the cargo transferred to the ships.

As the carts drew nearer to Lithius he could smell several scents of perfumed fragrance in the air, a smell he has never smelled before in his young life, a smell that he found very pleasing and somewhat soothing. He could see that the Draccus soldiers were ready for any attack. Heavily guarding these carts, the carts stopped before the young boy. Lithius moved, getting out of harm's way of being noticed by any soldiers. As he looked on, his interests perked on those that were in these carts and the servants tending to whoever was in them.

It was his first opportunity to see the Draccus soldiers so close to him. The boy could see that many of these men, these men whose skins were like a pale moon gray, hair short and all a shining black, so black that there seemed to be a blue tint shining in the sunlight. Their eyes were as dark as the night as the boy looked on. Lithius took notice of the Draccian soldiers' facial features, and besides the eyes, high cheekbones, there was almost a nonhuman quality in their long slender faces. The soldiers were considerably tall, much taller than Salvan and the other sailors from the ships that were unloading the large crates and boxes.

As all the carts stopped fully, the soldiers surrounded each of them, protecting them. Lithius looked back up toward the hill where the road went up and over and could see the Gwarvarik soldiers gallop off with the extra horses in tow that was used for the Draccus emissary to get to this village.

Young Lithius turned his attention away from the emissary and back toward the ship that Salvan suggested earlier that he should board. Lithius carefully walked up to the dock and up to the gangway of the ship on where two guards stood protecting the entrance.

"Hello?" the boy said cautiously as one of the guards looked down from the brow of his helmet and smiled slightly.

The guard uttered something that Lithius could not understand, a language he certainly didn't know and he was not about to bring out his sword knowing this would be a sign of aggression. The thought frightened Lithius, this was something he did not want to do, or did he want any more attention drawn to him.

"Boy, get away from those men!" scorned one of the villagers that was working on the dock in the boy's native tongue.

Lithius turned toward the source of the voice, there stood a man in his early twenties, "I need passage, safe passage to Draccus" The young boy explained as the villager approached the boy cautiously.

"Boy these are the warships of the Draccus navy, the dragon boats of the emissary. Try one of the other ships, now get away!" Then the soldier that smiled before yelled something to the villager that caused the villager to reply to him in like manner.

"What does the young boy want?" The guard said to the villager.

"He wants to gain safe passage to Draccus." The villager replied timorously as his dark brown eyes shifted back and forth between the boy and the two soldiers.

"What business does this one have in Draccus; this one doesn't look Draccus to me. Too frail, are you sure he's a boy, and not a girl?" This caused the three men to laugh aloud a bit at the young boy's expense.

The villager looked back at the boy, "What is your name?"

"Lithius is my name." The boy grew quiet.

"Lithius, huh, hmm, what business do you have in Draccus?" The villager said.

"And don't lie, boy!" the villager quipped.

"I am to see my uncle who lives there." In addition, Lithius began telling the same story as before as the villager listened and then translated to the soldiers.

"I will bring this up to the captain when he arrives, it will be up to him to decide if there is room for such. Does the boy have any coin, the voyage is not free, and by the looks of this lad, we couldn't get a good day's work out of him, not of less he wants to work in the galley?"

"Boy, do you have money for the voyage?" the villager asked looking harshly at Lithius.

"Yes, I have the coins, how many coins?" The boy was quick to ask.

The villager turned and translated what was said, the prices were ended to be the rest of the coins plus labor in the galley that is if the captain of the ship would allow Lithius passage. For Lithius, the story worked and now he realized that he would certainly be putting some distance between him and Kronus, and for now, that's all that mattered.

Lithius' work in the galley of the ship kept him below the decks for two days straight. Without little time for much else with the exception of needed sleep, he was left alone. On the third day however he was released from his duties and spent the entire day staying out of the sailor's and the soldier's way. He sat there up on the bow of the ship upon some crates held down by netting as he looked at the indigo sea as the main sail flapped and stretched in the wind as the ship continued southwest. In the horizon of the morning light was a faint outline of land and Lithius naturally assumed that this was the isle of Draccus.

The aid of his sword that he managed to keep hidden in his cloak attached to his backpack that made it possible for him to understand the conversations. He befriended several on board including the cook as well as one of the emissaries who heard of his story he had orchestrated since Salvan.

As he sat, there in the open air, alone with his thoughts. His own thoughts reflected on the capture of his people by the Tarvas. The Tarvas who raided his small village, The very same village that comprised mostly of old men, women and children, for the men were off in bands gathered to fight the wretched foes from the other side of the tall mountains. Lithius realized that the only reason he managed to escape from the tyranny with the loss of his mother. His dad already gone was nothing more than the conjuring of Kronus, who after all, used the boy in gaining the sword. Lithius thought about that for a moment as he wiped the welling tears from his face.

When Lithius looked into the mind of Kronus, he saw plans within plans, people, faces, and thoughts of revenge and deception. Lithius could remember feeling the hate, the betrayal not to mention the rise in frustration within Kronus. It was certainly clear to Lithius that Kronus meant to have the sword and at any cost no matter what!

Pitah Valgas, the very same sorcerer using some unknown sinister power was able to guard the sword for all these years. Some weapon that Lithius was sure that came from another world, another realm that Kronus must have stumbled upon somehow. Lithius could not see these thoughts from the old priest at the ancient temples of Adajahara.

"Pitah Valgas obviously knew of Kronus, Kronus feared Pitah Valgas so send in a boy, an innocent boy and somehow Pitah Valgas would not sense or at least worry about this boy," Lithius whispered aloud as his dark eyes burned with wonder and a sense of anger.

"Pitah" Lithius whispered as he thought about Pitah Valgas and the great leader of Draccus, a man named Pitah Morderra-Atrauis. Lithius knew the ancient scrolls from Adajahara were correct and the people of Draccus were the descendants of the Taltakkurdg-Kevnaps. Then another point entered his thoughts, something he himself has been burying deep within and that was, he was also changing physically taking on the physical attributes of those that were from Draccus, the light grey moon colored skin, and the dark orbs of his eyes. Lithius knew this had to be from the sword somehow, or a spell, a curse, but again, it was the sword he was carrying, a sword that Kronus would not stop to get.

Lithius looked over at the portside of the ship and could see at some distance the two cargo ships and far to their left the other "dragon ship." Lithius turned his attention to the pack and from within he brought up another scroll.

One of several scrolls included a map that he found from the galley below showing the interior of the island he was going to embark on his next adventure.

Lithius quickly looked around and noticed that the sailor and the soldiers were busy about the day, too busy to pay any attention to a quiet boy at the bow of the boat. As he turned around giving full attention to his scroll, this was written in the language that was certainly neither from the blue planet like so many of the other scrolls, but of the Taltakkurdg-Kevnaps. Its strange runes and symbols were impossible to read without the aid of the sword. Lithius had realized from the other scrolls he has read, those written by the ancient sages of old and those even older written by the people of the blue world stumbled on a power. A power that was as mysterious and as frightful to them as it was to the ancestors of those along the Adajahara region. In that moment, Lithius realized that perhaps it was the sword itself captured from the Taltakkurdg-Kevnaps. As he thought, he remembered one of the scrolls and concluded it was indeed Pitah Valgas who had the sword, and who as, as the boy seen, did those of the blue world captures. There was no further doubt in Lithius's mind that it was the blue world that captured and hidden both the sword and its secrets in the darkness of the Pitah's crypt in Adajahara. Somehow, Pitah Valgas wasn't finished even after death of his body. This thought further intrigued Lithius even more, something inside, deep inside of him warned that Pitah Valgas was still lurking around, even in spite of releasing the souls from the sword; Pitah Valgas would find a way around it. Lithius also knew that as powerful as the sword was, it was not the source of all his strength. After all, since he met Kronus's associate, Naverron, Lithius had the budding ability of telekinesis, the ability to speak to another with thought only. However, with this gift alone, Kronus attempted to use it to his advantage.

Very carefully, Lithius examined the ancient Taltakkurdg-Kevnaps scroll that may shed some light on this whole affair, while gripping tightly the hilt of the sword, the alien writings began to form lines, sentences of words that Lithius could understand

"The great leaders arose against those who called themselves earthlings, enemies of all the Taltakkurdg-Kevnaps, our people the righteous conquerors of this world over the diseased carrion have fully invaded. Our great ships that carried promise of our seed are all but destroyed and it is only we who are fortified on the worlds that remain. We have discovered great ancient weapons to fight against the earthlings and we shall once again dominate this weak planet like so many before it"

"Could this sword be one of those weapons?" Lithius thought as he finished the ancient scroll. There was nothing more, and it only raised more questions than answers.

As Lithius began looking at the map of Draccus, he heard a conversation behind him, he slowly turned and could see it was the captain and on of the emissaries talking to each other. Lithius put away the map quietly and gripped the concealed hilt of his sword in hopes of eavesdropping on a nearby conversation. In doing this, he could understand what the two were saying before the mouthpiece of the large horn that ran between the crates. Lithius was now sitting on the large black horn that ran along the top of the bow. "I can assure you that Pitah Morderra-Atrauis will hear of this" the old balding tall lanky man in late in life, spoke softly looking at the Captain.

"I am sure he will, and is everything, everything falling to plan?" the captain asked looking at the dignitary with some measure of concern. The captain was tall and built very powerfully. It was obvious to Lithius that this man was not Draccus, but of another nationality as the captain removed his headgear exposing his light blond shoulder-length hair. His stern blue eyes caught the black orbs of the emissary.

The emissary flashed a quick smile as he looked around to insure that the conversation went unnoticed. His long silver hair he pulled out of the way of his face that caught the sea breeze as he spoke. "Once those Gwarvariks starts indulging under the spell of the black lotus, they will be utterly mindless and Pitah Morderra-Atrauis will have no problem with sacking all of Gwarvarik, and with the aid of the puppets from the north, Adajahara will be ours and with it, its secrets."

The captain just looked at him, "Pitah Morderra-Atrauis will need an admiral to lead the attack Tiberius, and that name is the only one I have on the tip of my tongue." Lithius carefully listened without making a sound as he realized whoever this man truly was he didn't like him much.

"Thank your emissary, but does Pitah Morderra-Atrauis put trust in a Faedarish; after all I am not Draccus?" Tiberius the captain asked.

The emissary smiled again shiftily and replied, "You have proved yourself many times over again both in battle, and as a trusted officer in his service."

His voice almost faded completely in the breeze as Lithius strained to hear as he could see that there was still apprehension on the Captain's face.

"...Pitah Morderra-Atrauis is the true black lord of Draccus, and with his word, it is final, my friend, no need to worry about it a moment longer" The emissary turned toward the tents made for the perfumed women from Gwarvarik, "The Gwarvariks hadn't a clue." The emissary finished speaking just shortly before he continued to walk into the tent. With his hand on the tent flap exposing the beauty within and turning to the other man standing behind him with a cold smile, this caused the other man to speak.

"Lord, what of the women, gifts to Pitah Morderra-Atrauis sealing the treaty with Draccus and Gwarvarik?" Tiberius asked as he looked into the tent.

The emissary turned his attention back to the captain and shrugged his shoulders under the dark robe, "Pitah Morderra-Atrauis cares not for these whores, and he may take one or two for his concubines but as for the rest?" He shrugged his shoulders again and then replied, "May just be like the precious Gwarvarik seed, spilt as waste amongst the waves of the sea to devour." He closed with a cold smile as he closed the flap of the tent and his attention turned to the sea.

Lithius could see that this didn't sit well with the Captain, "What about that priest that I was told that attempted to persuade the king of Gwarvarik to head his warning?" The captain changed the subject causing the old man to look again at the captain, this time, sharper than before.

"Yes, Kronus has been nothing more that just a second rate magician. A born again looser!" The anger rose in the emissary's voice and he paused for a moment before continuing looking down and away from the harlots within the tent toward Tiberius. "A conning nuisance for one thing for certain. He comes from Rho-Haven, the desert region on where there are more of the likes of him, a wretched pain in the ass at times, but no matter, he will be dealt with." The emissary paused for another second.

"Kronus, a priest of an ancient order, and most like him, ancient and old. They tend to themselves in the temples far in the desert and live out their wretched and useless lives as such, but not this one. He is educated, a scribe if you would and chasing a dream, a useless dream at that."

"But some sort of a dream?" Tiberius asked.

"Somewhere he had uncovered some sort of ancient scroll deep within the desert that he spent years researching and uncovering dark secrets and history of people from other worlds."

"Other worlds?" The Captain quipped.

"Yes of long ago, with this knowledge were rumors of a strange and powerful magic, weapons that spit out fire and light that would set cinder to anything it was pointed at. There are other things, things I will not speak of here" His voice leveled to nothing more than a whisper as Lithius strained to hear.

"…Kronus have made a life of recovering such knowledge and to gain into his possession of such weapons and he will do anything to get his hands on them. This is all I care to know about his past. As far as the present goes, he is trying to gain favor with the Gwarvarik king to broker some sort of a deal by persuading the mindless twit who sits in control of Adajahara, the forbidden temples within." He paused only for a moment.

"I tried to probe his mind, he is difficult, but I will tell you that he knows something, something to certainly do with Adajahara and the secrets within. I have gotten the impression that he was recently at Adajahara, but he kept those thoughts guarded safely. It will be something that Pitah Morderra-Atrauis will contend within his own good time."

"Lord, so do you believe that there is something to the legends of Adajahara?" Tiberius asked with apprehension in his voice.

The emissary looked at the captain cautiously, "I believe that Kronus does, he has seen something, knows something, and more importantly Pitah Morderra-Atrauis believes in the legend especially in regards to the greatest of all the Pitahs. Dare I utter the name even in the light of day?" The emissary said with reverence in his voice. The captain just looked at him reading his face as the emissary broke into another quick ghost of a smile.

"Tomorrow we shall be home, I will have you in the audience of Pitah Morderra-Atrauis himself, and perhaps he can convince you that you are the right man to lead the assault on Gwarvarik from the sea. You should leave without a doubt of the plans from our great leader." The emissary said with a smile as he returned to the tent.

The young boy then looked upon the Captain standing there in his thought with his arm resting against his chest as another soldier came up to him, "Sir, I will be glad to be rid of the emissaries."

The Captain looked up at the tall soldier, "Soon enough, we head west to the sun and then bring us around ready for the dawn." The Captain said as he brought his other hand down.

"Very good sir" the soldier returned his salute and went to the end of the ship and out of the eyesight of Lithius.

The boy turned around and stayed out of eyesight from the Captain and the others until it was dark. The torches from the tents and the other ships sailing close by gave enough light for Lithius to see clearly enough. As he carefully made his way unseen to the galley, on which he filled his backpack full of provisions. Lithius then headed toward the bow of the ship and to the top of the crates. From there, he drifted off to sleep.

CHAPTER 6

▼

Lithius awoke around dawn as he could see the high cliffs of Draccus before him; the cliffs went hundreds of feet into the air, steep and jagged and neither sign of any dock nor a trail of any kind. As the ships, now in a single file behind the flagship, the flagship was making way through a narrow canyon carved through the sheared cliffs. Black wet rock that rose high above them and Lithius could see only a few circling birds from up high that flew out from the nests along the sheared face. Orders were given to bring down the sail as most of the soldiers were sent below to man the oars as the ship was guided through the waves deeper into the canyon.

Never before has Lithius seen such a place. From within, the sun did not shine as the canyon widened and snaked around each turn until the air grew cold and wet by the mist of the huge waterfall just in the distance. There just after the huge waterfall that fell perhaps five hundred feet down stood two magnificent solid iron doors that were as high as the canyon itself, one on each side that seemed carved within each of the walls. The ship continued to be rowed to the cadence of the drum propelling the ship further up to the waterfall. Lithius could see the other ships were on each side of the flagship. Then without warning, a sound that nearly shattered his eardrums rose up from the large horn of the ship as he scrambled to cover his ears.

The sound echoed up through the canyon, it was only one long deep sound that resonated even through his bones and then as soon as it started, it had ceased.

As the heavy wet air from the waterfall came crashing down and now has completely drowned out all other sounds. Lithius leaped down from the crates with all that he carried with him. He then moved to a dyer place on the other side of the crates and sat they're nearly motionless. As he could see from behind the ships, he could now see the two huge iron doors closing by a huge chain on each. Soon the huge doors closed sending a resounding sound that echoed up the canyon walls. Shortly Lithius felt as if the rising water from the waterfall was raising the ships. As he looked, he could see the rising water filling from the waterfall. Again, Lithius has never seen nor heard of such a thing as the ships continued to be raised by this marvel.

By midday, the ships were raised well over two thirds of the total height of the canyon and by late in the afternoon the waterfall had all but vanished. Lithius could see the ships raised up nearly level with the huge river that fed the waterfall. The boy, he could also see on either side of the river a huge village, and the villagers had all turned out to see the ships. Lithius could also see on each side of the river, huge iron wheels that rose high up in the air from the waterline. These wheels were along the side a huge building of cobblestones, each identical to one another and on each of these buildings bellowed steam and smoke, dark smoke that rose high into the sky. Lithius guessed it was each of the buildings that powered the iron wheels that bore the chain on each of the huge doors.

Within moments, orders were then given as the ship's oars once again followed the drums as the boast moved up the river. At the horizon, Lithius could see a huge black mountain that rose high against the white clouds in the distance. The ship was completely saturated by the heavy condensation as it pasted the village. Lithius found that once again, he was sitting upon the huge crates at the bow of the warship. The ship quietly navigated along the river as the sun began drying the wet timbers.

By evening, the ship went through a small set of locks, nothing like the huge lock that raised them far above the sea. By now, the dryer air had evaporated the moisture and Lithius' clothes were finally dry as the ship pulled up next to a garrison on where the ship docked. Here Lithius decided it would be a good point to depart with the others. As he left the ship, he followed the cobblestone road out of the garrison. Lithius headed through the small twisted oaks that lead into a large field on where he could see the bright stars above him and from behind, he had left the river.

Once he had safely crossed the field into the coverage of the mighty oaks, he decided to build a small fire after catching a rabbit for his dinner. Finally, he realized that indeed he had arrived at Draccus, "For what am I to do in this place and in a land who favors the Tarvas?" His blood began to boil as his eyes blazed with vengeance for those who were responsible of killing his family and all that he has known. Now he was in a land that he understood very little.

Lithius wasn't a dull-minded child; he understood that the people here that were Draccus were descendants of the Taltakkurdg-Kevnaps. The Taltakkurdg-Kevnaps are the same race that came from another world, the very same world that perhaps the sword was from so many, many years ago. From that world, where did the weapon, the sword originate from, and what other powers did the sword posses? These thoughts preoccupied the boy's thoughts from hatred. He also realized fully that the sword was somehow changing his physical appearance to those akin to this dark island. "Why is the sword changing me, for what advantage does it posses?" he said aloud as he drew it from its scabbard.

As he looked at it, the nearly translucent properties shined like a valuable stone as the firelight danced along the blade. His eyes darkened to two black orbs as his thoughts wondered at the possibilities. As he looked on at the blade he could see the reflection of his own face, for the first time, he saw the two bottomless pits of his eyes, and this nearly caused him to drop the sword.

He looked back at it again as if he thought his mind was playing tricks upon him, and indeed as before, his eyes look like the bottomless pits. As he stared as his heart raced, he could see nothing in them, not even the hatred he felt moments ago, nothing, and nothing at all and this truly frightened him.

He turned his attention away from the blade to the stars above him shortly and wondered that perhaps he had made the wrong choice to come here. He felt perhaps that Draccus would hold some sort of an answer, an answer he couldn't have found in Adajahara, though he looked.

He knew the sword on occasion had influenced him; more like possessed him to some measure in combat especially with the Lycoi, the wolfen beings that somehow served Kronus. The creatures his people did not know about, "What mysteries do they hold in all of this?" Lithius thought, as the fire grew small as he placed some small sticks on it as the fire snapped and crackled sending small echoes of sound into the woods from behind him.

Still holding the sword, he ran his thumb along the sharp edge ever so slightly. In doing so, slightly as he did, still he cut a shallow wound on his thumb as the blood oozed from the wound onto the surface of the blade. In that instant his mind reeled as his body became energized by electricity and a sharp burning sensation from deep within. He removed his thumb as quickly as he could, nevertheless, in his natural reflex, he was sent to the ground as his eyes lost sight of the surroundings before him as his ears filled with ringing. As he fell unconscious to the world around him, his mind raced through a corridor of his young life's events to a place, a place he had no idea, a place alien to his own surroundings.

As his mind cleared to this place, he could see dark brooding clouds high up overhead, and before him, an arid landscape filled with small brush, blowing dust and sand. The light, a single point of a bluish blur that broke beyond the clouds had shown through enough light for him to see on a small mesa a temple's silhouette at the top. He was drawn to the temple, a temple made of black obsidian stone. As he walked, drawn to the structure many miles, his spirit crossed the desert floor toward the mesa in blinding furry. From there, he then suddenly found himself at the foot of the huge temple. Stairs lead from where he stood to the great columns above him that held the roof of the massive building. There he could suddenly see a cloaked figure standing before the columns. The figure, this specter was carrying in its long ivory grip, a long staff. The boy could see little else as his attention fixed on the cloaked figure.

The figure came down the steps toward the boy, as he thought he was only dreaming. The boy was nearly naked standing there, he tried to move, but he could not, his limbs were numb as terror began to grip him.

"Fear not!" The left hand then risen, warning the boy as the voice deep like many waters spoke to him as the specter drew closer to him. Lithius trembled as sweat began to draw from his brow.

"Am I dead?" The boy asked as he found his words hard to speak, his own voice sounding unfamiliar and not his own.

"No" It said almost a whisper as the figure that stood nearly seven feet tall was now upon the boy as he stood there trembling before the apparition whose face was concealed by the hooded cloak.

"Where am I?" Lithius forced to say.

"No matter, important that you listen." The specter warned. The cloak that concealed his features seemed alive in a torrent of dark souls swirled around his body. It was more like a fog that at times grew shapelessly and sometimes coiled around the figure much like a serpent crushing the life of its intended prey. Lithius could see that this thing, this person was more like a phantom than a person, and he stood nearly naked and unarmed before this specter.

"Who are you?" Lithius gasped.

"I am he who was the origin of the sword you obtain." Lithius peered up to the face of the creature but he could yet see a face and he wasn't too sure he wanted to as he thought about it.

"Are you Pitah Valgas?" Lithius could see the name had some baring on the specter as the hood rose up a bit higher as Lithius could feel the cold gaze of the being peering deep within him.

"No" his mysterious voice said.

"Taltakkurdg-Kevnaps?" and again this caused a reaction with the being.

"No" Lithius was afraid of that answer as well. He wasn't sure to say next but to remain quiet only for a moment.

"I am the creator of the very weapon you have taken from Pitah Valgas." Finally, Lithius' fear had subsided enough after realizing that perhaps, perhaps if the specter does not kill him that he possibly might get some answers to the mystery of the sword.

"You have taken Talquardez-Solstas; you know it in your tongue as the Sword of Souls into your own very possession." The voice of many waters said.

"I have no sword on me here?" the boy rose his palms up toward the face of the hooded creature, "As you can see, I have not the weapon, I mean not here."

"Silence, you stupidly fool!" The strength of the creature's voice nearly knocked the boy down as he began to tremble.

"I was the one who knew you before you were in the womb. It was I who have sought you out when you were laying with your dead mother for it was I who had saved you from the same perils that your kin had suffered."

Lithius peered into the hooded cape as he cowered below the looming specter as he thought about what the apparition had just told him.

"I looked into Kronus' mind, it was him that saved me by some sort of magic, and I saw it in his mind!" Lithius insisted.

"Magic, no, it was I." The phantom leaned back a bit from the young boy.

"Kronus is simply a pawn who is privilege to certain things, certain things I want him to see. I used him for my purpose as I did with Naverron who at one time beckoned me to share my mind with him. How impossible that is to be." The phantom laughed as the mere sound of his laughter rang out through the surroundings.

The phantom regained his composure and leaned back toward the cowering young boy standing before him, "It is Talquardez-Solstas that has brought you here. Nevertheless, you posses the sword and none can take it from you." The creature warned.

"There is one who has tried to take this from me. Did you want it back?" Lithius introvertedly asked as the phantom was now looming over him.

"If I wanted the blade, I would have turned your bones to ash!" The specter rose as his looming dark shadow engulfed the boy seizing Lithius in fear.

"When you drew your own blood on the blade it has sent your spirit to this place, this place far beyond your physical world, do you understand this that I am telling you?"

"Yes, yes I do." Lithius were still assuming he was simply dreaming or perhaps the rabbit poisoned him somehow.

"You are gifted young Lithius." He could feel the being probing his mind, and the creature was far too strong to keep out of his own mind. He could feel the surmounting power peering deep into the innermost recesses of his soul, there was no mental rock, no nook, no cranny left unturned by the power of the phantom's probing. Unlike the rest that Lithius experienced, there was no sharing of thought in the transference of the experience.

"I know your mind young Lithius" His voice faded off like a whisper in the wind. The phantom grew quiet only for a moment.

"Your body dwells in the land of the children of the Taltakkurdg-Kevnaps and there in the land is the great ruler Pitah Morderra-Atrauis. He is an evil and twisted soul that does the bidding of his great master Hanhadra or Hamahadra, as I know of her, the dark goddess of the underworld. Pitah Morderra-Atrauis is merely her puppet and you shall be my instrument to the fall of Pitah Morderra-Atrauis."

"I am but a boy!" Lithius exclaimed, "Couldn't you kill him yourself, why must you need my help?" Lithius expected to die at that moment when the specter lunged forward.

"Not while Hamahadra is protecting him and his bloodline, it would raise a war in the heavens for millenniums to come. It is this reason why I have forged such a weapon, a weapon that will crush any foe, any adversary that should come against the one who wields it."

Lithius could not catch a glimpse of the face within the hood and he thought for a moment in silence that perhaps there was no face for him to see. He could sense that the being, this apparition was still in probing his thoughts as if the probes were icy hands, though the presence was not as strong as before.

"For lifetimes ago, unspoken ages, there were more of these weapons that the gods created to set forth balance, all are lost except for Talquardez-Solstas, Kaggur-Ohm, Dystrayd-Uttus, and the Staff of Hydrayn on which I hold here." He leaned the staff forward as Lithius could see symbols, strange runic signs. The phantom pulled the staff back.

"This is for another destined on a distant world" his voice seemed to ascend to the heavens above them both as he looked up. In that instance young Lithius caught a glimpse of something, something dark and sinister with eyes like mirrors, and then when the specter returned his attention to Lithius, the hooded cloak hid the face.

"You have the greatest of weapons, you will become more with it as it power grows within you. Now you must restore the balance and vindicate my coming upon the wretched children of the Taltakkurdg-Kevnaps. Through you I shall burn the seed of the Taltakkurdg-Kevnaps, and with the seed, the Taltakkurdg-Kevnaps are finished, and with that my young Lithius, so ends' Hamahadra who shall become weak and her body shall then accept my blade." Lithius could feel the hatred that was far surpassing his consciousness as though it was an eagle taking flight far above him.

"The whore is already on her throne, and upon her crown of abominations rests her minions. I see her sitting upon the dais, her thrones of ivory; she lifts her golden goblet of the blood of the damned to her lips. Drunk with the blood of the slaughtered that stains the venomous teeth of her condemning grimace. Her dark red eyes intoxicated peers on her children who worship her as their savior, the protector of their race." The hatred became that of a searing fire flashing and engulfing around them standing before the steps of the temple and Lithius was now prepared to be consumed by the flames.

"Many ages ago the sword was lost only to be recovered by Pitah Valgas, the sorcerer and husband of Hamahadra. Though his dark heart filled with pride of the power unleashed by Hamahadra in him, he did not come to fully understand Talquardez-Solstas, but yet he wields it upon man and beast, and many, many suffered" As he spoke, Lithius felt no compassion in his voice, only bitterness that stung the nostrils of the small boy like that of sulfur.

"Hamahadra grew pregnant and gave birth from her rotting womb the carrion that later grew" As the specter spoke, Lithius remembered the writing, the relief on Pitah Valgas' tomb showing the bloodlines. It was all becoming clear to him as then he covered his face from the scorching air to breathe.

"...But they attempted to deceive the father, so they died by the very hand that birthed them. Pitah Valgas grew angry in spite of the betrayal from his sons and with Talquardez-Solstas, he vowed to kill Hamahadra, but this was his own undoing. Bidding the aid of the children of the distant star seals him to a chamber upon which he died later. The chamber of which Talquardez-Solstas resided for many years long after the remnants of the children of the distant star mingled and became lost in your kind." The fiery hatred began to die out around them and far above them as a cool of dry air engulfed Lithius as he gasps for air.

"Hamahadra, husband less looks upon Pitah Morderra-Atrauis, king sorcerer of Draccus in favor and it is you that will steal her gaze from him with Talquardez-Solstas, the sword of souls as you seize his soul from his body." He paused for only a moment.

"Ascend to the throne of Draccus, orphan boy and avenge the murderers of your family, the Tarvas who lay waste and ruin to the Steppes of your people, fail me, and I will insure the hottest flames for thee." The phantom outstretched his left hand as he began to laugh, stretched toward the boy.

"Talquardez-Solstas will not fail you as you shall raise an army of the undead against the living flesh of Draccus and this alone, I ask for, as you shall pave the way of my coming. I will make you prince over all the flesh that resides on your world and men will tremble in hearing your name and draw there last breath if they should stand before you in battle. I imbue my powers into your very soul and you shall do my bidding."

Suddenly the staff in his right hand turned to a living animal, a creature like that of a striking viper that struck Lithius' right side of the neck. Horrified, he viper began injecting fiery poison into him as he attempted to get away from the snake but fell into blackness from the horror.

"In you are my plan and in you are the answers, my son." The voiced faded off into the whirling darkness as the boy fell deeper into the bottomless timeless pit that lead across the great seas of time and though the corridor of his mind.

CHAPTER 7

▼

As he awoke, he found his body cold lying where he fell with the sword beside him, it was daybreak, and he turned to see the fire has long been out. As he slowly rose up retrieving his sword, the young boy's vision cleared as his heart pounded in his chest. Buzzing filled his ears as he looked down at his right hand after placing the sword back in the scabbard. He noticed there was a small scar on his thumb; the scare was healed and old, as if the wound happened years ago. He reached up to his neck thinking it was all a bad dream. In doing so, he found with his right hand the puncture marks from the viper, the serpent who was once the staff, and to his horror, he realized it was not a dream at all.

Trepidation fell upon the boy as his feet gave out from underneath him. As his body began to tremble uncontrollably as he realized that, somehow this was all real to him as he was standing on the edge of the field in Draccus. The boy began to weep to wonder what evil, what menace had entered his body from the bite that struck squarely in his jugular. He knew his body was poisoned as his vision once again blurred and he became overcome by this dread.

Eleven years has passed since Lithius has arrived to the dark and foreboding isle of Draccus. Once hidden in the shadows of the ancient oak forest as only a specter, Lithius grew both physically and in his dark arts until such a time deemed by the phantom specter. The very same that saved the man when he was yet a boy so long ago, this phantom that would come to the young one in dreams and visions throughout these years. During this time, the work of the specter had gleefully transposed young Lithius into a man and the manifestation or the physical transference had taken hold of Lithius for the bidding his master in the netherworld. Lithius had grown cunning and matured masterfully making him a very implacable adversary. During this time, Lithius had found souls. These souls that were embodied in the flesh and blood of men and beast that went looking for the small boy, or haphazardly crossed deadly paths with him and Talquardez-Solstas giving even more power than ever before.

"Time has now come, my young acolyte to put our plans into action" The voice was laced with venom hatred as it carried through the wind in the leaves of the oak forest. Lithius kneeling by a small pool of water taking a drink on the twilight of an autumn night stopped as his black eyes peered into the clearing subtle pool. The reflection changed to one reflecting the surroundings of the netherworld of his phantom apparition he simply knew as "master."

There in the pool Lithius could clearly see the cloaked phantom walking down the steps of the black stone temple behind him. Lithius could see the living forces of the black cloak stirring around the figure. Lithius froze there as the water captured in the cup of his hands gently slipped through the clutches of his long slender fingers back into the pool with his agape mouth.

"Young Lithius" The phantom bid.

"I am here my Lord." Lithius' deep voice was just a whisper looking into the pool in half a trance.

"It is time for you to strike and fulfill my initial plans"

"To kill Pitah Morderra-Atrauis?" Lithius asked.

"Yes, and with his death the lineage of Pitah Valgas and Hamahadra is ended. Already war with Gaelund has drained the vibrancy of Draccus into infirmity. Already Gwarvarik begins to wake from the Black Lotus slumber and realize that they have been enslaved by the tyranny of Pitah Morderra-Atrauis and his lessen power. The fangs of the Tarvas begin to turn to the hand that has been feeding them as if the ravaged dog chained and pitted into a corner. It is time for you to rise and fulfill your destiny as the ordained prince of the dark lands of Draccus" the phantom paused for a moment.

"Go to the Keep of Pitah Morderra-Atrauis. Upon this obsidian mountain of Thuma-Attarrach and seize what is yours!" The voice of man waters disturbed the pool as Lithius leaned back only to peer back into the pool.

Lithius could only see his own reflection starring back at him, the phantom was gone, "Yes Master, I shall fulfill your bidding." Lithius then arose and turned toward the deep forest. Lithius traveled without a sound through the underbrush and concealed by the canopy of the trees.

As Lithius followed a scant trail, an ancient trail made by the deer that lead toward a small stream, he then followed the trail up through and across a small waterfall and further into the woods that led to his abode of moss covered stone and rock with a thatched roof. There he removed his bow and a quiver of black oak arrows next to an old wooden chair next to an oak table that contained scrolls, maps, and several brass and copper plates and a flask of water. He then whispered an ancient spell and a half-burnt candle on the table lit up without the aid of fire. There on the other side of the table was a fireplace, its mantle rested two Lycoi skulls, two of the very same that set out stalking Lithius when he first came to the woods so many years ago. As far as the remaining Lycoi that was somewhere in the oak forest only Lithius knew, his magic and legendary skills alone shunned any retaliation for their lost kin. Just out back of Lithius' domain was a small field and upon the field were a hundred staffs that stood straight up on their ends surrounded by discarded weapons, swords, shields, axes, bows and other trinkets from the dead. Upon these staffs were the heads of both Draccus and beasts that sought after him. The ghastly site was enough for most to turn away the other direction with the exception of the ravens who stripped away the flesh and sinew from the sun bleaching bone.

It has been sometime since there were any signs of an ambush awaiting Lithius to walk into the trap. While Lithius grew up in the woods, he rarely left the concealment within. During his experience he spent much time learning from his master and developing the skills, he had no time to look for trouble; trouble always without exception came to him. Among the outskirts of the forest rumors of something more sinister than the Lycoi awaited men who stalked after it, and even a name was given, the Brakar-Baine simply meaning "Evil Spirit," this was the name given to him. From an old hide that Lithius recovered from a hunter that stalked him for three days before Lithius grew bored and added a new soul to his sword and a fresh skull on a staff it read. "*I have been chosen to be the bravest amongst my village and the most skillful in the arts of tracking and the bow. I have been honored eternally to bring down the Brakar-Baine who dwells in the heart of the ancient oaks and plagues the night air of the living.*" As Lithius read from the writing of the skin that was nailed to this wall between the two Lycoi skulls wearing a smirk.

During the years, Lithius would visit the villages on the outskirts of the forest only at a distance and intentionally never wished any harm or bring any undesirable attention toward his very existence, but long ago, he had decided that he was through with running. Yet Pitah Morderra-Atrauis never ordered soldiers into the woods and as Lithius deducted, didn't care, or regarded it as some sort of legend or myth. A myth in Lithius' mind would be the very death of Pitah Morderra-Atrauis in the end. Still in spite of everyone that was ever sent into the deep woods to expel the life from Brakar-Baine never walked out again. There were others, children, women who would venture into the woods, Lithius would occasionally cross paths with them also at a distance unseen by them, but close enough for him to probe their minds. These were either the lost or the half-minded lot, these he would allow leaving with their lives, they were of no threat, and he didn't have time to indulge.

Lithius had the ability to cloak him for a series of durations to become invisible that would drain him most intolerably at first. In fact, the first time he was taught the spell, it nearly took his life, and it was of many moons before he would eventually attempt this again. With each passing time, he grew stronger. It was this spell he would occasionally use very carefully as he followed the innocent ones; this of course fed the flames of the legend of Brakar-Baine more so until eventually he stopped entirely.

As he grew, his invisibility gifting through spells was strong enough to cause his entire lair to become unseen for a couple of days at a stretch. This exercise in power would drain him completely but like an athlete, he too trained. There were other spells, teleportation like that of Kronus so long ago, but Lithius could travel at greater distances such as several miles at a time, this in addition, he had to continue to develop like a long distance runner. In the summer, he was literally able to use this power some fifty times in a row before he was completely out of the forest; this was as he figured perhaps one hundred miles or more covered by teleportation.

Unlike so many beliefs and myths about magic, it requires strength and endurance of mind, body, and will. Magic was not free, it had its price, and Lithius understood this far better than he was a boy. During his years, he mastered the bow, built his first boy by the age of fifteen fashioned after the Faedarish Bow, a very strong and powerful bow made of laminated compounds of oak, bone, and sinew. With a word he could kill, but preferred the bow, and if it was an important kill. Lithius enjoyed the personal confrontation that would lead to the use of his sword especially the matters of extracting a soul. Lithius had obtained other skills and spells, but for now, it was time for him to move on. For years, he found comfort behind such stall, it was time for him to fulfill his destiny, and besides, there were people at the top of his list after Pitah Morderra-Atrauis was completed. One of which was Kronus who was still out, and the news that would occasionally come from his master, was still seeking after the sword.

"Even Kronus serves a purpose in my plans" The master's voice echoed in Lithius' thoughts on the matter. There was also the matter of Naverron who betrayed him through the mind of Kronus's scheming thoughts. However, the course of laying waste to the Tarvas, though it was many years ago but Lithius wouldn't go out of his way to settle the score with Naverron. Naverron would come to him.

Now in the evening, Lithius would plan forth he ascension to the throne of Draccus as his dark lord has promised. He knew enough of Pitah Morderra-Atrauis, the tyrannical sorcerer king. Lithius was smart enough as to not undermine the king's power and skill. He knew no matter the spells and gifts that the lineage of Pitah Valgas would not easily be persuaded to suffer no longer his life to Lithius. One thing that Lithius counted on was simply the element of surprise, and of course, he was not very alone in this matter. After all, he had found a small army within the sword, an army that could not be killed. Lithius knew that the travel to Thuma-Attarrach would be a perilous one; at the foot of the obsidian mountain were the formidable three legions of trained soldiers and the garrisons he would have to slip by on the way up. Once passed the soldiers at the base of the mountain, he would have to stay off the roads, and paths of men. Moreover, the added challenge of the few of the Drakkars that can actually see through his powers of invisibility, this of course would not prevent Lithius from hiding from them. The Drakkars could spot Lithius from afar through the invisibility spell as if he was like any other man. Then there were the other beasts that he would have to carve through, and rumor had it that the mountain had its own brand of Lycoi imbued with incarnations and spells by none other than Pitah Morderra-Atrauis.

"What else should I suspect?" He said aloud in his thoughts as he began to pack up his important belongings as he looked around.

"The rest can stay, I will be back for them, someday, if I die, no matter anyway?" He smiled oddly at the thought of what he just said.

There was one soul that Lithius required, a special soul that would be a formidable army in its own right. Lithius would have to go and collect this prize on his way through the forest, he needed all the assurance he could gather in his favor on this venture. Besides, he wasn't dealing with an average mortal or a half-witted Lycoi. Lithius would be going against a very powerful foe that possessed a lifetime of power as king.

Pitah Morderra-Atrauis is someone that Lithius, though at a distance has been carefully studying relying on what his master had told him, rumors and gossip he would pick up along the way skirting villages. Pitah Morderra-Atrauis, a powerful sorcerer was constantly tending a weary eye. The Pitah would look for the slightest signs of a possible elimination of his power. Any Pitah was knowledgeable, as if this knowledge was second nature to spot out dark schemes brought up by the hopes and ambitions from his enemies who would triumph in his long awaited death. The ruler of Draccus, a ruler from a long bloodline that Lithius would, if successful, severs. Nonetheless, Lithius was not the first to attempt such a malevolent stratagem that's the outcome would give Lithius the throne. The tyrannical sorcerer-king ruled Draccus for nearly 74 years succeeding his father. Even in youth, his younger brother, the prince who in spite of being the only other offspring ended beheaded and his body ravaged by Pitah Morderra-Atrauis's very own pet Drakkar, which challenged Pitah Morderra-Atrauis ascension of the throne. How much of this was true? Lithius could only speculate, but since the prince, there were nearly forty attempts on Pitah Morderra-Atrauis life, and each resulting in a bitter failure.

Pitah Morderra-Atrauis over the years made uneasy alliances with the kingdoms of the north some had ulterior motives such as Gwarvarik that fell into the drug induced slavery of the Black Lotus, weakening the kingdom into submission. When the powerful addiction took hold of the entire kingdom that Lithius had passed through as a child, Pitah Morderra-Atrauis sent three legions into the land seizing the opportunity. When the capital fell, Pitah Morderra-Atrauis sent his trusted emissary to head as governor. The Tarvas who invaded from the north bellowed for a share in the spoils, Pitah Morderra-Atrauis forced into giving over a third of the land and its conquered inhabitants over to the red bearded savage warriors of the north. With this, Pitah Morderra-Atrauis continued to strengthen his ties and restore confidence with the Tarvas, a confidence that was nothing more than a façade. In the sacking of Gwarvarik, Adajahara the prize objective was now under the tyrannical sorcerer's control and the spoils within. Lithius did not hear in any detail if Pitah Morderra-Atrauis had found out anything that would tip him off to the young sorcerer warrior. Besides, Lithius figured that Pitah Morderra-Atrauis's was already finished when the boy sent forth the souls from Talquardez-Solstas against the spirit of Pitah Valgas, but Lithius understood that knowledge is power just the same. Having thought this, Lithius knew that Morderra-Atrauis would obtain something he could use against any foe he'd run up against.

Morderra-Atrauis certainly had the dark isle under his iron-fisted control since the beginning of his reign. One of the first things he had prepared was an exile of all foreigners from the land. Only natural born Draccus were allowed to stay, after the exodus, Morderra-Atrauis broke off any trade that his father had started with other countries from afar. Draccus over night were transformed into a self-sustaining power that broken any or all treaties with its neighbors. The second accomplishment that Morderra-Atrauis imposed upon his people was the banishment of the former country's religious practices with the devolvement of the Senate; Morderra-Atrauis were now in absolute power and did not have to answer to anyone. With the installment of his newfound religion worshiping Hamahadra, the god of the underworld and the eventual marriage to her, made him a demigod. With his dark reform, he executed many former priests, those that opposed him, former generals, governors, and other officials formerly serving his father. Those that escaped his cruel blade, the Black Corsairs his spies and most trusted of his soldiers were unleaded upon the countryside rounding any and all whom they deemed suspicious. Naturally many escaped by leaving Draccus heading south into Caledon, Gaelund, and the black forests of Gaelund before Morderra-Atrauis destroyed all of the southern ports and villages razing them to ash.

Morderra-Atrauis next plan on his agenda were to perpetuate his kingdom to the south in Gaelund. Building his new naval fleet, warships sleek in design sent forth by the very same river that brought Lithius from the sea to embark a black wave of destruction to the savage shores of Gaelund. Gaelund, in spite of the barbarity of its painted people, rose against the Draccus insertion. The various Pictish tribes of Gaelund did something that any scribe would bet his life against that was, the tribes untied for the first in history against one single adversary, the Draccus.

With the northern land of Gaelund occupied by the Draccus forces, Morderra-Atrauis caught wind that the Tarvas to the north were looking for an opportunity. The opportunity was nothing more to increase their borders and with the weakening borders of Draccus, Morderra-Atrauis struck a treaty with the king of the Tarvas.

The Tarvas accepted the alliance, and the king sent forth his savage warriors against the Picts with the Draccus. Gwarvarik's former king then took this opportunity of attacking the Tarvas occupied Gwarvarik frontier and managed to push the Tarvas occupation out beyond her borders.

Eventually Gwarvarik liberated herself from the Tarvas and then took the offensive sacking many Tarvas villages and returning several hundred years of pent-up retaliation that caused the king of the Tarvas tribes to recall his forces from Gaelund, but the Tarvas troops in Gaelund were at the mercy of the Draccus navy to transport them across the sea. Morderra-Atrauis did not intend to allow the Picts to gain an upper hand. The king of the Tarvas was certainly facing a very daunting insurgence of angry Gwarvarik armies. The King of the Tarvas was forced to plead with Morderra-Atrauis. Morderra-Atrauis continued as planned, even in spite of certain retaliation for the Tarvas, if the Tarvas would survive the Gwarvarik invasion.

By winter of that year, Morderra-Atrauis had secured the northern portion of Gaelund, as for the Tarvas a heavy bitterly cold winter spared them to the point of the Gwarvarik sword, this was something that Morderra-Atrauis hadn't counted on. With heavy Tarvas losses in the south, the Tarvas's primary focus was to defend the homeland in the thaws of spring. However, the winter was very hard on the Gwarvarik forces in the east and including the eventual withdraw in the frontier were forged by a new uneasy peace with the two northern kingdoms. The Tarvas king, not forgetting Morderra-Atrauis broke off the alliance with the dark isle and threatened an invasion, but without a navy, the Tarvas withdrew any further intentions of an attack on Draccus.

With the shifting of the borders of Gwarvarik, by the Tarvas forces in the occupied frontier, Morderra-Atrauis was left to his own devices with Gaelund. Yet another problem arose for the Sorcerer-King. Caledon threw their hat into the battle of Gaelund siding with the Picts, this of course persuaded Morderra-Atrauis to reconsider his plans on sacking the Black Forest, let alone, attempt to hang on with his foothold on the northern portion. With the added uprising within his own troubling land, Morderra-Atrauis finally withdrew his forces from Northern Gaelund. Too weak from the expenditures of war, Morderra-Atrauis was forced into squelching the growing resistance of his kingdom that merged into a civil war, a bloody war that nearly ruined his reign.

The Draccus army now divided, Hamahadra has summoned her great magic in giving Morderra-Atrauis the upper hand. This eventually the isle fell fully into his control. Once he had regained control, he retaliated against the leaders of the opposition by immensely torturing anyone that his dogs, the Black Corsairs brought into view. With no escape and a heavy cost upon his own people's blood and nowhere to run, Draccus fully submitted to Pitah Morderra-Atrauis.

It has been nearly fifty years since the civil war in Draccus and the landscape ravaged by war has been slow to recover. Morderra-Atrauis then realizing that he would not have a kingdom to manage to be keep on his present ambitions had decided to set them aside. He then began manufacturing and distributing Black Lotus oil, and a strong hallucinogenic drug, powerfully addictive extract from the plant as an export to certain countries. The plant, an herbal plant that grew indigenously amongst the Draccus landscape that was usually dried and smoked, which was common, but as addictive as the oil was forbidden for anyone on Draccus to partake. He opened the trade with other kingdoms, selected kingdoms. One of which was the Isle of Mannus, and the isle of Gran Cayna who fell in an addicting torrent that devastating hand of his controls that later became an intricate part of his kingdom.

Black Lotus was then spread out to other reaches with this a surplus of both revenue and resources coming in to strengthen his rebuilding of his army and with the fact his navy grew stronger. He then opened his borders up to those that he would find beneficial to his kingdom, engineers, scribes, and those he preferred. Once his kingdom regained to a bleak level of self-sustaining, he continued trade, by now many kingdoms, countries had forbidden the oil and the plant due to the de-habilitating mind controlling addiction. Morderra-Atrauis sought other avenues of income. One of which was the budding livestock and small agriculture advancements along with illegal importing to such countries through an underground network that eventually caused Caledon to pursue it ships against the "pirated" Draccus merchant ships. The newly traded strains of grain grew most vibrantly on the dark isle; this became his new gold that he traded heavily with the south. For years, the Black Lotus production was ceased and anyone caught in possession of the Sorcerer-King's plants were executed without exception. To this day, the Black Lotus grows wild, and only Morderra-Atrauis allows though his Black Corsairs direct contact with the substance. Lithius understood this was just a tool that Morderra-Atrauis would use in bewitching a society to fall prey to the ills of the oil or plant. Lithius seen this drug used on Gwarvarik that eventually fell to Draccus as he was growing up in the forest of his youth. Even in the canopy of the mighty oaks, the plant grew in the shade of the trees as a weed or a vine and never once did Lithius ever partake. The plants, so powerful as they were, if a man walked up next to one, and it's leaves would touch an open wound, or cut a man's skin, the man could and most often fell under the diabolical spell of the plant. Once exposed to the plant in such a way would eventually end in an addiction where it would eventually drive a man into a state of mindlessness, madness, and more often than not, death.

Lithius also understood that there were of course medical or healing properties from this plant. The Black Lotus plant would have to be processed in such a way, still the addictive properties could not be contained, and most of this knowledge was lost. It is rumored that Morderra-Atrauis and other powerful sorcerers knew the medical secrets of the plant. Lithius didn't give much thought into rumors and speculation.

The Drakkars, the beasts now in so very few in numbers, a creature with a lizard-like body covered completely in heavy scales with powerful web-like powerful wings. The Drakkar was also armed with its powerful legs and feet with sharp talons could strip the flesh of the bones of a man in a single swipe. Drakkars were the only animals that could digest the plant without any known effect.

These creatures, the Drakkars, as far as Lithius had understood were indigenous of this world and unlike so many other creatures that were transferred from other planets. Drakkars were always few in numbers and for many years were focal points of many legends that mainly resided on Draccus. In fact, the name Draccus is said to have come from the word Drakkar. Seldom seen, these winged creatures feed usually on large fish, small livestock such as sheep, goats, small horses, and calves and rarely hunt man for a food source. As stated earlier, the Drakkars, mostly in solitude, do feed upon the Black Lotus and other herbal plants along with wild berries, and occasional fruit baring trees seldom eat much else.

It is also known that these creatures only mate every fifty to sixty years and begin to bread within seventy years when they reach puberty. Most of the Drakkars seen today along Draccus reside up in the high peaks of Thuma-Attarrach. The Drakkars in general are rarely seen and do most of their hunting and food gathering during the twilight and dawn hours of the day. It is also known that outside the isle of Draccus, Mannus, and of course, Gran Cayna is very scarce. When Lithius was a very little boy, he heard tales from his tribal elders of such creatures up along the highest peaks of the mountains of his homeland, but very few ever saw.

Lithius read the ancient scrolls he had recovered during his stay at Adajahara, which the people from the blue world found great interests with these creatures and documented many accounts along the ancient temple region. As the years passed, they too like the people of that world had vanished. In addition, there were stories of several breeds of these creatures residing along the Black Forest of Gaelund and across the Caledon Mountains and eventually only several in Gaelund. As it stood, south passed the silver mountains across Anguaria and eventually Styga there hasn't been a sighting in several generations. Rho-Haven in the deep desert along the Dragoon Mountains as Lithius had read while growing up, there perchance are several families of these creatures, but Draccus from now on the name, has the lion's share.

It is also rumored that Pitah Morderra-Atrauis himself has several semi-trained to a various extent as his own pets, though too many this is highly doubtful. As for Lithius that spent most of his life growing up in the shelter of the ancient forest and it's vastness. Lithius saw two under these conditions, the Drakkars, a crimson red male and a deep cobalt blue female both on independent occasions flying overhead of the forest canopy from Thuma-Attarrach. The third, he had seen much closer that's maroon red and black spirit resides safely in Talquardez-Solstas after Lithius was nearly killed by the creature.

On an early summer morning, Lithius climbed above the floor of the thick forest to escape the heat and humidity by climbing to the top of the forest canopy. While enjoying early morning coolness, from up high, he had become an easy target for a lone male Drakkar. Without warning, the Drakkar snatched him up only barely getting the young boy in his grasp. Lithius drove the sword deep into the heart of the young Drakkar. His sword penetrated the natural armor of the creature sending both of them hurling toward the forest floor. Lithius scraped and bruised was fortunately enough to limp away from the encounter. There were tales of great hunters, men who thought themselves as powerful dispatchers of the Drakkar usually died in the encounter of such a creature than ranged in size of sixty to six hundred pounds. The biggest species of Drakkar resided in Draccus that could exceed several thousand pounds with a wingspan of well over a one hundred. As for the Drakkar that attacked Lithius would have easily killed the boy weighing in about three hundred pounds by Lithius's estimates after he had looked over the creature that meant to devour him. As for other dangerous creatures, the forest was full of them and unlike the Drakkars, there seemed to be no end in sight of a shortage.

In the forest that Lithius grew up in, where the Lycoi, the wolfen, and often called the wolf-men that showed remarkable intelligence in hunting and staying out of the sight of man. The Lycoi, larger in numbers than the villages like to pretend to be. There were also the dark emerald serpents, non-venomous but able to constrict the life out of various animals including full-grown men. There were also smaller venous snakes unlike the thirty to sometimes forty-five foot mammoth serpents, and the Drakkar panther, and some jet-black predators stalked Lithius from time to time ending up like the maroon and black Drakkar. There was the forest three-horned dark rhino that would be in small herds that would occasionally run into the snares of man. These forest rhinos were deemed by many as a prized possession. Lithius have raised two as his own orphaned by hunters. There were other animals, animals that you would expect to find in ancient forests, owls, birds, squirrels, and various species of bats, deer, wolves, and with them occasional elk in the upper grasslands and hills of the forest.

As for Lithius, he enjoyed animals, always had, with the exception of those that wanted to kill him, he would occasionally sit and watch the creatures of the forest. There were wild goats, kids he had captured and raised them as his own right alongside that of the three horned rhinos. It has been several years since the rhinos have grown and took off on their own, and it has been several generations of his first two goats that linger around his abode, mostly on their own as well. This was something that has never changed with Lithius, his love for animals, and of course the very same he applied to other humans. He generally didn't give much thought about them, if they didn't try to kill him nor were Tarvas; he could care less and hope that they would get on there way while observing them at a great distance. His master long ago had put incarnations, spells to protect Lithius's surroundings through Lithius. Since then, Morderra-Atrauis could not peer into the forest and find Lithius in the event that he, the sorcerer-king, or Hamahadra for that matter would uncover or reveal his mater's dark intentions through the boy. As far as Lithius was concerned, the forest in spite of the inherent dangers protected him as he grew strong and into a man.

Never once did Lithius ever set eyes upon any member of the Black Corsairs, Morderra-Atrauis's henchmen nor that of the Draccus soldier while living in the forest, so to the young boy growing up, the spell must have worked. Eventually Lithius gained the power of sealing most of his personal thoughts and mind from his Master's powerful mental probes when confronting him by means of visions or in dreams. Lithius knew his master possessed great powers, strengths that far exceeded his or Morderra-Atrauis's for that matter, but his master could not enter Lithius's physical world. If his master had a weakness, this of course was it indeed. If his master had this power, he of course would not need Lithius and Lithius would have died next to his mother so long ago.

In dealing with his master on many accounts, like that of Hamahadra, the master could only alter the weather, and with the help of their minions, could in fact extend their reach through the flesh and blood of their servants. Lithius did not possess the power, nor did he ever pursue the avenue of going into the realm of his master. Even as strong as Morderra-Atrauis is in the black arts, he too can only go in spirit, but Hamahadra however found a way to bring her husband across, she became the mother of his children, the very same who have long been dispatched by their father. Lithius did not give these things much thought; instead, he focused on the teachings of his master, which took much of his time.

CHAPTER 8

▼

It was now morning when Lithius arose from his sleep. Lithius then got dressed as he fastened his huge leather belt around his waist that contained the scabbard of his sword. Once he adjusted the belt on his waste, he then put his hair into a tight single ponytail, donned his quiver full of black arrows and fastened his bow securely on his back. Lithius then concealed all of this as best he could by placing his dark cloak over him. Lithius fetched his walking staff and headed for the door. He turned once more looking back to all that he had left behind realizing that he could have lived the rest of his life here in solitude just fine and walked out closing the door behind him.

He walked down to the stream; there he could hear the goats just on the other side of the stream. Within the undergrowth, the goats were rustling around foraging and paying no mind to Lithius.

"Goodbye my friends take good care of yourselves!" He yelled with a smile, a smile filled with a measure of regret. One of the goats came out and crossed over the creek to meet him, he bent down and petted the small animal as the others eventually came across and followed him along the damp wet path. They followed him for several hundred feet, turned, and watched him go into the woods.

Lithius walked for a few miles through the dark oak forest that lead to a huge rock along the way. He then jumped up upon the rock and looked all around him. The forest was alive with life, this didn't alarm him, in fact, this is what he usually woke up to for the past eleven odd years, when it was quiet, and it was time to worry.

Once he got his bearings, he then headed northward in the forest, a place he had known that was sacred to the Lycoi. In addition, the most ancient place in the forest and it would be here that he would require the soul of one of the most dangerous creatures in the forest. As he continued heading north, the forest grew darker and damp. Along the way he crossed over the paths of fresh Lycoi tracks, they were hunting once again, heading southwest, a track that contained what looked like three or possibly, more. It was hard to tell, the Lycoi would walk a single file in this matter to conceal their numbers.

As he walked up the small hills covered by the heavy oaks, the air grew damper, heavier with the moisture laden by the river that cut through the forest. He continued up the river to the verge of the waterfalls, three in fact that stair-stepped up upon each other. Once at the top, he turned further southeast on where the oldest of the oaks resided, he had been here before, and now he was in the oldest part of the forest, and the darkest. It was here that he would not have to worry about the Lycoi following him or running across the stalking path of a panther, or of the large serpents. As he carefully walked as quietly as he could, he then sat his staff cautiously against a few large stones. The rushing of the water-falls had quieted down from the distance he walked from and he drew out his sword. His heavy bow and sling of quivers rested against the rocks with his staff, and soon so, did his cloak and pack.

Armed with only his sword drawn he entered farther until the forest was as dark as night. The air grew still and as he looked up at the tops of the trees, he could see silhouettes of bats hanging upside down from the branches. Oddly, there were no birds, nor any other sign of life, and he realized that perhaps the focus of his attention for being here could have been visiting these parts recently.

As he continued stalking ever forward in the most ancient part of the forest, sweat gathered above his brow. His solid black eyes probed the woods for any sign of the most dangerous and sinister of the animals, he saw none. An hour passed by and shortly it was noon, though inside these woods it could have been midnight. He continued up to a path, a fresh path that gave a sign of what he had come for. Lithius then donned the spell of invisibility and followed the fresh path that led up the hill to the other side on which he most carefully entered. It was the mouth of a cave, the mouth was twelve feet high and the area covered by thick spider webs. He stopped short along the side of the cave's entrance. In spite of him being invisible, he knew the creature could sense that he was near, and he could not see the creature, but he knew likewise.

From years of experience, Lithius knew where this cave lead to, he has seen what he has some for many times in the past along this region, and every time, it rose the hairs on the back of his neck. The cave eventually led into the lair of one of the deadliest creatures in the entire forest. Lithius knew there was another way, a safer way, a way he quickly chose to take. He knew this cave would lead into at least several miles and within the cave, there would be too many places he could walk right into the ambush awaiting him and there were no second chances.

The stench was nearly unbearable as he decided another way, a safer way. He looked up above the cave's entrance and could see the top of the hill, using his power he was instantly at the top of the cave's entrance. He then removed his spell of invisibility and looked around him. He could see a few trees before him, below him the forest floor. Realizing where he was standing, turned once more, and vanished, he appeared next to a ledge that was hundreds of yards away. Lithius accomplished this in just a blink of an eye without a sound. He then bent down on his left knee; he then peered down the chasm. Lithius could see through the thick web of the spider of what he had come for. Down there it was, the slowly crawling beast moving through the bottom of the jagged dark pit. Protect by the web and low-lying brush that daylight itself would be only shown through a few minutes each day, it moved on over the carrion and bones.

As Lithius in silence peered on, he realized that he could summons one of the spirits within his blade to do his bidding. This would be too easy, and oddly, he had more respect for this ancient creature of the forest. This was something he wanted to do, something he needed to face, face to horrid face. Even now, if he managed to leap down through the huge spider webs and drive Talquardez-Solstas through the head of the huge creature, it was to be all too easy. Lithius could now only make out the giant black, yellow and red spider as it crept through the bottom of the chasm occasionally stopping and then moving slowly on. The horror of the creature would turn most men's blood to ice, as for the Lycoi; this ancient animal was a spiritual godlike creature. To Lithius, its spirit would be a fierce weapon to be collected with all the others in Talquardez-Solstas, which was drawn in his hand as he looked down.

This creature as far as Lithius knew about it, was something that he found out about within six years ago as he saw it feasting on a wild young rhino that was sick and dying. He remembered watching it bite into the tough hide of the small creature injecting venom, venom that paralyzed the small rhino while turning its inner organs to liquid. Then he sat there from a distance, gazed upon the giant spider as the creature was rolling the dying animal up in a cocoon, and dragging the remains off into the forest. Young Lithius at a distance, followed the spider up to the most antediluvian portion of the forest to feed on it prey. Lithius could remember seeing it eight ruby red eyes reflecting the dark light like stones. Lithius did not know how old indeed the spider was; the Lycoi's believed the creature was the first primordial thing on the isle, long before the race of man, drakkar, or for that matter, themselves and the forest, but rather the great forest grew and around the spider. If true, then this spider was truly prehistoric. As Lithius reflected upon these things, he looked up and around the ancient forest and could see the leaves beginning to turn colors as autumn was now becoming into season. He looked back down into the dark chasm and could see the spider had moved on.

Lithius appeared like before just in front of the spider from up high along the edge of the cliff in the heart of the great oak forest. Still out of the eyesight of the spider, Lithius could sense that the spider could sense something wrong; something it knew was being stalked. The spider stopped short with its two front legs before him in front of the opening. Just below the cliff a huge spider web was spun earlier that summer, in its snare were various decomposing small birds, bats and forest debris collected. Lithius could peer through some of the web and could see below that he was obviously in the spider's lair. The floor was filled with bones of carcasses, and Lithius could see the litter of years of remains ranging from small rhinos, deer, goat, cattle, Lycoi, and human. Lithius again used his powers of invisibility and leaned over to peer closer into the spider's lair.

"I know you are here," Lithius read with his mind a sinister cold ancient voice that seemed more like a screech. It was obviously the voice of the spider in his mind by telepathy. Lithius leaned back from the cliff surprised as his grip on his sword intensified.

"I cannot see you, no least not yet, but I will" The spider warned.

Lithius remained silent, "You are very near, near indeed," The huge revolting spider hissed.

Lithius could see the creature coming slowly forth under the huge web; he could see the eight blood red eyes glaring. Lithius made sure he was down wind of the spider, though there was no breeze, but the slightest would give the spider a good idea on where he was lurking.

"I feel you presents human," the spider warned as it were beckoning Lithius to engage in dialog. Lithius quickly assumed if he does partake, it could be possible for the large spider to zero in on his location on where he was standing and strike.

It was now fully in view under the web as its eight legs tenaciously placed themselves securely under the bones littering the floor. Its two large front legs poised itself up in the air as if they were antennas on locating Lithius from the air.

"Show yourself?" hissed the giant spider.

Lithius knew the spider could not see him if it could, it would of already strike. If Lithius moved ever so slightly, the spider would hear or now as a tip of the front leg has gently touched the solid rock canyon wall before it, while the other was still probing the air directly in front of the spider. "Smart move" Lithius thought to himself, the slightest vibration would tip off the spider. Lithius could see the spider hadn't figured out exactly where he was standing at, but his invisibility was limited by his strength and his endurance. His heart quickened as he stood motionless realizing that in time he would have to release the power of invisibility, once the spider would see him this close, the spider would have him in a fraction of a second. This thought would threaten the fiber of any man's wits, but not Lithius, this was more excitement than fear.

"Where are you human, I know you're near?" The spider hissed as it backed up from the wall of the canyon, turned making in spite of its huge size, little noise as it climbed up out of the canyon through the edge of the web on the far side. Once at the top, it turned to smell the scents in the slightest of the breeze, and Lithius could see the spider was not onto him yet.

"What fun is this?" Lithius asked himself in a thought.

"Tell me something spider?" Lithius said with his mind to the creature far over on the other side of the canyon.

"So you know how to speak?" it hissed with its back turned to Lithius.

"What is your name?"

"My name?" the spider quipped.

"How old are you?" Lithius asked.

"Older than anything in my domain, much older than you human!" The spider then released a powerful stream of web directly at Lithius, before the web material would hit Lithius, he moved a third of the distance of the canyon wall towards the spider.

"You have missed!" Lithius said with his mind.

The spider turned as if it could see Lithius and lunged upon his general direction, this proved a miss as well as Lithius appeared and was farther away.

"So there you are, and now I can smell your sweat, yes" Lithius could see his own reflection in the eight ruby red eyes of the hideous spider and the venom drip off the two big fangs of the spider.

"Yes I remember you." The spider said as it could see Lithius plainly with Talquardez-Solstas in his right hand in a formidable stance preparing for the spider's attack.

"It seems just like the other day when you were a small boy, still taking care of those goats?" The spider said with its voice half filled with contempt.

Lithius remained calm and quiet as the spider inched up ever so cautiously, "You are not the only one who visits upon the living from a distance my young human friend."

"I have seen your kind young wizard come and go, I even had the luxury of feasting on your kind a good many times as I will on you now!" The spider leaped suddenly towards Lithius, Lithius moved quickly and severed on of the front legs cleanly off the spider.

The spider hissed horribly, "I will kill your unborn for that!" The spider moved to the side very quickly throwing Lithius off into the brush. It then leaped up and came down crushing the brush where Lithius's body landed. The spider arose with its bloody wound, Lithius was not there, as the sword pierced the other side of the spider, it reeled around screaming and hissing again in the pain. Lithius was so much quicker as the warrior wizard cut two more legs out from under the spider.

"I have come for your soul great spider of the woods, and I mean to have it!" Lithius said aloud.

"You die now!" One of the spider's back legs lunged forward kicking Lithius squarely sending him nearly to the web that covered the top of the small canyon, on which would trap him. The spider turned hobbling to Lithius as quickly as it could leave a thick trail of blood and venom behind it scorching the rocks and ground. Lithius arose and leaped up in the air and somersaulting over the top of the spider's head driving the black sword into the skull of the spider, another leg caught Lithius in blinding speed that was now sending Lithius directly to the web. Lithius seeing this used his sword to cut through the web and Lithius fell to the bottom of the spider's Liar. Landing squarely, Lithius turned his boot-covered feet directly back up to the spider as sweat came down and stung his eyes.

The spider, severely wounded certainly had enough life in him to end Lithius as he stood there in two feet of bones and remains of the spider's kill over the years. Lithius looked around and among the bones of various animals, bones that seemed half melted by the venom of the spider as it injected its prey turning the innards into liquid were the bones of a couple of rhinos among the litter. The stench was burning his nostrils as he realized that he was in a fix, a slight fix. His heart pounded as the excitement rose, "That will hold you down a bit!" The spider said in its screeching voice as it attempted to recover; "Besides your bones will rest nicely there." The spider was having trouble talking, it was struggling with its words, and Lithius could tell that the spider was very old, and the wounds were now taking in effect, he could see the wound upon the head of the spider oozing out blood over its eight eyes.

"You have had your last meal upon the young rhino and the life of the forest!" Lithius then through his power in blinding speed through telekinesis was up on the ledge of the canyon as the spider limping turned to face him. "I am not so easy to kill, am I?" Lithius asked.

"Wizard, what do you want with me?" The spider asked. The spider was now growing more tired as he continued lurking for an advantage to strike at the one clutching the black translucent sword.

"As I said your soul." Lithius was without serious injury, both of the kicks from the spider's huge legs have bruised him as he smeared the blood from his bottom lip with his left hand.

"Why my soul?" The spider asked looking on at Lithius.

"I aim to kill Morderra-Atrauis and using your soul in doing so over there," Lithius pointed with his sword to a distant black mountain far off in the distance.

"Thuma-Attarrach…" Lithius was regaining his breath as he could see the spider weakening and struggling to keep its balance.

"I have lived a thousand lifetimes and my soul belongs only to the one who has given me life" The spider said as it began to lean to its left side and then sprayed the acrid poison in the air, Lithius avoided the poisonous cloud that would have instantly killed him.

"And whom might that be spider?" Lithius quizzed with a sweating smirk upon his face.

"Hamahadra." The spider struggled with the name realizing that this adversary was much too quick and has obtained the upper hand.

"What about Hamahadra?" Lithius drew closer to the spider with both of his hands on the sword poised at the giant spider.

"I am one of her favorite…favorite pets. She will avenge my death, young wizard fool," The spider was attempting to catch his breath and then fell to its belly and slowly rolling over the side of the canyon that fell on its back below. Lithius avoided the pools of venom bubbling up dissolving the first layers of stone and rock as Lithius looked over as he saw the spider struggling to hang onto its life as it flowed freely from its wounds with the oozing of the deep maroon pools of blood. Lithius stood ready summons the spider's soul with his sword poised directly above the body of the spider. In that instant the soul of the spider already rising from the body struggled lifeless towards the sword as if there was some sort of power unforeseen elsewhere pulling at it, then in doing so, Lithius realized the opposing force was coming from the cave far below. Lithius focused his energy on the sword's tip aimed at the dark smoky soul of the spider. The opposing force was intensifying and the young wizard came to the quick realization that the master of the spider, Hamahadra may be the one responsible. Talquardez-Solstas force was stronger and the soul entered the blade and having collected the soul,

Lithius disappeared and reappeared at the beginning of the most ancient part of the forest to collect his belongings and sheathing Talquardez-Solstas into the scabbard and grabbing his belongings, he vanished off into the forest across the stream.

CHAPTER 9

▼

As he quickly vanished from the area, behind him he could hear the wailing of a woman's voice filled with rage and bitterness. He knew it was Hamahadra's voice filling the woods behind him. "I will find you and kill your unborn!" her voice, an echoing scorn like heated flames igniting the very air around Lithius like a blanket of hatred spread forth throughout the forest.

"Now you've done it boy!" A voice within him sprang forth as he wasted no time departing out of the Lycoi's most sacred land within the forest, in doing so came a wind, a wind filled with horror and retribution for killing the most sacred animal among all others, and he knew with no uncertain terms, the retribution was meant for him.

As he ran utilizing his special powers that added him to cover much distance, though draining his strength, he knew that the oak forest could no longer be his home, nor was it safe for him any longer. Already, Lithius could hear the faint sound of drums off at the distance; it was no doubt, the Lycoi. In spite of his power of covering great distance, the Lycoi also through their primitive and near supernatural ways of bringing down their quarry would quickly pick up his trail though fragmented, would eventually find him, and bring him down. The Lycoi were exceptional pack hunters with their crude axes and spears, but they had physical strength, stronger than any natural man, that also towered over most as well.

By dust and nearly physically drained like a long distance runner with limbs and lungs stinging with great pain and fire, Lithius's chest swelled back and forth with his heated panting in attempts of fueling his body with the cooling oxygen. Sweat flowed freely from his pours as his legs trembled, shaking from the excursion of the great distances covered. His focus was on the edge of the forest, the edge he had seen a few years ago, a place he once stood at, the very same that took him nearly two days in his youth to travel with his magic, no he has nearly done it in a few hours.

He could afford to stop and rest, the drumming, though far behind him was as relentless as those following his broken trail were. As he continued to walk allowing his body a chance to recover from the exhaustive pace, Lithius, he looked to the northeast; he could feel that the forest's edge was near. Perhaps another mile or more, and past that was a small valley, a valley he stood on the edge concealed by the heavy growth of the forest as he watched the people work along the cleared fields near a village. He figured if he could make it to the village, least near it, he would seek protection from a building, and he knew there he would have half a chance to regain his strength. Besides, he figured, the Lycoi hated to be seen out in the open, out in the open in daylight in large numbers, but the daylight was leaving him quickly.

In a few moments and nearly exhausted, he could not summons enough strength to magically shorten the distance by his magical teleportation. He was finished as far as that went as he nearly collapsed over a fallen tree. His vision blurred and darkened by the physical exertion. Streams of sweat poured from his face as he forced himself to sip on water as his chest felt like it was being filled with the sharp points of knives. He was still in the forest, and it was getting darker. Half-clumsy, in a drunken-like walk, he forced himself to continue on heading in the same direction. Pressing on, he continued up a slope. Though a slight grade, it felt as if he was climbing the side of a steep mountain. As he continued switch backing up the side of the grade it brought him to the very edge of the forest. There in the failing light, he could see the village across a mile or more of open field. The village, dark silhouettes of buildings small made of stone and thatch roofs looked more in disrepair than he imagined. He couldn't see if it were abandoned by the villagers he once spied.

Behind him, ever so faintly the drums would be occasionally drowned out in an ebbing effect of the growing night breeze through the rustling of the forest leaves. He stood bending over frantically catching his breath, he had no choice, but to wait, his legs burned as if they were on fire. As he panted, eventually he caught his breath, and his lungs began to smolder like metal being taken out of the furnace as sweat drenched down from his matted hairline. He drank some more water carefully as not to cramp up. He turned once more to look at the distant village; it was at least a mile to the nearest building. If he would start walking now, he figured he could be there before the light of day would be totally lost by the coming of night. With that thought, he put his flask of water away and readied himself as he walked out of the forest, though tired and exhausted, walking out in the open was nearly alien to him, but there was nothing that he could do with it now, the forest home behind him was lost to him forever.

Lithius had carefully approach the edge of the old village and he could see it had been abandoned for sometime. As he drew closer to an old dark stone dilapidated building that seemed to be used as some sort of barn, he could see markings along the stone and peat moss side reflecting an old battle of sorts, a battle that he soon realized in the twilight of the coming darkness that this village suffered a Lycoi attack. As he entered the main village, the natural grasses and weeds had reclaimed the floor of the village, and in the tall withering grasses were the human remains, most showing that they were victims to the crude weapons of their opposers. The villagers, by the sight of the ancient remains had also gotten a few of the Lycoi before the wolfen overcame them in the end. Young, old, male, and female remains littered the inner courtyard of a forgotten battle of survival.

Lithius knew nothing of this attack; it seemed odd that the Lycoi, dwellers of the forest would come out in obviously large numbers to attack a settlement. He fully understood why the Lycoi were following him; he brought on the wrath of the forest when he dispatched the spider. The light was now gone and it was all he could do was to see and avoid stepping on the skeletal remains beneath him. As he continued on, he could see the tallest of the old buildings, an old windmill used for crushing the grain that the villagers grew to make bread and such. He decided that the old building would at least give him some limited protection. The structure, with ample height to give him a panoramic view in any direction around him, which is if he could make it until morning, a thought that was as remote, so he thought, as the idea, that maybe he might be lucky enough to have lost the Lycoi.

The Lycoi might have been as Lithius puts it, "…slow minded" but tracking, tracking tenaciously was one of their strong suits. Their keen sense of stalking, hunting in packs was definitely something to reckon with. The Lycoi, a blend of man and beast, more beast in these parts than those up near the borderlands of Lithius homeland and the countries just south of his native steppes that seemed more like a memory that belongs to another lifetime as he thought to himself. Still, the tribes of the Lycoi in Draccus were as deadly as any Lycoi as Lithius has ever known.

Up until now, the Lycoi in the dark oak forests mainly stayed among themselves for the most part in Lithius' experience. On occasion, Lithius was forced to confront these creatures, usually facing up to no more than two or three at a time.

Lithius figured the Lycoi allowed him to exist in the forest as long as Lithius would not go out of his own way and stay clear out of the most sacred of their territory. Naturally, Lithius broke this alliance with the slaying of the spider, obviously the Lycoi's most precious item. Lithius painfully realized that killing the sacred spider of the forest might have indeed brought on a bit more than he could chew, more than he cared to risk, or should have risked.

As he climbed up inside the old windmill towards the decaying loft, he managed to get high enough to swing for a rafter and carefully pull himself up and over the old beam without it coming free from the stonewall and come crashing down. There he cautiously balanced himself up on the beam and walked across the narrow center to the other end on where he climb a series of other beams to the top leading to the loft. From there, he scaled a couple of old timbers to the top of the thatched roof through a hole. There he looked around, the air was cool and damp now, all in a shroud of darkness. He couldn't see nothing clearly passed the village as the fog began to roll in. He looked straight up into the sky and could see the twinkling of stars, no moon, and no other source of light. The fog like that of long fingers stretching forth from the forest's hand came forth canvassing the valley before Lithius. The fog seemed to have a life of its own, and to Lithius's dismay, this would definitely give the Lycoi the advantage, morning to Lithius seemed like an eternity away now. He thought about climbing back down and taking his chances crossing the valley to the other side in darkness, he thought for a moment as long as he would keep running he might have a chance. This was a thought he quickly dismissed, he knew that his strength would soon leave him, he taxed his body enough, and he would have to face the Lycoi either way. He decided to overcome his fear and fight to the end.

Having come to this conclusion, he then went back down to the loft, there he could somehow fortify himself there against the aging stone wall and use his bow raining arrows down upon the assailing Lycoi, he had a window in two directions, before him, and behind him, not to mention, the floor of the wind mill far below him. He could make a good stand there, least until the arrows in his quiver would run out, then the Lycoi would have to be forced to climb up the rafters, most of which would not support the Creature's weight, a few of them would fall to their undeserving deaths in the process. Lithius also calculated that there might be a slight chance that he could then wait it out until morning, by then he would have more than enough strength, fully rested in so many words, and actually make a, "Damned good run at it!" he thought to himself.

Lithius knew that the Lycoi are terrible tacticians in battle, a siege upon the wind mill would be nothing more than a bunch of howling menaces throwing up their angry hairy arms clutching their crude weapons at him as he would play the waiting game long enough to recover. Lithius had enough food and provisions, his quiver was full, and with a few quick spells, he could double the arrows without taxing his strength much. He fully rested in his discussion; this was something that he could do as his confidence welled upon inside of him. Eventually the Lycoi would grow bored of pinning their adversary up in a stone tower that they could possibly knock down or set fire to. This was certainly the wisest choice that he could come up within considering his circumstances. On thing was sure in his mind, if it was his time to go, he would unleash the power of Talquardez-Solstas, his sword upon all of the Lycoi, and that would mean the abrupt end of his master's plans of dealing with Pitah Morderra-Atrauis.

There was obviously something in his mind he didn't calculate on, and having a thought about it would unravel his confidence in the whole matter, Hamahadra. As he began to think about this being, a goddess of some evil, some wickedness, he forced himself to remain focused on that which was around him.

As Lithius drew food from his pack to eat looking out into the night air, already the fog had rolled in blanketing the entire area in a thick silver layer impossible to see through. He sat down with his back to the wall under the window eating. As he ate, he knew that the Lycoi, though as primordial as the Lycoi were, the creatures could speculate the direction their prey is traveling and to where. They obviously knew this place, and they were not afraid of it, especially now with the villagers vanquished and with the possible aid of Hamahadra, he just may need to unleash the true power of Talquardez-Solstas.

The night slowly waned, seconds like minutes, minutes like hours. He thought as he looked about in the sea of darkness the true matter of Hamahadra, those things that his master, the maker of his sword have told him over time, was she truly a god. Lithius thought for a few moments, "…if a goddess, why the need of the Lycoi?" he mumbled slightly. Naturally, his mind began to wander, "If she is not a god, neither could be my master?" His thoughts paused abruptly as though he heard something, something like a twig or perhaps a dry decaying frail bone been broken underfoot. He turned slowly his attention in the direction of the sound he heard reverberating in the night air. His ears critically attune as his eyes pierced through the darkness. In spite of his keen eyesight, he could not see through the fog. He placed his hand firmly on the hilt of his sword as to draw its magic strength. The drums have all stopped by sometime, he knew for certain that the Lycoi were among him, though he could not see as if the fog was a shield to protect their detection. Lithius could not see anymore with the sword as before, he then realized that the fog was no ordinary fog, but something that

Hamahadra conjured up by the sent of her rancid hatred festering in the fog and beginning to come to his sense of smell. The odor came up to the window on which he stood nearly knocking him back. There was something else that he was picking up, a faint perfume sweet smell that was growing slightly thicker laced within the rancid smell that began to turn his stomach, a smell that was becoming ever so stronger over powering him, and then without warning, as fast as it appeared, it was gone.

Lithius, with hair still standing on end, turned around, and looked down below, down to the stony and straw-covered floor below. He could not see anything in the fading twilight. The air was considerably cooler as the fog had consumed the old windmill tower. In spite of his eyes, he knew for sure that there was someone, or something in there with him and it wasn't the Lycoi, least not yet.

"Hamahadra?" He faintly whispered with his eyes peeled down to the floor as he could see the fog acting like a large skeletal hand grasping and clutching the air around the floor.

"Yes" The response was a venomous whisper in his mind that began coiling like a large serpent on his thoughts and shooting shards of fear through his senses. The young lad could feel the power of this apparition and the surmounting feel of dread gripping tighter on him, and with it, the probing of his mind. Lithius reeled back to the cold stonewall with his back up against it with his sword drawn as he tried to close his mind off to her treachery.

"I have come to claim your soul as you did my pet." Her words in his mind were that of ice prickling his mind physically as the air around him turned bitterly cold. He struggled to close his mind off to her as she was beginning to read his thoughts, and in turn, he could see with his mind, she was not of flesh and blood, but a specter not fully in his world.

"Lithius is your name young Ramadan who bares Talquardez-Solstas, a sword of my realm, the greatest of all swords" Her voice faded away in somewhat of a surprise as her grip on his mind and thoughts loosen ever so slightly.

"I see in your mind that you are a slave of Mydyr" She then began to mock Mydyr.

"He used you to get Talquardez-Solstas from the greatest of all the Taltakkurdg-Kevnaps, the first and the most powerful of the Pitah." Lithius was struggling with all of his might to keep her out of his mind and in spite of the frost building up around him, he was showing signs of a great struggle as his nose began to show a slight sign of bleeding as her constricting powers were consuming him.

"Valgas, my child" her thoughts drifted away from the present, enough for Lithius to conjure up enough strength to throw off the great invisible freezing and constricting coils of her mind control. As he regained his senses, he felt another presence in a loud stone shacking clap of thunder that shook the building and nearly knocking him off balance, it was the presence of his master, the one that Hamahadra calls Mydyr.

Lithius looked down and could see a ghastly figure of what he considered Hamahadra's icy grey spirit, translucent specter and across the floor from her in the fog was the grimacing darker image of Mydyr as the air became electrified as the grip upon Lithius now removed. At this time, he noticed his nose bleeding, as he wiped his nose he kept still looking down with his sword in hand. He knew these beings were not ghosts, but of some sort of being in some other realm, a realm that he felt was close to his own physical realm, not quite his own.

As Lithius looked down upon the two, each on opposite sides, Mydyr in a black cloak that covered his skeletal-like extremities, a cloak that seamed more alive than of fabric swirling around his tall slender body, the creature focused his attention only to Hamahadra. Lithius, who was still bent down along the edge of the remains of the loft far above them both turned his attention towards the ghostly pale image that blended so well into the fog. The green and blue glowing lights around both these, as he suspects, supernatural creatures, a reckoning he has come to understand was poised to spring forth to escape by means of leaping down, that is, if he could survive the jump. As he looked on, he could see that Hamahadra had lost interest with him and was certainly more concerned with the presence of Mydyr holding a large heavy silver axe.

"You have meddled in my business long enough!" Hamahadra hissed at Mydyr. Her physical voice had a watery effect, though as bone chilling and as sinister as she spoke to Lithius earlier through telepathy.

"Guarding of the great Pitahs, the last of the wretched Tal-takkurdg-Kevnaps—You who sleeps amongst the scum!" retorted in like manner as Mydyr shifted the axe slightly.

"You have no interest in these matters on what I care to do with these mortals, what business is this of you Mydyr who hides in the shadows. Even in your own world, you are cursed and foul." Hamahadra countered heatedly.

"What of the boy?" She pointed upon Lithius without breaking eye contact with Mydyr.

Just then, before Lithius's own eyes the fog rolled back exposing the floor below and he could see that there was some sort of seal, a golden circle covered in runes that he could not clearly see, and in the middle it looked like the entire ground was giving away, and where the ground was, it was now gone. Lithius could see it wasn't a hole, but some sort of a passage leading somewhere, as it cleared, he could see more.

Still looking downward, he could see it was another world, a world swirling around like a whirlpool that was beginning to make him slightly dizzy, but he found himself drawn to the center.

"The boy is mine! He is nothing to do with you." Somehow, Lithius wasn't convinced that to be the truth and consequently neither did Hamahadra.

"You lie; you have sent him to gather an army to Pitah Morderra-Atrauis, this is your plan!" She shouted.

Lithius could see that this offset Mydyr somewhat as the dark specter looked up at the young man far above them, yet Lithius could not see his face concealed by the hood of Mydyr's cloak. "And what else did he tell you whore!" Mydyr stated looking back at the horrid looking apparition from across him standing there with the mighty axe.

"I've said nothing!" Lithius said with his mind.

"Silence fool!" Mydyr scorned in like manner to Lithius.

"You may see this through if you remain silent." Mydyr warned and then directed his attention towards Hamahadra.

"Morderra-Atrauis is already aware of the boy, and his attentions." Hamahadra clambered.

"No matter, he is grown too strong, and I have hid him all these years right under your very nose Hamahadra." Mydyr laughed slightly.

Lithius could see that she wasn't amused, "Talquardez-Solstas will fall into the rightful hands of Morderra-Atrauis and the house of the Pitahs soon enough." She then turned her attention to the young man poised with the black translucent blade in the shadows above them. Lithius knew that she could see him clearly as he looked away from what he was realizing was some sort of a portal in the center of the golden ring. A portal to another place, a place as he could see was a dark, and terrible place filled full of the horrors that were beyond his verbal skills to describe of such a place.

"I have come for him Mydyr, and hell awaits him and the sword on which I will freely take." Hamahadra smiled up at Lithius a most sinister and foreboding smile that caused Lithius's own blood nearly freezing within his own veins. Lithius managed to back up against the wall behind him fetching his pack and his bow and quiver.

"It would be far better for me to take my chances to attempt to scale down the side of this building and take my chances with the Lycoi," he whispered to himself as he went out the small window. In doing so, he slipped and fell, as he fell he managed to conjure a spell to ease his fall enough to keep his balance and using his powers, he dodged at great speed the few bands of approaching Lycoi. In a few minutes, his strength fueled by the new fear of Hamahadra put many miles between him and those he quickly left behind heading to the great mountain, the mountain upon which Morderra-Atrauis resides, the lofty dark peak of Thuma-Attarrach.

Far from behind him now, as he turned resting only a few moments, he could see a brilliant light, a reddish glow that dimmed into the vastness of a cloud-covered sky of darkness and with it an explosion that sent a shockwave that turned into a subtle warm breeze upon his sweating face. He knew without a doubt it was from Hamahadra and Mydyr and their magical powers, powers he found difficulty to understand.

Lithius turned away and was now safely away from the hordes of the Lycoi. It would be morning soon enough and he would find rest.

CHAPTER 10

▼

By morning, Lithius had stopped at a small brook and took on water, washed his face and arms from the sweat and dirt and then sat up on a large stone wondering about all the horror he saw from the night before and realizing how close he brushed with death. He realized now as he stumbled upon then, that if he unleashed the souls from the sword, he would have spent his only hope of fulfilling the destruction of Pitah Morderra-Atrauis and his henchmen, the Black Corsairs who in their own right were Draccus most elite soldiers in the skill of combat. Besides, Lithius wasn't sure that the souls, his army of the undead that he has collect over the years would have been any good against such an entity of Hamahadra or not, it was a risk that he wasn't prepared to take. In addition, he certainly remembered that of what Hamahadra said earlier that Morderra-Atrauis already known of him and the sword. He thought about that for a moment, he thought if this is a true statement, wouldn't Morderra-Atrauis has made some sort of an effort to come forth with some army against Lithius, as he thought about that for a moment, another thought came into mind. If Morderra-Atrauis knew the power of the sword, Talquardez-Solstas, then he may come up with adroitness, a cunning plan indeed. Lithius knew that the sword had its own curse, a spell of some ancient magic within it to protect the owner of the sword from departing with it by some sort of thievery. It was obvious, in death, all's fair, and the sword is up for grabs, or unless as Mydyr has put it in the past, Lithius gives up the sword freely.

Lithius also knew there was far more to Talquardez-Solstas than Kronus and for that matter, Mydyr was prepared to bring into the light. Lithius pulling out the sword by the stream and drew the blade close to his face for a closer examination. Lithius knew from his readings so long ago at the forbidden temples of Ada-jahara from the ancient scrolls that the sword had certain powers and warned of curses for those that wielded it, but more so for those that attempt to take the sword while the rightful possessor was still breathing. He knew that the sword would transform the one who bore the sword, the one who commanded the imbued artifact to whatever liking the sword found necessary. For Lithius, it was turning a fair-skinned Ramadan into that of a Draccian. Lithius was no fool; he also knew it was the power of the sword that has kept him alive for all these years. The sword giving him skills beyond his own to defend him from others, skills he now possessed that otherwise he would of never had achieved.

Lithius then put away his sword back into its scabbard, walked up next to the still small pool of water next to the bank, and knelt down next to the shoreline. He then attempted to beckon his master, Mydyr. He waited and tried several more times without success. He then spent no more time and got up, gathered his belongings and headed for the foothills under an oddly warm sunny day, a day like this he had seldom seen on this dark wretched island plagued by war and sorcery.

As the day continued, Lithius on foot making good time across the expanse of the valley that lead him further upstream the very same river he traveled up as a boy when he first came to this enigmatic interior of this land virtually unknown by the outside world. His mind on the thoughts of the outcome between Mydyr and Hamahadra, as he walked, he wondered if any luck at all, that should be owed upon him that Hamahadra is now dead. As for Mydyr, if he should have met his end, to Lithius, this was a thought that only disturbed him slightly. Lithius knew Mydyr was the one that saved him so long ago, but as he realized years ago, that Mydyr only had done this so the boy could eventually acquire Talquardez-Solstas and all being an active part of this horrid creature's plan, Lithius did his master's bidding. For Lithius a dark term was reached long ago, Lithius would kill Morderra-Atrauis providing that he himself would not end up dead in the process and help usher Mydyr as ruler or Pitah into this realm. In return, Mydyr would allow Lithius pursue his endeavors of slaughtering the Tarvas and freeing the Ramadans, his people. It is this soul reason that Lithius has fought, collected souls for his army of the undead use against the Tarvas. Personally, other than the deal he struck in so many words, over so many passed conversations with Mydyr, he could care less who would become Pitah of this island.

Lithius thought about the ancient giant spider, a pet of Hamahadra, the very same just the other day brought her wrath upon him. He needed the soul of that creature for his bidding against Morderra-Atrauis. Lithius realized that

Morderra-Atrauis perhaps is more than powerful enough to fight against a creature and Lithius may require more against the old sorcerer, and if Hamahadra herself is still alive, she no doubt has warned Morderra-Atrauis of the young man and the sword he possessed and the ultimate power. Lithius figured this is probably the course he should consider, after all, he realized that his luck was certainly waning. This thought alone caused him to smile slightly as he could clearly see Thuma-Attarrach before him, her dark obsidian snow-covered peak jetting up to the blue sky. This was certainly the tallest mountain on the island, and as he heard, years ago while eavesdropping on some villagers in the younger days. Those that traveled up the castle, which was near the peak, that one could see the entire sea in all directions, and on a clear day, the two major continents. To the north was Lithius's continent across the sea, and as far as the other to the south, he knew nothing of. From his understanding that no mortal has ever climbed up to the peak of the snow-covered mountain, the walls of smooth glass-like obsidian offered no path, and impossible to climb. For what little of a map that Lithius had in his pack, nothing tangible about the way to the castle of Draccus was shown, only a point of reference of such a place. The mountain, as he later found out by his eavesdropping adventures, he knew the mountain was an ancient volcano and in the crater, the original top of the mountain resided, blown off in the first eruption of eons ago, fell directly into the deep crater. The glaciers at the time melted, back filling the crater with water creating a huge lake, and the ancient peak became an island, and to Lithius, this island was called Wizard's Island, and the lake also has a name, a name simply called the lake on top of the world. On Wizard's Island, is the castle of the Pitahs, home of Morderra-Atrauis himself.

Lithius in his studies from the past knew that most of the people, those that were Draccians were descendants of the Taltakkurdg-Kevnaps, again, a race of warlike creatures from a distant world of long ago that over the centuries mixed their blood with the indigenous race of humanoids and those from the children of the blue planet. As for Draccus, it is known that the purest of the remnants of Taltakkurdg-Kevnaps world reside here, and as for Draccus, no other races truly exist. Lithius also knew the largest of all the cities and villages of Draccus reside at the base of the mountain along the river under the greatest of all the waterfalls of Caledon, the Illua Falls, Illua, an ancient name for "From Heaven" pours from the huge lake from the top of the mountain. The water travels through some sort of underground passage and from twelve thousand feet pours from the side of the mountain, free falling that great distance down the steep face eight thousand feet to the upper portion of the greatest of all the Draccus cities, Draccarium. Draccarium, the walled city, spires up from the lava earthen valley floor of fertile ranch lands and farms up along the river to the very side of the mountain fortifying the city as one of the most formidable strongholds of its inhabitants. Lithius understood the history, a violent history of Draccarium in his readings in his youth. The city in the beginning was nothing more that the ancient village belonging to the indigenous race before the Taltakkurdg-Kevnaps. Since the Taltakkurdg-Kevnaps, the land was brought under the harsh and unforgiving decree of the first of the Pitahs. It was Lithius's own understanding based on the ancient scrolls of the scribes of Adajahara that Pitah Valgas himself lived in Draccarium in his youth and his very ascension as successor of the Pitahs expanded his lands north to Adajahara, "And on that note, we know the rest of the story" Lithius smirked as his thoughts were on this topic.

As Draccarium grew with the expanse of the Taltakkurdg-Kevnaps occupation, great battles were waged, and for a time, Draccarium became the sole focal point of the Taltakkurdg-Kevnaps Empire on this planet after Adajahara fell with the destruction of the Taltakkurdg-Kevnaps stronghold of the lands north of the Isle. Since the first Pitah, Draccarium has never seen defeat, though many armies in the past have tried, it remained the relic of the Taltakkurdg-Kevnaps, now, long gone over a vast sea of time.

Lithius was now well into the foothills that gave way from the valley floor below, as he climbed, the old oak forests changed to barren landscape of open rolling hills of dried natural grasses to the beginning of the small pines. He was now well passed the mighty river, there were small villages, fishing boats not to mention small army outposts along the easier way of the river.

Lycoi was long behind him, he gave no other worry to the vast horde of them, now it was for any sign of Morderra-Atrauis awareness onto him. The earth beneath his feet was showing signs of more of the evidence of the ancient volcano looming up high above him. Though Morderra-Atrauis seems that it was just a few miles in front of him, the distance was deceiving. He knew it would take at least three days of travel avoiding Draccarium and the smaller villages before the foot of the mountain. He would also have to navigate through the thick pine forest up to the trail, the only trail leading up above the timberline on where the earth beneath his feet would turn into the obsidian rock and stone that harbored very few species in vegetation. He would be exposed to anyone coming up or down from the path. Though he felt confidant about his special powers, that of invisibility and his supernatural bursts of speed to outrun, outmaneuver those that he might run into.

If the numbers were few, he thought, perhaps an opportunity to add a couple of souls along the way. He certainly wasn't worried about the average peasant or farmer, they were of no matter to him, and chances were, they would pay no never mind to him. Besides, he fit in as a Draccian now, who would suspect? He knew of only of Morderra-Atrauis and his henchmen, the Black Corsairs, the soldiers, the Lycoi, and anything supernatural, on this island, and in his experience, which was more than enough.

Lithius eventually walked up to a small village of hill folk farmers, the village was small and he kept his distance as he checked his map, getting his bearings on his position, he looked up to see a tall dark Draccian woman taking notice of him. Her features were slender, hair well passed her shoulders, pitch black against her smooth white ivory skin. She was dressed in heavy denim brown and tan clothing carrying two buckets full of water from the nearby well to one of the small houses nearby. She stopped, smiled, and sat the buckets down easily next to her as she gave Lithius a quick smile caught in her surprise.

Lithius did not return a smile; instead, he removed his hood, exposing his face to the light of day. He noticed she smiled once more and started to speak, Lithius could hear fragments of what she was saying, he turned and motioned that he was having difficulty hearing her words and decided to walk up unthreatening towards her.

"I am sorry, I cannot quite hear you?" He said in her tongue, "Were you speaking to me?" He asked.

He continued to look at her, and the small village, seeing people about doing their daily chores, two men, and one looked like the village blacksmith glanced at him and paid no more attention to the traveler. The traveler was an older man with a wooden pipe in his mouth gently puffing on it, seeing that Lithius seemed to be a young Draccian male, also paid no further attention, and then went on with his daily business. Lithius, as he drew closer to the young woman, a woman he guessed to be in her early twenties, long slender face, and her eyes a dark solid brown, thin lips and long slender neck and about six foot tall wearing old leathered boots with the heels practically worn completely away. Lithius could see that in spite of her beauty, that her life was harsh and did show on her hands and her warn teeth.

As Lithius walked up to her, he could sense that she wasn't alarmed as he used his powers to penetrate her mind as carefully as he could so she wouldn't notice. He was looking for any sign of a trap, or information that would give any admonition in anyway that Hamahadra was correct in saying the Pitah was onto him and he was walking into a possible ambush. He could of avoided the village, but he also would have been wondering on the extent of the possibilities he was pre-occupied with, besides, it has been years since he last talked to a woman, or for that matter, another living soul outside of those trying to track him down to only kill him.

As he began searching her mind, he realized that she was very unaware and did not have the ability of telepathy. He could also see that she wasn't afraid in her mind of his presence; however, he did see that she recently suffered from some tragic news. As he walked up to her supporting, a façade of a smile, he could see what it was, she received news from someone, someone who looked like a soldier, an officer of the Draccian army telling her and her father that her brother was killed in a skirmish in Gwarvarik in the war. This caused Lithius almost, that is, to lose his smile completely, but that would seem odd, if she suspected a sudden change in his demeanor.

As he probed her mind, he found out other things, one of which she did not expect to see him, nor was she warned of such a cleaver plan from Pitah Morderra-Atrauis to look out for such a person heading from the west. Lithius could relax knowing from her thoughts, that the village, so it seemed through her, did not know anything of him, least for now. Lithius also found out her name, as he walked right up to her, he realized it has been a long time that he has seen a woman, and a pretty one at that. Still in her mind, he carefully uncovered other things that he found favor with, but naturally was keeping these thoughts to himself.

"Good morning, or afternoon," Lithius spoke with a smile looking up at the sun, "Should say afternoon, time flies in this good bit of weather that we are hav-ing today." He lowered his right hand from the brow above his eyes to protect them from the glare of the sun.

"Aye that we are" Her voice seemed relaxed with a flavor of excitement of see-ing a new stranger, and as Lithius was picking up in her thoughts, she was drawn by two unmistakable impressions. One is, she finds him attractive, and secondly, Lithius was the first male that she has seen at her age in quite sometime, as for the strangers, it has been a good long time. As Lithius could see, since the old officer had come to her village reading off a list of the casualties from war in Gwarvarik.

"Where are you heading?" She asked looking at him. He could see in her thoughts that she was just trying to strike up a conversation with him, she was naturally inquisitive.

"East" He could see in her thoughts that were a vague question, but he could see that on her face as well.

"I'm heading east past Draccarium. I have family there." He quipped.

"Any news of the war?" She asked as he could see that she was suspecting he was indeed a warrior, the bow, armor of sorts and the wide leather belt that contained the sheathed sword.

Lithius was careful with his answer, and slightly slow to respond, if he told her he wasn't a soldier in the war, like so many men his age, this would raise suspicion with her quickly, and the last thing he needed right now was to draw weary attention to him. He could peer into her mind openly enough to realize that any information that she has had was drastically outdated, but none the less, Lithius would have to be careful on what he had to say, who knows, perhaps another stranger would visit upon the small isolated village with conflicting news and he wanted nothing to do with that.

"The war with Gwarvarik has been over; the generals have put the entire country under Draccian Law. This has been so for sometime now; unfortunately there are Gwarvarik rebels who test Pitah Morderra-Atrauis..." As he continued to tell her of the information, she bent down, picked up the two pails of water, and began to walk up the dirt path to the village slowly listening to every word Lithius was telling her.

"What of the South?" She asked and he could see in her thoughts, that she was struggling with the name of the country, "Gaelund?" Lithius asked for her.

"Yes, I heard there is a very large forest, a darker forest than the one that Brakar-Baine himself resides in, in our own homeland?" Lithius stopped suddenly an as she turned towards him wondering why he stopped, he spoke, "What do you know of this Brakar-Baine?" This thought of hers came out of nowhere, there was nothing in her thoughts, and it just simply came out of her mouth and caught him astonished. He quickly recovered, with a smile, "It is true, it is impossible to know what is on a woman's mind." He said to himself.

"Brakar-Baine, the evil one has killed hundreds of men, mostly hunters, passers-by, women and children that were unarmed, and some say he is not a man, but an evil spirit to torment the innocent souls who draw to close to his forest, and lucky for you that you didn't run into him since you are heading from that direction?" She said as she continued to walk.

Lithius fuming within him of her misinterpretation of the whole event of him living in the forest, he had never killed women and children, or for that matter, anyone unarmed. "Perhaps, this one you call Brakar-Baine is nothing more than a legend spawn by some angry villagers, or perhaps to keep those from wandering too far in the forest and causing an uprising with the Lycoi?" As continue to follow her up to the village.

He could sense through her thoughts that she was weighing his words, "Could it be possible, I mean to say, just a story to keep innocent children away from those woods due to the Lycoi, and this Brakar-Baine had never truly existed?"

She turned once more, and before she spoke, Lithius knew that his suggestions had fallen on deaf ears, "Oh Brakar-Baine exists all right, wither an ghost or spirit, or an evil soul in the flesh, none the less, he exists!" she insisted.

"How do you know this to be certain?" He asked.

"My father has seen him from afar in the woods…" She continued to talk about a time, a few years ago when her father with some others traveled west to an old village that was attacked by the Lycoi, the very same as Lithius was assuming was the one he was in a day earlier. As she spoke, she told him about the fate of that village and its inhabitants.

"I have seen that village in my passing, please go on?" Lithius said half amused as she continued to speak about it under the strain of the weight of the buckets of water.

"Should I take one of those buckets from you maiden?" Lithius asked as she turned and smiled.

"No, it's easier to carry both than just one, besides this is woman's work, not the work of warriors, and what is your name, I mean, my name is Tyra, I am sorry, I should of told you earlier." He could sense she was truly embarrassed by this fact.

"None to worry, you were caught up by a stranger, I suppose it has been some time since you saw anyone new? My name is Brakar-Baine." Lithius said as seriously as he could.

She smiled, "Sure and I am the wife of Pitah Morderra-Atrauis himself, queen of Draccus." Lithius bowed and responded.

"My Queen" he arose with a smile. However, he was partially honest in his answer as he put more of his weight on his walking stick looking at her, as she seemed to pretend that she indeed was of royalty rather than a peasant girl. It was at that moment that he could see in her mind that she suffered another tragedy as the thoughts of a loss close to her heart. Lithius could tell it wasn't her brother, but what looked like perhaps her lover or husband perhaps, but it was hard to see. The thought vanished as quickly as it came. Lithius could see that her face changed to reflect the pain of the thought.

"Do I remind you of someone?" Lithius was bold to ask as he peered into her mind a little further.

"More like the moment, reminded me of a happier time." Tyra admitted as she dismissed the thought. Lithius could sense through his power that she was indeed telling the truth.

"Anyway, my name is Octavius, my dear lady" As he took, another bow like before, arising with a smile, and quite naturally he was lying, and he could sense from her thoughts that she found the name somewhat odd.

"Octavius?" She replied as Lithius could see she was wondering through her thoughts, "A name I have not heard in such a long time." Lithius read her mind as she pondered for only a moment.

Lithius could see an image of a small boy from her thoughts, a young Draccian who was killed in his youth by men, dark riders in black armor coming up a hill, a hill on the other side of the slope, the backside of the hill. As Lithius could see, the boy was trampled by accident by these riders, these riders who were the Black Corsairs in an obvious hurry. Lithius could see the young boy dying under the hooves of the Larnges, the large six legged beasts. It was also made clear to Lithius; this boy was someone dear to her, perhaps a childhood friend. Lithius could see this pretty woman has endured much tragedy throughout her life thus far. He lied about his name naturally; he picked the name from one of those villagers from long ago that attempted to kill him. Lithius's own mind reflected on a dark and raining day on which the man with the name Lithius chose and one other stalked him. Both lied dead and their remains consumed by the forest floor.

Lithius concentrated on Tyra who stopped looking back at him as they both followed the old path up the hill to a cluster of pines. "Octavius, come and talk with my father, I shall cook you a warm supper." She smiled, but Lithius could see the memory of the boy was fading from her thoughts and returning to the darkness of the sea of thoughts that rested deep in her own mind.

"Certainly…" Lithius responded with a smile, "That would be fine with me, so how much farther to your village?" He asked.

"Just up over the hill there, past those people whom have nothing better to do than to gawk at us." She hinted.

As Lithius looked passed her, he could see some of the villagers who has stopped at took a closer look at the dark stranger. "The main part of our village is just on the other side."

"So what is the name of the village?" Lithius asked as he remembered that his map really didn't show any sign of the village to speak of at all.

"Dearth" She continued, "A peaceful place, which is, if the damned Corsairs would quit frightening the elders, and leave our youth alone." She turned with a disgusting look that was obviously well warranted.

"What have they done?" Lithius asked and remained behind her following her nearly to the top of the hill.

"What haven't they done hoodlums of the Pitah, his extension of his maliciousness and cruelty?" She spoke quiet frankly, as her words did not betrayed her true thoughts.

"Dearth has lost all the young men, men suitable for husbands, men of your age because of the Pitah's war, him needing fresh bodies for this mindless war." Her option was tempered only to a fading whisper that was barely audible.

"Most of the nearby villages have been ransacked by the black plague you know as the Black Corsairs; I hate 'em." She then grew somewhat quiet now that she was in earshot of some of the villagers.

"I see." Lithius responded as his attention turned towards the blacksmith who was repairing a piece of farming equipment. "I notice your blacksmith isn't Draccian?" Lithius could see this man was not the tall slender dark type with white porcelain skin, but of a shorter, weathered, and stocky sort.

"Oh yes, that is Kur, a foreigner from Caledon." She replied as she flash the older man covered in dirt and grime with a receding hairline and a mouth full of teeth as he stood there looking at the two with some measure of contempt.

"I see they are not used to seeing strangers." Lithius added.

"No, unless it is the wretched Corsairs coming to collect taxes or men, and since we have no young men, they just come for the taxes and whatever else fancies their shameful ways." Lithius caught a glimpse from her thoughts that shown a measure of violence of roughing up some of the villagers and things far worse for some of the women, and he could see that Tyra has fell victim to several accounts of such cruelty.

To change the subject from what he was seeing in her mind, "Kur, is he a good blacksmith?" His swallowed attempt caused her to turn around at look squarely at Lithius as he could see her dark eyes welling up from tears.

"Yes, he is the best we have" She then turned and looked at Kur that began banging out the metal device on an anvil as he smiled back at her.

"Who is your friend their Tyra?" The blacksmith asked as he quit pounding long enough to get an answer back.

"This is Octavius; he is from a village east of Draccarium returning home from the northern war of Gwarvarik." She said as Lithius could see Kur's brow lift up, "Is that so?" Kur responded as he looked closely at Lithius.

Lithius could also see the others looking at him just as closely at the stranger as Kur was.

"Yes, he will be eating supper at my father's house tonight." Tyra said in a quick response.

"All right then, your father will find Octavius and his news interesting I'm sure." Kur then waited for no other response as he realized the metal was cooling as he continued back to work.

CHAPTER 11

▼

Lithius followed Tyra down the hill, he then looked at her shapely, and attractive features that her heavy denim dress attempted to conceal. Lithius also realized on how lonely she is, and how much heartache she has endured through which in some aspects certainly humbled any attention of him drawing closer to her. He wasn't looking for a woman, though plenty attractive, he dismissed any thoughts he was having deep inside of him that was attempting to well up in him. It was true, he has never been with a woman, never loved no other woman except of his mother. Tyra he found in the short time was something he didn't need to meddle with, and considering all things, she could be something he could grow accustomed to.

The two walked down the other side of the hill past the cool shade of the cluster of pines that Lithius looked for any signs of any ambush or being followed and found none. The village, the main part of Dearth was a small village, a village that consisted of a few cobblestone homes, a central building, perhaps of the elder council would meet. Lithius could see out in the open were a windmill, and ancient windmill, though in much better shape that the one he nearly was forced to stand against the Lycoi. He could see the windmill was working as he could see the building was used to grind grain and wheat into flour. The entire village came out to look Lithius over, and he could read the thoughts of many of these villagers, most were negative, but all were curious. As he walked on, he could see that the village contained mostly the elderly, only a few children, children that was not even in their teens, toddlers mostly. There were a few women like Tyra; they looked at both Tyra and Lithius most harshly. Lithius could sense some measure of contempt and jealousy but remained quiet watching the two walk on. As they did, Lithius could see the huge field of cattle, and other livestock in corrals and in a few barns and stalls. Beyond the village was a huge field of grain, and there he could see that the villagers, mostly older men and women working this field as tall columns of grain were cut and stacked, it was well into the time of harvest.

"We live here." As Tyra walked, up to a cobblestone two story home and behind the home was an old moss covered dilapidated barn. Lithius could see that the home of Tyra and her father had already going a fire in the fireplace as the chimney gave off subtle plumes of smoke.

Lithius walked up the porch, "Are you sure it is all right with your father?" Lithius asked causing Tyra to turn and look at him with a smile.

"Yes, he loves news, news about the outside world, news of what is going on, and it has been a long time since he has talked to a young man. Nonetheless, you are welcome here. Please come in." She kicked the door open and walked in with the two buckets of water.

"Father!" She yelled in her velvet thick voice, "We have a guest with us, a visitor." She continued as Lithius stood at the doorway, he didn't go in and found it odd to do so.

Lithius could see that the large room before him was well clean but dark as his eyes adjusted. He could see plush but crude furnishings, the fireplace and some tendering and wood beside it. From the hallway from another room that he could not see partially blocked by Tyra standing there smiling and motioning Lithius to come further inside, which he again stood right at the doorway on the porch. He has never been inside a villager's own home and found it odd and difficult to come in.

"A visitor?" an older voice, a man's voice asked from the other room as Lithius could see her handing the old man coming forth the water, "Just sit it in the kitchen and prepare the vegetables." He said as he went around Tyra and with a flashing smile, his steely blue solid eyes gleamed with excitement caught in the daylight of the open door, the doorway that Lithius stood looking at the old man.

"Please come in?" the old man insisted. He then offered his right-hand extending out to Lithius. Lithius smiled in returned and shook his leathered hand from years of toiling in the fields. The old man's hair was long and white turned by his years, his face was warm, and friendly that eased the uneasiness in Lithius.

"My name is Byris, Byris the elder to be exact; my son was called Byris the younger" Lithius could see in the old man thoughts, the latter he was referring to was an image, the same that Tyra had of her brother.

"Byris, I am called Octavius." Lithius shook his hand firmly with a façade of a warm smile. As Lithius gently probed the old man's mind, he could see into far enough to see that the old man bore no contempt, but wonder and fascination of the young visitor.

"Please make yourself comfortable Octavius" Byris pointed to a very comfortable chair next to the fireplace made of leather and animal fir on a heavy oak frame.

Lithius walked over to it, there was another chair identical to the one Lithius sat his pack down next to him on the right-hand side of the chair. He went to sit down on and began to get comfortable, after removing his cloak, belt, bow, and quiver of black arrows as he looked at Byris that sat down across from him still looking somewhat gently surprised.

"Forgive me young man, but it has been such a very long time since we had a visitor, a traveler coming through our village." He said with a smile, Byris was speaking what was on his mind.

"So what village do you hail from?" Byris quipped.

"Not so much of a village but of a place actually, east of Draccarium, south east, east passed the great river." Lithius of course was lying, besides as he thought, how could I ever begin to tell any of them, not to mention, Byris on who he actually is, and his true intentions.

"Pretty country down there, well much prettier when I was just a strapping boy" Byris paused as he reflected. Lithius was probing his mind and could see the landscape that Byris was remembering.

"Listen to me, an old man rambling on about days past" Byris looked at Lithius's pack, his cloak, and the belt that contained the dark sword lying in a pile next to the chair.

"You are a warrior, a soldier?" Byris was now focusing his thoughts on the sword, and Lithius could see it in the old man's mind, that in fact, Byris thought it was unusual.

"Yes, well, more like I was a soldier." Lithius stated.

Byris then spoke meeting his eyes with Lithius's black orbs, "What news of the south?"

"I am afraid I know very little about the war in Gaelund, I was released from service in Gwarvarik in the Northern provinces along the lands of the Ramadans." Lithius looked at Byris.

"I see, of course it is my understanding that Gwarvarik fell some time ago and the king executed along with the line of his family, and those that served his court, those that were not put to the blade where enslaved. I also have heard that Pitah Morderra-Atrauis's generals have been quelling uprisings, rebel forces in the former kingdom, this is true of course?"

"Yes, Byris, this is true enough." Lithius added.

"Forgive me for asking this, but how did you manage to come back home, I mean released from the Pitah's service?" This was the question that Lithius was waiting for and that he has already rehearsed several times in his mind already.

"I am from a small family, no other brothers, and when my father died, my mother and elders from the nearby village contacted the Grand Conciliate in Draccarium. Because of the law and stature I was released with no further obligation to the army, and my orders were to return home." Lithius could look into the thoughts of Byris and could see that this certainly made sense; after all, there was this law, that much was truth.

"I am returning to my father's farm and to take care of my mother." Lithius didn't like lying to Byris, though he found it easy to lie, and he could see he was quite good at it, but he was rationalizing the notion, if the Black Corsairs question for whatever reason Byris or Tyra, it would be better this way.

"Octavius, I have noticed your sword, odd type, I have never saw anything quite like it?" Lithius smiled at Byris.

"It is a sword I have found in the northern regions of Gwarvarik." Lithius answered, "There that was almost the truth," Lithius thought to himself.

"Oh, the bow you have is most unusual, it is not like the long bow, but of a fashion I have only heard about, it is a Faedarish bow, is it not?" Byris pointed slightly at the bow resting against the chair.

"Yes, well fashioned after one, I made that myself." This of course was the truth.

"There is this man in our village, a foreigner" He was cut off by Lithius.

"Kur, the Blacksmith?" Lithius added.

"Yes, that's right. You know him?"

"No, Tyra introduced me to him as we walked into the village earlier." Lithius smiled.

"Yes, I see. Anyway, he's from Caledon originally." Byris paused only for a moment.

"Poor bastard was part of the Caledon Emissary sent by his former king to accompany the emissaries to help construct a building in Draccarium. This was to show Pitah Morderra-Atrauis that Caledon wanted peace and an open channel of communication with the two kingdoms."

"What happened?" Lithius inquired.

"Pitah Morderra-Atrauis grew tired of Caledon and never really liked outsiders, but yet he loves waging war, war beyond our country's means." Byris added bitterly.

Byris could see that Lithius was looking a bit perplexed by his particular views about the war, but Lithius remained silent knowing full well that Byris, after all, was entitled to his opinion after losing at the least, his son.

"I have lost my son and my son-in-law in Pitah Morderra-Atrauis's own ambitions of expanding his kingdom through treachery and deceit and his bloodlust for war, so much it has turned this isle into a very dark and depressed land." Byris continued on speaking his views as Lithius nodded in agreement.

"Draccus is dying, has been for a long time, a very long time under the cruel yoke of bondage by the very hand of that man." Lithius knew that Byris is referring to Pitah Morderra-Atrauis.

"Oh I dare say that the Pitah is a man, though I seriously doubt it" Byris's own voice faded into a whisper as he looked over his shoulder to the open doorway once more and then back to Lithius sitting there.

"I'm sorry about that, anyway back to Kur, Kur is a very talented man, though he is imprisoned here amongst us and can never to return to his homeland." Lithius followed Byris's own thoughts and worlds as Byris continued to talk in a lower and quieter voice.

"Kur, spared with his life, more fortunate for him than the Caledon Emissaries that crossed Pitah Morderra-Atrauis." Byris flashed a smile.

"I see, and this man, Kur, was what exactly?"

"He was to help construct the Emissary Building with a few others sent forth from Caledon. Like him, the others, most were imprisoned in the harsh dungeons in Draccarium for a good many years, some died in the process, and others like Kur that survived were released eventually and sent to various villages in Draccus due to the war efforts. Kur, he is most fortunate of the rest, he had no family in Caledon, no wife, no children." Byris stopped and reflected for a moment before continuing as Tyra entered the room.

"Close the door and light a few candles, the sun will be setting shortly" Byris said before turning his direction towards Lithius.

"Kur is somewhat of a great hunter and bowman himself, I guess that is why I brought him up, you know, looking at your own bow and all." Byris then looked back at Tyra that closed the door, and then lit up a few candles in the room.

"Tonight will be our first frost I'm afraid and with it, a very cold winter, I can feel it in my old bones." Byris warned.

"Are you married Octavius?" Byris turned his attention back towards his visitor. Lithius could see out of the corner of his eye that Tyra was also listening and awaiting an answer.

"No" Lithius replied solemnly with a ghost of a smile.

"I see, spent most of your adult life fighting over there?" Byris pointed in a northern direction referring to Gwarvarik.

"Yes, I suppose that is a true enough assessment." Lithius added.

"Most of the soldiers seemed to prefer Gwarvarik; they end up staying there, good soil, good weather, and great pastures for raising livestock. Oh I suppose I cannot blame them though the dark hand of Pitah Morderra-Atrauis stretches across their well enough." Byris paused as Lithius could see that Tyra had finished with the candles.

"I will begin with supper father." She then walked away out of Lithius's eye-sight into one of the other rooms.

"That will be fine." Byris then turned once more towards the door and finding it closed, he looked once more at Lithius before lighting up his old wooden and stone pipe.

"Finest weed around." Byris lit the pipe and Lithius could smell the sweet cherry like flavor or gentle smoke rising slowly up towards the wooden ceiling.

"I am sorry for your loss Byris."

"Some has suffered more than I, this is for sure, the damned Pitah has sent his henchmen to villages to plunder, seize, and commit atrocities, unspeakable atrocities" Again, Lithius could see blurry visions of thoughts, violent and evil thoughts, also thoughts of Byris's thoughts of revenge.

"Tyra has suffered much more than any man could" Byris's thoughts were enough to finish the sentence, and Lithius knew what has happened to her on several occasions.

"You are a good man Octavius, I can sense that. Unlike the Black Lotus that touches the hearts of the wicked" Byris took a couple of puffs from his pipe.

Lithius could see in Byris's mind, that there was something more, a plan, and a dark plan. Lithius was especially careful now; he sensed that there was something Byris was scheming of has schemed with others, others from his village. Lithius had to be careful now, if he started peering deep enough in Byris's mind, there would be an exchange. Byris would be able to receive Lithius's own thoughts in his mind; this is how the gifting of telepathy worked. Lithius spent most of his life alone in the woods and his experience of how deep he could go before Byris would realize Lithius in his mind was severely limited do to Lithius's experience.

"There, I can see it clearly enough." As Lithius said to himself in thought. Lithius could see what Byris was hiding, the plan, the scheme of retribution against the Black Corsairs, and Lithius could see that the plan would unfold in a day or two from now, as he could see in Byris's own mind that the Corsairs would be coming upon the village in a day or two. Lithius could see in Byris's thoughts clearly enough now without probing further and risking detection that Byris and several others including Kur were planning to make a final stand against such odds. Lithius could also see that Byris and the others including Kur did not expect to win, but surly take a few of this twisted and malevolent physical hand of the Pitah.

Lithius then pulled back his probing of Byris's mind, and was now caught in his own thoughts of what was about to happen, and of course, what has happened thus far. Chances were good that the Pitah, Pitah Morderra-Atrauis to be specific that looms over the land like a dark shadow from a top of Thuma-Attarrach high overhead of the village in the foothills.

Lithius wondered if his own master was somehow destroyed, or was it Hamahadra. Nevertheless, Morderra-Atrauis had to know somehow about it and it was safer for Lithius to assume that Morderra-Atrauis did in fact know about it and the Lycoi employed by the evil hand of Hamahadra could still be a factor and on the move to this village following the scent of Lithius himself. If that is the case, as Lithius was thinking quietly to himself before Byris who took a couple of more puffs from his pipe.

"They could never withstand against the Lycoi, let alone the damned Black Corsairs," Lithius thought. If for whatever reason that Morderra-Atrauis did not know of Lithius and his own Master's plan, the element of surprise would surely be gone, and without a doubt, Morderra-Atrauis would be on to him.

As Lithius sat there weighing out his options, Byris sat there quietly for a few moments before speaking. "So you came from the west, any sign of the Lycoi?" Byris asked breaking up Lithius from his thoughts.

"Sorry?"

"Did you see any sign of the Lycoi on your travels thus far?" Byris took another puff looking at Lithius through the cloud of whispering smoke in front of the fireplace.

"In Gwarvarik, I saw a few" Lithius hesitated, "Dare I tell him about the huge numbers he roused up that may be bold enough to storm Dearth?"

"Yes I saw a few along the ancient oak forest, around an old deserted village just about a day's or so travel west of here." Lithius admitted.

"Deserted village? No my friend, not deserted, destroyed is closer to the truth Octavius" Byris took another puff.

"That village, well, it's been about three years since most everyone was outright killed, slain and left for dead." Byris went on to explain.

"It was certainly the Lycoi, over the years, the Lycoi have been growing in numbers in those dark woods, and rumor has it that other evils have grown powerful from the very same woods that now no man dares enter." Byris concluded as he drew from his pipe once more briefly.

"The Lycoi usually avoid settlements of such, don't they?" Lithius enquired.

Lithius could see that Byris was in his thoughts; Lithius refrained from using his powers to probe the old man's thoughts. He felts in doing so would be a matter of time before the elder would sense somehow find out.

"The Lycoi has been an enemy to all things righteous, all things pure, and an evil abortion upon the Gods" Byris took a long puff from his pipe and gazed into the fireplace before continuing.

"Since Pitah Morderra-Atrauis reign, back when I was a child, he had protected what little of the Lycoi that existed, all but a handful was left, that is until the iniquity cursed the land, that is, before the black hand of the Pitah turned his vengeance upon his own people, long before your time, I'm afraid." Byris took another puff as he continued.

"It is said the ancient fathers of the Draccians had the Lycoi as pets in the beginning, defying the Gods if you ask me. Anyway, the numbers of these beasts, these wolf-men grew in numbers, mostly along the ancient oaks hunting their prey, the deer, the woodland rhino, and other such and more exotic like the Drakkar. Eventually the numbers grew and the Lycoi expanded throughout the dark ancient oaks and across to other forests and even throughout the foothills of Thuma-Attarrach. As I grew older, the Lycoi also grew bolder, attacking small villages, first the livestock and then the old, young, and weak. Men drew to arms to hunt these iniquitous beasts. Yes, and for years, these abhorrence's rescinded to the shadows of the deep forests, that is until the wars began, that is until all the villages began losing those capable of hunting these beasts had to go off and die for the Pitah and his bloodlust desires for conquest." Lithius could feel the contempt in Byris's voice in both the Lycoi and Pitah Morderra-Atrauis, his ruler.

"Now the Lycoi's numbers once again grow strong, and three years ago the Lycoi attacked Sommer, the ruins of the village that you mentioned earlier, my friend." Byris puffed on his pipe once more before he looked back at Lithius firmly.

"Sommer lay in waste; it was Kur, and several others that traveled to the village that found of unspeakable horror. Kur sent one of the villagers back to get the elders. Upon doing so, we went to Sommer to see it first hand. There amongst the smoldering ash laid strewn across the village were the dead, mostly women, children, and a few of the men." He paused before continuing as his steel blue eyes looked away back into the fire. His gaze seemed to go off and transverse a sea of time back to the very day that he came upon the mayhem and devastation that befall Sommer for only a moment in silence before looking back at Lithius with an expression of disbelief still to this day.

"Not a living soul was found, all dead, even the sheep, the goats, and the fowl, nothing" Lithius could sense there was something more, something more that Byris was afraid to mention, but Lithius was patient.

"All the dead, the villagers were beheaded. Their very heads removed from their shoulders and placed on crude poles that circled the village. A most ghastly sight to be witnessed, there however, was a few Lycoi that the villagers did manage to kill lying with the dead. There were signs of large numbers of Lycoi, numbers that were hard to believe, never before have I seen such sign, such a violent attack on quiet villagers. Lycoi has never before attacked in such a way, even provoked, there was or is something dark behind all of this, no doubt it is Morderra-Atrauis!"

Byris was in full stride as his eyes lit up with the hatred and contempt for the Pitah, "We then burned the dead, and removed the poles, burned the whole lot that remained strewn throughout the field around the village, it was impossible to put together the pieces" Byris grew silent for a few moments.

"The Lycoi spared not a living thing, entire homes were destroyed, and the wheat, oats, and hay were torched." Byris was then interrupted by Lithius.

"Torched?" An odd look came across Lithius's face in disbelief.

"I know my friend, odd isn't, I mean have you ever heard of a Lycoi using fire. For years we have used the very same against them." Lithius quickly probed the elder's mind and could see without a doubt, that Byris was being honest on what he saw back then at Sommer and now.

"In spite of the law, we formed a group of, well, old men like me to go and to protect the women and children. We went to the ancient oaks and found a few of the Lycoi, yeah; they were of the same that attacked Sommer."

"How do you know that?" Lithius was indeed fascinated by Byris's account, after all, this was the first he heard about such a large attack by the Lycoi.

Byris looked at him with a ghost of a smile with his pipe in his mouth as he removed the pipe for a moment as he spoke, "They had collected trinkets and items from the village." Byris put the pipe back in his mouth and continued.

"We killed about twenty of them before it got too dark, before the others came for us." He took a puff from his pipe and looked at Lithius again.

"We fought for most of the night against these horrible creatures that is before the morning then we retreated. God knows how many we killed, not enough I am afraid. However there was one odd thing" He drawn from his pipe deeply and exhaled the smoke into the darkening air.

"The Lycoi were never before so organized as they came upon us. Unfortunately for us, we were losing men left and right, Kur was wounded in the process, we barely made it out of there you see. For whatever reason they did not follow us, there was only just a handful; they could have overtaken us easily enough." Lithius could see the perplexed look clearly on Byris's aged face.

"These are the darkest times Octavius my friend, hell of a time to return indeed." Byris drew from his pipe once more as Tyra entered the darkening room to light the fireplace.

"Supper will be ready soon." She smiled quickly at Lithius and then focused her attention back towards the fire.

It was dark enough now with the sun setting for Lithius to see a reflection of a small fire in the kitchen, the fire was obviously used for cooking and Lithius could smell the vegetables cooking in a slow boil.

"Smells wonderful" Lithius admitted as Tyra then went back into the kitchen when she was finished.

"You say that the Lycoi is using fire now?" Lithius asked.

Byris nodded accordingly, "Yes, and they have grown much wiser to battle now, never seen the likes." He admitted.

"And you think that perhaps Morderra-Atrauis is behind all of this?" Lithius quipped.

Byris leaned over his chair towards Lithius most seriously, "Aye, that I do. We are under the most evil of Pitahs. Morderra-Atrauis sleeps with the daughters of the underworld himself. He is the most wretched amongst men."

"I see" Lithius was a bit unnerved by Byris's own intensity and found it hard to look into the old man's eyes.

"Someone or something has been teaching the Lycoi over time on how to deal with us, how to fight. This of course has been foretold by a prophet."

"A prophet, what prophet?" Lithius was somewhat amused again.

"The very one that Morderra-Atrauis had taken into his dungeons, the one that came many years before from a distant land." Byris stopped shortly as he reflected.

"I believe he came to us about ten years or so ago, he was from, lets see what was it that he said?" Byris paused once more, as he reflected.

"Jah-Hadeim, from the desert I believe, yes, it was a place called Jah-Hadeim!" Byris admitted.

Lithius's heart began to race with excitement and anger, "What did this prophet look like?" Lithius asked leaning towards Byris who was sitting back fully in his chair.

"Odd you should asked, his face was covered in a dark mask of sorts, no one was to see his face, it was his religion, his faith, his walk with the Gods" Lithius peered into Byris's mind most carefully and could see the tall slender crimson robe figure through Byris's thoughts. The figure's face was cloaked by the hooded cloak that covered his entirety. His face, Lithius could see the black mask. Lithius of course saw this same figure before as a child, and Lithius had no doubt, on which the person in the red figure was.

"His name escapes me," Byris admitted.

"Kronus" Lithius mumbled under his breath.

"Yes, his name is Kronus, but how did you know that?" Byris was now looking oddly at Lithius.

"Oh" Lithius surprised that Byris had heard him recovered from his thoughts.

"I have heard of this prophet, this priest from Jah-Hadeim in Gwarvarik." Lithius explained wondering if Byris would believe him.

"I am sure you have, he is a powerful priest and has traveled to many lands in his lifetime that spans many a man's lifetimes." Byris went on to talk about the prophet.

"He came to us over ten years ago, blessing the villages, and acted like he was constantly looking for someone or something, least that was my impression of him anyhow."

"What happened to him again?" Lithius asked carefully as not to raise any suspicion.

"Pitah Morderra-Atrauis of course." Byris replied.

"Yes, but explain, what happened?"

"My friend, when Morderra-Atrauis found out that there was a priest amongst us; especially one who is gifted in prophecy, the Pitah sent forth the Black Corsairs who had him properly arrested like all the other priests." Byris drew in from his pipe as he explained.

"Everyone knows, including yourself, religion is forbidden in Draccus now, has been for quite some time." Byris looked sternly at Lithius.

"Yes, that's right, of course." Lithius admitted.

"What do you think happened to him?" Lithius asked.

"That is easy, if not dead; he resides in the dungeon atop of Thuma-Attarrach with the others, which is of course, the Pitah had not killed him. However, I doubt if he is still alive, let alone all the others that Morderra-Atrauis has imprisoned. You know that Morderra-Atrauis only keeps priests, shamans, healers, and the like in his dungeon. All the rest, well they rot in the prison of Draccarium." Byris looked at Lithius with another ghost of a smile.

"I see" Lithius paused for a moment.

"So you said that the prophet had said something to you, something about warning you of the Lycoi?" Lithius grew silent from his question.

"Did more than that I am afraid?" Byris arose from his chair and looked down at Lithius still sitting.

"He wrote his prophecy out and with his scribes, those poor souls that could read and write that converted to his faith, mostly village boys, still in their youth wrote out copies to give to all the village elders throughout the land, those who believe in such things." Byris said with a smile as he reached up on the mantle above the fireplace, brought down a wooded box, a long slender wooden box, and sat back down in his chair.

CHAPTER 12

▼

Lithius watched him as he opened the wooden box up by sliding back the wooden top exposing an oiled leather scroll that was tied in the middle by a leather string.

"He in fact knew his time would soon end upon his own capture, so he wrote his final words, his last prophecy that we all know of anyway." Byris began to untie it and opened the scroll.

Lithius could see that Byris was taken great care of the scroll as he unrolled it. "Though it does me little good, since I cannot read, could you read it out loud for me Octavius, that is, if you can read, if not I can have Tyra read it, she's read it so many times in the past, she probably knows it by heart?" He smiled as he handed the parchment over to Lithius who reached out for it.

"Yes I can read, thank you." Lithius carefully brought the lengthy scroll up to him and there was just enough light now from the fireplace for him to see the writings, the writings of the man that he believed long ago tried to kill him and take his sword.

"Before I begin, did this priest have both of his hands?" Lithius was compelled to ask before continuing.

"No, he had lost a hand long ago. Some say he fought a demon in some forbidden land, yes that's what I believe was said." Byris then readied himself for the reading.

Lithius turned his attention towards the scroll and began reading aloud; *"I Kronus, the last of the great Jah-Hadeim Servants of the Most High from the temple of Jah-Hadeim, May the Lord continue to shine his glory upon thee in the desert of this world."*

"I come forth from many lands sent by the one true God, the father of all gods, creator of all things large and small, seen and unseen. I bring this land a blessing that one day that you shall be free of the Desolate One, the wickedness that blankets this land and darkens the hearts of the righteous. For sometime, the Lord has shown me a forbidden land. This land of our ancestors who came from the stars and mingled so long ago with the race of people who dwelt in darkness and waged war with the heathen nations of the humanoid. The pestilence of the plagues that came from foreign Ships to enslave us in hard bondage and unspeakable deaths, the fathers of the Lycoi, the fathers of the Pitahs, and all that is an abomination of God."

The Lord has sent me to your dark isle first to offer your souls unto God so that he may show you everlasting peace that awaits each of you who believe in the hereafter and to strengthen you during these perilous times, these foreboding times of iniquity. Unfortunately I have come late, this is my fear, for another, another comes from the Forbidden Lands Afar, for he is the bringer of death and sorrow, of disease and famine, it is he that is the beast amongst the children of the Isle. It is he that I am speaking of that will bring havoc, war, and hatred amongst all men, turning brother against brother, son against father, daughter against mother. This harbinger of death, the Desolate One will bring forth a weapon, a weapon not of this world that will unleash its fury amongst the living flesh that none can withstand. It is this very weapon that I was anointed to destroy; it was the Desolate One that I fought and through my own weakness in Faith and understanding had lost my hand in battle with this demon, this prince of darkness.

I have come to warn you good people, the righteousness of Draccus of the danger you may hold upon your land. This evil dwells in the heartland, the bosom of your most sacred and darkest of places, the most ancient of places that shall begin poisoning the waters, the air, and the forests with his evil.

Mark my words, proclaim this prophecy of Kronus. For my time draws near as your evil king already seeks me out through his minions. Yet he is just a puppet in the great evil schemes, and he too shall fall to the sword of the Desolate One, for even his strong magic shall fail him as he bows down before the Prince of Darkness who shall rule all of Draccus, shall rule over the house of Morderra-Atrauis who now rests with his fathers.

You shall know of these end times when they come upon you my children of the light by the following signs carried in the winds of time by first my own demise by the hand of Pitah Morderra-Atrauis himself through his black hand of those closest to him that protect him so that he may fulfill his wickedness. Once I am gone, the children of the ancient ones, the Lycoi will come forth only after the land is barren of its youth and treasure fighting in distant wars draining the blood of the land. This of course will be the things yet to come, but trust me my children, they will come.

The Desolate One who has come as a child will grow into a man, and through him a menacing powers of magic and baleful works will come forth. From the Netherworld, a dimension of a ominous place that is nether physical of flesh and blood, he will open its doors, and upon this, a plague of iniquity whose chalice is over filling with the blood of the innocent shall rise upon Draccus and all of Caledon shall shutter and moan in horror as the malevolence shall reign. The Desolate One shall again appear as a man, a youthful man, a man of this nation, a man of the people and tribes of the Isle, but understand he is not of this land, nor is his intentions to be deemed true, but cloaked in self-ambition, retribution, revenge, and death. You will know him by his evil works.

He shall come to you as a friend, as a savior, as a warrior with unspeakable power, as a gifted healer, and scholar. You shall know of him through his works soon enough, but least of all, his manner. He shall come upon you as a man returning from a far away place, with wonders, he shall swoon many in deceit and he shall raise a holy war amongst the children of Draccus. You shall also know of him by many names, you shall know him from his true name, the Desolate One is called Lithius"

Lithius paused for a moment, knowing that Kronus was writing about him, this wasn't religious rambling, but of a calculated warning, a warning in hopes that would disrobe Lithius and turn everyone against him. Lithius looked quickly at Byris who sat there listening serenely before raising Byris's own suspicions on why Lithius has stopped.

"Lithius is indeed the Desolate One. He is a man who has dwelt amongst the great evil Pitahs and gained power through their ancient tombs in the Forbidden Lands, the lands of Adajahara. The Desolate One who has conversed with the walking dead, and obtained many a dark magic through deceitful means learned to him by unmentionable ways. He will come, my children, bare witness to the things to come as a sign.

Upon my passing, the Lycoi shall grow in numbers and wisdom of war. They shall attack in organized numbers and fashion, they shall attack villages, razing them to ash, they shall kill their adversaries and spare no one, and not one living thing shall escape their fury, their hatred amongst men. First, it will be small settlements, and then villages, even the black hand of the Pitah will be bitten by the children of the ancients. This will be the ushering sign of the Desolate One. Now arrow, nor sword, axe, or bow shall defeat him, only faith shall subdue him and send his bone to ash and dust. From the ancient oak forests shall rise the gateway of the dimension of the Netherworld, and from this portal of wickedness shall come forth the gods of the ancients, and the dead shall be his army, and none shall stop the horde, take my words as a warning upon this land. As the Desolate One shall become Pitah, look for him in the high places of the land, look for him against the surmountable armies as they bow down to his might."

Lithius then rolled up the scroll, his blood as hot as smoldering iron leaving the foundry's tough. The warning from his enemy was filled with lies about his character; this alone he wished Kronus death many times over again.

Lithius then handed the scroll back to Byris who then put it back in the wooden box and upon the mantle. "I am afraid if I was caught with that writing, that Morderra-Atrauis would take a dim view upon my life." Byris said with a smile as he looked back at Lithius who was very aggravated by the information he had just read.

"Do you believe in this prophecy?" Lithius was careful to speak, he wanted to say something else, something more, but remained silent for an answer.

"I am not a religious man myself, I just keep it to aggravate the Pitah, and I think you know I hate the Pitah."

"Aye, this I know, and I also know that is treasonous alone Byris." Lithius said without a smile in a sullen voice.

"True enough, true enough." Byris freely admitted.

"I keep the scroll as perhaps a warning, especially after what has happened with the wars, and the Lycoi, why a man has to wonder though, wouldn't you say?" Byris asked.

I suppose" Lithius then peered into Byris's own mind. Lithius didn't care if Byris would notice or not, at this point, Lithius fully intended on keeping his secrets to himself, no matter the outcome that will soon unfold.

Lithius looked up and could see Byris smoking his pipe and looking towards the door. "I must shut the door, wouldn't want the Desolate One to come in, would we?" He said with a smirk.

Lithius could sense that his identity was safe and above suspicion. Beside, Byris was slightly preoccupied by his plans with the coming of the Black Corsairs he was expecting in a day or two.

As Byris closed the door and returned to his chair, Lithius looked hard up at the wooden box, "Why do you keep that out in the open?" pointing to the box on the mantle.

"No matter, soon it won't matter much anyway." Lithius understood what Byris was truly meaning.

"There is another great evil in those old oaks, before, and since the attack at Sommer, those that dared to enter those woods, seldom did they ever see the light of day again. Those that did vowed never to return."

"What?" Lithius now had to concentrate on what Byris was saying, he thought he'd missed something and could sense that there was more that Byris wanted to say, wanted to talk about those ancient oaks that he grew up.

"Because of the Lycoi, is that what you are talking about, sorry?" Lithius ventured to ask.

"Partly, but there were other creatures, dare I call them creatures, more like spirits, inexplicable malevolent in nature" Byris paused and drew from his pipe once more.

"Some say there is a huge ancient beast, more hideous that the Lycoi, some say it is a spider, an eight-legged warrant of perilous death to those that fall prey to the likes of such an imaginable beast. I have never seen such myself, but there were others, mostly before my time that has said they have seen it from a distance. Now, of course, who's to say, it has been years since anyone has made it out from those woods. There is of course another, Brakar-Baine, the spirit that preys upon the woodsmen, or those that ventured in." Lithius almost smirked and had to turn away slightly from Byris.

"What of this Brakar-Baine?" Lithius inquired.

"An wicked spirit that resembles a boy, or a young man in nature, but moves through the forest as if he was the wind, silent and deadly, cunning and treacherous, unmerciful and of course, malicious intent fills its heart."

"Really, and have you seen this spirit?" Lithius said as seriously as he could as not to raise suspicion to Byris's accusations.

"Yes on two separate accounts, about four years ago. I watched him through the woods, once, he was on top of a large bolder, he was overlooking a small clearing, and in the clearing, he seemed to be watching the small heard of Rhinos. There were three bowman that had him dead to rights, when oddly as if the spirit could sense danger, he turned and before an arrow could pierce him, he was gone, too fast to see, too fast to track. Without warning Brakar-Baine killed the three. I was close enough to get a shot off, I released my arrow, and again, before the arrow got to him, he vanished out of thin air. I left as quickly as I could." Byris explained.

"Through the years Brakar-Baine grew as a man would grow from a boy into a man, and many died by his hand, the time before the one I mentioned, I have seen this apparition as a child swimming in a cool dark pool along a creek. The spirit arose from the water naked and ran off. I tracked the spirit as best as I could, but never was successful." As Byris spoke, Lithius remembered that day, the day that he saw a middle-aged villager hunting him.

Lithius remembered a different version of the story, one slightly different. Lithius didn't run off, instead he grabbed his bow, notched an arrow, turned and shot at the villager, the very same he was now sitting next to years later. Lithius's arrow hit the top of the left shoulder of Byris, greased him. Lithius let him live and didn't give chase. Lithius found it odd then that he didn't, and now, odd that he would run into the very man, the only man that he ever missed with his bow. Lithius wasn't too sure if he was glad he ended up missing or not at this point with everything thus far unfolding before him.

"Brakar-Baine, this creature, do you believe he is part of the prophesy?" Lithius asked.

"Perhaps" The old man turned his attention to the cooking going on in the kitchen.

Lithius had forgotten about Tyra, and he realized that she was in earshot of the entire conversation. "Tyra!" Byris snipped.

Lithius using his powers reached out in thought to Tyra and he knew she was standing over the boiling pot of vegetables as she dropped in fresh dough into the thickening broth of the vegetables. His mind met hers, she was thinking on how long it has been since they had company, a young male warrior in their presence returning for home. There was nothing more now that she was thinking about, and Lithius knew she hadn't realized the warning of Kronus that was now like a small stone caught in Lithius's boot.

"In a few minutes father" She responded.

As Lithius went to sit down at the quant. wooden table, the scent of warm food that was displayed in hand carved wooden bowls was already poured along with a loaf of fresh bread no more than a day old. This was Lithius's first warm meal that he hadn't prepared himself since the invasion of the Tarvas upon his people many years ago. As he thought about that fact, a wave of melancholy came briefly upon him. Lithius grew quiet as Byris seasoned his portion of stew.

"Dig in, my friend." Byris mentioned smiling at Lithius.

"Thank you, it looks wonderful Tyra." Lithius quietly responded only making quick eye contact with Tyra sitting across the small table from him.

She just smiled and looked over at her father sitting at the head of the table. Lithius noticed the kitchen was small, mostly wooden and clay bowls, a few cast iron pans, and a big pot over the small fire that Tyra used to prepare and cook the stew. The house was small, a typical thatched roof, cobblestone home covered in moss due to the weather of this island.

Lithius thoughts changed to the warning of Kronus onto these simple people, and his mood changed to something closer to anger as he thought to himself for a moment while he began eating the stew. "Some Prophet indeed"

"He must have realized where I headed somehow and followed me here to the isle" He then looked over with a glance towards Tyra, "This is very good," as he flashed a smile and continue to eat.

"A charlatan, I should have killed him when I had the chance, see if I make the same mistake again!" Lithius was in his thoughts.

"Who is a charlatan, and what is a charlatan?" Tyra spoke up looking at Lithius.

"Excuse me?" Lithius stunned, for his thoughts he kept to himself without saying a word. Lithius looked over to Byris as he himself shrugged his shoulders. Byris looked over at his daughter for an instant before he spoke.

"Octavius didn't say anything except he thought the stew is good, and indeed it is." Byris seemed a bit perplexed.

It was obvious to Lithius that seemingly unknowing to Tyra, she possessed the power of reading another's thoughts. Lithius realized this was somewhat of a fluke for her.

"I am sorry, forgive me, I thought you said something Octavius." She humbly said before continuing eating.

"It's okay, it's getting late anyway, and I must be going." Lithius then arose from the table.

"Nonsense, it's dark, too late to travel, it isn't safe my friend, not in these hills," warned Byris who had nearly a half of mouth of food, as he looked somewhat surprised at Lithius standing before him, "Please, and you can stay in the loft in my barn this evening."

Lithius could see the dismay in Tyra's face from the corner of his eye as he looked upon Byris, "I travel best at night, and I can make up much ground."

"Was there something wrong with the food?" Tyra asked as Lithius could sense a hint of remorse in her voice, but the fact is that she was capable of picking up his thoughts; though he closed his mind in the case, she would realize her gift.

"No, it was wonderful; it is the first home cooked meal that I have had in a very long time." Lithius confessed.

"My friend, it is very dark out there, and there are reports that the Lycoi is forming in great numbers to the west." Lithius knew this was true enough; he was, after all, responsible for that. However, he was somewhat stunned that Dearth found out about that, or it could have been something Byris was just saying in hopes that Lithius would reconsider.

Lithius wasn't going to probe his mind, Lithius was doing that too much earlier, and realized this could have risen Tyra's gifting somehow and he was not going to chance it now.

Nevertheless, there was a small part of Lithius that did want to stay behind, a very small part of him, something deep inside began stirring when he looked at Tyra, she is a beautiful woman, and he thought, only fleetingly the possibility of staying in Dearth. This however would not work, he realized that his presence being here was certainly placing the village in great danger of the Lycoi, especially if they picked up his trail somehow; the village would not be able to withstand an attack and would be another Sommer.

"To be honest, I would love nothing more to stay, but I am afraid time is against me already." Lithius looked at Tyra as he could see her eyes welling up with tears.

"I am sorry to upset you, Tyra, I think you are a wonderful person, a woman with a good heart, and I hope that you shall find a husband to replace your loss." As he said that, he realized that he just made a terrible mistake.

"How did you know I am a widow?" She was very perceptive and now put Lithius in a bind as he could feel not only her eyes upon him, but that of Byris.

"I don't, I just felt that you have suffered a loss, sometime in the past, am I correct in saying so?" Lithius figured it was a quick response, quick enough perhaps that it wouldn't raise any more suspicion. He waited for a response only for a moment before he continued, "I realize that the Pitah's greed and war has cost this country much, and I believe everyone has greatly suffered, that is why I presumed in saying." Lithius then waited as he could see Byris agreeing with a nod as the old man continued to eat.

"Yes, I suppose that is true enough, yes I lost a husband as well as my brother" She grew silent as she reflected upon her loss.

"I am so sorry to have brought this up, I would do well to remain silent and keep my thoughts to myself" Lithius needed to change the subject quickly, "Anyway the stew was wonderful, and I thank you" he turned his direction back to Byris that was now looking back at him.

"…for the use of your barn. But if I travel through the night, I can be passed Draccarium and upon the following day, entering my father's land." Lithius concluded.

"Yes, but at night?" mussed Byris. "…well it looks like that there is no changing you mind on this, my young friend." Byris looked over at Tyra that seemed more discouraged that her father could not persuade Lithius on leaving tonight.

"Pack up the bread and some of this stew that he may eat along his travel" Byris then arose and shook Lithius's hand.

"I understand you are anxious to return home, we have not had a visitor, especially as one as young as you for quite some time. I will be glad when the sons of Draccus return from this horrible war, and also put an end to the Black Corsairs!" Byris stood there smiling at Lithius.

"Yes, indeed. Has anyone ever tried speaking to the Grand Conciliate on these matters?" Lithius asked looking sternly at Byris.

"Yes, of course, at first it did little good, but over time, Morderra-Atrauis has replaced members of the Grand Conciliate with his own, giving him even more power than ever. Now I am afraid, you know, complaining will only get one killed."

"Pity" Lithius said softly as he headed for the living room. He knew from before that Byris was expecting the return of the Corsairs, and he knew from Byris's thoughts, that this time will be worse than ever.

"Is there anything, anything I can do to repay the hospitality you and Tyra have given me?" There it was a chance for Byris to mention about the thing that most troubled his thoughts throughout the day.

"No, nothing you can do, except…" Byris put his hand on Lithius' right shoulder as they walked out of earshot of Tyra towards the living room.

"Take Tyra with you, there is great danger in the village coming forth in a few days, and I cannot asked her to stay, she has, in the passed been a victim of the Black Corsairs' cruelty. She is a very fair looking woman, and she needs not to suffer any longer" Lithius certainly did not intend for this and looked surprised at Byris.

Byris feeling Lithius's attention, "Listen, true I have not known you for more than just a few hours, but Octavius, I know you are a good heart, take her to Draccarium, there she has relatives, an aunt, her mother's sister, if she is alive, she will take her in, if she has passed, Tyra has cousins. I know this is a great thing I am asking, would you consider this" Lithius getting over his surprise could see it was extremely hard for Byris to ask of this.

"I am in a hurry" Lithius wanted to say more, but Byris touched him and Lithius thought of what the Black Corsairs, and he knew this was a way to get Byris daughter out of the way of the violence coming forth.

"She will not slow you down, and she certainly knows the way" Lithius obviously had nothing to do with going by Draccarium, his intentions were to find a way along Thuma-Attarrach and face Morderra-Atrauis as he was trained for, and now this. If Mydyr were still alive, he would certainly be disappointed at the very thing that Lithius was about ready to do.

"If we get into some sort of trouble, I cannot guarantee her safety." Lithius was compelled to say.

"Better chance with you, than by herself or for me for that matter." Byris mentioned, "She can fight, but with limitations of course, so will you do this?"

"She will need to travel light, I have my own to carry, and she cannot slow me down." Lithius warned.

"I understand."

"Besides Byris, she might not want to go?" Lithius asked with a slight puzzled look on his face.

"She is my daughter, I will contend with this, nothing for you to worry about my friend." Byris added.

CHAPTER 13

▼

Lithius prepared to leave, he put his pack on last, and his bow and a quiver of arrows, adjusted his girdle that contained his sword and scabbard.

"I shall wait outside, see that she carries the food, it will take how long you figure to enter Draccarium with two people?"

"If you leave tonight, like you plan, you should end up where you need to be in two days. When you get into Draccarium, passed the gates, she will find her own way at that point." Byris said somewhat dejected, "I cannot have her, my only living child suffer so much, do you understand?"

"Yes, yes I do" Lithius certainly understood, but in spite of this, he felt conflicted.

"I'll be outside waiting" Lithius then turned for the door, he looked back only once forcing a smile across his face, for he knew this would be, without a doubt, his last time seeing Byris alive.

"I'll take the best of care I can for her safety." Lithius did not wait for a response, turned towards the door, and walked out closing the door behind him. It was dark and the air filled with the autumn coolness. Both moons were in nearly full phases, and he had more than enough light to see in spite of the spotted cloud cover. As he stepped off the porch, he looked up at the night sky, "Yet another delay" He didn't seemed so conflicted, he understood fully what would of happened if she stayed, she no doubt would end up as dead as Byris, and perhaps, even worse. He knew there were worse things than just dying, especially for a woman, he remembered his mother and what the Tarvas dogs did to her before she died in the high mountain pass, a memory that always triggered both remorse and rage in his heart.

Thinking of this fact alone in his thoughts, Lithius knew he was making the right choice, and if Mydyr were still alive, it would be something that Mydyr would have to wait upon. For Lithius, this was something he had to do, there was some purpose, some grand design why he met Tyra, and the village of Dearth that was, least for now, beyond his total understanding. "If I am as evil as that hack Kronus claims, then why do I do this?" Lithius scorned in his thoughts. Lithius could hear stirring in the house he just came out from, he could hear Tyra's voice but could not make out what she was saying, other than she seemed angry and bewildered why she was leaving. Lithius could hear Byris's own voice reminding her that she needed to get on with her life, and Dearth was not the place for her any longer, then Lithius heard the old man's voice fade as he continued to listen to the conversation.

Lithius turned west, the sun was well down, and he figured that it was nearly ten or passed as he looked up at the stars. To the west as the slight wind blew from that direction, he could sense there was trouble in the wind, a warning, a deadly harbinger with it. There was no tangible scent in the air, but he knew that Hamahadra was somehow alive, and with her the Lycoi horde. As he stood there as if he could peer into the wind, he was beginning to see that the Lycoi were definitely on the move, they were skirting the tree line of the great forests west, and were quickly approaching Sommer. As he stood there in a near trance, his full attention given to what he was seeing in the gentle wind, a wind that most would not feel, a sense of over whelming death for anyone caught between Sommer and Dearth. There is no mistake, the Lycoi was on to him, but were having great difficulty tracking him, though he realized if it wasn't for Hamahadra, the Lycoi would of never have gotten this far in the first place.

Lithius turned towards the silhouette of Thuma-Attarrach, and it appeared looming over him in the moonlight, reflecting both hues of silvery blue and orange, the hue of light given from each of the moons. Lithius's perception into the mystical world grew suddenly in this moment as he gazed up at the mountain; he realized that the lower portion of the mountain was stirring. The Lycoi there were on the move, forming and banding their resources together as if they were preparing for Lithius. Lithius could also sense it was Hamahadra a part of that as well, but yet there was something else, and as the mild breeze changed to that of the west to the east only momentarily, he picked up there was another, a single presences, a strong dark presence, a male presences, an evil presence. This presence was none other than the evil Pitah himself, Morderra-Atrauis. Lithius has become aware of his powers increasing especially since he has left the ancient forest of oaks, shortly after the demise of Hamahadra's favorite pet. Lithius, though focused on the presence of Morderra-Atrauis, briskly came to the stark conclusion that the Pitah was realizing the movement of the Lycoi, the Lycoi along the timbered slopes of the mountain, Lithius perceived that the sorcerer king's presences wasn't certainly directed towards him, least not yet, it was something more like an observance the Pitah was sensing. Lithius figured most quickly, the Pitah wasn't a fool and it would only be a matter of moments before Morderra-Atrauis realized that the tumult was Lithius's presences or worse yet, his intentions. Hamahadra may likely have warned Morderra-Atrauis of his coming, "…why not?" Lithius thought, "There was nothing keeping her from doing so, unless her powers, perhaps her conflict with Mydyr caused some sort of unforeseen predicament.

As Lithius stood there contemplating this fact after the wind once again changed back to the westerly direction, the air grew still, and his near trance-like behavior faded giving way to the reality about him. He looked over at the doorway and porch of Byris's home. He thought all about the things he has just seen in the wind and realized, if he indeed headed up towards the mountain, he would have walked perhaps right into an ambush.

He wanted to warn Byris, Lithius wanted to go right inside and tell him of the Lycoi danger, who he really was, the full measure on why he was here, and more importantly, what his intension were with Morderra-Atrauis. Lithius realized he couldn't, that would be the last thing Mydyr would ever want, the more people knew, the greater the risk was that the Pitah would indeed find out, along with an accurate description of Lithius no doubtfully taken by a poor victim suffering only moments later with his or her own life, no, he endangered the village enough. Lithius decided that fate would have to run, though he loathed facing it, its course upon the village of Dearth, and specifically the matter of Byris and his plan with several others to make a last, but futile stand against the Black Corsairs. However, by what Lithius saw in the wind, the Black Corsairs may come across another Sommer and finding everyone dead. Unlike the Black Corsairs, the Lycoi are only butchers, not a race that rapes the flesh of neither men nor women. Lithius also thought if the Lycoi attacked Dearth, Dearth would indeed fall, many of the villagers would be hunted down and killed, and this would take time, as they would be looking for him. This of course would buy some time, that is if Hamahadra didn't see through this, didn't know. If she did, or does, she would simply warn the eastern Lycoi, those that dwelt along the dark tall pines of Thuma-Attarrach. He thought about these possibilities, the road to Draccarium would certainly be safer; none would certainly expect that he would be traveling with a woman, and especially to Draccarium.

"This just might work" Lithius thought to himself as the doorway opened fully. There in the light of the fire in the living room, he could see Tyra prepared for travel, walking stick, and pack wearing a heavy waxed denim dress coat that would protect her from the cold rain, leather pants and what looked like a good pair of walking boots. Lithius could also see Byris who kissed her on her forehead as she bent down to hug him. Lithius could also sense that she was saying her final goodbye, she was weeping, and Lithius knew her perception was true about her father and the last of seeing him. Lithius dismissed his thoughts and focused on this moment he was witnessing of the two.

As he watched, he wondered, there may have been a time where he could have said goodbye to his parents when he became of age and it was time for him to go on his own, needless to say, he was never afforded that opportunity. He smiled slightly at this heartfelt moment, "Least you have closure Tyra, and for you Byris" His words were only in his thoughts as he looked on.

Moments later, the door closed behind the two, Byris said to his daughter a final goodbye and a blessing, a hope for her future as Lithius noticed that Byris was overcome by the moment, he loved his daughter, and it showed.

Lithius in this moment, though yards away, imagined briefly for a moment what it could have been like for the both of them, no war, no terror or hostilities from a tyrannical king, she, Tyra living with her husband, a farmer in this very village.

Lithius imagined, Tyra and husband with Byris with his grandchildren all together, eating, and celebrating, or something." Lithius thought to himself as he watched. "Not in this life" He answered sharply back to himself under his own breath, "…not in this life."

Tyra in the moonlight was especially beautiful, her dark eyes seemed like a twin abyss, her slender nose and cheekbones caught the moonlight, she was a fair Draccus woman indeed. Now she was leaving the only thing she clung to so terribly unyielding, her father's presence. Lithius remained silent as they walked out of the village, Lithius could see her, from the corner of his eye on his left as she would turn and wave, sobbing. He pretended not to notice and continued up the path that lead to another path turning south passed Kur's place, and within a few moments completely out of eyeshot of Byris. Lithius walked passed the point on which he first met Tyra and continued heading south in silence as she cried. He wanted to hold her, her pain was something he didn't care to see, it bothered him, he didn't grab her in fear she would think her life would be in danger. However, he couldn't go on pretending that he wasn't paying any attention.

He turned, stopped, and faced her. "I can only imagine on how you are feeling, life here is hard, hard for a good many people, you have suffered so much and I am afraid if I comfort you, you will take it wrong and—"

He was cut off when she lunged forward and hugged him as she began to cry bitterly. He stood there in the moonlight and held her for a few quiet moments; he could feel her fears, her uncertainty, and anxiety. He just held her, this was the first woman he has ever held, and it was something that felt odd at first, but seemed somewhat natural. He realized that he had feelings stirring about her, but he kept them repressed. Lithius was certainly going to do what was expected of him, but he also knew there were dangers about and as much as he wanted to stand there holding her, he knew this was valuable time, and a vulnerable area to be at.

"Come we must go, we must make up some time, yes?" Lithius said softly and as concerned as he could be.

"All right, okay" She had trouble talking caught in her emotions. Lithius had his map handy, and with the light of the moons, he could easily read the map. He knew this trail, if it was the trail indicated on the map would lead to Illua River, the biggest river of the country, the very same he traveled upon from the ocean so long ago.

"Looking at my map, the very same I used to stumble upon your village with" He attention turned from her own thoughts to the map that Lithius was holding before him as he continued. "...This path, trail leads to the main trail along the river?"

"Yes, yes it does. I know the way." She said as she wiped the tears from her eyes.

"Okay then." He rolled up the map and placed it in the inside pocket of his cloak. "We have a few miles along this path we must cover, it will be at least morning before we are to be about Draccarium." He turned and with his walking stick began walking along in silence for most of the way to the main trail.

Once they reached the main trail, it was early in the morning, the sky cleared completely and the stars were mostly faded from the wash of the moons. "It will be the harvest moons perhaps tomorrow night." Lithius turned towards Tyra who was right behind him step for step.

"Yes, I suppose so." Lithius retreated in silence for only a moment longer.

"Your father told me of an aunt you have in Draccarium?" Lithius asked to strike up a conversation.

"No, well, I had an aunt there once, long ago, not anymore." This caused Lithius to turn once more as he continued to walk.

"Really?"

"Yes, I have no one there anymore, anyone that I have met." This bothered Lithius.

"Your father told me that you have other relatives there?" He almost stopped.

"I do, I just never really met them, besides with the war and all, I do not know if they are still alive or at the very least, still there." He could sense the concern in her voice.

"Yes, okay, but what if" He stopped himself; she had enough on her mind and didn't want to trouble her any further, least not today.

"Never mind" Lithius turned once more in front of him.

They walked until early dawn, the day thus far was clear, and they were indeed making good time, they reached the main trail earlier and began heading east along the very wide Illua River. Lithius didn't see any boats, nor any sign of trouble. The air was still, but he knew that the sun would be warming up the upper atmosphere and that would stir up a breeze, and from there he would take another "reading" to sense with his developing powers. He could hear Tyra's breathing and her ever-increasing heavy footsteps behind him.

"We need to rest, you are tired, and we can catch our breath up there along those trees and get some of your great stew in us. Would that be okay?" Lithius turned briefly towards her as he pointed up at a small cluster of trees.

"Oh, that would be fine." She smiled at him and continued to concentrate on her walking. Lithius knew she was growing tired, no sleep, and her world turned completely in disarray, and a rest would be good.

Within a few minutes, they reached the top of the hill and found two perfectly good stones to rest upon while Lithius helped remove her pack. She then took out two bowls covered in animal skins to protect the stew from spilling, flask of water, and the remainder of the bread. The two ate, mostly in silence as Lithius could see the uncertainty in her eyes growing.

"How long have you been away from home?" She asked in between bites.

"Going on thirteen years all in all." He finished the mouth full of food fully realizing he was sharing the years he was away from his homeland, he wasn't going to lie any longer to her if he could help it.

"Thirteen years?"

"Yeah, there 'bouts." He continued to eat.

"How old are you really?" He could feel Tyra looking at him.

"I guess that would make me about twenty-three or so, give or take a few months."

"You began fighting when you were in your tenth season?" She nearly exclaimed.

"Well the truth, yes, fighting for my life actually, and I haven't quite found the time to stop fighting I guess" He grew silent.

There was a moment that the two were silent; it was Tyra the first to speak up. "The Pitah ordered your family to send you off to war at that age!" Her statement was more like that, rather than a question.

"The Pitah, though I think, had nothing to do with it." He felt very odd about telling her this much, he could see she was growing even more confused about the whole affair.

"The war for me began in the Ramadan lands, and it was from where I am really from." "There, I fucking said it, okay, I fucking said it, now are you happy?" The latter statement he thought to himself, and with that, a sea of relief came upon him, nearly overcoming him.

"Wait, what were you doing there in that land? Was your father in the Grand Conciliate there?"

"No, Draccus has no interests with gentle people, shepherds, and those tending to flocks of animals that live a simple life. A place where at one time, children grew up lived and married to raise children of there own. A peaceful life, and for too many, a boring life to live like that. Having compared my life, to the life that my family wished for me, I would have chosen the latter I'm afraid." Lithius concluded.

"But you are Draccian?" She asked.

"What I appear isn't exactly so." He grew silent again as Tyra oddly began understanding.

"I know that you are a good man, my father said so, and there is nothing to make me think differently about you. I do know you are a complicated man." She said as she smiled slightly.

Lithius looked at her in a gentle surprise that she was taking the conversation so well, he thought she would quickly turn and run screaming "You filthy liar!" he thought. He certainly did not want to tell her anymore and he would have to stop her questioning if that was to be the case.

"You think I am complicated? Okay, I think you are right, and for that we should finish eating, you will want to sleep, and we cannot sleep here. I mean to take you to Draccarium, and from there, you may do as you wish." Lithius tone changed to one more of concern for her safety than wanting to spend a few minutes answering additional questions, besides, it was safer if she knew nothing about him, least for her.

He then spent a few minutes looking at the map and checking their progress with Tyra. Shortly, the two were off again and by mid morning the two were just a couple of miles from Draccus's largest town, Draccarium and behind the city, loomed Thuma-Attarrach. The path or trail turned into a cobblestone road, already there were shops and a few houses along the way. Lithius and Tyra were passed by several horse drawn wagons, and a few of the Black Corsairs on huge Larnges poised along the way, Lithius spotted one sitting upon a black Larnges, he was different, though in the same armor, helmet and black heavy cape, there was something unusual. Lithius only stopped for an instant to peer upon the man that paid no attention towards him, the Corsair wasn't a Draccian, but a man of another race, Lithius found this odd, but realized what race this man was. Though Lithius could only see the man's eyes and bridge if his nose through the turban cloth that came down from the back of the pointed dome helmet lined with animal hair, a thick hair dyed of black. The cloth of the turban helmet concealed a man's identity but also used to keep the dust from his face, but it wasn't enough to hide his color of skin. A pit hit Lithius's stomach as he turned away and his anger rose nearly overtaking his senses. Lithius was able to probe these minds especially. All were in fact looking for anything suspicious or closer to the truth, anyone hauling anything of any value so they could later relieve the valuables from their victim's dead hands however, this man was different.

Lithius wasn't easily allow this opportunity slip through his fingers, only for the present time with Tyra in toe, and knew this man would remain there along the side street. During that morning, Lithius understood their intentions, those who were the Corsairs, and they had no knowledge, least of all those along their watch, had any idea about Lithius or Tyra. They in fact paid no real attention at all of them. Tyra was concealed enough to hide her figure, and like Lithius was dressed down enough not to raise a second look from these cutthroat thieves.

Lithius walked ever so closely to Tyra speaking to her softly and lowly that others along the crowded way could not hear he was encouraging to continue a bit further until they reached an inn. There, Lithius guided her in, and purchased a single room. There, he instructed her to freshen up and get some sleep, there were things he needed to do as he sat his bow, quiver, and his pack down and left. He would come back to the room and sleep upon the floor in a while. She did as instructed without hesitation, the trip thus far had taken its toll upon her, a rest would do her good, besides, Lithius wanted to go back and visit the Black Corsair that he found of interest.

CHAPTER 14

▼

Lithius crossed the street just out of sight of the foreigner, the foreign Black Corsair who was still mounted on his six-legged powerful Larnges. Lithius was certain it was the same man. As Lithius took a side street and an old alleyway, he was close enough now to clearly read the man's thoughts, he too was looking for anyone that he could either take advantage of to fill his pockets or his desires upon the women.

"Scum!" Lithius drew out his small blade that he had found so long ago in the Ramadan frontier and hid his arm with the dagger within his cloak. Lithius was right, the man was indeed a Tarvas, and as he peered into the mind of this man, Lithius found out a few more things, the Tarvas has been to the mountain before, high up along path that led into a cave; from the cave, Lithius could see there was some secret passage. The scene changed abruptly when there was something that caught the attention of the lonely Black Corsair, Lithius was seeing it through the mind of the Tarvas Black Corsair, several others coming up to him, they too were Corsairs on Larnges. Lithius put his dagger back his belt, ebbed back into the shadows of the alley, and waited using his powers to peer into the mind of the Tarvas that was unaware.

Through the physical senses and mind of the Tarvas, Lithius could clearly see and hear the conversation that was beginning from the three riders approaching. Lithius could see the lead man; it was an officer judging by the polished silver helmet above the turban black fabric and fur. His uniform, other than an insignia of his rank, a rank that Lithius wasn't sure about was something this man had on his black leather and mail armor in comparison to all the others with him.

"Good morning Captain!" Lithius could hear and see clearly through the Tarvas.

Lithius could see the captain return a half-formal salute and begin to talk, "Anything to report?" Lithius could see the captain remove the turban vale from his face; he was certainly a Draccian like the others.

"Nothing sir, nothing of interest." The Tarvas answered back as the others remained silent.

"Good." The Captain and his Larnges approached the Tarvas closer as he continued to speak.

"Major Urlez reports that scouts have picked up movement, a rousing among the bastard children of the Pitah" Lithius could see clearly in the mind of the Tarvas that the Captain was referring to the Lycoi along Thuma-Attarrach. Lithius quickly probed the mind of the captain. In doing so, he realized the captain was also unaware. For Lithius, the officer would have more information than the Tarvas and probing his mind would be more useful. Lithius then broke off his mind from the Tarvas and focused on the officer. In doing so, he completely read the officers thoughts and feelings not to mention, see, and hear from the officer's point of view physically.

Lithius could sense that this office had a very low opinion of the one called Urlez or for that matter the Lycoi, "~. What of the Lycoi?" The Tarvas asked.

"Nothing to worry about, there is no threat upon Draccarium, however we are to ride out to Dearth" Lithius rose slightly when the name of the village was mentioned.

"Dearth?" the Tarvas quipped.

"Nothing going on there, just a routine patrol, a routine patrol!" Lithius could feel that the Captain didn't care for what Lithius read as, "a cutthroat scum"

"So far, this guy I like" Lithius thought to himself referring to the Captain.

"I want no funny business or the actions one would take upon innocent people when riding with the major, do you understand?" The Captain asked the Tarvas.

Lithius could see through the Captain the expression in the Tarvas' eyes. The innuendoes of the Captain did not set well with the foreigner.

"Understood, sir." The Tarvas answered.

"Meet us at the Ugly Unicorn in half an hour, I will gather the others." The Captain return the salute and Lithius grabbed enough from the mind of the Captain to fill in any details of Wizard's Island or the exact way of getting there and quickly broke off his link to the Captain's mind. "What luck!" Lithius thought to himself.

The Tarvas sat there in his saddle, Lithius knew right were the Ugly Unicorn, an inn down at the riverfront. Lithius readied himself again, he wasn't going to let this Tarvas scum get away, Lithius already formulated a plan, a plan that might just work with a little luck, physical prowess, and "a shit load of magic!" he thought.

Lithius withdrew his dagger once more, linked up to the unwary mind of the Tarvas, and after seeing a window of opportunity. Lithius through his stealthiness and blinding speed jumped up on the Larnges and with one hand covering the face of the Tarvas from behind, and with the other hand firmly placed on the dagger, Lithius slit the throat of the Black Corsair before the Tarvas realized he was already dead let alone slashed deeply from ear to ear. Warm blood began to ooze slowly out of the fresh wound, as Lithius seemed to master the measure of time that nearly stood still, his dagger already placed back in his belt, and he was off the Larnges before the animal realized it had another occupant. Lithius hit the ground before the body of the Tarvas whose hands and arms were coming up slowly to the fresh gapping wound that jetted out arterial spray slowly with every pulse of his beating heart. If there was a witness that would of seen this horrid event of murder, he would only see a dark blur of Lithius and the Black Corsair falling from his large animal after developing a fatal wound showing the area about the falling man in a rain of arterial spray of his own blood.

Lithius could see the terror in the foreigner's eyes as Lithius watched in slow motion the man fall back from his saddle and onto the ground. As time nearly standing ever so still, Lithius grabbed onto the man's scalp and quickly ushered the body down the alley from across the alley. This caused a physical drain on Lithius, once in the alley, Lithius released his spell, time then resumed as normal around him. Lithius glanced around, and realizing he literally got away with murder, turned towards the dying Tarvas. Without saying a word, as the Tarvas was slipping into unconsciousness from the sudden loss of blood, Lithius began removing the Tarvas' outer garments. Once the Tarvas was finished, Lithius was disguised as the Black Corsair after chanting a short spell that removed the blood of the now dead Tarvas whose heart grew still. Lithius then placed his right hand firmly on his sword, and within a few moments, Lithius looked physically exactly like the dead Tarvas, like so many years ago as Talquardez-Solstas transformed Lithius from a Ramadan child to a Draccian, the sword through Lithius's command transformed him into the likeness of the one he just slain. Looking down at a reflection of a tranquil pool of blood, Lithius could see the transformation; the magic from the sword had taken hold. Lithius was now gone from the alley and upon the great six-legged beast. From the conjuring and the gift of reading the minds and thoughts of the men, he knew enough to ride along as one of the Black Corsairs; his plan was beginning to unfold now. He planned on riding as one of the Black Corsairs, and in doing so; he was going to help rid Dearth of the pestilence of these men finally. If he could help it, Byris would not have to die, and if everything worked accordingly as he thought about it, Tyra wouldn't know the wiser.

In a couple of hours later, as the plan was succeeding as Lithius hoped it would, the Captain had in his company of twelve Black Corsairs heavily armed riding up to Dearth. The village appeared empty; there was no sign of livestock, or the inhabitants. Lithius sensed that Byris was indeed near and watching all of them as they rode down along the main path of the village.

The Captain ordered the men to ready their arms and prepare for an ambush. Lithius peered into the mind of the Captain, Lithius could see that the Captain was certainly concerned about the possibilities of the ambush, but Lithius could also see in the mind of the Captain, that the Captain had absolutely no intention of attacking or plundering this or for that matter, any village under his command. Lithius could see that this man wasn't responsible for the attacks in the past, not like the minds that Lithius probed on the way, many he rode with were veterans of rape, murder, and old fashion robbery. In Lithius's own mind, they were all going to die as sure as he was sitting as one of them, not one would escape his blade of retribution.

Lithius purposely fell unnoticeably behind the eleven before him that rode surprisingly through the village. "Byris, can you hear me my friend?" Lithius sent out through telepathic means.

Lithius said it once more in like fashion and could sense that Byris could hear his warning, but Byris didn't have the gift or the ability to answer in like manner.

"Old friend, this is Octavius, I will cut these foes myself, have your men at the ready when the attack commences, it is not your mind playing tricks, and you must trust this message." Lithius could somehow feel that Byris heard him, but didn't trust the message given. Lithius brought up his bow, notched a black arrow, and shot the one directly in the front of him, the arrow penetrated through the back of the neck and through the throat, sending the man to his silent death from his saddle and before his body hit the ground, Lithius sent two more to their death. The count was nine left when one of the others turned from the single file column entering the village to see what the noise was only to find an arrow piercing his armor breastplate. The Black Corsair sent out a loud grown of pain as he sank into his saddle and began to loosen his grip and fall. The others bolted headlong into Kur and the others that just jumped out of concealment fir-ing off arrows. Lithius then, like before, grabbed his sword, and transformed into his physical being before the Tarvas disguise.

Lithius in plain view threw down the turban helmet exposing his face in plain view as the sound of battle began to ensue. Lithius removed his sword from his scabbard and brandishing the deadly sword he leaped off the Larnges jumped through the air striking another rider who was heading in the opposite direction of the attack from the front. Lithius drove his sword through the chest of the man sending both him and the man to the ground from the hooves of the huge beast. Lithius sword consumed the soul of the one he just attacked. Lithius removed the sword and in a blinding speed managed to dodge several arrows from two other of the Black Corsairs. Lithius caught a moment behind one of the villager's house, with blood oozing down the translucent blade upon the guard of the sword; he caught his breath just long enough to hear Kur's final order before being cut down by an arrow released by a Black Corsair. Lithius knew there were three left, the Captain, and two others, he also knew that, Byris and four others were alive. Lithius sheathed his sword, and drew out his dagger and again through his magical means with blinding speed jump upon the back of the Larnges that contained in its saddle, the bowman that killed Kur. Lithius drove the dagger up through the back of the upper neck into the back of the skull of the man, killing him instantly as the Black Corsair dropped his bow and his arrow flung loosely from its notch.

Byris confused, saw Octavius on the Larnges and realizing it was his friend turned and fired an arrow into the Captain; Lithius rode his Larnges into the other standing next to him that managed to get a shot off into Byris. Lithius drew out his sword and in lightening speed, severed the head from the shoulders of the bowman that sent Byris down to the ground on one knee. Lithius turned and could see Byris had been mortally wounded and was now dying. As Lithius leaped off the Larnges, the battle was over as quickly as it started. The others, the remaining villagers, two indeed were wounded but had certainly enough life in them to harm Lithius who stood there with his blood-soaked sword, Lithius raised his hands up in the air as he spoke.

"I am Octavius, friend of Byris that has come to help fight against the Black Corsairs, please bring down your weapons!"

Lithius then sheathed his sword once again and drew near to Byris who was looking up at him with only one eye open, his right. His teethe were clinched together as his face was riddled with pain as Lithius could see the arrow's shaft squarely placed in his chest.

"It is I, Octavius!" Lithius knelt down before Byris who was gasping and coughing up a mixture of oozing blood and saliva.

"I cannot believe it is you my friend, I don't understand how you got here" Byris was having a hard time speaking.

"Where is Tyra?" Byris reached out and grabbed Lithius left shoulder with his right arm and clutched the young man's shoulder in pain.

"She is safe, safe I swear it." Lithius looked into the dying eye of Byris.

"Thank you for all of" Byris's voice faded into a cough.

"It was my honor my friend. But I fear there is nothing I can do for you, the arrow is deep"

"I know" Byris returned as the other two villagers drew nearer.

"Take good care of my only daughter" He paused as his look in his eye began to glaze over from the intensity of pain subsiding into death.

"Soon I will be with my fathers and my son who await for me on the other side my dear friend of much mystery"

"I will take good care of her" Lithius didn't know how he would, but he couldn't say any different not to a dying man, and his first, his truly first friend that caught him by somewhat of a surprise.

"I go now" Byris then rolled over as the grip on Lithius's shoulder gave way. Byris was gone from this world and heading to those that awaited him on the other side.

Lithius arose with his eyes watering as he looked at the other two, Lithius could hear off in the distance another battle, far to the west of the village, the Major and his men rode headlong into the Lycoi, the very same that were tracking Lithius from days ago. Lithius then turned his attention to the men before him; they were as old as Kur and Byris.

"Each of you take a Larnges, behind you to the west is a vast number of Lycoi that are fighting the Black Corsairs. Don't ask me how I know of this, but you must trust me know, waste no more time and run for your fucking lives to the north, and keep riding until you reach the safe haven of your people you have hidden. Gather them and head north to the fishing villages, there you will find safety in there numbers." Lithius warned.

"How do you know this?" as he turned to the west peering with his failing eyesight.

"Go or be dead like the rest of these men!" Lithius drew out his sword as the two men, though still confused began doing his bidding. Off into the western horizon, blood curling screams and cries carried ever so faintly in the wind, barely audible, but discerned clearly enough by the remaining standing in the village.

Lithius then walked over to the fallen Captain who now fully expired and looked down upon him, the Captain's body rested face down in the mud, "Wrong place, right time" Lithius then took the gold coins from the fallen, and it was quite a sum and buried Byris behind his own home. On his way back from the house, Lithius filled his quiver full of arrows and anything else, which was very little he needed, Lithius then mounted a Larnges that was growing somewhat edgy due to the Lycoi and killing to the west. Lithius watched from the saddle long enough to see the two remaining Dearth men take off in a northern direction for a few moments until they were out of eyesight of Lithius.

Lithius sat there looking around at the dead, his plan had been a success up to entering the village, there its primary objective had failed, he couldn't save Byris, and no amount of magic that he knew could bring him back alive, and what was he suppose to tell Tyra anyhow?

Lithius pondered that for a moment, she would never understand his power, let alone failing to safe her father's life. No, this was something that he would have to keep secret. Lithius turned his Larnges back to the direction on where he left Tyra, his hopes was that she was still resting, fast asleep and would awake and find him there.

Lithius rode off leaving Dearth for good as he thought, there was nothing left there to come back to.

CHAPTER 15

▼

Lithius walked into the room to find Tyra still sleeping, he had completely shed the Black Corsairs' garb and sat there in the chair, the fast ride back, the day's adventure and battle, and the fact of not retaining any real sleep in a few days wore him out completely.

When Lithius finally awoke from the comfortable chair, he looked over at the bed and could see Tyra was gone. It was obviously nightfall as he could see the stars in the dark sky through the window next to the bed as moonlight from one of the moons shown in through allowing enough light for him to see clearly around him. As he arose to his feet, he heard someone on the other side of the door in the Inn right next to him; he drew out his dagger as the key tumbled the lock at the door. The door then opened slowly and the light catching Lithius directly in the face made it nearly impossible for him to see as he brought up his free hand to his brow to see through the light, there he could see the fine-figured silhouette of a woman, it was Tyra. He withdrew his dagger quickly, put it away inside of his belt, and quickly apologized as he allowed Tyra to enter the room. His eyes were now adjusting to the sudden darkness as Tyra then lit up a candle that was furnished in the room. It looked like she was carrying a bundle of what appeared as clothing. As his eyes adjust well enough, he could sense he was still very tired and sat back down in his chair.

The sweet-smelling perfume then filled the air around him, he looked over at Tyra, and her hair was wet and needed to be combed as she then sat down the bundle of clothing on the bed. She was dressed in a very nice light blue and white maiden's dress, though not fancy in design, but practical and the fabric not as heavy as the denim that Lithius could see was the bundle of clothing. He could see that the clothing was clean, and next to the foot of her bed, were her pack, walking stick, and her boots.

"Sorry to have wakened you, Octavius." She said as she turned to face him. Lithius took notice on how pretty she was, she obviously washed the dirt from her, bathed, and had time to shop at the market while he was sleeping.

"That is all right, I guess I just need a few hours of sleep."

"A few hours, really?" She commented.

"Late yesterday, all of today is closer to the truth I would say." She said with a smile.

Lithius found this at first hard to believe, "I slept all of today and part of yesterday?"

"Yes, afraid so." She smiled once more.

Lithius looking perplexed turned to face the window once more, realizing he was tired from sleeping and the grogginess was leaving him. It was the first good sleep he has gotten in some time.

"I went shopping earlier waiting for you to get your rest." She added.

"I see." Lithius then got up as the perfume was consuming he senses, he felt drawn to her beauty, and this was something he certainly was not used to, these feelings; he needed to get his mind on something else. In a moment, something did come to mind, by now the Lycoi had come upon Dearth, finding nothing but fresh bodies strewn about, they would have ransacked the village and possibly burned it to the ground before moving on. Lithius figured that they still would be after him; changing identities would not change his scent. He also knew that Draccarium was a city entirely too big for the Lycoi to attack, and the village that he was in now, he was safe, they wouldn't dare attack. Without Hamahadra, Lithius figured that they, the Lycoi would give up the chase and head back to the ancient woodlands.

Lithius had certainly obtained enough information from the Captain of the Black Corsairs and his men to know a good idea what was in store for Lithius on his way up to the summit of Thuma-Attarrach to Wizard's Island and the entrance there of. He also knew in some measure of the great dangers of the thick pine forest leading up to the tree line of the mountain and the creatures that lurked there in the darkness.

The magic and conjuring of the past couple of days drew enough energy from Lithius, but he knew enough that Talquardez-Solstas was the center of his strength in magic, Mydyr's most powerful weapon ever created was this sword, Talquardez-Solstas. The possessor that brandish this weapon would over time, grow in strength and power. For Lithius, over time, he has grown in both in physical strength and power, the sword enhancing his gifts, and adding skill far beyond his years, Lithius had everything he needed, except one thing, one thing the sword couldn't do, and that was companionship. He looked back once more at Tyra which was spending this time combing and brushing out her long black wet hair before the mirror on the desk as she sat on an old wooden chair.

"I would imagine you are ready to go on to Draccarium?" Lithius looked at her reflection in the mirror as she shortly stopped brushing as he spoke before continuing.

"Yes, whenever you are ready, tomorrow morning would be fine." She flashed a nervous smile as her dark eyes looked back at him with the mirror.

"Great, did you eat supper already?" Lithius responded.

"No not yet, and this Inn has some good food."

"Good, when you are ready, I will meet you down for some supper." Lithius then got up and hesitated on grabbing his sword, it would be safe; anyone that would try to take the weapon from Lithius would suffer a fate worse than death as he was warned by Mydyr so long ago. It would look odd for Lithius taken a sword on where he was about to go.

"I will go and bath now" He then left the room and headed to the bathhouse he remembered seeing on his way into the Inn.

Once at the bathhouse, his first bath in such a place, he found a bit awkward, but the hot water soothed him as his clothing was taken out to be clean. After his bath and his clothes cleaned, he purchased a pair of new knee high black boots, a new cloak to replace the old and frayed. His new leather boots added spring and comfort to his steps, besides they were the best that the gold could buy. The other pair, a pair he took from a hunter that attempted to kill Brakar-Baine a few years ago, and then the boots were old and they were just a size larger than what Lithius needed. These boots fit well as if they were made for only him.

As he walked back to the Inn on where he would find Tyra waiting at a table for him, he passed to men, older men in the marketplace, they were well to do judging by the clothing and jewelry. He couldn't help but overhearing the two in a spirited conversation of some news, they both had heard.

"I am telling you, it's all the fault of Pitah Morderra-Atrauis bleeding this country dry," One was saying to the other as Lithius stood out of eyesight of the two for a moment.

"…The Lycoi had grown very bold to have attacked a main column of the Black Corsairs!"

"The lesser of the two evils I'm afraid." Added the other with half a smirk as the other nodded in agreement, as the first continued to speak his point.

"There was another column that I heard about that according to the Lieutenant of the post said it looked like the Captain fell to another type of tragedy, most different that the Major." The one grew silent only for a moment, shifted his eyes to see if anyone was eavesdropping on their conversation. Lithius turned his back, knowing he could use his powers if need be, but felt there was no need.

"Yes, my friend, he says there was a village uprising in Dearth of sorts, a few stood against the good Captain." He paused as the other interjected.

"As good as the Captain may have been he was running with a vile group of cutthroats."

"Yes, indeed. They found a Larnges from one of the Black Corsairs less than one mile from here, empty saddle and no sign of its rider. The Lieutenant ordered a search but came up short, nothing." He shrugged his shoulders in a perplexing manner.

"What of the village elder, did they question him?"

"What elder, there was nobody left, nothing much to find after the Lycoi had their way to the village." The first added.

"Where are the foul Lycoi now?" The second asked.

"The Lieutenant who is now in sole charge of the outmost" The two broke out in momentary laughter as if they were mocking the officer's leadership skills resumed speaking to one another.

"…says that the Lycoi in large numbers changed direction and were heading north following what scouts believe are tracks of two or three Larnges, perhaps the assailants that survived the battle with the Captain and his men possibly. Who's to say, but the Lieutenant rests that the Lycoi, possibly several hundred—" He was cut off by the other standing there.

"A couple of hundred!"

"That's what the Lieutenant suggested." The two broke out in laughter again.

"Absurd! No such thing!" The second said in a mocking defiant tone.

"Well it was certainly enough to finish the Major and his ruffians to the quick." The second stopped laughing and that sentence wiped the smearing smile off the second's face.

Lithius began walking once again as not to bring any notice to their attention as he headed back to the Inn.

Once there in the Inn, there were rumblings of solemn conversations throughout the main floor of the Inn. He knew what the discussions were about, the demise of many members of the Black Corsairs and the attack of the Lycoi on Dearth.

Lithius found Tyra who had her hair pulled back in a single ponytail, her face had glow the moment her eyes made contact with Lithius as he smiled and walked up to the table and sat across from her. She was looking even more beautiful than ever. As he sat down, he knew she hadn't heard of the news buzzing throughout the village about Dearth. He didn't know how long that would keep, if he could manage to avoid her hearing of such news, he could get her to Draccarium. He realized that she would eventually find out, but that didn't have to be tonight.

"Did you order yet?" Lithius asked as she smiled in return.

"I am waiting for you, Octavius."

Lithius picked up the wooden plaque that contained the menu of food that the Inn offered, "Looks good." Lithius commented.

"It is, the steak is wonderful, though the salad and greens could be fresher."

He looked up from his wooden plaque and smiled, "I bet you are right."

A waitress in leather and dark denim then went to take their order, "You make the choice for us Tyra." Lithius asked.

"All right" She then turned her direction to the older woman who took the order and left.

"You know it's only less than a two-hour walk from here to Draccarium, if we leave first light, we should be there by breakfast." Lithius could sense a measure of excitement to Tyra's voice.

"Yes, that is true enough." Lithius then looked around the main floor and he could see up at the bar from across the smoke-filled room several local villagers in heavy conversations about the turn of events. There were several at various tables between Lithius and Tyra from the bar all talking amongst themselves, the room was filled with many people, some regular villagers, others from out and about the local area. There were no soldiers or members of the Black Corsairs amongst any of these people. Lithius began gently probing the minds of those that looked somewhat suspicious in their elements. Lithius found in a few moments, nothing to concern himself with, and those along the bar, they were full of themselves as they discussed the issues that were raising fear amongst the villagers of a possible attack.

Lithius then turned his direction back to Tyra who was looking down at the top of the table in her own thoughts.

"You look simply wonderful Tyra." Lithius said softly.

She looked up at him, her excitement turned to concern of uncertainty, and Lithius needed no special spell, gift, or magical knowledge to understand why.

"Thank you" Growing silent once again as she stared at the tabletop.

"I know this is a huge change for you" Lithius's heart was oddly, as he thought, pulling towards her once again as he found it rather difficult to speak to her, he grappled for the cup of cool water to coat his drying mouth and to give himself a moment to select his words. It was far easier for him to kill a man than to say the things he wanted to say to her right now.

"What is?" She looked up directly at him as he cautiously sat his water back down to the table.

"Leaving your father I mean, leaving the surroundings that you are accustomed to for so long, this is what I mean." His words were subtle but with purpose as he looked into her eyes.

"I see, I suppose so" Her voice faded as he strained to hear them.

"I hope that I still have family to claim me in the city. You see, my father has not kept up with my mother's side of the family for some time, they're not very close you see." Lithius continued to listen.

"Perhaps you have employment for me at your farm?" She questioned looking at Lithius hard, "Or was that a lie too?" She was perceptive; perhaps she gave more thought to their discussion from the other day.

Lithius's face welled up with blood as he hated to lie or continuing being deceptive to her, especially now. He returned the sharp look, took a moment before answering knowing full well the gold coins he acquired at the battle in Dearth was certainly a very sizable sum, so much in fact, he could quite easily buy a farm. "That's it, I could buy a farm for her, and she could live out her years at her very own place" The idea vanished with the thought, "The first thing she'd do is to return to Dearth, and there she would once again fall upon heartbreak." His focused returned to her still looking at her.

"No, I have no farm, least of all not in this land." She reeled back in her chair in somewhat of surprise.

"I knew it, I mean I figured that as much about you, and what of your mother, let me see, there is no mother either, is there?" Her anger turned to mockery, and that was something he could not tolerate.

Striking his fist like a hammer upon a blacksmith's anvil, the table shook nearly spilling the contents of his wooden cup and knocking the wooden menu tablets to the floor certainly got her attention along with several others.

"Enough!" Lithius exclaimed his voice pointed like a fine tip of a sword piercing her chest.

"Enough already" He turned his attention around to the others, who then realized he was looking at them, in turn directed their attention to what they were doing before his sudden outbreak.

He could see she was upset by his reaction, "You need not know anything more of me. I am nothing but trouble in the most worst of ways." Lithius explained.

"So everything you told me and my father is a lie?"

"Pretty much, yes." His voice lowered.

"Did you lie about your name as well?" She said lowly.

"Yes, that too, does that surprise you?" Lithius returning a fierce look at her leaning towards him as to be somewhat courteous so others would not over hear them talking.

"If my father was here, he'd—" She was cut off by Lithius.

"If he was here, I wouldn't need to be, would I?" He then leaned back at his chair, disgusted mostly with himself forever having to lie, and he was wishing that they had met entirely on different set of circumstances.

The two were silent only for a moment, Lithius realizing that he was no longer hungry and looking across the table at Tyra that couldn't even face him now as she was beginning to sob. Lithius arose from the table and went to the room. He gathered his things, laid the heavy bag containing the gold coins, and opened the window. He felt very bitter about the whole thing, the outcome of Byris that lay buried and Tyra realizing that most of what she known of Lithius was built upon a lie. He went back towards the door, looked into the mirror, and saw his reflection, a reflection of a Draccian. He stood there only for a moment as he saw himself. He gripped the handle of his sword tightly as the anger of his reflection and the events the last few days mounted to a summit as high as the lofty peak of Thuma-Attarrach looming in the window.

"Change me to whom I truly am I am Ramadan!" He wasn't sure if it was going to work; after all, it wasn't he that first changed from a Ramadan boy to a Draccian in the first place. Later he found it was Mydyr all along that did it from afar when Lithius fought Kronus.

As Lithius stood, his hair turned to a dark brown with highlights of lighter brown and red, his skin began changing to a darker olive color and his eyes returned there thin almond shape showing his green eyes and pupils. He then could see the white in his eyes; he was now back into his natural self. It was the first time he has seen himself, and for the first time as a man before the mirror. His anger subsided as the change continued. He wasn't as tall, but his shoulders were wider and his arms thicker with muscle as like his legs. As he stood there, he realized his physical strength. His high cheekbones and thick brow came in along with his slightly widening nose; differ from the long sleek beadlike nose most common with the Draccians. He was still indeed very tall, and as he looked into the mirror more closely, he realized, he had favored his father in so many ways. His chest expanded filling out his garments nicely, he was indeed powerful, and now it showed, all those years of training and living a life in the woods has certainly shown.

He had to adjust his girdle, the wide belt that contained his sword, he then went to the bed, grabbed one gold coin from the pouch, put on his leather gloves, and adjusted his pack, grabbed his walking stick and headed out the door. He realized that Tyra would not recognize him in the least; there was nothing in common, with him now in this shape, his true self.

As he slowly approached her, the food was just being delivered to the table, he had no intention of sitting, and he could look over and see her crying a bit, wiping her eyes with silver or pale white handkerchief. The waitress remained quiet as she placed the meal and walked away.

"Fool!" Tyra cursed herself under her breath, "You could have handled this so much better."

"Excuse me?" Lithius said as she turned to look up at him, she recognized the voice, but as she looked up at the foreigner who appeared odd, a mist of confusion covered her.

"Are you talking to me?" She asked.

"Yes" Lithius could see that she had no idea who he was, even though he was in Octavius' clothing and walking stick.

"Pardon me, but Octavius wanted me to give this to you, says it will cover the cost of the meal. He also says he is sorry for the deception and has made good of any pain he might have brought to you, it is in your room, upon the bed." She looked surprised still, and wanted to ask this foreigner a question. Lithius was standing around he was leaving her there; she became more of a problem to him now.

"Where is he, where is he now?" She asked frantically.

"He is gone my lady, went out the back way." Lithius pointed towards the other side of the Inn.

"You sound just like Octavius, oddly you are not him, but yet you wear the same clothing, similar walking stick and bow and pack. Who are you?" Her voice raised in anger, as she was feeling bewildered and somewhat betrayed.

"Lithius, my name is Lithius." As her mouth opened in realizing the name, as she covered her mouth with her hand, "Others such as you, yourself, have referred to me as Brakar-Baine, my lady." He walked out of the room into the darkness. She arose and ran to the door of the Inn along the wooden boardwalk of the village.

Lithius was well across the street in the shroud of darkness there he could see her clearly under the light of the main lamp above her head illuminating the sign of the Inn. She began to realize that somehow Octavius, Lithius, though physically different were one of the same, and that childhood monster, Brakar-Baine was nothing more than the man her father trusted with her safety. Lithius could sense these things from his vantage point.

"Goodbye Tyra wished we had met in another time, in another place." He then faded into the darkness of the night heading for Draccarium.

CHAPTER 16

▼

Oddly enough, for Lithius, he felt better; he was back on his own with one single objective in mind, Morderra-Atrauis. Yes, he thought deep within himself as he cut over the main rode and within a couple of hours later away from the city lights of Draccarium along the lower slopes of Thuma-Attarrach. He thought of Tyra, the look on her face of the gold coin she'd find and her future, for the most part, that is if she'd play her cards right, was secure, and for that, he thought no more about her. He was now entering dangerous territory now, he knew no matter what identity or disguise he would use, Hamahadra knew what he naturally looked like, and assumed that Morderra-Atrauis did as well, in spite of this, he felt good about his decision of changing to his natural self, seeing himself has he naturally is.

He had gained enough information from the various minds of the Black Corsairs to navigate through the perils of these woods. Normally, the Black Corsairs, those chosen to visit Morderra-Atrauis, went along the path above the city that coiled steeply around the mountain like a coiling serpent. The trail lead to a cave, from the cave there was a secret and heavily protected passage that lead to an opening several thousand feet above the end of the main trail. From there, under the waterfall, the hidden opening lead to another wide but steep path towards the top of the mountain, there, the path led to another cave, and like the first cave, this too was heavily guarded. That cave led to a trail on the top of the summit that overlooked Wizard Island far below in the lake. The trail then turned and led downward into the crater, from there, a bridge, a drawbridge lowered would allow the men to cross over to the Island itself. Upon the top of the wooded island of pine, the original top of the mountain long before it blew in a volcanic eruption was Morderra-Atrauis's castle spiraling steeply up in the air made of the obsidian and marble stone.

Lithius could see from the thoughts of those he took them from, the entire castle, rooms, and especially the dungeon far below the castle, it was here that Lithius would find Kronus, and among the old priest, that is, if still alive, others who Morderra-Atrauis secretly placed to rot the rest of their lives in darkness. However, there was something else; something that Lithius could seem to get his arms around, the Captain had thoughts of something else, something more sinister below the dungeon, another level entirely. Mydyr spoke of this place long ago in Lithius' teachings vaguely as if it were Morderra-Atrauis crypt or source of power; perhaps secrets of the Netherworld, Lithius didn't receive any additional information about the likelihood of this place. He wasn't certain if the place even existed at all. There was nothing in the thoughts of these men of these men, any of them that have actually been there themselves.

Lithius now with bow in hand kept from the trail, following along the direction of the path from several hundred feet below the trail in the dark woods, there were the Lycoi who were much larger, and as reports suggested, smarter than any Lycoi that he had ever encountered. There were other things, things that he picked up from the thoughts of the Black Corsairs, ghosts, apparitions, and ghouls that Lithius found difficult to ponder. Yet, there were thoughts of those he took from that have seen what they thought were ghosts. Lithius didn't have much difficulty believing these things, after all, he knew that all things carried with them some sort of a life force, a soul; after all, his sword collected these souls to be used in the bidding of the one who possessed the sword and his experiences with the ghosts of Adajahara. It was those other things he was seeing in the thoughts of those men he had probed, of strange creatures, creatures that seemed more of spirit than of flesh, and were these things somehow creatures from the Netherworld, something like the world of "...Mydyr or that bitch, Hamahadra?" Lithius thought.

By daybreak, he was nearly halfway to the mountain using his magic and at the timberline. He had to be careful, his power to transcend distances quickly was wearing on him, the mountain was steep and now he was near the face of the huge cave and already he could see the guards, four Black Corsairs standing towards the mouth of the cave brandishing large axes and pikes.

The air was especially cool and dry, as he turned around to the westerly direction, he could nearly see all of western Draccus. He could peer as far as the hills passed the very oak forest he spent most of his life at, and beyond that, the dark horizon. He looked towards the north and could see the ocean from afar, and to the south, the great river changing direction to the west as if it were a large snake across the farmlands and forests. Also to the south, he could see dark brooding clouds coming his way, and with them, much rain. The building storm was a good day away if not more; he knew he was at least ten thousand feet up from the rolling hills and valleys below.

Lithius in concealment thought about disguising himself as a Black Corsair once again, but he had no Larnges, he didn't care, he knew those that were guarding the entrance would need orders, a scroll of expressed permission to enter the cave to continue either by the Grand Conciliate or by Morderra-Atrauis himself. Lithius realizing this from the thoughts he acquired smiled and took out his map, rolled it, and changed his appearance once more as a Black Corsair. He then backtracked down away from the opening of the cave, and walked along the trail up to the cave's entrance. He appeared as a Draccian Black Corsair to them through use of his conjuring magic.

Lithius transformed the map into a written statement from the Captain's memory of orders to audience with Morderra-Atrauis inner staff of the Grand Conciliates' plans or initiatives for the Pitah's approval, complete with signatures. This was going to work, or there would be four dead guards, Lithius reassured himself.

"Good morning!" Lithius exclaimed breaking the conversation of these guards now turning and looking upon him.

"Yeah that it is." Said one of the men, an obvious leader of the guards.

"What brings you all the way up here?" The leader spoke looking at Lithius suspiciously.

Before Lithius could answer, "Where is your Larnges?"

Lithius had the map rolled up in his hand and went to hand it to the leader waiting to see the scroll. The leader opened the scroll, looked up at Lithius only for an instant, and back at the writing as the other stared at Lithius as if without warning they may have to strike him down.

"The Lieutenant sent me afoot the day before; he could not spare a Larnges, besides I am on his shit-list about something." The others laughed as Lithius saw a smile stretch across the face of the leader.

"I see, so I haven't seen you around before?" The leader looked up at Lithius with one eye squinting from the light of day.

"I got transferred from the south, from Dartanian."

"Dartanian?" Lithius realized the leader seemed to know of this city to the south.

"Yes."

"Shit, I am from there, is good ole Kellingar still in charge?" Lithius could peer quickly enough into the leader's thoughts that this Killingar was nothing more than a local magistrate in Calpurnium. It was obviously a trap.

"Kellingar?" Lithius asked, "I don't know of the name, unless you are talking about that old codger in Calpurnium that thinks he's the next Pitah." Lithius answered back. "You must be thinking of Mandigar, Colonel 'Iron Fist' Mandigar of the Dartanian post before he was sent to Gaelund, right?" Lithius probed enough into the mind of the leader to convince him and the others that Lithius seemed authentic enough.

"Yeah that must be it?" Leader handed back the scroll to Lithius in displeasure wearing a coy smirk.

Lithius rolled up the scroll and placed it safely in his inner pocket of his cloak, "Are we finished here, I do not want to keep the Pitah waiting." Lithius responded with a measure of satyr in his voice that raised a smirk from all the others standing before him.

"Sure, you know the way?" The leader asked.

"I've been briefed but this of course is my first time."

"Stay along the lighted path, do not stray off, or it will be your last." The Leader warned and then stepped aside allowing Lithius to pass through.

"Take a torch from the bin below. There you will receive any additional information, in addition do not forget to sign in, that way we know who you are if you should stray away and find yourself dead." The Leader smirked once again.

Lithius didn't respond, he just continued down the dark path away from the cool dry air into an air that seemed damper and dismal, an air he remembered as a youth in Adajahara. As he walked down the cave, from the entrance which was purposefully kept dark as not to give its location to onlookers or those far below, the cave dipped downwards steeply veering left and then to the right and back up steeply to the top. By now, it was certainly dark; Lithius had difficulty seeing well enough. Once at the top crossing over, Lithius began seeing some sort of a soft orange and reddish glow, it was the torch light. He was soon up before the bin, and standing there were several heavily armed guards. Lithius presented his scroll disguised as an official document allowing him access to the castle far above. Here he noticed that the cave narrowed and the walls were of obsidian that reflected the light a good distance adding brilliance in seeing much farther.

Lithius wasted no time, and signed the book after being briefed, these men were more serious about their tasks and Lithius refrained from using comical conversation, he kept his answers short and to the point. He then was given the torch after entering the name, a name he wrote down as Byris Dearth. He didn't know

Byris's last name, it was never told to him, and perhaps, Byris had, like Lithius, no last name. He then followed the path, he was briefed if he left the lighted path along the way, he could be lost in some sort of inner cave, a labyrinth of smaller caves, chasms and black abyss' along the way, or become dismembered or wounded by the sharp obsidian shards protruding from the walls like many did before.

As he continued, he noticed the path was both wide and well lit, oil torches, lamps along the way made it easy to travel even with Larnges. The floor was dirt and obsidian crystals from the years of travel, it was certainly a path well maintained.

Lithius continued climbing up the slopes within the huge cavernous cave up to a level area on where he had to walk a mile deep into the mountain, he couldn't see the other end, not from where he was standing, it was too far, and the light reflection made the illusion that it was closed by a wall of fire. As he continued to walk, the air in spite of the torches were cold and damp and already condensation was upon his hand and fingers carrying the torch. He pressed on and once on the other side, a steep turn to the left, he ascended upwards above the great strait of passage he just walked through. As he though, it was much wider, darker, the torches were along the path only and the walls he could barely see on either side, little reflection was given as he continued to climb up the cave's switchbacks. It would be easier for him to ride a Larnges up through here, but if the animal spooked, it could very well through him to his death.

Lithius continued for nearly another two hours until the air changed to a wet turbulence with the sound of rushing water. He was now beginning to see natural light up ahead, and there he would find the final set of guards of this great cave under the waterfall, the highest falls in all of Caledon. Shortly the sound filled his ears, and the torchlight flickered along with the others as the turbulence of the wind created by the rushing water, the torch never went out and Lithius could clearly see, his clothing was drenched.

There before him under a spectacular waterfall, a sheet of water plummeting down thousands of feet stood four guards. Illua Falls, the source, or beginning of this magnificent waterfall was still hundreds of feet above him, fed from an underground stream from within the mountain were also the beginning of the Illua River. He walked up to them cautiously as one of them took his torch, he produced the scroll once more, as one looked it over, gave it back to him and realizing Lithius was new, pointed to the direction of the path that lead from the falls. From the opening of the cave to a trail wide enough for two Larnges in tandem as he continued to walk up the steep cliff away from the main waterfall to a safe location on where he could take in the warm sun and the view of the falls without getting more damp and cold. The mist from the falls caused a beautiful rainbow and shards of color against the black obsidian from the bright sunlight. The waterfall was at least a couple of hundred or so feet above him still. It almost made him dizzy as he looked up at wondrous site. He turned around to face the trail and continued towards the second cave. The air became breezy since he came from the southern face of the mountain, he entered from the west, and he naturally took note of that fact. Once on the northern face of the mountain, high above the tree line, he stopped long enough to peer off into the blue horizon of the great expanse of the sea.

He took a moment and pondered the events that lead him up to this particular place. He was made an orphan from the Ramadan war with the Tarvas, and through a magical intervention of Mydyr, he was spared from certain death of succumbing to the harsh elements of the high pass in the Catanbar Mountains or the even crueler whip of the Tarvas slave masters. As Lithius looked, he could barely make out the high peaks of the Catanbar Mountains, the tallest of all the mountains in Caledon, his world. Lithius remembered the journey from the high mountains to the steppes and crossing the Iratirus River that led him to Naverron who betrayed him in Kronus' plot in obtaining the very thing that kept the boy alive, Talquardez-Solstas. Lithius' life had served a purpose thus far, trained and educated to stay alive, arming himself with both magic and imbued by the sword in skills that surpassed most swordsmen twice his age. His life's journey came to this one particular spear point, to kill Pitah Morderra-Atrauis so that Mydyr would become ruler, and for Lithius, that is if he survived the confrontation, he would have his way with Talquardez-Solstas against the Tarvas. To Lithius this was still the plan in his heart, he wanted to free his people, but the years in Draccus, though despised by the local villagers as Brakar-Baine and hunted accordingly because of nothing more than superstitions and popular beliefs that he was the personified evil in the ancient oak woods. Lithius, in the eyes of these local simple-minded people was responsible for a various unfortunate acts and things based upon these local superstitions. Lithius often thought, as he grew older, how much Mydyr was responsible for in this aspect. Lithius never really had much of a relationship with Mydyr, servant-master relationship at best, nevertheless, Lithius had a strong measure of respect for this being that dwelt in a world much different from his own physical world and understood even less about the Netherworld. Lithius would often ask questions, after all, he had an inquisitive and sharp mind, but his questions were often sidestepped or dismissed by his master that educated him beyond his years in these matters of the Netherworld, and the creatures like Mydyr and Hamahadra that dwelt there but had a strong influence upon Lithius' world.

Lithius in the beginning thought of these beings as godlike, and he realized that Mydyr and the likes of him preferred that notion. As Lithius grew older and wiser, he come to a realization, an epiphany actually, that these beings were not gods, but powerful entities of another sort, something darker, something more mysterious, something that could possibly be destroyed or killed. Lithius realized at least for Mydyr, that these creatures were not all knowing, put very powerful and perceptive nonetheless. He kept these thoughts to himself, deep within him actually, he didn't want to give the impression that his opinion or thoughts on this matter would change, oddly, and he kept these thoughts to himself in the event that he would need to draw from these for whatever reason in the future that he may need.

Lithius trusted Mydyr, after all, the being did save his life on a couple of occasions including Lithius' first encounter with Hamahadra back in the village of Sommer. Lithius trusted Mydyr because of these things, but he also felt there would come a time that he may have to confront Mydyr that would alter his servant-master relationship in the future and prepared for this event no matter how serious it may become. Lithius wasn't afraid of death, he wasn't ready to die yet, he wanted retribution for his people first, and killing only one, Tarvas wasn't even a drop in the bucket in the comparison of contempt he had for those cruel people.

He turned to the west and looked up Draccus far below, the Pitah with his bloodthirsty quest to expand his kingdom in Gaelund, and to the north in Gwarvarik cost this country too much, and in Lithius' mind, over extended Draccus' resources. Lithius' eyes shifted back to the north towards the sea, already the Pitah had many Tarvas men within Draccus, obviously serving him in the Black Corsairs and in other offices and positions. Lithius didn't know the extent of the Tarvas in Draccus, he certainly didn't like it, and in fact hated the thought of it, and for that alone was enough to make Pitah Morderra-Atrauis his enemy.

As Lithius' eyes turned back to the west, he heard rumors of the war in Gaelund, that many after being faced with harsh and costly defeats and high numbers of casualties has turned their attention on returning to Draccus and raise a civil war in hopes of brining the Pitah to the reckoning table. As low as the general moral is in this land, Lithius figured with a sizable force led by a charismatic general returning with armored troops, the spark would ignite of rebellion, even in spite of the Black Corsairs, the people would rise up and demolish any of the Pitah's remaining loyalists which would be very few in numbers.

As Lithius thought about these things briefly, he noticed something that caught his eye from far below the mountain. As he peered, he could see a huge number of Lycoi, hundreds of them sweeping north in the valley far below leaving a small grove of oaks upon a meadow in the open. At first, Lithius thought they were perhaps going forth against the remaining villagers of Dearth, but the change in direction and the unification of the larger Lycoi joining them from the forest pines of the mountain as he could see were in large numbers as well were indeed up to something completely different. Lithius could see several villages on the other side of the valley, small, and defenseless. As Lithius watched, the combined Lycoi forces turned east to the mountain and Lithius, as he watched closely, realized they were after him. The climb would take a couple of days, steep, and some would die in the process, unless there was another passage, a passage he had no idea. One thing that was for sure, they were on to Lithius, and so were Hamahadra and Pitah Morderra-Atrauis. Morderra-Atrauis had to know for sure that Lithius was so close. Lithius wasted no more time, he ventured to the second cave, and he was fully prepared to cut his way through the top of the mountain if he had to. As he cautiously approached the opening of the cave, like the other before this, he was greeted by four guards; he quickly probed their minds, and could see to be on a lookout for anyone new, perhaps a foreigner, and not to let anyone in or out of the cave. The Pitah had no plans or news of anyone needing to audience with him. In fact, unyielding orders were given to arrest anyone claiming to see the Pitah. Lithius could since this news was fresh, just dispatched by an officer of the Black Corsairs, a commanding officer himself to these men.

To Lithius' surprise, three of these four men were Tarvas; they were the first to die as their heads were quickly separated from their shoulders before they had time to react. For the forth, Lithius wasted no time on severely wounding the leader, severing his right arm and left leg from his body by the singing sword of Talquardez-Solstas. The wounded Black Corsair was slow on his axe, and he paid for it dearly as he was bleeding to death.

"I am he that you have been warned against!" Lithius shouted as he heard others from within the cave come forth meeting his blinding fury of his sword that cut deep into the flesh of the remaining four, sparing none. He then covered in blood spatter on his face, turned from the fallen dismembered bodies to the leader who was fading fast in a pool of dark blood.

Lithius with his sword clutched in his right hand, with his left he grabbed the skull of the dying leader and began drawing his thoughts, anything that might assure Lithius in his quest to the top of the mountain and down through Wizard's Island.

Lithius didn't get anything new, but confirmed some things that Lithius doubted from the thoughts of the others. This was only a beginning of his battle to the top; the cave was on level of weariness of an intruder. Lithius looked at this man and like before, conjured up the spell that transformed him to look exactly like this man. He then drove his sword into the bosom of the fallen leader and drained the body of the man's soul.

Lithius then disappeared into the darkness of the cave with eight bodies behind him testifying to his skill as a swordsman and assassin. Little did Lithius know, but the beginnings of the Civil War of the land was becoming fact with the black sails of the ships returning from Gaelund were already upon the Illua River far away with bellows of smoke beginning to rise in the distance.

Lithius using his special abilities ran through the lower part of the second cave with torch in hand, as his approach the second level, a steep level, and one much darker; he was forced to slow down. He could hear the rushing of the water, the underground stream, or river on the other side of the obsidian walls, but this too shortly faded as he continued to ascend towards the top.

He approached the opening several hundred feet away, he was faced with a large number of the Black Corsairs coming at his direction carrying torches, he stood there yelling a warning that the intruder was near and is coming in this direction. As they approached him, he realized that the disguise had worked and the men, twenty in all rushed passed him on foot, and behind them, two men upon Larnges. Passed the two, there was none he could see, he then with his powers, leaped up and dispatched one of the riders, he took his bow and fired directly upon the other before he had so much as a chance to warn the others. Lithius then used the great woolly beast out of the cave and heading through to his surprise the brilliantly reflected fields and patches of snow. He followed the trail up higher along the edge of the crater. There he could clearly see the wide lake and far below on the other side was Wizard's Island, and upon it stood the castle stretching forth up to the sky. He could see small figures of the Black Corsair bowmen reading themselves upon the wall armed with bows awaiting the attack, the attack of one man.

Lithius stood there upon his saddle and quickly realized that Morderra-Atrauis was indeed expecting him, after all, he couldn't just ride up to the castle, though his disguise might get him right up to the castle, but none the less, would allow him to enter beyond the walls. The men that he had just fooled would quickly find that they have been hoodwinked and would come after him. Lithius wasted no more time, he then transformed his features to the Likeness of the Captain that he fought against in Dearth, and it was his only chance of getting close enough to get near the Pitah let alone inside the castle walls.

In a few minutes upon the fast and powerful animal, he was upon the drawbridge that was raised, he yelled up at the guards of the castle and ordered the drawbridge to be lowered, and he had important news to deliver to the Pitah. Lithius was hoping this would work, or he would have to attempt his magic in lowering the bridge, and if successful, he wasn't sure how much strength would be required to do so, and more strength her cared to wager.

CHAPTER 17

▼

The bridge in a moment later was lowered and Lithius quickly rode across and under the bowmen's eyes from above that were trained upon him, there were a small cluster of guards that came forth heavily armed.

"Good to see you, Captain!" One of the men said, a Lieutenant that Lithius ever so quickly probed, he was a friend of the Captain.

Lithius returned a smile and dismounted the beast, as those were ready to lead the animal by the reigns away.

"Good to see you, as well Sariusen!" The disguise was working so far, as Lithius then carefully focused his attention towards Sariusen's thoughts. Lithius could see that there was some confusion in the man's thoughts, but he could clearly see that they, the Black Corsairs were definitely preparing to protect the Pitah at all costs from an assignation attempt upon their ruler. There was something else, something that was as new as the information of this assailant and that was the information of the Lycoi.

"As you can see, Nathal" Sariusen was using the captain's first name in referring to Lithius in a low-keyed voice so the others wouldn't hear the Lieutenant speaking to the captain, his superior by first name.

The Lieutenant turned towards Lithius, "...I have doubled the bowman, and have sent reinforcements to the entrances to be on the watch, no doubt passed them on your way here?" Sariusen asked with a smile.

"Yes, you have done well. Keep the drawbridge up at all times, let no one, absolutely no one enter. This bridge does not come down for nothing, understand?" Lithius was firm.

"Yes sir, you heard the Captain, raise that damned bridge!" Sariusen bellowed.

The two then walked right up to the gate of the castle which raised enough to allow the two in, "Same for the gate my friend."

Again, Sariusen barked the orders of the captain before drawing his attention to the ranking officer.

"Nathal, we just got word that the Lycoi—" Lithius cut him off.

"Yes, overran Dearth, killed everyone there that was still in the village when I got there with my men."

"Right, but there is a rumor, that your men might have been killed by others, other than the Lycoi, is that true?"

Lithius stopped walking, turned to the Lieutenant and with a serious look, "No, it was the Lycoi, and they put down the Major and his men."

"Yes, you are the only one that made it out of there, but some said you were dead too, I found that hard to believe and hoped that you would of made it out alive, and thanks be to the gods, you are!" Sariusen then put his hand firmly on Lithius's shoulder.

"Thank you for your prayers, now lead me to the Pitah at once, I must tell him of the looming danger of the Lycoi joining with the tribe of Lycoi about the mountain." Lithius could sense in the eyes of the one he was deceiving through his disguise as the man's friend, Lithius could see a look of fear and concern of this news.

"Nathal, the Pitah is not seeing anyone, and rumor has it, he is far below." Sariusen looked down at his feet and Lithius could see in Sariusen's mind of a place far below the dungeon.

"Take me there, he shall see me!" Lithius ordered.

"Nathal" Sariusen's voice lowered as he drew nearer to the captain so others could not hear.

"I only know of a place where he is at, never been there, know nothing on getting there, nothing of the way, and none of us here know of the way Nathal, you know that?" Sariusen looking somewhat perplexed at Lithius as he spoke.

"Right, yes you are right, so show me who does." Lithius could see in the mind of Sariusen that it was someone on the inside being revealed. Someone that surely would know the location began revealing itself from Sariusen. Lithius could clearly see in Sariusen's own mind though the young sorcerer's power that it was one of images of the Pitah's acolytes, a shadowy balding old white haired ugly twisted figure called Aberdan that Lithius was seeing in the young officer's mind.

However, Sariusen grew weary of what was happening, Lithius could see this in the young officers thoughts, Sariusen was realizing quickly that Nathal wasn't whom he seemed to be, the young officer had a limited understanding what was happening to him, and an exchange of thoughts between Lithius and him began.

Before Sariusen had a chance to warn the bowman above who was looking the other way, looking outside the walls for impending danger, the danger was obviously within. Lithius with lightening reflexes grabbed his dagger, struck Sariusen in the side of his neck, ripped through, and over the officer's windpipe and jugular veins rendering him incapacitated to talk. Blood gushed into the air and upon Lithius finished the job, grabbed Sariusen, and entered a dark corner of a small entrance to a building, a small stone building out of the eyesight of anyone. Lithius realized by shear luck, he got away with killing Sariusen. Lithius was in the young man's mind and thoughts long enough to realize, the officer was a good man, an excellent quality.

"Too bad for you, that you are fighting on the wrong side my friend." Lithius said in both speech and thought to Sariusen who was dying and thrashing about only for a moment before his death. It was the last thing he heard was Lithius' words.

Lithius then decided quickly based on Sariusen's thoughts of Aberdan, which Aberdan would be forced upon death before revealing the location of Morderra-Atrauis, and Lithius had no time for interrogating the old crone. Lithius knew the last location of this man, and he meant to find him in a hurry, before the others would return.

Lithius left Sariusen's body after hiding it in that room, closed the door, and with his powers literally transferred to one location to the location that he found in Sariusen's thoughts. It was the first time that Lithius was able to cross from one point to the next without taking a step, he was stunned, and he wasn't for sure how he did it, if at all it was he. As he looked around, he found himself in a room, a very large room within the main floor of the castle. There he saw an old man, Aberdan leaving quickly. Aberdan obviously saw him first; Lithius took off after him and caught him in the dark hallway that leads to many rooms.

Lithius spun the old frail skeletal of this dark robed man around quickly with Lithius placing the bloody dagger to the old man's throat just as the old man hissed and went to spit upon Lithius.

The old man, as he hissed, Lithius could see two long upper fangs, long and ivory. This caught Lithius by surprise and there were much more to Aberdan that obviously meets the eye at first glance.

Lithius avoided the spittle and knocked the balding old man's wrinkled head up against the marble wall, "Listen I do not have anytime for you!"

The eyes of the old acolyte widened and darken to a maroon solid color, Lithius looked into the solid dark red eyes of the old man, and Lithius felt no fear from this man, only bitterness and contempt of its capture.

"I have even less for you, Ramadan!" Aberdan commented through thought as Lithius realized the old man was probing his young mind.

"Tell me where Morderra-Atrauis is and I will spare your life old man." Lithius realized as he spoke through thought, that Aberdan was wise protecting his thoughts from Lithius.

"Spare my life?" Aberdan mocked as he continued speaking, "I see through your disguise and your heart, you shall not spare my life!"

Just then the old man pulled out a knife made of some sort of bone and thrust it directly into Lithius' abdomen. Fortunately, the armor mail of Lithius's true attire protected him; the knife's blade shattered and Lithius threw the old man to the floor and kicked him in the belly knocking the air and strength out of the old one.

This in fact open the old man's mind just long enough to allow Lithius to peer inside, Aberdan then revealed the location of Morderra-Atrauis deep underground and the entrance to the underground passage from the dungeon. Lithius kick the old man once more with his boot, and Lithius using his powerfully entered the mind of Aberdan. The old man couldn't recover, and Lithius knew he was killing him. The old man went to conjure up a spell, a spell that could easily kill Lithius, but Lithius saw this in the old man's mind and like a striking viper, Lithius poisoned the mind of the old man with confusion and kicked him yet again sending dark oozing blood from the corner of the old man's mouth. Stench from the mouth of Aberdan began to fill the room like a rotting carcass.

"Tell me; show me, what I want to know." Lithius said through thought as he frowned down upon Aberdan in his natural form for all to see since Aberdan could see through any disguise that Lithius could have mustered.

"No!" The old man struggled, but he was too beaten, too weak to attempt to close his mind.

Lithius peered in and saw lifetimes of torture, sinister evil and hideous misgivings, and deed that this man, Aberdan had committed or watched Lithius again saw things he wished not to, this man was powerful in the ways of magic, far exceeding Lithius' true talents. Lithius realized immediately, if he didn't surprise Aberdan, or if Aberdan was waiting in preparation or in ambush, Lithius would be dead by now.

There was something, something far more in the mind of Aberdan other than the images of cruelty and hostilities. Aberdan was a creature, not necessarily a

Draccian, but something much more, something much darker and Lithius had no time to reflect, Aberdan was a deadly being.

Lithius drew out his sword and the old man looked up to see his end quickly approaching him. "You have the sword; you have Talquardez-Solstas, the mighty sword of Pitah Valgas from his crypt in the forgotten temples of Adajahara!"

Lithius then felt the first signs of fear from Aberdan as the old man reached up most feebly to thwart off the impending blow from the sword.

"And you shall become part of it!" Lithius sent the sword into the chest of the old man, with it; he twisted the blade that made the body of Aberdan snarl with pain as the sword extracted the evil soul of the man from his now frozen body, free of life of the soul inside.

Lithius, sword in hand turned and left the body in plan sight, suddenly Aberdan's mortal remains turned to a pile of ash upon the dark stone and marble floor. With Lithius' newly acquired thoughts of Aberdan headed down the hallway and down a flight of steps across yet another room to a door that stood two very tall and powerful Tarvas guards dressed in dark leather but bare chests, exposing their over developed muscles. They saw him coming, Lithius could see that they were not easily frighten and stood nearly a full head taller than he stood. He threw his dagger into the forehead of one of these guards, the one on the left that was raising a silver scimitar up to his waste to prepare to cut Lithius in two.

The strike sent the dagger, the Ramadan dagger deep into the Tarvas' forehead rolling back both his eyes looking up at the handle of the very knife that killed him, he dropped his very large scimitar sword on the marble floor that rang out filling the entire room. This guard, the one struck with the dagger, reached up with both his massive hands and pulled the dagger out. Lithius was stunned, the other guard, the one on the right readied himself with his huge double-bitted axe.

As Lithius looked, the one on the left pulled the dagger from his forehead, sending a stream of oozing blood and grey matter of his brain upon his face and floor as he collapsed dead, the dagger then freed from the grip of the hands and fall skimmed across the floor to Lithius' boot. Lithius cautiously picked up the dagger with his left hand, and without taking his eyes off the remaining Tarvas, placed the bloody dagger back in his belt.

"Once, long time ago, I went to give this to a man, he didn't want it, thought it was too valuable for me to give it away I suppose. He said I would need it someday. That day is certainly today, wouldn't you say?" Lithius grinned coldly, the look must have nerved the remaining Tarvas a bit, but only for a second, and without a response, the Tarvas guard lunged forward with his axe blurring through the air to protect him from a sword attack and offer Lithius a fatal blow in the process.

Lithius dodged the attack, faster on his feet than the Tarvas, Lithius counter struck with his sword across the back of the Tarvas' calves, cutting through skin and sinew, but not enough to lose the balance of the man, but give him something to yell with pain about echoing throughout the room and filling the ears of the living.

The Tarvas turned and came towards Lithius like before, Lithius turned out of the way from the mighty momentum of the axe. The Tarvas couldn't stop as easily with the wounds, blood leaching down from his caves sustained by Lithius and fell through the opening of the doorway and stairs down to the dungeon. Lithius could hear the man stumble and fall down the steps and the accompanied sound of the axe falling along with him. Lithius smiled once more at the painful sounds coming from the constant failing and rolling down these steps as he entered the doorway following the bloody path down the winding and dark way to the dungeon.

As Lithius began to walk down the steps, he could hear the Tarvas hit the bottom, and in doing so, the axe that manage to fall following him and the sound, the thudding sound of the axe striking flesh. This caused Lithius to smile even more, "A dead Tarvas is indeed a good Tarvas."

Lithius then using his magic closed and sealed the doorway above, anyone would find it nearly impossible to open the door, and it would take a heavy battering ram to break through the iron and oak six-inch door.

Lithius turned to look at the Tarvas, the fall killed him, and broke his neck, but the axe imbedded deep in the chest of this giant of a man had a very pleasing touch to Lithius. A small dark pool was forming around the dead guard caught in the flickering torches mounted on the walls by iron crude placements. Lithius could also see other doors; smell the dank must air in the hallway. The doors, smaller than the main door, fashioned the same way, there he could see slats and a slab of iron with a brass handle fashioned on hinges, these slats were made to look in on prisoners. Oddly, these doors were open, exposing the cells within. He realized that he was the only one standing in this room.

"Where did they go?" Lithius said aloud as he walked up to a torch, removed it with his sword in the other hand still drawn, he looked into a room after walking over to one of the opened doors. He peered in, and could see old straw, the wreaking smell of stench and saw nothing, no sign of anyone living or dead in any of these cells. Lithius then drew the disguise of Aberdan's physical form. He didn't have a lot of time, they, those from above would have to be upon him soon enough. Lithius with the disguise of Aberdan might be able to fool a guard or two in the event he should come across more in his search for Morderra-Atrauis. He wanted to find one man, one man that caused him trouble in the past that nearly got him killed, and Lithius meant to find him; it wasn't Morderra-Atrauis, rather the old priest, Kronus.

Lithius knew of the secret entrance to the lowest point within the bowls of the island, it was located in the last lowest level of the dungeon. Lithius checked every room on his way down to the second level of the dungeon, and still nothing, he thought perhaps that Morderra-Atrauis might have already done him a favor by killing the Priest, the charlatan years ago. As he looked on, he thought of what Aberdan had said about the sword, and if he, Aberdan knew, so did Morderra-Atrauis and Kronus could have given them all information about the sword in the first place, regardless, the Pitah knew of its existence and its power.

Down in the lower level of the dungeon, Lithius came across two additional guards, like the other two; these two met their deaths suddenly and violently without warning as they recognized Lithius as Aberdan. One of the guards through Lithius' mind probing found the cell that contained Kronus, Kronus was yet alive, but held in the third and final level of the dungeon, hundreds of feet below the castle. Lithius' prowess gave no indication to the six guards at the bottom floor of the dungeon, and like a breeze, Lithius separated bone from flesh, limbs, and heads from those opposing him, his disguise of Aberdan was working without a hitch.

With a new torch in hand in the darkness of the lowest level of the dungeon, Lithius found the door, the door that sealed Kronus from his freedom. Lithius put his hand up against the cold rotting wood of the door covered in moisture, years of dust and abandoned webs. Lithius realized that there was someone on the other side; he heard a sound of feet in the hay. Lithius opened the door with an iron set of keys he took from one of the dead guards. Across from this room, was another room and it was in this room Lithius would find the secret passage that was well hidden.

Lithius turned the lock and with all of his natural strength, opened the door and inside he could see a dark looming figure between the stench and filth. The odor nearly brought tears to Lithius's own eyes as he entered the torch into the room on where he could make out a figure tarnished by years of imprisonment, long dirty white hair, beard, a hooked nose and two blue peering eyes through the single bone hand attempting to shield against the blinding light. There standing slouched by malnutrition, old age, and poor health stood nearly toothless was Kronus. Lithius could see the stub of his arm where his hand and a portion of his forearm were released by him as a boy in his first encounter in Adajahara so long ago.

Lithius felt a moment of pity and as he walked most carefully in this room shedding the disguise of Aberdan from him. Lithius careful of taking the keys with him from one of the guards he had finished killing and mindful of guarding his mind and thoughts from Kronus. Lithius realized, perhaps by the light and years in the worst conditions imaginable, that Kronus didn't realize who this dark and powerful figure was. Kronus' eyes began to adjust, and Lithius could see etch on the cold dungeon walls of stone and rubble was "God has forsaken me." Lithius took a hard look at that, it was written in Kronus' native language; Lithius translated it in Ramadan and spoke it aloud.

The old and nearly dead man began to cry; he understood the language of Ramadan and began sobbing. "The living god has brought a dark angel to come and end my miserable life."

"Perhaps." Lithius spoke in Kronus' native tongue, Kronus was far too weak from years of abuse and treatment, his mind did not possess the power to read Lithius' mind. Still Lithius would not let his guard down, but just went through Kronus's thought, that's how Lithius was able to find the old man's words in the first place, his language of the desert people of Rho-Haven.

Kronus got down on his knees looking bitterly at only the feet of Lithius, "Who long have you been here?" Lithius asked.

"I lost count, after five years of being here. That was long ago I'm afraid."

"What do you know of Morderra-Atrauis, old man?"

"A cruel and horrid man, dare I say a man at all."

"Go on, tell me more Priest."

"Yes, certainly, but I can only tell you of what I know, he is more of some evil beast, some abomination, an abhorrence, a detestation, an odium of all things righteous and pure." Kronus kept looking down as he spoke.

"I see do you know where he, Morderra-Atrauis is at?"

"No my lord, it has been many years since I have looked upon the face of revulsion. I know of nothing more, except he is the evil one foretold in the ancient texts he has sealed up from the relics of his kind."

"What kind would that be?" Lithius quipped.

"He is the purest of the Taltakkurdg-Kevnaps bloodline. It is written in the ancient text, he will be the one to user the pestilence and plagues upon the nations and kingdoms of this world, but there is more, something far more sinister…" Kronus lowered his voice as he trembled.

Lithius could see in Kronus' mind of a creature like Aberdan, but more power-ful with the fang-like teeth, and Lithius could see this creature, the one called Morderra-Atrauis transformed in some evil apparition that was beyond Lithius' own words, a demon of sorts sucking the life's blood out of its victims.

"Did him or any of them" Lithius could see others, others like Aberdan doing the same in the old priest's mind, "…bite into you in such a way?"

"No my lord, for if they did, I would be dead or like them." Lithius could see into Kronus' mind for the explanation he had just said. Lithius needed to get Kronus' old mind off this evil; Lithius could see it was distressing the old man nearly beyond his own means.

"What of these Taltakkurdg-Kevnaps?"

"Cruel taskmasters from another world" He paused thankfully off the subject of these strange horrid creatures that through his old mind resorted to as simply demons.

"You mean from the Netherworld?"

"No, a world far away across the stars my lord." Kronus grew silent.

Lithius didn't want to hear religious rambling from this man so he changed the subject quickly; Lithius could see in Kronus' own mind there wasn't much good for him to find useful. Lithius could see nothing useful for him in his quest for Morderra-Atrauis in the remaining thoughts of Kronus.

"What did you do to end up here?" Lithius quipped.

"I preached the good news, the gospel of the living god, giving hope and love to the broken people of this cursed and wretched land."

"And that was it?" Lithius retorted.

Kronus's balding head nodded accordingly, "What about the boy?" Lithius eyes narrowed upon the top of the old man's head, the old man was slow to answer through his own confusion.

"Boy, what boy my lord?"

"The boy from Adajahara, the boy from Gwarvarik, the Ramadan boy that you would have killed?"

Kronus looked up only at the boots of that man, Lithius could tell through the thoughts of the old priest's mind that he was having trouble connecting his thoughts of the young boy made mention.

"You know the boy, the sword?" Lithius ejected.

"Oh yes a fool's errand. Lust for power, lust for glory" The old man began to weep again.

"I was deceived in my own pride" Lithius could see in the old man's mind, the thoughts of the young boy were coming back to him in good detail.

"The boy, so I was told was killed, the sword forever lost in the forests of this wretched land, not even the Pitah himself could find it, and so I'm told."

"By whom were you told by?" Lithius quipped.

"A foul nature of a man called Aberdan, an evil sort, heir to the throne."

"Heir, really?" Lithius was shortly amused.

"Aberdan, though more Draccian than Taltakkurdg-Kevnaps blood has been chosen to succeed, the Pitah, Morderra-Atrauis grows very old, lived many lifetimes among men, and it is said, Morderra-Atrauis has no kin, no children from his seed that has lived to carry the crown."

The old priest was nearly naked and Lithius could see that this man has been whipped and tortured of the heavy scaring. At that moment, Lithius felt in his heart, deep within, that he was not going to kill him. He could sense in the mind of the old man that he was truly repentant of his misdeeds, besides, the old man actually believed in his heart that the boy was dead and because of this, that the old man fell out of favor with his God.

Lithius drew back from the mind of this man, he saw enough to know that this man, if left alive, would spend the rest of his days in a clouded mind and spirit on the road to redemption of sorts. To Lithius, this and all the torture he received under the care of Morderra-Atrauis was more, much more than any punishment that Lithius could ever fathom to offer.

"The boy did not die." Lithius whispered barely audible, but enough to feel the hopes rise in the old man.

"The boy lives, where is he?" Lithius could see into the mind of the old man as the old man looked back up at the boots of Lithius.

Lithius could see no malevolence or contempt in the old man's thoughts, "Yes he lives, but he is a man now."

"Oh, yes, I suspect that is so." Lithius smiled as he looked at Kronus who had come to the realization of the boy after all these years would be a man now.

"If you see this boy I mean this man, tell him that I am truly sorry, and ask for his forgiveness, I mean no harm to him and I am indeed sorry for any misfortune" Lithius left the room and was gone without a sound, nor did he care to listen to anything more.

CHAPTER 18

▼

Lithius opened the other door across from Kronus who was still talking and unaware Lithius left. Lithius closed the door behind him, locking it. This door was much easier to open and to close and the cell was clean of filth and debris. Lithius wasn't a fool; he knew this room never contained a prisoner. He also knew there was no one in the room before entering it.

Lithius with torch in hand sheathed his sword and there on the wall were shackles, he turned counterclockwise the left shackle and the wall behind it opened slowly as he heard off in the distance considerable pounding from above, he knew they, those out to get him realized he was within the castle. He entered the secret dark entrance, and there he found was a lever on the other side that he pulled. Pulling on this lever caused the secret passage wall to close completely sealing him in the passageway.

The air was considerably damp and cold, not to mention, pitch dark. He could see ancient stairs leading steeply down, he could see thick dust laden with moisture on the steps, and from it, and he could see footprints, fresh human footprints, and only one set leading down.

Down the stairs, he went without giving a sound other than the torch flames licking the dark dank air coming from below. Lithius continued on, moving further down the stairwell to the first landing, there he could clearly see the footprints, whomever it was, the person, Morderra-Atrauis, was in a hurry.

A few minutes later, Lithius was standing in front of a huge massive door made of the oddest stone he has ever seen. The door reminded him of something he had seen in Adajahara, though this was much bigger and impossible to move. As he looked down, he saw a large iron path of metal in the floor made of the same material, he could see the door had just been open recently, and of course closed. He looked up along the edge of the door and could see huge iron hinges, massive in size to hold the weight of the door. Where the iron path met to the door, he could see a large steel wheel; this wheel rode on the iron path. Now Lithius would have to find a way possible to open the huge door that stood ten or twelve feet up, and no idea on how thick it was. He could see something faded in the door, a faded paint in dark colors, some sort of words, too far-gone and impossible to read and decipher.

He looked once more at his torch, and noticed that the flame was dancing, as he looked up and around, using the flame to find the source of the breeze, in which he did, it was not coming from the door, it was sealed. He then found the source, to open shafts on the side leading up to the bottom of the lower dungeon a hundred or so feet above him. He looked up at the ceiling from where he stood and could see it too was made of the same material, a rock that looked or felt like smooth granite, but a dingy grey or white in color.

Lithius also found a small rounded rectangular steel object just out of the range of the iron circular path; Lithius realized this was the pathway of the steel wheel that the door's weight rested on as it traveled. Lithius turned and looked at the steel boxlike device and saw two buttons made of some material that was neither stone nor metal, the buttons, one on top the other, green on the bottom, and a red on the top. Closer examination he could see a third below, smaller, and not a button but a silver metal surface that was recently free from the disturbed dust and debris, same for the surface on the green button. Lithius then back up from the small device that was fasten into the hard wall. He looked at the door, the tracks at the bottom on where, possibly, Morderra-Atrauis stood, and realized that it was this device that opened the door somehow, and when he carefully pushed the green button, nothing happened. He pushed it once more and again, nothing happened.

He stood there brining up the thoughts of Aberdan, Aberdan only saw the doorway from this side that Lithius was facing, Aberdan was never or at least Lithius never retrieved the thoughts that Aberdan may have had about what lurked on the other side.

Lithius stood there in silence for sometime thinking, pondering and going repeatedly on Aberdan's thoughts. Suddenly Lithius saw something, a stronger darker and more horrid nearly human shape come into mind from Aberdan's thoughts it was Morderra-Atrauis. Morderra-Atrauis in his natural form of sorts, the demon-shape, nearly looking like a man, though a Draccian, yet different, favoring more like the images and reliefs that Lithius saw so long ago in the crypt of Pitah Valgas in Adajahara.

"Yes, that's the one I am to kill!" Lithius thought aloud. As he stood there drawing upon his own thoughts as a child in Adajahara, the ancient reliefs from Pitah Valgas' tomb began to make sense, began coming even more clearer. It was Pitah Valgas and his army shown fighting these creatures, these part Taltakkurdg-Kevnaps, Draccian, demon-like creatures that fed upon the week, the innocent, and the blood of mankind.

As Lithius' own mind raced, he realized that the very sword he possessed, the Talquardez-Solstas itself was a weapon used to kill these sorts of creatures, in fact, perhaps the only weapon to successfully do so. Other things, pictures, and runes became even clearer to him while he stood there before the massive door. Lithius realized that Pitah Valgas, this Taltakkurdg-Kevnaps was an alien from another world, the world that Kronus mentioned; it wasn't a legend, or rumor, but truth. This fact didn't alarm Lithius at all, it was the fact that somewhere along the way, these demon-like creatures that disguised as Draccian and mankind. The reliefs also showed that these creatures though were, at the best of Lithius' interpretations were of Taltakkurdg-Kevnaps origin, but there were those from the "Blue planet's" origin that were mysteriously converted to these creatures by some sort of transference that happened after an attack from the ones that seemed turned originally, that is before the great fire destroyed them. Lithius eyes ablaze with this enlightenment realized that the relief in the tomb of Pitah Valgas was reflecting the creatures of the likes of Morderra-Atrauis and Aberdan that managed to survive throughout the seas of time. Some of those bits and pieces of dark passages of thoughts Lithius had acquired from Aberdan were starting to make sense, and what roll did Mydyr and Hamahadra truly play into all this.

Lithius focusing on those thoughts that could possibly help him with the huge massive door was at hand, he needed to figure out the secret to opening this impossible structure, as he focused, he could see a key in the thoughts of Aberdan with Morderra-Atrauis at this particular point. It as a key, a key went into the silver shining keyhole, Lithius could see Morderra-Atrauis turning the key. From this, then Morderra-Atrauis pressed the green button, the door was beginning to open and then Aberdan in some argument or heated discussion was told to turn away and head back up with the other acolytes, those of the same likeness of the creature within Morderra-Atrauis and Aberdan.

"The others, those that followed the Pitah, were they now?" Lithius wondered as he trekked through Aberdan's thoughts. Then there it was, Aberdan and the Pitah growing in fear, both that there was one among them that would betray and kill the ruler of Draccus, it was this specific thought fueled by Hamahadra raising suspicion caused the two to plot the deaths of these men, Lithius could see Aberdan was instrumental in this. It was Aberdan that went out and killed these other men, these others who could challenge the throne, the very same that fed on the blood of the prisoners and others. Now dead, the threat was removed. Hamahadra was the engineer, the fabricator and accuser a lover of Aberdan as well. It was she to persuade Morderra-Atrauis as his successor for a darker and deeper plot, a plot that Lithius could only see in so many parts, but not enough for him to put it all together. Lithius found there was something missing, something not said or told to the author of these thoughts that Lithius was reflecting upon. Lithius realizing, he had to focus at the task at hand, after all, he had the entire army of Morderra-Atrauis behind him, it would only be a matter of time before they would be upon him, that is, if they found the entrance to the passage down here.

Lithius looked at the ancient control with the torch drawn up next to it, and there he could see the odd-looking silver keyhole. Lithius then sheathed his sword, and drew out the dagger. He then worked the tip into the keyhole, and with some force in hopes of triggering the tumblers to open, he then carefully turned the keyhole one way, and then to the other partially, he tried again. On the third attempt and ruining the lock, he turned it to the right drawing from Aberdan's memory. He then tried the green button, with it pushed in, a large winding mechanical sound began filling the tunnel he was in, and with it, the massive door that Lithius guessed weighed tons, opened as the large steel wheel creaked and moaned along its path. Lithius removed the dagger setting the keyhole back to its original position. As the door opened, Lithius peered in; it was absolutely dark as a slight breeze of damp cool air came forth to greet Lithius with the torch. Lithius then carefully entered the tunnel beyond the doorway. He then found a second control identical to the other. He then noticed the key, on a chain, still in the keyhole seen from the torch's reflection. He then realized that Morderra-Atrauis must have been in a hurry. Lithius could see only one set of footprints made in the dampness and dust on the odd stone floor. Lithius looked back towards the heavy door once more before he turned the key and pushed the red button, in turn closing the door and sealing him in on the other side. With a loud noise that echoed throughout the tunnel sending a small tremor through the darkness, the door was closed. Lithius took the chain and key from the keyhole and put it around his neck.

He drew back his dagger for the sword in his right hand and proceeded through several yards into the tunnel made of this solid odd whitish stone. The air was old and damp and moisture accumulated from his brow and saturating his hair as he walked.

On the wall before him was some sort of small lever, he was careful; it was small in a rusty steel rectangular box. He stopped looking at it, it look as if it were made of ivory, but a material he only seen once in Adajahara, but no idea of its true nature. He reflected on Aberdan's thoughts, again, Aberdan, known to Lithius, had no idea, no thoughts of what lied beyond the great door. Lithius could see that the moisten dust had been disturbed on the small lever, small enough for a couple of fingers from one hand to move either up or straight down. Lithius turned the lever up, and then like a flash of lightening throughout the tunnel that startled Lithius immensely, the ceiling above him lit up an odd soft glow of light. There were four long tubes what looked like glass, three were filled with an odd light that ran six feet long, and there was an odd buzzing sound from these lights that began to grow steady. The sound soon quieted down within a moment, Lithius' eyes were adjusting to the brightness. He could see other sets of these tubes encased in these rusted steel frames. As he stood there allowing his eyes to adjust to the strange light, the light began to seem an odd dark amber color and the buzzing sound stopped. He looked as far as he could see and could see these lights separated from one steel encasement to the other by about twelve feet. He could see ten of these encasements, some, only had one or two of these strange light-emitting tubes giving off light, other had three or four and was naturally brighter. At the end of the tunnel that ran straight and level was two steel doors, much smaller that the great door of the odd stone. Lithius could see there was a small illuminated rectangular region, small and flush with the smoother white stone around it.

The walls around him, he could see paintings, symbols in red and yellow he could not discern in spite of the sword. However, below these large symbols of the ancients, he could see writing, scripture of sorts below the symbols. He had no need of the torch in this light, but he didn't trust the odd light just the same and decided to leave the torch lit and continue to take it with him.

"What gods have created all of this I wonder?" He whispered to his amazement standing there now before one of the scriptures under the symbols. He recognized the scripture as Taltakkurdg-Kevnaps, like some of the symbolic writing in the ancient tomb of Pitah Valgas and seen nowhere else by him. He used the sword's magic power as the sword itself began to glow a dull amber color. This caught Lithius' attention for he only saw this once before in Adajahara when the spirits attempted to kill him. He could feel the hair rose upon his neck and without warning; he turned slashing his sword, cutting through anyone or anything standing behind him. There was nothing, nothing but the damp air and the wall on the other side of the tunnel that spanned across twenty feet. He realized that his nerves must have been getting to him; this was a very fear-provoking ancient place, a place that Mydyr had not ever trained him. Lithius would have to draw from his first experience of the tunnel he encountered long ago in the cave leading to Pitah Valgas' tomb. There was something different here, other than the odd lights, below him, Lithius could see a second set of footprints, not that of Morderra-Atrauis' that lead to the two twelve-foot high steel doors closed shut. Lithius could see these two footprints were standing just moments ago standing behind him. The tracks led nowhere, came from nowhere as if the one that made them descended out of thin air.

"Ghosts don't make footprints," Lithius looked back down to them from above and again at the footprints, they were sandaled, perhaps a soft sole to give off no nose. The prints were narrow and favored a woman's foot, he could tell no more from them.

Lithius wasted no more time, he walked up to the twin doors, and on the rectangular shaped steel plate, he could see only on glass-like button, a dim blue illuminating light behind the glass reflected an arrow symbol pointing down. He realized a premonition rather, if he pushed it, the doors would open, and again what would be waiting on the other side, and realizing that Morderra-Atrauis could be waiting in an ambush.

Lithius looked around him; there was a small corridor that leads to a set of stairs in a dark recess to the right of him and the two doors. He went to look, and the sword began to change to a dull burning amber. Whatever was causing the sword to do this, he realized it was down there along the stairwell in the darkness waiting for him. As he stood there, he remembered it was the spirits in Adajahara that caused the sword to illuminate. He decided to try the button, take his chances there. He turned and was now back in front of the doors, he pushed the button and like he expected drew back his sword in the ready, that is, if there was something ready to pounce on him standing there. As the two doors opened quietly, he could see nothing but a small cubical made of mirrors and metal railings. He could see his reflection in the glass, the cubical had no other doors, and again, like the tunnel, it had its own strange light, but it wasn't amber, but a dark mysterious blue light. He cautiously walked in and the doors closed behind him suddenly causing him to turn abruptly. He backed up against the far wall of this strange cubical. There he noticed a set of buttons, two, like that outside the cube beyond the doors, an arrow symbol pointing up, and another down. That was the only two he could see. He also could see the set of his own footprints and that of

Morderra-Atrauis. He could also see that the arrow pointing down had recently has been pushed.

He then pushed the down arrow and the whole cube seemed to move downward making his stomach shortly rise up to his chest. He realized the entire cube was moving quickly downwards, as for his torch, it was running out of oil quickly and it began to smolder filling the cube up with smoke. Still, the cube propelled downwards deep into Thuma-Attarrach and Wizard's Island's bowls. Lithius felt helpless, as there was nothing he could do, he felt trapped and he felt his fear surmounting.

"Fear is the greatest enemy, I will not give into this," Lithius whispered as he could hear the cube mechanical sounds and air passing around the outside of the cube. The oil torch was completely out and he lowered himself to the floor to breathe in the damp air free of the smoke with his sword ready.

The cubical descended further and Lithius realized that he must be hundreds of feet below from where he started. Finally, the cubical slowed down and then eventually stopped. The doors opened quietly and Lithius could see the smoke from his torch below out of the cubical, he could also see the cubical opened to an entrance of a hallway, washed in this soft blue light. Lithius cautiously left the cubical, and like before, the doors closed behind him. The cubical was still motionless on the other side, it wasn't rising. He felt safe as he removed his left hand from the closed doors, then, without warning; the cubical inside gave a mechanical moan and shot up through the ceiling to return to where Lithius had found it.

Lithius turned away from the doors; he could hear the cubical rise faster, and faster. He drew his ear next to the doors and listened until he could not hear the cubical ascend no longer. Lithius realized he was far deeper than he thought earlier, perhaps thousands of feet below the lake. He turned as walked away from the doors; there he could see the same control, a blue glowing glass-like button with an arrow symbol pointing upwards. He figured same process in returning. He walked down the ancient tunnel that led directly to a chamber filled full of large glass-like windows built into the huge odd stone-like walls, there he could see that these large places were filled with some sort of amber and dark red fluid, and in there, amongst the fluid, creatures. Beings that Lithius has never before have seen, some hideous, others less intimidating, all dead. There were three along each side of the wall, six in total, and all six had a being in them, all different. Lithius walked up to each of these containing transparent windows to examine these creatures. None looked either Taltakkurdg-Kevnaps or his own, let alone from the Blue Planet. The chamber and the environments that contained these creatures were well lit, and the place was not damp, but rather warm and much dryer. The chamber led to another and larger room, Lithius using a conjuring spell of invisibility realizing this would draw from his physical strength, slowly and carefully walked into the larger room paying attention to anything, or anyone that might be in there, let alone his sword hinting there might be spirits within. Lithius could see only strange, very foreign equipment, tables with blood, dried blood and fluid stains on the shining metal tables that glowed reflecting the blue soft light from above. There were strange lamps of sorts, these rested directly above these tables. Lithius could see restraining devices, tools, instruments some covered in ancient stains, some clean with the exception of the dust collecting over time and the huge cobwebs over most everything in this room. Here the air was considerably dryer; wide-eyed he walked through and saw many devices, some with lights, some with tools and applications he had no idea of their uses, and others, he had a good idea of their practicalities. He then focused on the tracks of Morderra-Atrauis as they lead out of the huge room to simple stairwell down several feet to a smaller room.

Feeling somewhat safe, he ended his invisibility spell, and returned to his natural self. Lithius realized that the reason that Mydyr never discussed or trained on these things was a simple deduction; Mydyr hadn't a clue about this secret and ancient place in detail. Lithius had to concentrate on getting through the maze of these chambers and rooms; the dry air was quickly absorbing any moisture around him, including the footprints of Morderra-Atrauis. Lithius could spend anymore time contemplating the relationship of the origin of the creatures like that of Aberdan and Morderra-Atrauis, let alone the relationship of the Lycoi with them. As Lithius dismissed this thought, leastwise for now, he realized through the thoughts of those he took, there was certainly a strong, but hidden, almost a unconsciousness of these two kinds, there were other things, things he would have to reflect on much later, that is, if he wanted to survive passed all of this. For one thing as Lithius noticed, all that he saw was made by the hands of the ancients, the Taltakkurdg-Kevnaps from a distant world, and somewhere in here through the labyrinth, he would find Morderra-Atrauis.

Hours passed quickly deep in the bowls of Thuma-Attarrach as Lithius found a great hall, there along each side of the walls made of the ancient stone of the mountain, carved within were twenty or so encasements like the ones he saw earlier that contained various beings that were preserved in fluid and gasses. As Lithius stood there at the great hall, the ceiling that stretched up high into the darkness supported by great pillars of the very same odd white and grey stone, ten per side, perhaps ten feet in diameter, the floor was of a very smooth odd stone, a dark red color. Lithius stood there in the doorway and conjured his spell of invisibility. He was hidden by whatever would be lurking in the darkness.

As he walked in stealth, he continued as his sword remains from detecting spirits in its amber glow. Lithius obtained the sword for most of his life, still Talquardez-Solstas held secrets and mysteries that perhaps would take all of Lithius' live, if fortunate, learn them all. Walking down the middle of the great hall, a distance of several hundred yards, Lithius caught a glimpse of something, something oddly familiar on his right. As he stopped and turned, he could clearly see a creature in the glass encasement. Lithius stood there only for a moment and realized that this creature was indeed something he recognized, not wasting any, more time; he briskly walked over to the large encasement built into the obsidian wall. As he looked at the dark figure, to his astonished surprise it appeared to be Mydyr floating in the dark orange and red fluid.

"Master?" Lithius whispered.

Lithius was certain it was Mydyr, there in the dark cloak, looking more like black oil or thick fluid rather than fabric that robed the skeletal creature. Lithius in his amazement could see that this body reminisce of this being, was in fact, in physical form submerged in this fluid. The body was indeed lifeless as Lithius lifted up his left hand outstretched on the thick glass. Lithius also noticed that the glass, along the edges had some sort of runes etched in it, symbols, writings that his sword's magic couldn't or didn't translate to him. It was useless to find out anything from these writings. Lithius had to assume that Mydyr was now dead, if not, this creature was no doubt the same sort of being as Mydyr.

Lithius backed off from the glass; still his mouth was agape from the ghastly site, and the thought, that this may indeed be his master.

"So the witch of the underworld won over you?" Lithius whispered in reverence.

He stood there thinking, at first, what would be the point to continue with his quest, if indeed his suspicions were true. He quickly dismissed that thought; Morderra-Atrauis was an evil man, an evil being, a tyrant amongst his own people. Mydyr did save his life at least twice, once as a boy, and once in the remains of Sommer. Lithius figured in spite of Mydyr's possible demise, it was the very least he could do. Then his mind went to Byris and Tyra, they suffered more than enough besides. As Lithius stood, he became reaffirmed in his conviction that Morderra-Atrauis and the likes of him had to be destroyed.

Lithius caught a reflection of something behind him off in the distance from the glass, he couldn't see himself because he was still invisible, his sword shown no sign of change, therefore he could only assume it was not a spirit. He turned to face the direction of what he caught a glimpse of. Lithius could barely hear a sound, but it was there, it was the sound of footsteps running down the hallway, but Lithius could only catch small infractions of an image, an image of a human shape. Then there, he could see as it stopped looking down the hallway before the entrance that Lithius came to the great hall, the specter stopped, it became more visible, something like smoldering smoke before becoming more solid. Lithius realized it wasn't a ghost, but a woman, a blonde woman about six feet tall, very shapely, and powerful, a woman in her late or early thirties in age, and certainly not a Draccian. Her long straight blonde hair fastened in a tight single pony tale behind her, she was carrying a bow, a quiver of arrows, a sword that was in her right hand, and just enough leather light armor to cover her large breasts and waist. She wore leather sandals that strapped around her calves of her bronze legs. She also had some sort of black fabric bag strung over her shoulder. Lithius though invisible to her, found cover behind a pillar as he looked on in fascination.

"What would she be doing here?" He whispered under his own breath.

She turned, seemed somewhat frustrated, and he realized that she was looking for him, and perhaps, she was the one that came up behind him from above, and she could have hid out in the stairwell. However, she wasn't alone there; Lithius knew there was spirits along the stairwell. Lithius could see her face clearly, she was remarkably beautiful, and her almond eyes like emerald green in spite of the dark red, maroon, and blue lighting. Lithius quickly and cautiously probed her mind, he came to the sudden conclusion, she is a thief, and somehow knew of this place, and has been here before, with others, men, two, both of the same nationality, a nationality that Lithius did not know of.

Her invisibility spell was indeed a charm, a charm she wore about her neck on a leather string, the charm failing her as Lithius peered her thoughts, the charm only for short, very short durations of invisibility. As she trotted past him, he followed her; she was the author of those very same footprints that puzzled him earlier. As she trotted, she gave no sound; Lithius of course did not either, though it was much harder for him in doing so. He could sense from his gathering thoughts from her mind, which she knew this area well, and this time she was alone, her male accomplices were not with her this time.

"So how did you get in here?" Lithius said to himself following here down a flight of steps into another room. If she uses the charm, Lithius would have to wait until the charm would again ware out, he wouldn't be able to find her.

As he peered into her mind, he could see there was indeed another way, a secret "back door," another way in and out. Lithius could see clearly, what it was, where it was at, and following her far enough, realized the route. Lithius had an escape route. As he followed she slowed down and used her charm, she sensed somehow without turning around, that she wasn't alone, that there was something behind her, she was gone.

Lithius knew enough, he knew she was a thief, been a thief for most of her life and comes from the south, far beyond Draccus, but he could not discern from originally. She has been in so many places, and as far as the other two, Lithius caught several impressions from her thoughts, they were thieves as well. Both were her lovers, though each of them did not know they were sharing the same woman. Lithius found that amusing, the men, the thieves were from Faedaria, which is where she met up with them. They, the three did several "...jobs" together, most of which were in Faedaria, that is before the authorities caught on and consequently a bounty on the three.

"There!" he saw her again, as the charm was wearing thin again; she was hiding behind some soft of a large metal cabinet, looking in his direction. Lithius knew he would be safe, and she would again take off again, and again, he would follow. He could sense that she was very perceptive and could feel Lithius inside of her head, though not knowing who or what exactly, she was beginning to think that there was or is a demon after her, her heart began to race.

Lithius could also see the times that she has been down here before using the secretive back door, the second passage down here. Through her mind, he could see all; he could see all that she has taken with the others, ancient artifacts, gold, silver, and anything that they, the thieves thought of interest. However there was something, something that she, herself were looking for, something the others didn't want any part. As Lithius probed her mind even deeper, he could begin to see what the item was, the memory, the thought was becoming clear.

Lithius could sense that she was waiting for the demon, or whomever it was that she felt was being followed by, there, the image came, it was Aberdan, Aberdan that she saw earlier which Lithius was indeed. This caused a smile on his face, and there was one other, Lithius, his natural physical self she saw, and in some measure found him pleasing to her eye.

Lithius concentrated on the item, the item that this woman found risking her life for, it was some sort of relic, a powerful relic, a relic of green, a glowing emerald behind a shield of glass, lights, power or energy that Lithius, or for that matter, herself didn't understand. Lithius could see in her thoughts, in her mind, that this item, the source of unexplained energy was responsible of the mystical power feeding these odd lights, and energy responsible of keeping the place warm and dry. The Thief, as Lithius could see was becoming very alarmed, and her only thoughts were to leave this place at once.

Lithius could care less of such a device, and sitting there invisible and separated from her only a matter of several feet, probed her mind for any sign of Morderra-Atrauis and the possibilities of his secret lair down here. As he probed even harder to be passed her surmounting fear, she panicked and ran off. Lithius didn't need to follow he obtained enough, in her thoughts, he gathered a dark place guarded by two heavily armed Lycoi before an iron door. These Lycoi were nothing like the ones he had dealt within his passed, they were huge, much more powerful, and there weapons were not of bone, stone, or wood, but refined steel. They were something that the three thieves would avoid at all costs, and there were more throughout the area, patrols, and sentries of them just ahead of where he was sitting in some measure of distance. The door had strange symbols, and as Lithius probed more before she could get out of his range, the symbols were indeed runes, ancient Draccian runes, a warning, a curse, "...That's it!" Lithius exclaimed nearly out loud breaking into laughter.

Lithius shed his invisibility, she was far enough gone, he could sense that she would come back another time, a time where her nerves would gather enough courage to come back looking for what she intended on some other time, it wasn't safe down here. Lithius knew that Morderra-Atrauis was on to him, and the closer Lithius would get to him, the more dangerous it would be for the young warrior sorcerer. Morderra-Atrauis would no doubt double the guard; double the numbers of these great and powerful Lycoi. Lithius, from the thief's memories and thoughts, these Lycoi served whatever was on the other side of the iron door; this alone convinced Lithius that the Pitah was using these creatures as his personal guard.

As Lithius sat there on the table, he knew that his invisibility could get him close enough to these guards, that is, if Morderra-Atrauis didn't warn them somehow, but he couldn't pass through quietly enough, they would pick up his sent regardless, it would result in swordplay against their huge axes. Their physical strength was too much for him to withstand, it would take finesse and some fine talent with the sword—Lithius was certainly not going to under estimate these creatures let alone Morderra-Atrauis. Lithius also realized that he had a small army of undead within Talquardez-Solstas to use in the event he would become overwhelmed by the Lycoi or Morderra-Atrauis himself.

In just a few minutes, as Lithius thought things through, he heard the feet of many, he knew it was the Lycoi off in the distance, and with them, Lithius could sense Hamahadra, she was beginning to sense Lithius's presence. Lithius's fear instantly rose as he reeled off the table with his sword in hand, as he drew near the opening of the room before him; it was another long and large hall, exactly like the great hall in every detail except different creatures caught in the great glass encasements. Lithius could see a huge number, possibly thirty to forty Lycoi, the Lycoi like the guards before the great iron door.

It would be impossible for Lithius to fight through this alone, before the horde of Lycoi was the specter, the horrid Hamahadra in spirit form above them with a staff in her right hand as she began screaming and moaning as she looked directly at Lithius with contempt and utter hatred in her eyes. No invisibility spell would save him from her.

"Bitch!" Lithius blurted as he sheathed his sword and gathered his bow and notched a single arrow. He conjured a spell as he released the black arrow from his quiver taking careful aim at the abortion. The single arrow as it flew through the air turned to several arrows, all which whisked through the air of the great hall before him directly at her. The arrows passed through her without effect, however the arrows brought several Lycoi screaming and thrashing to the ground. Lithius shot several more times, this time directly at the approaching horde, killing several, and wounding many. Hamahadra screaming obscenities and ill will towards Lithius, he abandoned his bow and drew his sword. Hamahadra seeing this drew violently back as the blade's tip pointed right at her head as she loomed over Lithius. Lithius instantly realizing the fear of his sword in a blinding blur lunged for her, the sword penetrated his physical realm and entered hers, striking her in the breast, she reeled and countered with her staff sending Lithius across the room and into the desk, crushing the desk beneath him. Lithius regained his footing; his chest swelling from the blow realized his blade didn't penetrate deep enough. She lunged forth, over extending herself with the staff, missed, and Lithius disembowel her, spilling her intestines unto the floor, though not in his physical realm.

Hamahadra, fell, dropping the staff to the floor, and in doing so, the staff was oddly in his physical realm. She fell clutching her wound and intestines as blood oozed from her mouth. Lithius wasting no time leaped up through the air and severed her head from her shoulders as he body convulsed violently. Lithius turned to face her body and the horror-stricken Lycoi who stopped in their tracks just yards away from Lithius and their fallen Goddess of the Netherworld.

"Join your spider!" Lithius then dramatically drove the sword deep into her body that loomed now lifeless above the floor. Talquardez-Solstas then drew her soul as the blade turned to an illuminated green. This sight nerved the Lycoi and sent them scattering in retreat.

Lithius withdrew the sword and her body vanished like that of clearing smoke into the air, Lithius let out a great sigh of relief, as he realized his chest was bruised from the impact of the staff. He then walked over to the staff, picked it up and realized that this was no ordinary staff, but one of great magic and power. He knew this staff could of easily have killed him, she didn't use the magic of the staff, her bitterness and hatred blind sighted her attempts to kill him with. Lithius thought, "She underestimated me greatly"

The Lycoi were coming back with renewed vigor in greater numbers. As Lithius looked out from the room to the great hall before him, the sound of marching feet filled the air; they reformed in an army to protect Morderra-Atrauis marching with weapons drawn. As far as Lithius could see, the Lycoi coming forth, realizing this, he had no other choice.

Lithius drew his sword at the horde approaching and released the spirit of the great spider from Talquardez-Solstas, "Seek out and kill every breathing Lycoi in the bowls of Thuma-Attarrach, I command you!"

Suddenly the sword wined and turned to an illuminating dark blue as a plasma stream of light gave way to the horrid specter of the spider as it turned towards the Lycoi.

Lithius sheathed his sword and gathered his bow and the quiver of arrows as he watched the spider begin its violent attack on the Lycoi as their weapons were useless as drawing an axe through smoke. The spider began dismembering the Lycoi, spreading body parts, organs, and creating a lake of blood, screams, and howls filled the great hall as the spider systematically destroyed the powerful army. Lithius watched carefully as the great spider eventually killed all in the great hall and went after those that were fleeing for their lives.

"This is why I had gathered the soul of the great spider, Mydyr." Lithius said aloud. A few moments later, Lithius gathered his things including the staff of Hamahadra and waded through the carnage to the other end of the great hall to another large chamber, there he could see the spider beyond driving back the remaining Lycoi to their bleak fate. Lithius outstretched his sword from his sheath and collected the fresh souls of the fallen Lycoi, the room filled full of plasma light in a rainbow of colors as Talquardez-Solstas collected.

CHAPTER 19

▼

Upon his completion of a formidable force of these powerful Lycoi, he sheathed his sword. Lithius turned to the left and knowing exactly the route from the female thief the path and location that might lead to the iron door, it was much darker and down the narrow steps chiseled out from the black obsidian. Lithius stood there at the top of the steps looking down and then back to his acquired weapon, the staff. The staff was well over six feet in length, felt like oak or some sort of hard wood, there were runes, symbols, writing carved in, but he could not read them, they, the markings looked like the markings on some of the walls, Lithius assumed the writings to be of Taltakkurdg-Kevnaps origin in nature.

Lithius could hear from behind him the spider off at the distance killing all those it found. Lithius understood the spider, the spell, and magic of Talquar-dez-Solstas would bind the spiritual creature, the soul of the animal continuing with Lithius' commands, that is, until the spider was finished. Upon finishing, the soul would be released freely and to Lithius, the spirit would enter the Nether-world with all the other souls that are freed from their worldly bounds that bind them amongst the living.

Lithius concentrated his energy and thoughts on the new staff, he concentrated even more to see if he could conjure it to offer light, in doing so, it began illuminating, from the top of the staff a brilliant silver light shown and the markings illuminated offering enough light for him to see clearly as he descended down the stars. The air became much cooler and with it, the surroundings became dark and dank. The scent of "old death" came into mind, as if some ancient corpse were left, though unseen, to rot.

Lithius with his right hand drew out his sword, no change in the translucence of his dark blade. He continued further down the steps without a rail to the very bottom. There Lithius could see a very large pool of water as black as oil though it seemed from the black shining obsidian. Lithius's chest pains subsided, knowing his ribs were still intact and suffered only from the bruised flesh and muscle. His armor, his chain mail took the brunt of the impact. As he looked upon the great pool contained by a two-foot wall that went as far as the light would allow contained the water that was nearly up to the top of this wall of obsidian. Lithius turned and could see a tunnel, the tunnel that would lead to the iron door. He then released from Talquardez-Solstas two spirits, two Lycoi, and commanded them to seek out the two huge Lycoi guards and wait for his coming.

The two went as instructed, within a few moments, shrills, howls, and the sounds of metal striking stone were heard before a blanket of silence. Lithius knew the two large Lycoi guards have been dispatched.

Lithius with his staff in his left hand, sword in right, walked down the tunnel to where the two Lycoi spirits under his control stood by the iron door and the bodies of the two dead, Lithius collected these as well into his sword.

"I might as well use them to" He looked up at the two looking back at him with a measure of disdain and contempt for him and his power, Lithius paid no mind.

"Open this door now!" The two did as ordered; the door was heavy and buckled under the strain. Lithius had already deciphered the writings from the female thief's mind as he walked down the long steps. The warning was nothing more, it was the charms that Lithius was concerned about, and these charms kept the door magically sealed by whomever were behind them, no doubt Thuma-Attarrach. However the Lycoi, the souls were of spirit, and it took something of spirit to break the charms, and consequently break the magical seal. The door gave way and nearly broke off the hinges.

"Bring forth from whoever is inside, bind him well!" Lithius on the ready as the two entered the room without a sound and Lithius could hear an older voice, filled with terror attempting to withstand the Lycoi spirits with his magic. Lithius then entered the room, this small chamber and there he could see Morderra-Atrauis in the flesh for the first time.

Lithius with his sword drawn, ready for anything, could see the dark cloaked image standing before the candles that filled the backdrop, there were other things in the room, silver, gold ornaments, ancient in origin, weapons, weapons of little meaning. There were scrolls under the blanket of dust, and before Lithius in the middle of the dark room was a sarcophagus of ivory, the heavy ivory lid hand carved with horrid scenes of the Netherworld, least that was Lithius' interpretation, and likewise the sides with spells and charms.

Lithius approached next to the sarcophagus and looking at Morderra-Atrauis who was subdued as the Lycoi bounded him with their massive hands around his own now behind his back.

"You are the bastard child from Ramadans" Morderra-Atrauis spit at him, Lithius didn't care as he looked down and saw dirt, dirt in the sarcophagus and thought this odd.

Lithius looked up and in the Draccian tongue, "The keeper of Talquardez-Solstas, not bastard." Lithius glared at him.

Upon the mention of the sword, the captured Pitah hissed at Lithius as if he were a huge cat, Lithius could clearly see his fangs, "Aberdan did the same thing before he died."

Morderra-Atrauis uttered a deadly spell, before he could finish, Lithius countered with a crushing magical blow that broke the Pitah's lower jaw.

"Hard to speak with a broken jaw, isn't it?" Lithius said aloud guarding his mind most carefully.

Lithius sent two more powerful spells that acted as fists upon the chest and abdomen of the old Pitah, Lithius could hear the Pitah's frail ribs crack under the invisible punches as Morderra-Atrauis' face began distorting by the pain. Lithius could sense the power ebbing from Morderra-Atrauis; his strength was far stronger than the average man in spite of his ancient age was. Lithius could also see only partially in the Pitah's mind his true nature, Lithius was standing before the most ancient of the creatures, half Taltakkurdg-Kevnaps in nature as he stood well passed the height of Lithius and a size more of the ancients. Lithius also came to the realization the magical light of the staff was somehow the source that was draining this blood-feeding creature, a parasite of the living.

"You were never really a man, where you?" Lithius spoke through telepathy.

"A man?" Morderra-Atrauis answered likewise through telepathy.

"A man has a measure of life in him" Lithius could clearly hear his cold harsh words in his mind, oddly, Morderra-Atrauis wasn't attempting any mind controlling or probing tricks, and Lithius wasn't giving in and sent two more spells that hit the Pitah again, striking pain throughout his body.

"Please I had enough!" Lithius could see dark blood oozing from the Pitah's wrinkled ivory pale chin from his blue lips dripping upon the floor.

Lithius tried entering deeper in Morderra-Atrauis's mind, "That won't work either." Hissed the ancient being as he was attempting to look at Lithius as he continued to speak,

"You do know that you shall never see the light of day again, do you?"

"Do you think you can stop me?" Lithius retorted though still refraining from thinking less of Morderra-Atrauis' powers.

"Me, no, I am too old, too tired"

"You mean Hamahadra, the Lycoi?" Lithius quipped.

Morderra-Atrauis broke into a cold slow rolling laugh that daunted Lithius, "I see you two have met, this time she will finish the job. But my question is, will it be before my death, or afterwards young Lithius?"

"Hamahadra is dead; do you not recognize the staff?"

A cold hard gleam of Morderra-Atrauis gave to Lithius, "What?"

"She is dead, and so is the Lycoi I am afraid. This is her staff, do you not know it?" Lithius could see it hurt Morderra-Atrauis' blood red eyes to gaze upon it, his eyes looking more like some crazed beast, perhaps a demon, something other than human. In that instant, Morderra-Atrauis raised his hands as he uttered an ancient spell that bound both of the Lycoi spirits, freeing him from them, as they were helpless in seizing him as if they were contained in invisible cages.

Lithius drove back as he was stunned by this quick maneuver from Morderra-Atrauis.

"I do not know of that staff, perhaps it was from Mydyr she got it from?" Lithius looked up at him, returning the cold hard look. Morderra-Atrauis could see the spell worked and took his attention towards Lithius.

A sinister smile broke across Morderra-Atrauis' narrow face, "Oh yes, your master"

"What about Mydyr?"

"…Did you not see the physical form in the great halls above?"

"Yes, but something is telling me that wasn't really him." Lithius insisted.

"Oh, it is, his physical form from the world on which he lived, though not of this world that you and I reside, but a world just the same" His voice faded slightly as he had great trouble with the physical pain and the light.

"You see, Hamahadra took it, took him, and brought him to me through her powerful magic and encased him with the others."

"The others?" Lithius asked most curiously.

"Any who was a threat to either I or my bride." Lithius understood Morderra-Atrauis referring to his bride as Hamahadra.

"They are from different worlds as well, different realities if you would, some by great distances. All beyond your comprehension I'm afraid." Morderra-Atrauis added as Lithius could feel a new vigor of strength flowing through Morderra-Atrauis, a supernatural strength nonetheless. Lithius, straining and using his power and the staff could feel Morderra-Atrauis loosening the grip the young warrior sorcerer was having.

Lithius was silent for a moment attempting to gain the upper hand once again, and then spoke under the strain with a grimacing glare, "Hamahadra and Mydyr were from these places?"

"Yes." Morderra-Atrauis looked back down at his own feet as he arose from the pain, and Lithius could see Morderra-Atrauis was beginning to conjure his deceitful thoughts.

"Down here, the worlds would meet, many of these worlds that Hamahadra knew of, knew how, a portal of sorts created by the most ancient of my people." Lithius, under the strain of the powerful and sinister black magic of Morderra-Atrauis, saw the spell in the old creature's mind from eons of years before, remembering this spell, Lithius could see he was losing and the spell was now affecting his physical strength like an invisible constrictor coiling around him ever so tighter.

"Many worlds, worlds in different realms, dimensions, and dominions have such portals of great power and magic. Hamahadra understood this, the secrets, and at seldom times could transverse these distances in as much as becoming physical in this realm that you and I reside. Mydyr tried several times, but could not, only to appear as a phantom, a ghost or shadow of what he is in his realm." Morderra-Atrauis grew silent as he began to smirk.

Lithius probing Morderra-Atrauis mind, could see the spell was twofold, one against the power of the light, and the second to crush the breath out of Lithius.

"Mydyr if successful would have devoured this realm and all we knew into a world of living hell of his own design like he has done in other worlds. Hamahadra, my beloved, kept these kinds at bay. Lucky for you and all that lives in this realm, she was successful in killing Mydyr as well as all that you have seen from the other room." Morderra-Atrauis paused seeing the spell was working to his satisfaction.

"You may say in so many words, that Hamahadra saved everyone from a true hell indeed." Morderra-Atrauis smirked.

Lithius strength was diminishing even more, "Mydyr was the strongest and most driven, he could affect things in this realm, such as saving you, saving you like the others to do his bidding, you are nothing more than a mindless pawn shown a few tricks but of no real power to speak of."

"What others, where?", Lithius attempting to draw nearer to Morderra-Atrauis, but failed and realizing the old one's sinister trick, shot a bolt of pain towards the old sorcerer, in all of his hopes to muster enough of this strength towards the mind of Morderra-Atrauis.

Lithius realized quickly it was obviously enough to throw Morderra-Atrauis off guard and reeling him back, it was enough to release Lithius from the magical coils that bound him, enough time to quickly recover from the serpentine grip.

"Do you think that you were the first that meddlesome Mydyr has attempted to mold into an assassin to kill me or Hamahadra for that matter?"

Lithius could hear Morderra-Atrauis laughter as he quickly arose at tried to reacquire his spell upon Lithius, Lithius at the break of Morderra-Atrauis' strong holding spell, countered it and applied the ancient spell towards Morderra-Atrauis with alterations that Morderra-Atrauis found himself check-mated and suffering in the grip of the younger sorcerer.

"You are good my young friend."

"I am not your friend, you demonic blood thirsty beast!"

Lithius quickly realized that Morderra-Atrauis was actually talking to someone else, or something else that he could not sense or see in the room, and with that, Lithius' mind slipped enough for Morderra-Atrauis to gain an upper ground on Lithius.

This was only momentary as Lithius countered once again sending a bolt of pain, and in a mental transfer of spells and conjuring, the pressure of Morderra-Atrauis' was indeed felt upon Morderra-Atrauis himself rather than young Lithius.

This allowed Lithius to see further in the mind of Morderra-Atrauis exposing thoughts and memories of the most wretched of deeds and the Pitah's blood cult of venomous vipers known as his acolytes, all the same bread as Morderra-Atrauis, all some sort of a vampirism, something Lithius himself had really no knowledge of before hand. Still Lithius could not see far enough into Morderra-Atrauis's mind. Lithius could see from the old sorcerer's mind eons and countless blood sacrifices as Lithius understood as some sort of ritualistic blood feeding upon the young, especially virgin women, preferably those entering adulthood.

Just then, Morderra-Atrauis had regained the upper hand and it was Lithius sent smashing up against the cold damp stonewall in pain as the old sorcerer stretched out his hands towards Lithius suspended against the wall.

"The magic from the sword, the sword cuts both ways, does it not?" Morderra-Atrauis toyed and continued in spite of the pain of the coils, the invisible coils binding and paralyzing him, breaking Lithius' thoughts and the mind-link long enough for Lithius to somewhat regain his composure from the hideous pictures he was seeing and work against the spell at hand.

Lithius also could tell that Morderra-Atrauis was fully aware of what Lithius was doing; he either was too weak to stop Lithius from probing. Lithius' powerful endurance of pain was saving his life, as the coils grew no tighter that bound him against the wall. He could feel Morderra-Atrauis strength of his spell leaving him.

"It becomes part of you, giving all that in its possession the gifts, the magic, and in return, it will consume you, and you shall become part of the sword and its eternal reward. Your soul it will require as well, just as you have fed it souls, it will feed upon yours" Morderra-Atrauis grew silent again for a moment as he strained to maintain Lithius, Morderra-Atrauis realized he was losing ground, his young enemy, Lithius was now breaking free of the spell.

"We really are not that different." Morderra-Atrauis accused as he continued, "You gather souls your own way, and I do it by other means." A ghost of a smile cracked across Morderra-Atrauis pale white moonlight glow of a face. His eyes were on fire by the pain and hatred, filled to the rim in bloody condescension towards the young sorcerer that was struggling towards him to kill him. Lithius filled with white-hot hatred, his face distorted by the pain, emotion had only one single thought, only one single monumental picture in his mind, and Morderra-Atrauis didn't need to probe Lithius' mind to know what he was thinking.

Lithius could sense Morderra-Atrauis in his understanding of Talquardez-Solstas was telling the truth, least as far as Morderra-Atrauis understood it; there was no deception in his fading voice.

Lithius struggled ever so slowly towards Morderra-Atrauis, sword poised for the blow, the final blow that would send this vampire sorcerer to the netherworld.

"Lithius stood there poised for the final attack as he carefully listened and thought oddly that Morderra-Atrauis was taking the time to explain all of this to him. Morderra-Atrauis was indeed dying as Lithius probing his mind, in control of the ancient thoughts of Morderra-Atrauis continued to utter coughing up blood. Lithius could see deeper, ever so slightly into the mind of Morderra-Atrauis, enough to see the truth, or at least Morderra-Atrauis' interpretation of the truth in his spoken words.

Lithius could sense that there was something great and terrible from behind him, as he slowly turned it was a hideous creature, much taller than he was, strong and powerful, eyes of emerald rage. The creature tried to grab Lithius by the throat, with one quick move of Talquardez-Solstas, the creature was cut deeply in both arms. The tall and powerful creature, a torso and legs of a huge man reeled back and vanished. Lithius turned once more to Morderra-Atrauis who turned away heading into an opening of growing light, and with this, the spell, like the creature, dissipated freeing Lithius fully.

The light grew into a large circle and faded showing the figures from behind some sort of a binding illuminating field, something of great power that separated his own world from that of the other world like a huge mystifying window and Lithius figured that somehow in that instance, a portal was opening.

Lithius turned to run as the static and lightning seized him in its grip, and like a whirlpool, Lithius was physically drawn into it. In the force, he lost the staff as he could see his feet leave the world he was just departing. He looked up to the other direction as his body twisted in the turbulence of the great whirlpool of static and flashes of light into the other dimension.

CHAPTER 20

▼

Lithius landed hard upon the bright hard stony ground and rolled, losing his grip of his sword that fell next to him. He, without hesitation grabbed his sword as the wind rushed passed him as the static discharge danced off his body dissipating in the hot dry air. He turned to face the figures he saw from what he realized was certainly a portal that opened taking him to this strange place, and the world he left behind. As for the creatures, they were blurred significantly in Lithius' struggling vision to the bright light and heat, the heat by the way, was more unbearable seeming to sear his lungs and nostrils.

Lithius' own body trembled as he struggled to maintain his balance, the portal journey though as short as it was in time, it took from him his physical strength just the same. His eyes clearing he could smell the heat from his leather and coat of black chain mail armor. Already the heat was pouring down from his forehead, as he stood ready for these creatures clearing in view. He could see that these creatures, naked from any clothing were male and odd looking.

The young sorcerer stood poised to embrace the attack of these great and powerful creatures, the likes he has never seen before. As he stood there, his vision cleared to see that these powerful male creatures were walking, stalking towards him, their skin was dark and dirty, covered in dust and dirt mixed with their own perspiration. He could see bat-like wings, a wingspan as he could figure were some fourteen feet perhaps affixed to their shoulder blades, he also could see that these two creatures had powerful tails behind them that they whipped around, back and forth cracking the air as they snapped the tails like a bull whip. Upon their hairless bodies, their ugly baldheads, and upon their brow horns, horns something like on cattle. Lithius could see their jaded solid eyes that seem to catch the brilliant sun shining like emeralds. Their noses, pointed snorting air through their powerful lungs, their massive powerful arms, bigger than most men's legs were ripping with muscles as they stretched their hands, long powerful fingers with talon-like fingernails to tear the flesh from the bone on whoever was unfortunate enough to be caught in their grip.

As Lithius looked on upon these slowly approaching two identical creatures that stood nearly eight feet tall in height and weighed to Lithius' guess, at least five hundred pounds. Their teeth looked more like the fanged leopards than human, their lips thin and ivory, and their ears, as the wings were webbed and bat-like pointing up straight in the air above their bald scalps.

They hissed and howled the howling unlike the Lycoi; Lithius guessed was simply a signal to others that they have found their prey. Lithius unlike any other man that would have just turned and ran away. Instead, he just stood there focusing on the two as still and as motionless as a marble statue, poised for the attack.

The two then stopped short, turned slightly to each other, and then began circling Lithius, sizing him up. Lithius tried to enter the minds of these beasts but could not, either he could not read their thoughts or speak to them through telepathic means, this was certainly a first, continuing to keep his stance as he kept a careful eye on each. The two, they crack the air with their whip-like tails that were at least ten to twelve feet long around him as to spook or send fear into him. Lithius could see one turned his head, though keeping an eye on the small frail figure in front of him to howl and flap his huge and powerful wings sending up dust into the air.

"Howl all you want fowl beast!" Lithius scorned slightly changing his stance with his sword pointed to strike at either beast.

"Just the two of you, perhaps you should wait until the others come, make it a fair fight, shall we?" Lithius taunted.

From the other, his tail nearly hit Lithius' own face like a darting viper striking its prey, Lithius moved even faster than the cracking tail sending nearly three feet from its length as the beast let out a blood curling shrill of pain nearly turning Lithius' blood to ice in his own veins. His sword signing it's death song in the air returned even faster towards Lithius on the ready as he decided to end this charade, this pensive dance of death to an all out attack. In blinding speed, speed greater than the whip-like tails, he severed the very hand armed with the dagger-like talon nails of the powerful hand, the creature reeled back as he brought his bloody stump of an arm for a shocking close examination as he realized that this little man took his hand off.

In doing so, Lithius spilled the creature's intestines with the sweep of his sword cutting deep into bone and muscle sending the screaming creature slumping over into his wound as Lithius leaped into the air like a striking scorpion taking flight driving his sword deep into the neck, separating the spinal column from the base of the massive skull. This intern sent the beast to his knees, paralyzing his body. The other creature at the heels of Lithius lunged forward; Lithius knelt down thrusting his sword up over his shoulders into the massive chest of the charging beast. The sword drove deep as the shorten tail snarled around Lithius's armor shearing the chain mail from the leather. Lithius arose pulling the sword from the falling beast and managed to get out of the way, as the beast fell face down nearly crushing the young sorcerer. Lithius then leaping like before drove his sword in the back of the beast's skull sending brain matter hurling into the air with the spatter of blood that covered Lithius' face as if it were rain.

By now there were others coming forth from the haze, from the dust that encircled Lithius due to the fighting. Lithius realizing that he could not fight all of them, as some were coming by flight from their massive wings above his head lashing their tails. Lithius drove his sword into the dead, summoning their souls to his bidding.

"Now fight these winged demons!" In doing so, the sword released the spirits of these two fallen beasts as Lithius fought for his very own life as the whip-like tails tore into his leather and into his flesh from all directions, tearing deep cuts into his skin as if the tails were like razors, no matter how fast he'd move, there were just too many. Lithius continued fighting, dismembering limbs, heads, arms, and legs, whatever he could get as the numbers of these beasts continued growing. Wounded, he summons more of the fallen until he reached a point that he could get a quick breather as the bodies began littering the brief barren landscape before him, then another greater number would show, he had no choice but to pour out the sword's keep of the souls it contained. A whole army of souls entered the battle, killing, dismembering, and gaining the upper hand, the tide was slowly turning.

As he noticed the cuts into his own flesh, he looked up to see even more of these very same beasts coming forth, he frantically continued harvesting the undead army of the fallen until eventually he was clearly winning the battle. As he looked around, great numbers of these beasts, the living coming forth from the barren rocky hills in this desert landscape came forth engaging the spirits of the fallen without success.

As time progressed, Lithius was now far behind the battle in a few moments of time, tired, and bewildered, his body, and sword soaked in blood and sweat. He stood there panting hunched over in pain, the heat was almost too much alone for him to handle as he panted attempting to catch his breath, this place was draining him, and it was becoming impossible to move as he was realizing that he was being poisoned. The wounds stung as he used his magical healing powers, but this alone was not enough to overcome the wounds right away. For Lithius, this took some concentration, concentration he needed to use on getting his bearings; he then fell due to the lack of blood to his knees in the mire of the battle. The air around him filled full of the stench of the dead and the screams of the dying and howling from the creatures in the distance.

The magic was beginning to take hold, but with expense. Lithius was now too tired to fight and barely could lift his head up as he fell completely down in the blood soaked ground as his ears began to ring. His chest on fire, he continued concentrating on his magic. It was the only thing that could save him as he realized that these razor whip-like tails contained venom that was spreading throughout his body. The venom burned, stinging him immensely. Fighting the wave of nausea and unconsciousness, he continued conjuring, mumbling his healing spells as he felt his heart skipping beats and his body trembling with the sweat stinging his eyes that he was not able to close due to the paralyzing effect of the poison. His vision did leave him, save for only shadows and he felt at this point, that he wished he only had a cool drink before passing over, for he knew his death was very near.

When Lithius awoke, it was night, at first he thought he might be blind, but as his stinging eyes ached along with every fiber of his body, he knew he was indeed alive, though barely. He tried to move his head, but he did not have the strength and soon passed out once again. When he came around again, the brilliant sun was setting, and his body hot from being exposed to the elements, it was silent around him. He knew he was alone, and could not hear any of the sounds of the dying in the distance. It took much for him to move his heavy arms and nearly impossible to move his legs, but he managed. He realized it has been over a day of lying there in the rocky dirt now matted with his own blood and sweat along with the dead. As he rose in a sitting position, he realized that as far as he could see, there was nothing but the dead as far as the eyes could see. Lithius realized that he had beaten back an army of impossible numbers with his swords power, though as he thought, drained his army of his own along with nearly his life.

Lithius lifted up his sword as hard as it was and chanted a conjuring spell that he used to bring whatever souls that may have remained back into the custody of his sword, and in doing so, great numbers of souls the sword harvested from the countless numbers of these beasts. Lithius, leaning up against a dead body, his back resting against one of the ones he had slain held the sword with both hands as he struggled until it was finished, and in doing so, collapsed into unconsciousness. It was morning when Lithius had enough strength to pick himself up on his own two feeble feet; he was now standing on his own. As he looked in all directions, all's he could was the fields of the dead looking through the great fields saturated in the heat.

Lithius who suffered much was able to stand as the heat waves from the sands before hi to the west rose up against the reddish sky, a strange color without the promise of rain, for there were no clouds.

Lithius reached out with his sword, a summoning up the ancient spell, he conjured the souls of the fallen. Within moments, Lithius collected enough souls a thousand times that of what he started out. The young warrior-sorcerer, severely bruised, welted and cut stumbled to put his sword back into his scabbard as his blistering parched lips as a swollen tongue was in need of quenching. He looked to the east and using his right hand as a roof above his brow to offer some shade from the brilliant sun to see what strange place he was at, and to see if there was such a place to find water. Nothing but the rotting carcasses of the fallen in the sand, so he turned his direction to the south, there at least amongst the thousands of fallen bodies of these strange creatures, he could see the hills and if he could make it, a least a day's walk, two or more as he was judging by his wounds. He knew he would never make it to those hills, he lost too much blood, he lost too much moisture, and with no water, he would be as just as dead as those he killed.

Lithius knew he wasn't anywhere close to Draccus, let alone his own world, he was to die in a world far from his own. This was to be his second time in his life that he would ever feel so very helpless. He thought about that for only a moment, and this thought aggravated him, the thought of him dying all alone in such a strange place. He realized through a ghost of a grimace on his sunburned face, that he would die trying, he would die trying for the southern hills. He began to walk and stumble through the vastness of sand and the dead bodies, the horrible stench of dismembered rotting bodies and the sun boiling the spilt blood in the sand.

A few hours went by, Lithius continued as best he can, he was far too weak to use his magic, and for the sword and what was left of his armor. Lithius, realizing no longer need, he removed and discarded in the sand, in doing so, he realized he was upon his last breath and no closer to the hills to the south, the heat was too much, hotter than anywhere he has ever imagined.

Lithius spent the last few minutes of his life praying to his childhood gods and then fell completely amongst the dead face down into the hot sand.

"So this is how I am to die…" He faded off into darkness, nothing more, no pain, and no worries.

"I guess if you are just going to give up, Pity" It was distant voice of a man in Lithius' darkness.

Lithius attempting to focus his remaining strength on the voice, it was coming back to him, the words tinged with bitterness, mockery, and very condescending. In his mind, it was dark he couldn't see nothing or feel anything. His physical body lay still paralyzed by the onset of death.

"You crossed over into this realm and now you are mine for the taking" The voice faded off into the distance, still froth with the emotions Lithius perceived earlier. Then his mind opened up, he could see a very dark and gloomy place, a place covered in mist and fog under a cloudy sky of a full single moon, but a moon unlike his own, neither looked like this moon Lithius thought to himself.

He could see a haunting foreboding specter, the moonlight dancing off of this hooded and horned creature came into light enough for Lithius to make out, this creature, this being was of some supernatural being. The creature laughed with a most sinister of voices that, if Lithius were alive, so he thought, that would chill his blood to ice, nor was that bad enough, but Lithius could see the ghostly apparition was stretching forth with his right arm. In his outstretched right hand extended was a chain and upon this chain of silver were human half-rotting skulls, three in all in various stages of discomposure.

"I have come for your head to add to this chain of mine!" Lithius could see the skeletal face under the hood of the phantom's gory face. Lithius could see only one eye, a human eye in the left, and upon the chain, Lithius' eyes locked, those fastened skulls. In the demonic apparition's left hand stood above the specter's head was a scythe towering up into the ghastly and grimacing moonlight sending sheens of a silvery reflection.

"You cannot kill me demon, I am already dead." Lithius used every muscle to strain to say the words as the dampness penetrated his bones.

The horned hooded skeletal apparition turned his attention more acutely to Lithius, and in this, the silverfish moonlight reflected off the face, showing the horrifying features. The creatures teethe were anything like human, they were long and sharp dagger-like teethe of bone and ivory. Lithius without his sword and unable to move, surely hoped that he indeed was already dead as the apparition moved without a sound, that is, with the exception of the sound of the chain and skulls dancing off the links that connected them to the chain itself.

"Dead, no, but I will remedy that" The voice filled full of the very same contempt and haunting laughter came nearer to Lithius who was standing squarely on his feet in the fog.

As the apparition drew nearer to him lowering his right arm with the chain, resting on his right shoulder now drew the scythe with both of his skeletal hands. Lithius could see the heavy iron breastplate of the apparition and on it was writing, runic symbols, and above the symbols was a larger one, one of an upside down star etched in the plate. Lithius with now time left tried once more to turn and run but couldn't move to protect himself, let alone draw his arms up to protect himself from the impending deadly blow from the phantom's weapon.

"Shit, I am already dead, what do I have to fear?" Lithius could almost feel himself sweat as his heart raced, seemly to leap from out of his own throat as he thought to himself.

With everything Lithius had, he raised his arms and conjured up a spell of brilliant light that burnt away the fog around him and blinding not only him, but also the apparition. The spell seemed to work hearing the chain and skulls fade off into the distance as his eyes were adjusting to the darkness.

Lithius then realized that he was save, and stood there with his shoulders slumped from exhaustion. Just then at that moment when he looked down at his feet, he heard the blade of the scythe move through the air and the pain of his head removed by the cold bitter blade and knowing he is now truly dead. As his vision blurred by the blinding light and the whirling in the air from the weapon's deadly blow that decapitated him from the rest of his body. The taste of his own blood filled his mouth as he realized his head fell to soft wet ground. He could feel no pain, but he could hear the sinister phantom come up to collect his reward, Lithius' severed head. The young warrior sorcerer's body fell limp and headless as Lithius' vision faded to a sea of blackness and surely, there was no more doubt Lithius, he was indeed dead.

CHAPTER 21

▼

A large clap of thunder from overhead and the deluge of rain, in literal sheets of water came down upon the dead in the arid desert landscape, the sand soaking up the blood and water before in a few minutes before forming small streams of water rushing down through the valley of the fallen forming small ponds. These ponds merging and becoming small lakes, and the rain continued raising the bodies of these dead as if they were driftwood. Across the vastness of the dead from the foot of the hills to the south rode a double column of soldiers in armor, the rain was letting up now as these men of nearly three hundred rode with purpose with their maroon and gold banners leaving the nearly two-hundred thousand foot soldiers in like armor behind. The lightning's reflection of the storm dancing off the brass and silver armor against of these soldiers as they rode under the ill-omened sky undaunted by the storm's hold above in the direction of the epicenter of the fallen. In the front of the of these powerful black and brown horses, riding on a white and grey steed was a powerful man, his piercing green eyes under a dark tan heavy scornful brow, and behind him, his closest captains, and beyond them, the gallant soldiers of his elite cavalry. They wasted no time through the valley of the fallen beasts towards the center of the former battle with only the sounds of the thunderous hooves and the clanging of armor of these men.

In a few moments, they found what they came looking for, there lying in a pool of water and blood laid the dark clothed body of Lithius face up towards the sky. "There, there is the sorcerer that Tiberius has prophesied!" As the leader of these men drew out his long silver sword as the tip pointed to the body.

Two of his closest men along with others quickly dismounted and waded through the mire to grab hold of the body. One of the captains removed his brass helmet with the long maroon single column of horsehair above it turned to face his leader who sheathed his sword looking down from his horse to them standing there.

"Kromaethius, he is barely alive!" The rain was nothing more than a drizzle as the desert began to draw in the standing pools of water and blood.

"Is he with sword?" Kromaethius' deep voice answered back.

"No sir!" Some of the others began looking around for Lithius' sword while the two captains began tending to Lithius.

"Be warned, find the sword, but do not pick it up, if that sorcerer has breathed in him, the sword will kill anyone who touches it—Least according to the superstitious Tiberius!" Kromaethius looked in all directions, and all he could see was the fallen beasts. He looked back to the double column of his men and they could see the fear in their eyes. He turned more acutely towards them and spoke loudly.

"Men, these beasts are dead, no longer part of the living, they cannot do any harm!" Still it was a ghastly seen, something Kromaethius would not forget throughout his life and he knew in his men at well.

His words did little comfort, but for his men, in spite of their own feelings and beliefs, they would obey their leader unto their deaths. There was no sign of any other creature, literally thousands upon thousands of them fallen with no sign of any other lying next to them and no sign of this army that slain them ever leaving the valley. This fact alone troubled and even nerved Kromaethius, with all this, save one, it was like to him, some force came down from the heavens and destroyed these beasts. The rain was gone and only a cool breeze caught in the banners of the cavalry flapping in the breeze. Kromaethius looked once more at the captains dragging Lithius' body up closer to Kromaethius.

"I found his armor and his sword!" yelled one of the other officers drawing the attention of Kromaethius away from Lithius to the location. "Bring them here to me!" Kromaethius barked looking back down at Lithius and then back to the men gathering Lithius' belongings. "Again, do not touch the sword or the scabbard!" In doing so, the men did exactly what he ordered. Kromaethius leaped down from his horse and walked over to Lithius grabbing a handful of Lithius' scalp and lifting his head up towards Kromaethius who stood well over six and a half feet tall.

"Not what I've imagined, he is strong, powerful, and young, not old, not feeble like one would expect from a charlatan of these sorts." Kromaethius nefariously smiled releasing his grip.

"Will he make the journey back to camp?" Kromaethius asked the men holding Lithius up.

"I do not know, not much life in him, could die any minute, wounded and weathered real bad." The captain said half spooked from the environment.

"Hope he lives long enough to tell us what has happened here." Kromaethius said looking at the other men coming forth from the mire with Lithius' belongings. "Put those carefully on my horse, if there is any truth to Tiberius, it will be I who will suffer from such things." Kromaethius ordered.

In a few moments, Lithius was slumped over the rear of a horse and all went back the direction of which they came to the legions of the other solders without another word or without incident.

Three days later on the march back through the hills that lead directly into the tall silver-capped mountains and deep wooded valleys of pine and heavy timber. The army continued south until they approached a river, it was here at this river that the army rested for only a day before leaving the alpine valley into the plains. From there it was another week's march down along the river to a large walled city with brass and gold spires and domes above the granite walls of stone.

"What is the status of this sorcerer?" Kromaethius asked one of his captains, the golden and reddish haired stern man.

"Sir, he still lives, but has not regained consciousness, your surgeon says that he was poisoned by some strange venom, and of course nearly roasted to death by the desert, his will is strong."

"Must have some powerful gods on his side?" Kromaethius returned with a smile.

"Yes, true!" The captain returned with a smile.

Kromaethius turned his direction before him to the city, "Those beast sir, what of them, I know you do not want to talk of these things we saw, but the men will surely speak of these things and the senate will want a full report, they will want an account of everything that has happened." Kromaethius turned once more to his captain.

"They will get their account, we came to fight the foreign armies as Tiberius foresaw in his visions, and we found this great army laid waste in the desert, and we found what Tiberius was looking for. In the process, we did not lose a single cohort, let alone any single man. The senate will be grateful for that, won't they?" Kromaethius answered.

"Yes sir, but this foreign army, what nature of vile creature, these demons?" The Captain's voice was froth with concern and fear when he began peppering Kromaethius with questions.

"Vorenus, I will hear no more about the talk of demons. These creatures, these beasts are nothing more." Kromaethius hissed.

"If people, the citizens of Kobar catch wind of these strange beasts as demons, there will be no holding back the panic and hysteria. This is why I left a legion of men to burn and destroy these bodies—Besides Vorenus, if they were demons sent by the gods, they would not be of flesh and bone, would, they, and they would not have died by sword, axe, and spear, would they not?" Kromaethius answered with a question of reasoning to Vorenus.

"My lord, but where did these creatures come from, what manner is of these beasts?" Vorenus quipped.

"Kromaethius looked once more towards Vorenus, "Your guess is as good as mine dear Vorenus, but they were of flesh and blood and as accessible to death as we are, correct?"

"Correct my lord." Vorenus answered back.

"Titus Pullo can be trusted and dispose of the bodies, and what is left, the desert will consume the rest, will it not?" Kromaethius asked the troubled Vorenus.

"Yes, yes on both counts my lord." Vorenus reluctantly answered. However, he was assuring himself in the matter of Titus Pullo.

"For the sakes of the gods, I know only as much as I do, my friend." Kromaethius witticism was warm, "And the senate will know even less. However" Kromaethius slowed his horse down from the paced march along the road leading into the city to draw closer to Vorenus before continuing with what he had to say, as he knew the other captains were listening to the conversation.

"If this young Sorcerer lives, regains consciousness, let him explain, besides Vorenus, he's the only one outside of Tiberius Gieus Trontipolli who can, yes?" He said with a smile as he continued, "If this sorcerer warrior dies, with him, all knowledge of all this dies with him, correct?" He closed with a smile.

"You wish him dead then?" Vorenus responded.

"No, though I think his living will cause more questions to be raised by my captain than not." He smiled back at Vorenus before taking the lead of the massive army and turning once more to his captains.

"Take the legions to the south of the city; take the thirteenth cohort with me and you Vorenus into the city along with our friend!" Kromaethius barked.

"They will wait for the senate's order from there; stage them there amongst the three forks of the river!" Kromaethius then continued to ride into the city's huge gate of iron.

"Yes sir!" Vorenus then transcended the order and the huge army broke in smaller groups around outside of the city of Kobar, marching south along the road.

Along with the thirteenth cohort rode a covered wagon pulled by a team of horses that carried the surgeon, Lithius, and the medical supplies into the city with the trumpets blaring throughout the city of Kromaethius' return into Kobar.

Once inside, the thirteenth cohort followed Kromaethius through the winding streets of the ancient city to the center. There, the Thirteenth Cohort came upon marble columns of the capital building with grand architecture of like marble and stone with a golden top and upon it, a godlike statue of a man baring a shield in armor and his massive sword pointing up high in the heavens. The cohort stopped in formation from Vorenus' orders. There were in the center of the stone courtyard before the building from all directions was the attention of Kobar's citizens of slaves, merchants, and other onlookers.

The marble and stone steps leading up to the great pillars were filling up from those from inside, men dressed in white and blue tunics and robes, these men of means were members of the senate, and some came up and greeted Kromaethius. Kromaethius dismounted then removing his helmet walked up the steps, two solders carefully grabbed Lithius' belongings including the sword that was contained in a wool bag and followed him. An older silver haired man with a broken disjointed nose from battle years before smiled and embraced Kromaethius with a smile.

"Any truth to Tiberius' rambling?" The senator said after he embraced Kromaethius.

"Some." Kromaethius answered to him as the other senators surrounded them as the thirteenth stood in formation.

"In the cart below lies the man that Tiberius prophesied about, least I think, for he was the only man found amongst his enemy." This struck the senator oddly but dismissed it quickly knowing there will be time later.

One of the other senators, an older man stood forth and spoke up, "What of the army, what casualties?" Everyone silenced as Kromaethius began to speak raising both, his hands up gently to the senate brood.

"No casualties suffered from our force, the enemy, those that Tiberius prophesied, these foreign army set forth to invade our sacred nation were simply destroyed." In his answer yells and signs of jubilance broke out, a swirling battery of questions overwhelmed Kromaethius, impossible to answer.

"Enough!" Vorenus barked, shouting over the mob of questions, "My lords there will be a proper time for this, this is not the time, and we have our army to the south waiting for your orders in leadership in this matter." Vorenus grew silent as Kromaethius smiled.

"Forgive Vorenus, senators, he is right of course. Let us discuss the matters at hand, shall we?" As the tall and powerful dark man walked up the steps with the senators following suite into the building.

"Vorenus!" Kromaethius turned once more to the captain at the foot of the steps facing him. "Disband the thirteenth; have them return to their families. Take the man we found, under guard and under the care of my surgeon to the sanatorium. Once this is done, go home and be with your wife and I will call for you later." Kromaethius turned away and headed up the stairs to the top of the landing into the great foot of the columns.

"Yes sir my lord!" Vorenus returned to his men and released them to return to their families and await additional orders.

The mob in the streets and courtyard disbanded and the city returned to its fevered pitch of marketing and bustle.

Once inside passed the columns of marble, Kromaethius turned to the silver haired man, "Porcius my friend, we need" as he put his left hand on the right shoulder of the aging senator causing this man to turn towards him as they stopped walking as the other senators returned to the chamber.

"We have the sword that Tiberius talked of, and have precaution of what Tiberius had warned us about. We need Tiberius to confirm this." Kromaethius was stern in both his manner and his words as they both turned towards the two men carefully carrying the large bag.

"Any truth to it?" Porcius asked looking hard at the bag.

"No idea, I would not venture my men to test that theory, besides, there was enough that I saw to see that this old man, Tiberius was right so far." This caused Porcius to take his eyes away sharply and look into Kromaethius' eyes hard.

"Really" Porcius voice somewhat shaken.

"Certainly, I will send my messenger to gather Tiberius at once." He then smiled a bit, "Now take your place and the rest of the senators will be here to give you another type of battle my friend." He said with a smile and leaving Kromaethius with his two men.

Kromaethius has already known of the battle that Porcius is speaking about, the barrage of questions, most of which that Kromaethius had no answer about, and he realized that rumors would be already forming leading to conjecture and more unanswered questions. He would have to be careful and deliberate in his answers to best-set aside further doubt.

"You two men sit the bag down, and you are released." The two did as instructed, the bag certainly was not heavy, but the two men were relieved just the same, as they returned a salute as they left the building. The bag rested at the feet of Kromaethius as he looked down. As he thought about the warning of Tiberius of this sword, a weapon so powerful, so deadly it would simply kill any man, any man who would touch it while its master still breathed. Any part of the sword itself according to Tiberius would strike any man dead in his tracks and with it, his firstborn in his family, and their first born as well.

There was nothing much more that Tiberius could say about this sword other than it was made of a magical foreign material unknown to any weapon smith or blacksmith among them. As Kromaethius stood there contemplating these things, his mind also reflected upon Tiberius' prophecy made no more that two moths ago before the senate that riled up the call to arms and eventually appointing Kromaethius as leader and supreme commander to lead against the onset of an invasion of an army. As Tiberius simply described as a formidable powerful army that no man has ever stood up against, ever, and nothing more was said.

Kromaethius was charged to lead a quarter of a million men from all quadrants of his Kobarian nation, gather a force to meet against this vaguely described army of doom and defeat it while the nation rested with such a small force to defend itself in the event that Kromaethius had failed. A risk that Kromaethius wasn't prepared to make, but regardless of what he thought of the senate's choice in the matter, he would obey. As far as Tiberius was concerned in the eyes of Kromaethius, he was nothing more than that of a charlatan, conjuring up visions, working up the superstitions of the people and that of the senate. Tiberius was nothing more at that time than a soothsayer that bore no real truth, his prophesies a wash in Kromaethius' eyes, nothing more than a keen perception on Tiberius' part to make him appear even more apparent with this supernatural or religious calling of a prophet of the gods that is until now.

Kromaethius was now faced with the artifacts and the fulfillment, no matter how vague, that there was something more to Tiberius' prophecy. How was Tiberius to know of an army that would be in the desert of Ravarak in the first place? The one, the sorcerer from distant lands who would wield the sword that would have so much power it would unleash legions of soldiers from the heavens to thwart the attack and intentions of the army of doom so described by this prophet. This troubled both Kromaethius' lack of faith and reasoning. How did this man, a priest could know of such things? This questioned burned and consumed Kromaethius on his way back to Kobar.

Kromaethius, the supreme commander and a veteran of many battles including the civil war of Kobarian itself knew that these things were impossible. The simple logistics of the thousands upon thousands of these beasts with no sign of supplies, no sign of support could not have happened, neither could they come out of thin air, but still all signs pointed that way. The purpose of this sorcerer warrior was somewhat a mystery, after all, Kromaethius thought, he was certainly not Kobarian, a foreigner, what would he gain by helping the Kobarian nation?

Kromaethius bent down and firmly picked up the bag and walked into the chamber, he would have to leave his thoughts on this matter and deal with the senate that were congregating before him.

CHAPTER 22

▼

As he walked into the center of this building, the voices and conversations filling the chamber abuzz hushed as he sat down in a large chair place below the amphitheater of the senators. Kromaethius could see that there were still some senators coming forth to be seated glaring at Kromaethius, some with eyes of contempt, others with eyes of praise and thankfulness that the nation was spared, all with a measure of questions within their gaze upon them.

Kromaethius has undone his girdle containing his sword and daggers, rested them upon the cool floor next to his bag, and rested himself in the large ivory chair looking back at the senators, pages, scribes, and court.

A very old man, a senator living an unique age carrying a staff of wood and ivory with the aid of two young pages on each side of him to keep him from falling, his eyes so sunk into his skull and covered by cataracts preventing him from seeing clearly enough, smiled at Kromaethius absent of teethe.

"General, it is good to see you again." As he outstretched his right skeletal hand towards Kromaethius, who carefully returned a smile and gentle with his handshaking as not to break the old man's ancient bones in his hand or causing any discomfort.

"And good to see you, Markus Tarrilium, Senior Patriarch of the Senate of Kobaria." Kromaethius then grew silent as Markus turned to face the senate that was growing restless once again. Markus raised his staff, pounded the foot of the staff against the marble dais, and spoke in a rough ancient voice.

"Senators of Kobaria, I call this session into order, we will continue on the matters we discussed previously another time. For our son, the son of Kobaria's own has returned to us to give his account of the matter of the prophecies of

Tiberius!" The senate grew suddenly still hanging on every word that the senate's patriarch was stating.

"It is my pleasure to say that her borders are safe, the people and citizens of Kobaria are content in the matter of security thanks to our leading commander by the will of the gods that favor our great nation. It is because of this fact, that I Markus Tarrilium welcomes General Kromaethius testimony of all that has happened since his departure to engage the enemy forces is the desert wastelands of Ravarak." Markus Tarrilium concluded with three more loud taps of his staff and was ushered to his chair right of Kromaethius to the far end of the chamber that was raised up on a high dais overlooking the proceedings of the senate.

A senator arose, a dark complexion of waxy black hair and beard with shimmering black eyes arose to speak. He, this senator of Ravarak decent, and as Kromaethius remembered, this senator was a former chieftain of one of the major tribes of these desert people before they untied with Kobaria peacefully years before. "Senator Jobbah-Lum of the district of Ravarak now has the floor." Markus Tarrilium spoke.

Kromaethius could see the former chieftain turn his attention from Markus Tarrilium to the general and begin to speak to him as a servant brought Kromaethius a goblet of wine. "General Commander Kromaethius, tell us, did you find this army, this army of doom as foretold by the prophet priest Tiberius?"

The room was still as Kromaethius accepted the goblet of gold and crusted jewelry, careful and planning his words delicately after sending the servant off. "Senator Jobbah-Lum, I did find an army indeed, north of the Tybarkan Hills in the vastness of Ravarak, as foretold by Tiberius, high priest of Kobaria, the prophet of the gods." Kromaethius took a sip of his wine never removing his eyes from Jobbah-Lum.

The senate chambers erupted in buzzing with the response causing Markus Tarrilium to regain order and control by using his staff against the hard stone dais that rang out. "Silence!" Markus Tarrilium yelled and reminding the senate audience of no further disruption and the necessity of order.

The large windows from up high offered more than enough light in the smoky atmosphere caused by the dust and incense burning into the air. "From what direction did this army of this doom that would befall us come from?" Jobbah-Lum asked.

"From all directions, from the north, east, west, and south. Impossible to ascertain the exact direction where this army marched from, that is, if you all it marching." Kromaethius did not afford another question as he arose from his chair and continued speaking given his attention away from Jobbah-Lum towards Markus Tarrilium looking on.

"If it pleases the senate, I am prepared to give my account now; in perhaps this would answer already many questions that the senators like Jobbah-Lum may have sir." Kromaethius waited for a response from Markus Tarrilium as there were a rumbling going on in the horde of the senate.

"Silence!" Markus Tarrilium turned once more to the senate, "Another man speaks out of turn, and I will have them removed!" Markus Tarrilium turned his attention back to General Kromaethius.

"Yes, precede son of Kobaria." He motioned with his left hand while his right firmly gripped upon the staff.

"Thank you." Kromaethius then turned his direction to the senators and continued to explain the events leading up to the desert valley of Ravarak, north of the Tybarkan Hills. He talked for the good part of an hour up to the point on where they reach the valley of the fallen.

"There we found the valley and among the valley there laid thousands of the dead, not one survivor amongst them lived, save on, the sorcerer warrior though, most of the life within him gone. Among the dead, we recovered his sword which I have in this bag below me." Kromaethius went on to explain in great detail that the army, this army of doom fell upon a terrible force that left no trace, no weapon, and more importantly no dead of their own, nor any sign of the direction and whereabouts of this force that utterly crushed this army. Kromaethius could see from the responses in the senator's eyes, and seeing them whisper upon one another, that they were indeed having a difficult time believing the General. Kromaethius found it hard for him to believe what he saw.

"I know this sound preposterous to say the very least. Need I remind you I had a quarter of a million men and three hundred of my finest cavalry with me at hand among the dead? Also Titus Pullo, captain of the legion to tend to the dead will attest to these I say." Lithius grew quiet, returned to his chair, and drank once more from his goblet.

The senate was only still for a few moments before Jobbah-Lum moved to have the floor only after talking to a Ravarak rider, a scout he trusted that spoke to him closely. Kromaethius could not hear what this rider could say to Jobbah-Lum.

"Jobbah-Lum has the floor, thank you, Kromaethius for your detailed account." Kromaethius nodded and remained quiet, now it was time for a barrage of questioning. The senate, many in the senate would want to justify the massive spending of the force to meet with this army only to find out this army of doom was already defeated. Deploying an army wasn't cheep, and as Kromaethius often said, it's all about the denary.

"General Kromaethius, for me, your words about the condition of the army you were charged to fight against is true enough, they have been decimated by forces we are yet to understand." He was interrupted by the wave of chaos that arose be his response as Markus Tarrilium arose and feverishly attempted to gain control as the senators shook their fists into the air demanding answers.

"Silence, silence now bellowed Kromaethius' voice over everyone in the room aiding Markus Tarrilium to gain control which worked.

Markus Tarrilium's earlier threat stood good as he had guards remove four senators from the room and tossed out of the proceedings before Jobbah-Lum could explain.

"A few moments ago, a trusted scout returned with the account of his own words on what he saw and what others of my people, the tribes of Ravarak saw, also citizens of Kobaria." The room grew quiet allowing Jobbah-Lum to continue.

"Your words, interpretation of a great man such as yourself General Kromaethius of the account in the valley beyond the Tybarkan Hills even find you in near debrief, wouldn't you say." Jobbah-Lum extended his right hand and arm towards General Kromaethius.

"Yes, I saw it all first hand, and I find it hard to believe, but none the less, it is what I saw." Kromaethius countered.

"Indeed" Jobbah-Lum responded and then began to attest to what the scout reported.

"My people say the words of the prophet are true" He had to pause because of those around him that were once again consumed by the fever of the religious connotations of their beliefs in the prophet and the gods, but not disruptive enough for Markus Tarrilium to act upon as Jobbah-Lum himself continued to speak.

"It is true, there was indeed, no other sign of an army that fought against this wicked and cursed army and surely no one man could ever fight against such odds, the purpose of this sorcerer warrior is a mystery that can only be explained by himself or by the prophet Tiberius himself. As to General Kromaethius' account. I find truth in his words, and with that Markus Tarrilium I yield the floor." Jobbah-Lum then left the room with his servants and scribes. Kromaethius realized there was something more going on with the former chieftain, but to as what? Kromaethius had really no idea.

There were several other senators, those with less compassion than that of Job-bah-Lum asking a battery of questions and it was nearly dark when Kromaethius and the senate disbanded and the belongings including the sword left in the bag were confiscated by the order of the senate until such a time that the High Priest Tiberius would examine the artifacts. Kromaethius found it odd that Tiberius did not show up during the proceedings, however he would be there the following day even if under arms, he was to be sequestered by the senate for further questions like that of Kromaethius to appear again the next day.

The nation of Kobaria could not afford to have a quarter of a million armed soldiers camped outside the walls of Kobar, and like the thirteen cohort was released to return to their respective cities and lives ready for the next bidding of assembly by the senate. Word from the chief surgeon confirmed that Lithius was still barely alive, and unconscious. No known medicine, or treatment was to be used against such poison, the usage of leaches proved ineffective in drawing out the poison as the poison in his bloodstream were killing the leaches. It was also made known that Lithius, a human like that of the Kobarian was from a race, a species not known of the people based on their understanding.

"Lord, I do not know why or what means this man lives" The words of the surgeon rang out in Kromaethius' thoughts as he was resting in his own bed in the still of the night on a hilltop safely behind the walls of Kobar as he found it impossible to sleep.

"Truly, what manner of man is this" Kromaethius asked himself.

By dawn, Kromaethius alone finally went to sleep, an uneasy sleep filled with nightmares and vivid dreams of the events, and things he saw and wrestled with his mind. When he awoke, a female slave, an older woman in black clothing woke him up gently informing him that his bath has been drawn and that there were men waiting in the courtyard for him, one of which was Vorenus.

"Feed them Atrilla, show them our hospitality while I bath and get into the proper attire for another day of relentless badgering." He said sarcastically as he rose out of bed completely nude before her and walked across the room on where there were two other slaves, one an attractive female, and a manservant, a bald older man that looked away from his nakedness.

"My Lord, do you need me to come with you to senate?" Kromaethius looked upon his old servant.

"Yes, Jonah, that would be wonderful, ready you're writing utensils and ink, there are others waiting for me in the courtyard, and see to their comfort afterwards." Kromaethius then tuned away towards his bath.

In a course of one-half an hour, he was dressed in a dark blue tunic and robe, upon his head was a matching blue turban that covered his long brown hair. This fabric of his turban ran down his back, this fabric would protect his neck from the elements offering shade and protection of the cold bitter winter or the blazing sun from the summer months. Kromaethius refrained from wearing jewelry except for the silver and gold ring that had a black diamond stone that looked more like that of an eye given to him by his late wife, a woman that he loved so dearly worn on his right forth finger. A wife now a few years gone that died of the civil war along with most of his family. Dressed in his flowing garb, the color, and fashion of his tribal ancestors of the foothills of the great mountains in northern Kobaria he donned for today's long drawn out session with the senate. This, like many other sessions he suffered from, would or should be over least with his part by today's end, least so he hoped.

As he walked into the courtyard of his very nice and plush villa, he saw Vorenus, his most trusted captains, leader of the thirteenth cohort. There was one other, a fellow officer, Magnus Potaro, an officer native born from the southland of Kobaria that was a former officer under Vorenus who was just as close to Kromaethius as Vorenus was to him.

Kromaethius saw those eating fruit and wine that Atrilla and a couple of other servants had put forth on the wooden table. "Thank you, Atrilla, you all may go and leave us three here." He smiled at her warmly.

"Oh, a general that thanks his slaves, what would people say?" Vorenus said with a smile and thanking him for breakfast as Kromaethius embraced Magnus Potaro kissing his bearded peppered colored beard. "I see the gods have kept you Magnus Potaro, my friend." He said in laughter as he kissed his other cheek.

"Yes, yes my friend." Magnus Potaro said.

"I can see citizenship has been good for you thus far." Kromaethius quipped.

"Yes, indeed, and it is something you should try." Sneering back at Kromaethius as he turned and embraced Vorenus in like manner before he continued.

"The men, they have all returned for home?" Kromaethius asked with a strong measure of concern.

"Yes, certainly as you ordered." Vorenus grew serious, as he was automatically able to transfer his demeanor from friend to soldier under and awaiting orders of his chief officer.

"Good, good then." Kromaethius then sat himself at the head of the table as the other two seated themselves and continued eating the fresh fruit and bread.

"Vorenus, any word on the status of that sorcerer?"

"Yes, the surgeon was just here a few minutes ago, he said nothing has changed, something like this man is in some deep slumber that cannot be waken, no doubt works of the poison in the wounds and in the man's blood." He concluded as Kromaethius continued to gaze strongly before relaxing shortly drawing a few grapes.

"How are the wife and your children Vorenus?"

"Fine, they give you their love and told me to thank you for keeping me alive so far." This caused the three to laugh amongst them before Kromaethius returned his gratitude of Vorenus' family.

"You must thank them all, your wife is the most beautiful creature I have every seen, and her daughters, thanks by the gods, take after their mother!" All broke out in laughter again.

"But Vorenus, you do not fully realize how generous the gods favor you on the blessing of having a family so loving, so close to you as they are—I say these things, because, heaven forbid, you lose your family, then you will only realize what you truly have" Everyone was quiet as Kromaethius spoke in seriousness.

"…And if I allow you to die in battle, I feel that I would never forgive myself, nor would I receive any piece from the scourge of your three daughters and your wife through eternity." He removed his hand from Vorenus' shoulder realizing the mood changed too dramatic for the beautiful morning as the sun was rising into the courtyard above the blue clear sky.

"Besides" Kromaethius turning his direction from Vorenus to Magnus Potaro with a gleam in his eye, "Don't you think that Vorenus' youngest daughter favors after my likeness more so than his?" Magnus Potaro nodded as the burst of laughter from all three ascended to the clear morning sky as Kromaethius mockingly pointed at Vorenus.

Later, Kromaethius appeared once again before the senate with his small entourage, and as before Kromaethius sent the bag along with two of his slaves. Today, it will be Tiberius that will open the bag and through him extract the sword and the belongings of the strange sorcerer warrior that Kromaethius and his army recovered. Today, it will be Tiberius who will be sitting in the chair before the senate. As for Kromaethius and his entourage, he will be seated to the right of the senate on the main floor across that of Markus Tarrilium. In addition, the surgeon will give his testimony on the stranger's condition and some insight to the ailments or whatever else he could possibly shed some light on this subject. As for Kromaethius, his thoughts on the subject should be laid to rest as far as his responsibilities were concerned with the senate, "Sooner the better and as soon as Titus Pullo could return to Kobar after destroying the physical remains of those hideous creatures, the better it would be for everyone." Kromaethius thought to himself.

Looking around, Kromaethius could see Vorenus and Magnus Potaro shaking hands and greeting some members of the senate as Porcius came down to speak with Kromaethius wearing a warm smile. Jonah, Kromaethius' slave, a highly educated scribe brought out his writing board, ink, and quill. Jonah began writing on the parchment as Kromaethius turned his attention back to Porcius that was now standing before Kromaethius, causing Kromaethius to rise and greet him.

"Wonderful job yesterday my friend." Porcius smiled again as he shook Kromaethius' hand.

"I wish that I only had more answers to the senate's questions." Kromaethius returned a smile.

"None the less" Porcius looked down at his own feet for only and instant before locking eyes with Kromaethius hesitating to ask a question.

"What is on your mind?" Kromaethius asked politely.

"Oh, Yes" Porcius stumbled in his thoughts before continuing, "This so called sorcerer, what manner of man do you think he really is, I mean do you think that this man is some sort of powerful magician?"

"Oh?" Kromaethius seemed a bit relieved to this question.

"I only saw him that first time; he was near death, looks to me a tall and strong man, a man perhaps in his late twenties or so. A man I would probably not give a second look on the streets myself. That was the only time I personally examined him. Though looking back on that" Kromaethius grew quiet only for a second as he noticed Jonah looking up at the two and realizing that Porcius was hanging on his words with a measure of wonderment.

"His clothing, an odd material, strange. I mean to say, it looked like wool or something of that nature, but felt so oddly, I have never seen such fabric. Strange that I would remember that now." Kromaethius gave an odd smile.

"Again, I wish I knew more about these matters." Kromaethius concluded.

"Yes, yes indeed" Porcius could see the troubling thought in Kromaethius and it was genuine. "No matter, we will find out more in good time. Say, Tiberius is here among us today in Kobar, he should be" Porcius turned towards the opening of the chamber and there were many of the senators, scribes, and clerks all busy amongst their business. "…here anytime." Porcius turned once more to Kromaethius, said his goodbyes, and walked off after seeing another senator that Porcius had some sort of urgent business.

Kromaethius sat back down next to Jonah quietly without saying another word to anyone, in a few minutes Markus Tarrilium called the senate to order as everyone began sitting themselves down. Magnus Potaro and Vorenus returned and seated themselves. A hush dampened the senate chambers as Markus Tarrilium recapped yesterday's events and reminded everyone in the large chamber that non essential people and staff should leave, Kromaethius noticed there was far more people here than yesterday. News in Kobar travels fast, and any kind of news, especially that of bad news travels even faster.

Markus Tarrilium continued to give in some detail approximately this session and a warning to the senate and all in the room his lack of tolerance with outbursts. Some people were now leaving, Kromaethius' entourage stayed as Kromaethius noticed his own surgeon was entering a room. Kromaethius could see the surgeon was looking for Kromaethius, the General raised his arm and motioned the surgeon to come to him after the surgeon, a man in his late forties, medium build, and bald cleanly shaven wearing a light blue tunic walked with haste to where Kromaethius and his men were sitting.

The surgeon sat to the right of Kromaethius, "Tell me, how is our visitor?" Kromaethius whispered to his surgeon while not taking his eyes off Markus Tarrilium and the senate.

"Same, he is in a very deep sleep state, he still breathes, but his condition has not changed. If this keeps up, he will surely die, I give him perhaps, two maybe three days more" The surgeon paused long enough for Kromaethius to turn his attention directly to the surgeon with a serious look.

"I am doing everything I can, I believe it is the poison, a poison I know nothing about, any known cure, tried everything. And now, the poison has infected him physically."

"Whatta mean by that?" Kromaethius asked lowly with a small measurement of frustration seasoned in his words.

"His eye General, they grow an unnatural red and my staff at the sanatorium grow afraid. Any man as I said before, would be dead long ago from the wounds, from the poison, dare I call this one a man?" The question presented struck Kromaethius odd.

"Healer, what would you call this, if not a man?" Kromaethius wondered.

The surgeon just sat deeply back in his chair without an answer, "I am sure you are doing everything you can, keep me informed of any other changes." Kromaethius turned once more towards Markus Tarrilium who was opening the floor up to discussion. Kromaethius noticed that Jobbah-Lum was not among the senate and this made him wonder, "Could he have gone to the valley north of the

Tybarkan Hills for himself, surely Titus Pullo would have more than enough time to destroy the bodies in fire" Kromaethius thought to himself, "Besides, the least these people know of these dreadful creatures, the better!" Kromaethius then focused on the matter at hand, the senate, the second day of this session.

It was Magnus Haltus that received the floor, he was one of the leading senators, a right winged conservative and usually a pain in Kromaethius' ass, a native of the city of Kobar that was in the pockets of the city's most elite. Kromaethius didn't like the man, the mere sight of this man made him somewhat ill. It wasn't the fact that the man was physically odd, Magnus Haltus was a tall slender man in his forties, and he and his family lived up in a terrace beyond Kromaethius' own villa just a stones throw away. Kromaethius just despised this man, he was corrupt and power hungry. It was made clear that if Markus Tarrilium would pass on in death, it would be Magnus Haltus who would be the senate's whip as it were. This man, Magnus Haltus had what many referred to as a man who had the best of everything, slaves, servants, three wives, the best education that money could by and every possible fortunate stroke of luck throughout his life. Kromaethius had nothing but contempt for this man, even before the Civil War, Magnus Haltus was a senator, and unlike most of the former senators that found their heads on the pikes before the main entrance leading into Kobar, Magnus Haltus escaped every trial and every investigation. Kromaethius understood as so many others did, he, this man, purchased his verdict and his way to remain a senator, and not only that, the next Senior Patriarch of the Senate of Kobaria.

Kromaethius realizing once this would happen, no doubt, Magnus Haltus will make life for the General Commander impossible, and in fact, force Kromaethius to resign to a life of retirement. There were indeed too many events leading to the cause of the bad blood between the two from the start.

In the beginning, before Kromaethius took the reigns of General Commander, a title that he earned through the seven long years of the Civil War and the annexation of Medhoria to the west by brutal bloodshed to become part of Kobaria increasing the nation to nearly two thirds, Magnus Haltus opposed him, restraining his power and leadership.

Kromaethius realized as the nation was beginning to, the reason for the struggle with the war in Medhoria was because the hindrance of the senate dictating strategies and fighting the war from within the chamber walls. Rather than relinquishing their leadership to the generals and officers and the countless soldier actually fighting the war and the epicenter of this travesty was none other than Magnus Haltus in Kromaethius' eyes.

Kromaethius was deliberate in his accusations against Magnus Haltus in anything that he could possibly muster up in good reason against this man for the years of pain and frustration, and he realized if Magnus Haltus would become the next Senior Patriarch of the Senate of Kobaria, he was finished as a General. One thing that kept the likes of Magnus Haltus and his minions at bay, which were quite a few. Even a few senators he had in pocket, those spineless sorts that were all part of the right-winged conservatives that so much as not to take a piss on their own without Magnus Haltus' approval, was the simple fact that the common people of Kobar or for that matter, Kobaria regarded Kromaethius as a national hero.

In the beginning of the Civil War when Dalmatius, the former General Commander lead his armies against the tyrannical powers of the former Kobarian regime, the former king and his senate. Halfway through the war, Dalmatius died, leaving Kromaethius as the next in charge. The men, the soldiers, and most of the country were with Kromaethius who literally went out in near treason a few seasons earlier in spite of orders from the former senate and crush Medhoria's capital stronghold with less than half of the army that was against him.

The Civil War ended with the fall of Kobar, and the people wanted a new king, and Kromaethius was to be this king, but this wasn't the dream of Dalmatius in which this man, Kromaethius, most admired and learned much. Kromaethius restored the Senior Patriarch of the Senate of Kobaria, a man who was imprisoned most of his life in contempt of the former king, it was Markus Tarrilium that Kromaethius came for to free, and he, Markus Tarrilium was the first Senator of the new Kobarian government.

The first acts of Markus Tarrilium, actually since the first day of being free, he wanted to take every senator into trial for treason against the citizens of Kobaria and fully restore the Senate to the dream and vision of Dalmatius, Markus Tarrilium and a good many others. The new government forming when surprisingly fast in Kromaethius' mind, sure it wasn't perfect, not with people of the likes of Magnus Haltus in the General's mind, but there was nothing that Kromaethius could really do about it now.

Kobarian society prospered well in peace, libraries, and schools for the youth to educate, military training went leaps and bounds under Kromaethius' watch. Now, deep inside himself, he too realized that his time as General Commander of Kobaria was beginning to draw to a close, and his successor would obviously be someone that the Senate would find to be easily controlled, and no doubt, it would be someone that Magnus Haltus would hand pick. Besides, as Kromaethius thought, Magnus Potaro might be right, he should begin to embrace the thought that retirement would be not such a bad idea after all as he glanced over at Magnus Potaro looking up most disdainfully at Magnus Haltus as he was beginning to speak.

CHAPTER 23

▼

Kromaethius turned to Vorenus who was looking at the General and rolled his eyes. Vorenus couldn't stand Magnus Haltus and if there was anyone in the kingdom who hated this man more, it was without a doubt, Vorenus. This caused Kromaethius to smirk and turn his attention away from Vorenus to the senator speaking.

"...I would like to thank the leadership of the senate that is responsible for this massive military undertaken to the north"

"There it is, you son of a bitch, taking credit, and publicly and politically putting the responsibility back on the senate, maybe you are not the horse's ass I thought of you to be" Kromaethius smirked again to himself realizing that Magnus Haltus let him off the hook as far as the accountability of financial responsibility. The senate was always short on memory when it came to who order what and when especially when they get the final bill, and again sending a quarter of a million men on a march to the north was anything but expensive.

"...Having said this" Magnus Haltus raised his right-hand arm towards Markus Tarrilium sitting there in his chair, "...Your leadership in guiding us to make the right discussion on sending the army north to intercept the enemy foretold by the High Priest of Kobaria, Tiberius Gieus Trontipolli, seer of the gods." Magnus Haltus took a brief moment lowering his right arm, his left clutching his robe and tunic turned to Kromaethius with a shallow smile and then with his very same right arm extended it to the General Commander.

"I would also thank and address the very son of Kobaria himself for his leadership and his speedy interception to engage the enemy, though, they enemy forces he had already found decimated—Still the same, my humble thanks." He bowed slightly, but Kromaethius could feel the sting of his so-called humility and not so hidden innuendo.

"Fuck you, and fuck you again Magnus Haltus." Kromaethius thought to himself. As for Vorenus, he was a little less subtle as he whispered his remarks under his breathe just audible for those who sat directly around him to pick up, one of which, Magnus Potaro who agreed.

"I would also like to thank General Commander Kromaethius for his testimony of his accounts to the valley north of the Tybarkan Hills." Magnus Haltus lowered his right arm as the senate began to clap and cheer as Kromaethius arose and thanked those that were honoring him, and he turned to Markus Tarrilium and bowed before sitting, "My god, I turned into a real political kiss-ass, haven't I?"

The senate grew quiet and with Magnus Haltus, still having control of the floor took notice that Tiberius Gieus Trontipolli had not arrived yet and made mention. "Since Tiberius Gieus Trontipolli, our beloved high priest has not arrived yet; I would like to ask Captain Vorenus Scaythe of the house of Magnus to take the chair."

"Shit!" Vorenus vented whispered, Kromaethius turned as was just as surprised as Vorenus with Magnus Haltus suggestion.

"What form of trickery is this?" Kromaethius asked to himself.

"Why do you call this officer?" Markus Tarrilium quipped looking somewhat puzzled and concerned.

"We have the testimony of his ranking officer already with General Kromaethius?" Markus Tarrilium asked in return.

"Yes, yes I know, and General Kromaethius' testimony as fantastic as it might sound, is beyond reproach."

"Then why question Captain Vorenus Scaythe?" Markus Tarrilium insisted.

Just then, there were several tall crimson red robed men, all-tall, slender build standing in the chamber's entrance. In the center, the tallest and oldest, the old silver haired man carrying a dark oak staff was Tiberius Gieus Trontipolli with his rose-colored cheeks wearing a matching red cap that fit tight made of silk resting on the crown of his head. The attention of him and his entourage of priests entered the room by introduction of Markus Tarrilium. This of course, his arrival could not happen any sooner for Vorenus who physically shown sign of relief as all stood as the priests entered the room.

Tiberius Gieus Trontipolli walked up to the main chair while his priests formed behind the chair in line facing the senators, as soon as the high priest sat himself, everyone else resumed to their seating with the exception of Magnus Haltus who still had the main floor.

Magnus Haltus began to speak, "Since Tiberius Gieus Trontipolli has graced our presence, and I believe we should not keep his valuable time. We will leave your matter for another time Magnus Haltus."

Kromaethius could see that Magnus Haltus seemed somewhat startled that Markus Tarrilium forced him to yield the floor before he had the chance to bring forth Vorenus and as he sat, gleamed a sharp look at Vorenus' direction. As Kromaethius looked on at Markus Tarrilium, Magnus Haltus sat himself with the others. Kromaethius then looked at the high priest who sat there comfortably before the senate mob. Tiberius Gieus Trontipolli wasn't moved in any apparent way, in fact, he seemed to embrace this session. Kromaethius did not know Tiberius Gieus Trontipolli and really actually spoke to him directly, even for a General Commander of Kobaria, he could not just come up and hold audience with this man. To speak to Tiberius Gieus Trontipolli directly was impossible, unless questioning him in session with the senate, and even then, Kromaethius figured it was taking unnecessary chances of insulting the High Priest unless you were a senator. In the days before the Civil War, the High Priest would never set foot in the Capitol building to hold audience with the senate; the senate was beneath the High Priest that clung to the ancient traditions of old. In fact, in the most ancient days of Kobaria reckoning, the days after the fall of the great empires, the country was lead by the gods through the High Priest and unto his priests, then to the people, but that was nearly two thousand years ago. The Hieratic order of the priesthood and their beliefs changed drastically since then, but in spite of these changes, there were still some ancient pious traditions these people still clutched most desperately. As for Kromaethius, these priests, the hieratic order of the nation's faith wasn't Kromaethius' own, nor in his belief system. Kromaethius could careless what offended this man, this proud man to elevate himself through this hieratic organization, the High Priest or what religion he stood for matter precious little to the General Commander. To Kromaethius, the hieratic order was nothing more than a controlling form of government over the minds and hearts of those who could not or would not think for themselves. If up to Kromaethius, the hieratic order would have been abolished, but it wasn't up to just him. Kobaria and its people in general are a superstitious lot that held the priesthood in the highest regard, and the matter of the High Priest to many was the vestige of the gods in this man. However there was something to this man, somehow, through some means, he could see into the future, least enough of vaguely describe the "army of doom" so Tiberius Gieus Trontipolli called it, enough to pinpoint their exact whereabouts for Kromaethius to find them.

That wasn't the only thing that Tiberius Gieus Trontipolli was right about, there would, in the midst of the army be of a powerful sorcerer that would enter from another world and stave the advancement of this army. There were certainly more to it, this prophecy that Tiberius Gieus Trontipolli told, and to Kromaethius, much he wasn't telling. Perhaps today there would be shed more light, and Kromaethius could see a glimpse into some secret into the prophet's source of knowledge. Kromaethius would not settle for the religious answer that these gods only speak to and through Tiberius Gieus Trontipolli directly or through his priests. Today would be in fact an interesting day.

"Thank you blessed Markus Tarrilium; yes there are just not enough hours in the day to get the work of the gods done." Tiberius raised his multi-ringed cluttered right hand up, with his left hand firmly placed on the staff standing firmly on end next to him in the chair as if it was the scepter of the throne.

"If it pleases the senate, I would like you to have read the scroll of this prophecy to the senate before I begin to deliberate further with these fine men of Kobaria." The high priest was looking up at Markus Tarrilium.

"Yes, yes, do you have the scroll?" Markus Tarrilium asked as everyone was still.

"But of course." Tiberius Gieus Trontipolli then motioned one of his priests from behind the chair to produce the holy parchment. The priest, a younger man, and by the looks of it to Kromaethius, a man in his early twenties, "Rather young this priest is?" as he produced the scroll.

Kromaethius thought to himself looking down at Jonah to insure he was writing everything down and then turned his direction to the priests. "I would like Magnus Haltus to read the prophecy marked and outlined before the senators so that they may hear the words of the gods, specifically of the words of Phaetius our chief god, the keeper of heaven, the most holy."

Kromaethius could see that Magnus Haltus was surprised and troubled by this request and before he had a chance to recant or reason with the High Priest, that is, if he dared, Markus Tarrilium spoke.

"That would be a wonderful idea, what a blessing indeed that Magnus Haltus should read from the sacred scroll." Markus Tarrilium gleaming at the befuddled senator as he spoke, certainly now, Magnus Haltus could not refuse.

The young priest then walked over to the wall, the stone wall that came up from the floor about five feet, and beyond that, the amphitheater seating of the senate assembly to hand the scroll to a senator that intern handed it to another and yet another until Magnus Haltus received it. Magnus Haltus opened the scroll, began reading it to himself, and then stood up as the priest turned to face the High Priest while standing quietly up against the wall.

"From the crimson line, my lord?" Magnus Haltus questioned.

"Yes, from there, that would be fine my child." Answered Tiberius most gently and patiently awaiting the reading.

"Behold the words of Phaetius, sacred keeper of the heavens and all that is within" Magnus Haltus began to read. Kromaethius leaned up from his chair and resting his face in his hands with his elbows resting firmly on his thighs, he listened carefully as the senator continued to read.

"...I bring my most humble servant a word of warning, a word of peril upon the people of Kobaria of a great evil that shall befall upon the northern boarders of this land. In the desert, you know of Ravarak, there just beyond the Tybarkan Hills and the great army of doom shall come from within the sands and from above gathered by the great evil one like locusts upon the nation they come forth. This army, this army that this world has never seen before shall devour men and beast alike with no mercy. Men shall cry up to me, but I will not offer any relief to the plague, for I have already seen this, and I shall bring a deliverer amongst them. He will fight against the evil one, the great chief of iniquity, and from the deliverer I sent forth, a great weapon to smite the pestilence. This deliverer is not of this world, but yet a man, a warrior, a possessor of imbued incantations and knowledge. He will come, and with him, the weapon that is also not of this world, this weapon, children of Kobaria will know this weapon, it is of a sword, a black sword crafted in the foundries of the netherworld. This weapon shall not be taken from the deliverer, for it possesses great strength, great powers that will kill all those that attempt to remove the weapon from the deliverer while he yet breathes. You shall know that I am god through this battle, through this army, and through my deliverer. Nevertheless, he is not enough, children of Kobaria be warned that a great evil exists in your land from the army and you must meet with this from the north. The great evil will feed on the souls and blood of the children of Kobaria. The deliverer will find this evil, seek it out, and destroy this terror"

"Stop!" Shouted the High Priest as he arose from the chair looking up at Magnus Haltus and then to Markus Tarrilium before continuing. "We know that this army truly exists and were destroyed exactly where Phaetius our lord told us, and you have the deliverer among you along with the very sword our god talks about, yes?"

"This is so," Magnus Haltus claimed pointing over to Kromaethius' direction, "Tiberius Gieus Trontipolli it is Kromaethius that has the weapon, and the deliverer!" This caused a minor eruption that Markus Tarrilium had to contend with before allowing Tiberius to continue with what he was about to say.

Kromaethius noticed the High Priest turned sharply to Kromaethius. "You, you have both the deliver and his sword?"

Kromaethius stood up with the large bag in his hands, "Yes, the sword I bring here today for you to examine." The room quickly quieted down as Tiberius Gieus Trontipolli motioned two of his priests to retrieve the bag from Kromaethius. "The weapon of Phaetius belongs with us until united with the deliverer, and what of him?" Tiberius Gieus Trontipolli quizzed, his demeanor seemed changed, and he was more into a rush, a need of urgency.

"Where is this deliverer, what have you done with him?" Tiberius Gieus Trontipolli words half filled with contempt for Kromaethius.

"As I explained to the senate yesterday, he was found nearly dead, I have put him in my care with my chief surgeon. He rests under my care at the sanatorium!" Kromaethius barked back in aroused anger, as his men including the surgeon stood up with him. Kromaethius was indeed angered with the prophet's meaning of his words.

The sound of the Senior Patriarch of the Senate of Kobaria's staff butted up against the floor several times as the senate broke out in a blizzard of remarks to one another and unto the hieratic order and Kromaethius' entourage.

"Order, I demand order!" Markus Tarrilium hammered.

"I demand to see him right away!" Tiberius exasperated.

"You will not!" Kromaethius bellowed back not intimidated in the least from the High Priest.

"You dare defy the High Priest of Kobaria?" Challenged Tiberius Gieus Trontipolli.

"No, I challenged the prideful and accusing man called Tiberius Gieus Trontipolli!" This was a delicate but challenging move on Kromaethius' he was as confrontational as Tiberius was to him. If Kromaethius acknowledge that he was challenging the authority of the office of the High Priest, the hieratic order would naturally demand his life for heresy. Since Kromaethius made the distinction clear that he was challenging the man, not the holy order or office, this was of another matter indeed, a matter that Tiberius Gieus Trontipolli was not prepared to enter with such a physically powerful man as Kromaethius. Kromaethius had successfully disrobed the High Priest, separating him from the hieratic order quickly.

"I found this so called deliverer, a man near his own end, surely he would be dead now if it were not for my surgeon. If you were here yesterday, you would have known of these things. I have given this man, this so called deliverer of the very best that I have" Kromaethius put his hand on the shoulder of the stressful surgeon as the senate mob quieted and began seating themselves to listen. Kromaethius turned to face his others and motioned them to be seated.

"You do not believe that this man is the deliverer?" Tiberius Gieus Trontipolli is setting a trap with this question towards Kromaethius still standing.

"That this man was sent by Phaetius himself to be our deliverer, is that what you mean dear Tiberius Gieus Trontipolli?"

"Yes this is what I am speaking about!" The priest was angry that this man was challenging him before the senate, before his own order of priests.

"You do not believe in the gods, do you?" The slippery character asked without waiting for a response from Kromaethius.

"I did not know my personal beliefs were to be on trial this day before you or the senate, but since you asked drear Tiberius Gieus Trontipolli" Everyone was hanging on Kromaethius' word.

"Sure I believe in the gods, to an extent, to a measure, I also believe this man that I have discovered, no doubt the very same you speak of in your words" He was cut off by Tiberius Gieus Trontipolli.

"These are the spoken words of Phaetius, not mine!" Retorted the bewildered priest.

"So it seems" Kromaethius wanted to say more, but what he wanted to say would put him on the receiving end of the executioner's axe. He would keep his thoughts to himself, least for now.

"You have his sword, and if the condition of this man changes, I will send for a messenger to inform you. Until then, no one will see him." Kromaethius knew he was in the right, this too was an ancient tradition if one who is in the care of another such as this. It is up to the one who provides the care in so many words, is in charge that is until the person in question regains his health or consciousness to make up his or her own mind on which this person wishes or not to see.

"General Commander, surely I can see him now, I realize that this man may die, or near death, but surely I can speak and minister to his soul?" Tiberius Gieus Trontipolli spoke with a transparent emotion of concern as Kromaethius could see.

"No, if he is who you say he is, and then he already knows Phaetius on a level we will never come to know yet alive, yes?" Kromaethius checkmated Tiberius Gieus Trontipolli ploy.

Without giving Tiberius Gieus Trontipolli a chance to retort, Kromaethius asked Markus Tarrilium for the surgeon's report of this man that Tiberius referred to as the deliverer.

"If the High Priest has any more he would like to say or should he yield the floor to the surgeon?" Markus Tarrilium asked of the priest.

"We shall keep the artifacts of the deliverer safe in the temple's keep, which is until the deliverer is able to collect them." Tiberius Gieus Trontipolli suggested to the senate and he turning once again to Markus Tarrilium began to speak.

"Since this is a spiritual matter, the state of the nation will rest this between you and that of whom found him, this man, this deliverer." Markus Tarrilium added.

"By all means, this is certainly fine with me, who am I to stand in the way of Phaetius and his priests." Kromaethius sat back down sending a cold smile to Tiberius Gieus Trontipolli in doing so.

"Thank you, General Commander, most gracious" Tiberius Gieus Trontipolli said lowly and regaining his calm.

To Kromaethius, these words were translated as "And fuck you Kromaethius" This caused Kromaethius to chuckle a bit to himself; he managed to upset the hieratic order.

Porcius then arose asking for the floor as Tiberius Gieus Trontipolli surrendered the floor momentarily.

"I put to the senate, that this man, this deliverer will remain in the care of Kromaethius, he gives us no reason to speculate his grand care in this man. It is his honor to take care of this man, it should be our discussion that this man that Kromaethius has found on behalf of our nation while acting as an agent of the senate, that this being, this person, should be nothing less than a ward under tradition to Kromaethius. That is until this man, if this man recovers that is." Porcius remained standing as those around him began to stir. It was now clearly time to vote on this measure, a measure that really was nothing more than a formality, a formality that will keep Tiberius Gieus Trontipolli from gaining any possible control of the care provided by Kromaethius, "…a smart move indeed by Porcius." Kromaethius thought to himself as he sat there sternly.

"Does anyone oppose this proposed measure?" Markus Tarrilium put forth into motion.

"Yes, yes I would like a moment." It was Magnus Haltus none other looking down at Tiberius Gieus Trontipolli for a moment and then back at Markus Tarrilium for approval to speak, in doing so another senator arose from the side of where Porcius sat demanding to be heard also.

Markus Tarrilium spoke up in his old raspy voice, "You may speak first Magnus Haltus."

"Thank you, Senior Patriarch of the Senate of Kobaria. I realize it is a sacred tradition to follow in regards of caring for those who cannot care for themselves, but because of the spiritual impact of these events, the prophecy, and the whole affair—Should the care of the deliverer of a nation not be put into the charge of anyone man? Because of this fact alone, these circumstances, I move that the state of the nation is far too great for anyone man to be responsible for this unique individual. I say no to this!" His opinion raised concern for both the left and right wing of the senate.

"Order, order" Senior Patriarch of the Senate of Kobaria stammered with his staff in hand.

"Thank you, Magnus Haltus, now for senator Crando to speak." Markus Tarrilium spoke signaling the young vibrant senator representing the northland district of Kobaria, from the very same region that Kromaethius' tribesman lived.

"I understand the concern that my dear associate Magnus Haltus has just spoken and I appreciate this concern, however I cannot agree with him on this matter" He was cut off by the uprising by the mob of senators from speaking. Markus Tarrilium regained control as the priests and everyone below remained quiet.

"…Thank you" Crando was allowed to finish, "As I was saying, I must uphold the sacred tradition no matter the condition, the situation. Our fathers in the past were faced with the similar conflicts. However, we shall resolve these issues by resting in the tradition. With abandoning our traditions, we abandon ourselves in the process, no matter how grave the situation maybe. If we vote on this, and this motion of Magnus Haltus passes, then not only would this tradition be ended, but what next, which other tradition, law, or belief that we hold dear and sacred to us will we abandon?

I say we uphold this very sacred tradition, this motion by Magnus Haltus should not even be considered among us. General Commander Kromaethius, is he not the very son of Kobaria that you yourself has said yesterday and again today? Is General Commander Kromaethius honorable to lead a quarter of a million of Kobaria's finest no matter the outcome against this army of doom told to us by Phaetius through his prophet, this very man to insure the safety of Kobaria? Is this not the man that has faithfully served the senate, brought in Medhoria, and aided immeasurably to the liberation of Kobaria in the Civil War? Yet according to the suggestions of my fine colleague, now the very same man I speak of should not be trusted none the least with just one person in his care!

No, I say we uphold the honor, we uphold the sacred traditions, and we uphold what makes us all proud Kobarians!"

The entire senate arose to their feet in praise of the senate speaker and from the other side, those closest to Magnus Haltus opposing bitterly as Kromaethius could see the look of discussed up on the brow of Magnus Haltus.

Porcius arose after Markus Tarrilium commanded order once again. "I move for a vote against the motion, and for the motion of allowing the sacred tradition we speak of to be continued in this matter to continue to allow Kromaethius to care for this man!" Kromaethius could see the disgusted look upon the brow of Tiberius Gieus Trontipolli as well.

The staff of Senior Patriarch of the Senate of Kobaria was raised high as all came to order and the vote cast before senate. To Kromaethius' honor, the vote passed with only six opposed. Kromaethius would continue the care of this person.

Because of the outcome of the vote, the High Priest in his anger left the room with his priests following behind. Kromaethius turned to Vorenus sternly and deliberately with his green eyes blazing, "Send a detachment over to the sanatorium, I want him watched every hour of every day, nobody, I mean, nobody except the good doctor here and his staff access in or out while this man recovers or whenever the gods feel that his time is through with us."

"Yes sir, right away." Vorenus then got up and left quickly from the Capitol building before Magnus Haltus would move to have Vorenus himself before the senate.

Time continued to drag for Kromaethius, there was a brief lunch, and the senate reconvened on where the chief surgeon of Kromaethius spoke before the senate giving medical details of the condition of this man, omitting what he personally told earlier to Kromaethius, especially about the eyes.

It was made clear by the surgeon that it was up to the gods as far as the final outcome of this person, wither he would pull through this or not. The senate was rest assured by the very brief questioning so it was not to detain the surgeon from his duties. Kromaethius and his entourage were then dismissed from this session that was drawing to the close. A measure was taken in the end for a list, a set of orders for Kromaethius and made clear. Kromaethius was to do everything in his power to save this stranger at all costs. If the man should indeed die because of the wounds and condition of his nature, Kromaethius' responsibility in this matter was resolved. However if this man was found to have anything but Kromaethius' best intentions, Kromaethius would be held accountable. His second standing order from the senate was to send word to Titus Pullo to remain north of the Tybarkan Hills to aid in the further investigation lead by Jobbah-Lum and his men.

Kromaethius in his hopes, Jobbah-Lum would not find a single beast left after Titus Pullo destroyed the bodies, bones perhaps, but not a clear picture, to Kromaethius it was a waste of time. Titus Pullo and his legion would be returning by late next week at the very latest. As far as the hieratic order in the charge of the "sacred weapon," this was a genuine relief to Kromaethius; he had no interest in religious artifacts.

Besides, he was tired, and needed much sleep, he would worry about his worries tomorrow as he walked with Jonah back to his villa. Jonah, a quiet man only troubled Kromaethius with the status of Kromaethius' household affairs. Kromaethius was patient he was concerned for the well being of his slaves and servants of his home and treated them most kind.

CHAPTER 24

▼

Lithius' mind and soul was trapped within his comatose body that barely hung on to live, the reality where his shell of an existence lies motionless on the table. For those around him, for the healers, the doctors that cared for him, they knew they done all that they could do and the mercies were up to the gods. The poison that was running through his veins were unknown to them as they tried everything, and now, it was just a matter of time, time that is before they would lay this foreigner's remains for good.

However, unknown to the healers, Lithius was very much alive and in his mind, his spirit was just beginning to realize that he was not indeed dead, that the powerful vision of his head separated from his shoulders was nothing more than that, a poisoned induced vision brought on by the venomous unrelenting powers of the creatures he had dispatched. Flashes of Morderra-Atrauis and those events leading up to the teleportation into the strange world that his paralyzed body rested in was all untwining. Lithius, realizing the gods were not done with him; the authorities would not release him from his body and slip off into eternity that his work was far from finished.

Lithius was regaining his strength even through the toxic poison through his very veins. His love for Tara, his hatred for Morderra-Atrauis and the Tarvas was keeping him alive. As beads of sweat began, to form around his eyes and forehead, his fingertips began to twitch and he began feeling the painful numbness through his extremities and with these signs of life, there was certainly hope.

As Lithius was ebbing his spirit back into his body from the darkness within, the high priest across the great city lie twisted and contorted in a horrible death, his face bore the horrors that killed him and next to him, the Sword of Souls that rested ever so coldly on the floor.

By the following weeks, Lithius reunited with his sword was strong enough to be moved, though his body healed from the wounds, though weak resided in Kromaethius' home. Lithius whose eyes were two smoldering blood red eyes void of anything human, were to crimson orbs of blood. His face darkens by the poison with the rest of his body. A mask was made of lightweight breathable material to hide his features from his black cloak that would conceal his burning supernatural eyes amongst the people. His character became also as dark as his attire as he grew intolerable to ignorance and his impatience for the bureaucracy of the government that surrounds him was at times, too much. For Lithius to bare the thought of allowing Morderra-Atrauis to raise arms against him and the country that regarded Lithius as the deliverer from the evils prophesied in an ancient religious text burned his soul, was something he would not allow. His power and strength has grown tenfold since the battle into this realm. One of the things Lithius had figured out was the language of Kromaethius was a slight dialect of the spoken language of the apparitions of long ago back in Adajahara. Lithius studied the writings of the language without the aid of the sword, in fact Lithius' knowledge and the magical abilities eclipsed the sword with the exception of gathering the souls of those fallen by it. Oh yes, Lithius understood that the sword he carried, in it, deep within still had other secrets yet to surface, these things he was patient, like the years before hand, the sword brought these mysteries to light.

In the coming months, Lithius was beyond suspicion of the Senate and was free to aid Kromaethius into searching for Morderra-Atrauis who was gathering forces far north among the Germanic tribes. Lithius under orders of the Senate and the command under Kromaethius were sent to the north with Kromaethius along the region where Lithius was found. From their Lithius spent many hours tormenting Morderra-Atrauis, his power far greater than that of the old Pitah in the matters of mental telepathy reading the thought of the ancient sorcerer king of Draccus, but far enough away not to hinder the old man physically, least not yet, and likewise Morderra-Atrauis knew this. As long as Lithius grew stronger, as long as he was alive and on the same plane, the same world of existence, Lithius was a hopeless thorn in Morderra-Atrauis of making a kingdom there on the blue planet, a planet called earth that was light years away from his, and for that matter, Morderra-Atrauis, and Lithius' home world.

Lithius who had a passion of learning history found many secrets of this place called earth, how the great kingdoms in the ancient past formed into two great kingdoms and then finally into one before the great upheaval, before the one called the "Great Prince," the one who deceived and destroyed. Lithius spent time showing Kromaethius these things, these things that Kromaethius personally for several reasons would not understand entirely and disbelieved much in regards. His friendship also began to wane from Lithius growing uneasy with his magical and foreign powers, his abilities to read minds and look deep into the hearts of men. These things made other men that were growing fearful of the dark one who concealed his face.

Lithius understood their fears and in some measure played upon them for his own benefit. Kromaethius on the other hand would not let this intimidate him in anyway, Lithius knew this, nor did he try to parlay this with the General. During these months, Lithius foiled many of Morderra-Atrauis' intension and through Lithius' insight and aid, gave Kromaethius many winning battles now in the southern provinces of the Germanic lands. However, there grew talk of an army so great to the north beyond the hills and mountains along the black forest that raised the superstitious fears among Kromaethius' men. Kromaethius paid no mind to this kind of talk, propaganda sent through spies and others to counter the morale of his forces. Lithius on the other hand could see into the minds of those captured. Lithius could see there was some truth some measure of reality in there minds of these things from this region far to the north.

By the fall of the following year, Lithius growing no closer to Morderra-Atrauis under the leadership of Kromaethius that was governed by the senate departed Kromaethius camp on his own to seek out Morderra-Atrauis and end this once and for all. Lithius threatened that the longer Morderra-Atrauis lives, the stronger he would become, since Morderra-Atrauis was not of this world, like Lithius himself, Lithius would go and confront him.

There were things that Lithius understood. Things he's seen both in this life and when he was near dead let alone, from his home world, and the battle he nearly died in. Lithius realized that for many years through powers of Morderra-Atrauis and his knowledge of these portals that allow creatures from various parts of the universe, dimensions entrance to and fro. Lithius understood that Mydyr and the likes of the bitch, Hamahadra. Lithius was clearly beginning to understand the knowledge of the portals and the conjuring behind it. He realized that he may be able to return to Draccus and his home world would come to him soon enough, but Morderra-Atrauis would be destroyed first and time was of the essence, he realized that if Morderra-Atrauis realized that Lithius was drawing too close, Morderra-Atrauis could escape through one of these portals.

With the great winged army of Morderra-Atrauis destroyed, this didn't stop the ancient Pitah's ambition, only postponing the inevitable. Lithius realized also if he killed Morderra-Atrauis before he would obtain the final key to the portal, Lithius might never see his home world again.

Lithius would just have to chance it; he would have to find Morderra-Atrauis and the evil within him nevertheless. Lithius' departure of his own ambition put Kromaethius in a position that the General would have to answer for, this of course, going against Kromaethius' orders to remain with him was something that would strain Lithius' relationship with the General. Lithius couldn't dwell on that, besides he realized that Kromaethius considered him as a "freak of nature" and others called the sorcerer an "abomination." Lithius grew tired of these things that others thought and felt about him, besides as he figured, they were right, he had nothing to do with this world, and limiting his feelings made things easier for him, besides being on his own was something he was certainly used too anyway.

Through his magical powers, he traveled unbelievably fast through the land gaining great distances from him and Kromaethius and his legions. Lithius by the first day put more than five-hundred miles between him and the General. Stopping only long enough to check his surroundings by a map and gathering his location, he was off again on the second day. He could feel Morderra-Atrauis presence growing stronger and with these feelings, he realized that Morderra-Atrauis could also sense his growing presence as well. Lithius' use of his magic was like that of a beacon for Morderra-Atrauis that was now heading quickly west into the lands of the Gaul. The Gaul and the Germanic tribes were always at an uneasy peace, Lithius realizing that the Gauls would never allow the major forces of Morderra-Atrauis' armies within their borders would only mean that Morderra-Atrauis would be traveling in a much smaller band if he continued heading west.

By the fourth day, Lithius was well past the northern mountains and into the region of the black forests along the eastern edge of the Gauls. For Lithius could not go any further using just his magic allowing him to cover great distances in very little time. Lithius, close enough to Morderra-Atrauis could sense that there was something that Morderra-Atrauis was after, not so much as an escape as to some sort of a place, not a portal, but a place of great power that may give Morderra-Atrauis an advantage over Lithius. Lithius using another means rather than probing Morderra-Atrauis over great distances attempted to see what might be this thing, this place that Morderra-Atrauis would abandon the great numbers of his armies that were turning southwest along the Germanic frontier in hopes of confronting Lithius. That is when, the moment Lithius could see in a small still pool of things to come in the near future, that Morderra-Atrauis in his cunning had manage to send with this Germanic army of over three hundred men lead by an acolyte from Draccus, a sorcerer in his own right. Lithius also realized that this creature was of the same blood-feeding creature as Morderra-Atrauis and also that Morderra-Atrauis had opened the portal in the north to bring forth this acolyte from his home world. That wasn't all that Lithius was seeing, that this acolyte had the ability to shroud himself up until now, and something that Lithius didn't realize that there could be others and that he was falling into a possible trap.

As Lithius looked into the pool seeing all of this, Lithius smirked at the small force heading in his direction, he realize that the acolyte was powerful and at one time may have been quite a problem for him to deal with, was nothing more than a pawn in allowing Morderra-Atrauis time, time to recover what? Even the pool and Lithius' conjuring could not bring into focus.

The acolyte was still over a good days traditional ride, most of the soldiers that rode with him were of light armor and about thirty bowman, and the rest, nothing more than heavily armed tribesmen with sword and axe. Lithius decided he would not engage, but would continue on to the direction of Morderra-Atrauis through the lands of the Gaul. He would stand a far better chance of not being noticed as one man, rather than bringing attention upon himself fighting an army of an invading army. Lithius was also formulating this possible trap into his favor. The Gauls might see this small army as an invading force, the Gauls nevertheless would meet head on with this army and looking into the pool of still water as he leaned over, could see already that the few posts of the Gauls had already took notice. If the acolyte continued heading west forced by Lithius own direction to Morderra-Atrauis, they would follow up to the point that the Gauls would stop them, and if the acolyte did press the issue, that perhaps, the uneasy peace would become war.

Lithius smirked again, arose and walked along as a normal man through the dark forest for the remainder of the day before commandeering a vacant boat and heading quietly along in a slow-moving river that emptied into a large lake. There he lifted the sail and without the aid of any magic crossed well over well into the Gaul lands. By the time Lithius landed his small boat, the army lead by the Acolyte was stopped by the Gauls, Lithius could see through the means of magic looking into another pool of water could see that the Gauls were no match for his magic and his men. Nevertheless, this broke the peace and now this would bring down the fury of the Gauls. For Morderra-Atrauis, and his small force, once word would get out through the kingdom of Gaul, he would have to carve his way back, or realize that his unfortunate-failed plan may cause Morderra-Atrauis to flee through other means, means that perhaps Lithius would be forced to stay in this world.

After traveling north west, Lithius was three days travel from Morderra-Atrauis and through Lithius powers, he sensed Morderra-Atrauis no longer, and as for the acolyte and his army, they have been forced to head east on a retreat. Lithius realizing that his fears of losing Morderra-Atrauis had happened could only hope that the acolyte may know something, something that would be a key on Lithius' return to Draccus and his world.

Since Morderra-Atrauis seeming gone, Lithius using his powers crossed into the land of the Germanic tribes out of Gaul. In doing so, the acolyte that led the small army was also mysteriously gone. Now Lithius feeling very alone, a different feeling of alone, an alone of hopelessness stood there in an open field in the chilling rain of late fall. Across from him was a small village barricaded by a wall of timber and upon it, Germanic archers war between the two nations have broke out and Lithius knowing that far to the south, Kromaethius would receive word.

Lithius looking across the field adjusted his cloak and began walking slowly to the village. His physical form changed into that of a Germanic warrior and assuming the looks of a that person he found in the woods a half day earlier, Lithius embraced the notion as bitter as it seemed that he might be on this world for a very long time. Peace came to mind when he thought there just might be a secret or three left in his sword. Besides, on his way to this village, he was forced to do a little carving for himself and within the sword rested the souls of those he'd fallen awaiting his bidding, and realizing this with his left hand resting upon its hilt, he smiled and concluded; after all, certainly he is never really alone.

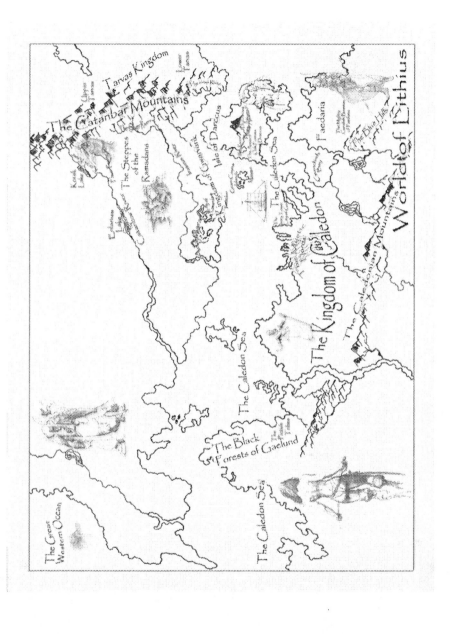

978-0-595-40947-1
0-595-40947-4

Printed in the United States
60266LVS00004B/197